# Fotheringham's Fictionary
## of
# Facts and Follies

## Other Books by Allan Fotheringham

*Last Page First*

*Look Ma, No Hands:*
*An Affectionate Look at Our Wonderful Tories*

*Capitol Offences: Dr. Foth Meets Uncle Sam*

*Malice in Blunderland, or, How the Grits Stole Christmas*

*Birds of a Feather: The Press and the Politicians*

*Collected and Bound*

*The World According to Roy Peterson:*
*Roy Peterson, with the Gospel*
*According to Allan Fotheringham*

# Fotheringham's Fictionary of Facts and Follies

*Allan Fotheringham*

KEY PORTER BOOKS

**National Library of Canada Cataloguing in Publication Data**

Fotheringham, Allan, 1932–
       Fotheringham's fictionary of facts and follies

ISBN 1-55263-357-8

       1. Canada—Humor. 2. Canada—Quotations, maxims, etc.
       2. Canadian with and humor (English) I. Title

PN6178.C3F66 2001      971'.002'07      C2001-901687-5

The publisher gratefully acknowledges the support of the Canada Council for the Arts and the Ontario Arts Council for its publishing program.

We acknowledge the financial support of the Government of Canada through the Book Publishing Industry Development Program (BPIDP) for our publishing activities.

Key Porter Books
70 The Esplanade
Toronto, ON, Canada M5E 1R2

www.keyporter.com

Design: Peter Maher

Printed and bound in Canada

01 02 03 04 05 5 4 3 2 1

*For Quinn, Hunter, and Lauren*

## TABLE OF CONTENTS

There is a historic, framed photograph hanging in the Ottawa Press Gallery. The time is 1957. New prime minister John Diefenbaker is strolling down from Parliament Hill, on the slope toward Wellington Street. Walking with him are a half-dozen reporters. All middle-aged—as he was—all in respectable tweed jackets and ties, all respectful and very deferential to the great man, all with their notebooks at the ready, tape-recorders blessedly not having been invented. It is a great, iconic tableau.

When the expanded press corps boarded the Diefenbaker campaign plane five years later, the *Toronto Star*'s mordant wit Val Sears announced, "To work, gentlemen. We have a government to overthrow." Such was the disastrous development of the Dief's relationship with the press that, coupled with public disillusionment, led to his eventual downfall.

There are now, in 2001, more than 450 accredited members of the Ottawa Press Gallery—too many of them former disc jockeys from afar (as was Brian Tobin)—and so many of them who probably think Diefenbaker was a German colonel.

Val Sears, famous for his put-downs, used to celebrate his birthday in his own Toronto home. He would invite everyone who was any-one and then—on the principle that he was paying for the booze and the food—insult them outrageously. One birthday, John Ralston Saul—long-time companion, as we know, of Adrienne Clarkson—arrived late as the afternoon grew on. Just in from a flight from Europe, he raced in with his shirt exceedingly crumpled from the journey. Host Sears admonished him: "John, you really should get your shirts laundered. Adrienne's family, as you know, has been in the business for years."

Sears's attitude to a prime minister—and to a future Governor General—illustrates exactly how the roles of the press and the politicians have changed. There ain't no respect any more.

The Woodstein Twins—Bob Woodward and Carl Bernstein—were responsible for it all. Actually, it was Richard Nixon. After the young *Washington Post* reporters exposed the president for the liar and shyster he was over Watergate, enrolment in American (and Canadian) journalism schools soared. Everyone who could learn to type saw in every minor municipal councillor a potential thief or embezzler. Everyone wanted to be a Woodward or a Bernstein and, if not immortalized in a Hollywood hit, at least worthy of overthrowing the local police chief for cheating on his expense account.

I guess I learned that words were weapons when I worked on Fleet Street in the 1950s, where ten competing papers—manned by assassins at the typewriter who would demolish each other in print—could be found later hilariously toasting one another in the best pub around the corner. There is no hypocrisy—leaving alone politics—more droll than among journalists.

The magic of words, however, was learned in a one-room schoolhouse three miles outside Hearne, Saskatchewan. It was run by the schoolmarm, who in those Dirty Days of the Depression was never paid any money but was compensated by room and board with a nearby farm family whose kids went to the same one-room schoolhouse where I learned to read and write.

I didn't write my first column until the age of thirty-six. I graduated from the University of British Columbia at age twenty-one, and as outgoing editor of *The Ubyssey*—the famed producer of such minor personalities as Lister Sinclair, Pierre Berton, John Turner, Val Sears, Ron Haggart, Joe Schlesinger, Sandy Ross and Helen Hutchinson—I assumed I could immediately master a high-profile column at the *Vancouver Sun*.

Higher minds in the lofty executive towers thought otherwise. They were entirely correct. At age thirty-six, when I was eventually given a full-blown prominent column, it was the best thing that ever happened to me. By that time, all the blokes I had gone to university with had taken over the town. Art Phillips, who used to make a million bucks on Howe Street while on summer vacation, was mayor of the town. Peter Butler was the most famous libel lawyer in the country, next to someone in Toronto named Julian Porter. I could just call up any heavy-hitter in town and get the drift. As well as the lies and gossip at lunch.

By that time I had also roamed the world and had learned a little about it. I had travelled Europe from Finland to Morocco, and gone through Poland on a Vespa scooter, the Soviet Union from top to bottom in a Volkswagen and the Orient down to the Vietnam conflict. Today I've been to some eighty-nine countries on all the continents on this funny globe, including Antarctica, where I held hands with a penguin on Christmas Day. You can't be a journalist unless you travel.

Those early days were a heady time to be a scribbler. But something, of course, was lost along the way. John Turner found this out, to his regret and resulting failure, when he returned to politics after a too-long stay on Bay Street. When he left Ottawa, the ambiance was still such that he could sit down with a few trusted buddies from the Press Gallery and toss back a few noggins on the unspoken understanding that what was bantered was all off-the-record.

When he returned to Parliament Hill after his exile in Toronto, the atmosphere between press and politician had completely changed—a result of the Woodsteins. Nothing was off-the-record, and a journalist could not be seen in a restaurant with a pol lest one be accused of being a paid whore. It climaxed, as we all know, with Pamela Wallin (who held no real animus for Turner) asking him on national television whether he liked the gargle a bit too much. Which naturally is like asking someone when he stopped beating his wife. (They have since kissed and made up, and are good friends again.)

This scribe's relationship with those at the top—as the snippets in this tome will indicate—have been interesting, to say the least. I first wrote about Brian Mulroney before I met him. In July, 1975, the day after the Conservatives announced a leadership convention to succeed Robert Stanfield, I wrote, "So the Tories have finally set a date to send off Robert Stanfield. The new leader of the party will turn out to be, next February, one Brian Mulroney, a young Montreal lawyer with the gift of the gab who was a former aide to Davie Fulton and is now on the Cliche Commission. Remember, you read it here last."

I had been following his career from afar. You didn't have to be too bright to realize that the Tories, out of power almost the whole century because they couldn't break into the Grit stranglehold on Quebec, could never get to 24 Sussex Drive until they had an easily bilingual guy and—in the television age—one with a beautiful wife (hello there, Jack Kennedy). It seemed an obvious slam dunk.

Two weeks later, Miss Framsham, my secretary at the *Sun*—the world's best, and with a plummy Brit accent—buzzed and said there was a "Mr. Mulroney" on the phone from Montreal. (Friends used to say, "Surely her name really isn't Miss Framsham?" Of course not, I would explain. Her real name was even more dangerous. It was "Mrs. Robinson.")

I picked up the phone and didn't even say hello. I said, "When did you first decide to run for leader?" The answer: "The second time I read it in your column." I dubbed him The Candidate from Whimsy. He and his lovely wife, Mila, who could work a room better than any politician I have ever met (including her husband), became friends. Whenever he phoned he would always say, "This is Whimsy." It was a standing joke.

He lost, as we know, his first try to Joe Who, then undermined Joe Who, as we know, and succeeded the second time around. We remained friends and I had easy access to the many 24 Sussex parties and dinners. My friends in the Ottawa Press Gallery were, naturally, at first jealous. Then concerned. A few trusted ones suggested that I was getting a little too close to a prime minister I was paid to assess objectively—and it was hurting my reputation (such as it was).

They were right. One Sunday at about noon, on the dock of the guest house at Harrington Lake, about a half-mile down the water from the prime minister's summer house in the Rideau hills, where I was visiting with a Quebec girlfriend who was a close friend of Mila's, a speedboat zoomed up. The waiter in the speedboat was carrying smoked salmon, scrambled eggs and champagne.

I decided my buddies in the Press Gallery were right. My employer, Southam News, had offered me the position of Washington columnist for their newspaper chain, which stretched from Montreal to Vancouver. I suddenly realized it was a very good offer—and retreated there for five years to "cleanse" myself from a too-close relationship to a man I was supposed to be examining. When I got back, my columns apparently were no longer regarded as amusing. The lunches Mila and I used to enjoy at the National Arts Centre patio, always with a press aide (chaper-one), dissolved. Such is life.

One day, as the Trudeau era was winding down, the phone rang. An anonymous voice said, "Paul Martin Jr. will be running for the Liberal leadership," and hung up. I'm not even sure I knew there was a Paul Martin Jr. at that moment, but after investigating his Power Corp. connections in Montreal, I ran a blind item in my column suggesting that he was going to emerge from corporate invisibility into politics.

Some time later, I was emerging from the Ritz-Carlton Hotel in Montreal near midnight when a couple approached me on the sidewalk. "You're Fotheringham," the male member of the duo accused. I, a modest man, allowed that that might be so. "Mulroney has warned me about you," he said. "He says that you invent a politician, puff him up like a balloon, then stick a pin in him and watch him deflate."

"Of course," I said, "that's how I make a living." Martin dropped off his wife, took me to his office, opened a bottle of whisky, and long into the night we became friends.

There have been, it must be admitted, more than several e-mail messages reminding this imaginative scribbler of my responsibility for Stockwell Day—apparently having touted him early on (again, someone I had never met) as the solution to the Canadian Alliance's search for a bilingual leader who could break into Ontario without a squeaky voice and a contrived haircut, not to mention contact lenses. This, alas, is true. Being an honest man, I must admit to some responsibility for inflicting on the nation a charming, glib person who has the attention span of a hummingbird. (I did not, it must be mentioned, invent Mackenzie King, nor Laurier. I digress.)

The Stock has a c.v. that includes having worked on his father's fishboat as a deckhand. He rode a bulldozer in the Far North, dabbled at McGill but never finished, was an auctioneer in Kelowna, actually raised chickens in his car, dabbled at the University of Victoria but never finished, spent some time as an interior decorator, dabbled at his Alberta Bible College but never finished that either—all before entering politics riding the Albanian-style, landslide voting patterns that pass for democracy in his home province.

His colourful career pattern would do well for an Ernest Hemingway or a Jack London—or even a newspaper or magazine columnist. It is, however, not the ideal background for someone who wants to be prime minister.

As I sit writing this, in a valley in the Roussillon in southwest France, looking out over endless green vineyards stretching through the hills to the Spanish border, it occurs to my evil heart once again that there is nothing like being a journalist. You'll never be a millionaire as a journalist, goes the saying, but you can live like one.

A spring spent in the Roussillon and then in Mougins on the French Riviera, followed by a visit to friends in Paris and then a wedding in London, Ladies' Day at Ascot in the Royal Enclosure and opening day at Wimbledon is not the usual fare of a dull lawyer or dutiful doctor, but a scribe with wit can manage while writing about it—and letting the expense-account boffins figure out the details on their own.

Some selections in this book show my love for travel (just as others show my hatred for some politicians). You can't show the sharp without the dull.

Bruce Hutchison, the finest writer in the land, used to write Lester Pearson's speeches and then sit in the Press Gallery above, writing about the speech just delivered in the Commons. Blair Fraser, of *Maclean*'s, had the ear of every cabinet minister. I used to have lunch with John Turner's wife, not to mention Mila, not to mention that fateful smoked salmon brunch at Harrington Lake. It's a good life, being a scribbler; you meet a lot of funny characters along the way— and most of them are found herein.

P.S. I like most of all the piece on Bobby Orr. Under *O*. Enjoy.

**AIR CANADA** The Air Canada jet is crossing, hour after hour, some of the most compelling scenery in the world. The Canadian Shield, the dappled summer squares of grain on the Prairies, the Rockies, the Pacific fjords. And Air Canada, our national airline, attempts to bully passengers in window seats to lower their blinds to blot out our country—so that those who are unable to read can view an American movie devoted to the sight of blood.

It has already been established that there is not a Canadian bright enough to run Air Canada, the airline having filled all its top positions with Americans.

Holly Harris, the Georgian hired in 1993 to save the country's flag carrier, who the last time I looked had not taken out citizenship papers, did what any Georgian could be expected to do. He hired some design experts to paint the Air Canada tail green to symbolize our vast forests, the maple leaf symbol a new red to illustrate our autumn trees and the background white to show our snow heritage. The only thing missing is a Mountie with a lisp as a drink-serving steward. (Who did he hire to do this? Of course. A San Francisco advertising outfit, for a mere $1 million.)

Gayle Christie, a Toronto Tory, says she was qualified for her appointment to the board of directors of Air Canada because she can drive a car. Does this increase your interest in (a) flying Air

Canada? (b) wanting to take the train? (c) urging the expansion of the runway at Gimli?

Someone who likes the scenery pays as much for his seat as does some dolt who would rather watch a darkened screen full of the Indiana Jones stuff of mindless violence that is right out of children's comix. But Air Canada is blind, just as blind as its passengers who are not capable of reading.

**ALBERTA** The key to understanding Alberta is androgen. Androgen rules business. Androgen permeates politics. Androgen affects Alberta's relations with the outside world.

Androgen, for those who are feeling lost in this exposition, is the male sex hormone, and the aura it projects, the insecurities it hides, the locker-room mentality it bolsters explain the new rich kid on the block—the province of oil and cowboys and nouveau riche swagger. It is a strange province, aggressive in its stance and surprisingly chippy toward outsiders.

Alberta is the male animal in a swagger. The need to prove one's self in the primitive manner of a bull in rut makes the atmosphere of the place resemble an entire province posing for hairy-chested aftershave lotion. There can be nothing more ludicrous than a grown man with a paunch teetering about Calgary streets on the high heels and pointed toes of cowboy boots, attempting to capture some primitive cachet from some distant past. If the foot is a sex object, as a trendy new doctor tells us, Alberta is abrim with fetishism and eroticism.

Alberta is the most "American" of the ten provinces—surpassing even Ontario, where centre-of-the-world Toronto in its penis envy wants to be New York (when actually it's a failed Boston).

In pioneering days, with cheap land available for homesteading, enterprising types from Montana and Idaho came across the border to establish vast ranches in Alberta. After the Second World War, the Leduc oil strike south of Edmonton introduced the province to liquid gold. It needed to induct experienced oil-and-gas veterans from Oklahoma and Texas who knew their onions. The Yankee go-for-it ethic is well grounded in the province that is "different."

The costume parade affected by otherwise normal businessmen is, of course, a sham because Alberta is not the rural backdrop for John Wayne that it makes itself out to be. Since the Second World War Canada has had the fastest urban growth rate of any country in the world and Calgary is the fastest-growing city in the country.

The look-alike wooden boxes move in uniform phalanxes over the dun-coloured plain on the outskirts, resembling from the air the shantytown dribbles that cluster at the feet of some African centre. The skyline of the city is now a cardboard cutout, the towers reminiscent of the Gotham City background for a Batman comic. Topping it off, of course, is the insane bulbous knob of the Calgary Tower.

Architecture has a way of revealing the personality of the inmates. If the structure is such an icon as a legislative building, an entire province is unfrocked. Seen from the opposite bank of the North Saskatchewan River, the *fin de siècle* pile of stone that is the Alberta parliament in Edmonton is bathed in a soft roseate glow and there is almost a Roman look to it. Snatched from its depressing surroundings, it could fit into a minor European capital. It has imperial pretensions. The building on the bank of the Saskatchewan wants to be more important than it is.

There are misapprehensions abroad (meaning east of Kenora and west of Banff) that Fort Knox is to be dismantled and moved to somewhere between Pincher Creek and High River. There has been the impression given that the total blue-eyed Arab population of this province, like some test-tube generation raised in a hermetically sealed hothouse, is to vault into hitherto undreamed-of affluence that will place them—somewhat like a German shepherd's whistle—somewhere beyond the rest of us and out of reach.

But Alberta is still, to an outsider, a surprisingly primitive place. In booming Edmonton, so many faces on the street are square and rough, so many parkas and tough boots remind the visitor that frontier and bush and farm are still close. The *Toronto Star*'s Ottawa columnist, Richard Gwyn, viewed Alberta in a western swing and the entire province's squeals of pricked pride some weeks later were reminiscent of a high-school orchestra reacting to criticism. The chauvinism of the place reeks, wafts upward from the rough sidewalks and emanates like perfume from the conversations.

Most important, though (and this is the point the panjandrums of central Canada most dangerously ignore), is that Alberta feels frustrated, trapped, the only province besides contented, serene Saskatchewan without access to the sea. Alberta is a muscle-bound Switzerland. She aims to do something about it.

There is in this aggressive stance against the rest of Canada something else that is a little disturbing. It is there in the huge billboard that first greets the visitor at Calgary airport: "English is the international language of aviation."

Somehow, there is the need to exert muscular dominance. Alberta voters do not pick and choose: they stampede. Two of every three Albertans vote the same way—an aberration in the political mosaic that makes up the rest of Canada. They are con-formists with a vengeance—the only province that sends only one party to Ottawa.

The base of it all, the folk rite that reveals the soul, is the anachronism called the Stampede, which every summer allows the abandoning of the frontier strictures that are in play the rest of the year. It is like some ancient Greek festival, when societal rules were set in abeyance for a set duration. Men who decline to swear in front of their secretaries are suddenly revealed as raunchy gropers who establish that the barriers are down in the after-office parties in the suites in the Calgary Inn. They treat women as they would a horse. Stampede Week is when the Albertan climbs down out of his after-shave lotion ad and attempts to emulate the caricature. The boys are out of school. It is a strange province.

• See also "Klein, Ralph," "Lougheed, Peter" and "Manning, Ernest."

• See also "Edmonton."

## ALMOST, LORD
• See "Black, Conrad."

**AMBER, ARNOLD** There were really only two important people on one frenetic sprint from the bottom to the top of Europe in June 1980. One's name was Pierre Elliott Trudeau. The second, almost as important, was named Arnold Amber. Most everyone in the country has heard of the first chap. Almost no one—aside from his mother—has heard of the latter.

Arnold Amber is a short, unobtrusive chap with a hairline that long ago surrendered. He once used to run a counter-culture paper in Toronto in the days when those causes were popular.

In 1980, he was in charge of the TV crew that recorded Mr. Trudeau's every jot and tittle, and the people around Mr. Trudeau—since the picture box rules the world—jiggled and shook at the approach of Arnold Amber, a humble dictator in the age when puffery is king.

Aboard the Canadian military jet that zipped us from time zone to time zone, eating inedible Armed-Forces food, Cabinet ministers arrived and disappeared, vague MPs got free lifts and Justin, being given a crash course in how to mug for the camera, was shoved front and centre.

Small corporals and large customs officers were trampled in the rush to accommodate Arnold Amber's army of technological instant historians. Is there a need of special cars to speed Mr. Amber and his acolytes to a predetermined spot the minute the Trudeau jet jounces off the runway in Venice? Rome? London? Stockholm? Mars? Arnold Amber speaks and Patrick Gossage, the prime minister's press secretary, gargles and obeys. Mr. Gossage is a man of great high humour but he knows that the camera is a simp and people with typewriters spell capital T, which means trouble in River City.

Typewriters analyze. Cameras record fake non-events which, in the jargon of the prime ministerial staff's non-language, is a "photo opportunity"—a phony happening contrived for the electronic chaps who need a thirty-second clip. It is a symbiotic process. The electrical chaps are assigned a mindless gap to fill; the Trudeaudiatrics plot each day for arranged piffle that will make *The National*.

That's why the bustling Arnold Amber was there. If he doesn't get the shot, he's sacked. If Patrick Gossage doesn't get his man in the shot, he's sacked. It's the open marketplace—like hell.

• See also "journalists."


**AMBITION** Journalist John Schreiner wrote: "It is hard to imagine a successful politician without ambition."

Well, I'm not sure. I don't think I agree.

I can think of quite a few. I think of Stanley Knowles. I don't think he had any personal ambition. He wanted to help people who needed help and he sat, every day, as you could see on your Question Period TV screen, in the well of the Speaker's table, perhaps not understanding everything that was going on but willed there by Pierre Trudeau because he knew he belonged there, an icon of the Commons.

I can think of Gordon Fairweather from New Brunswick, Ged Baldwin from Alberta. I don't think Audrey McLaughlin was personally ambitious. Nor was Ernie Winch, the working-class socialist in the B.C. legislature who saw his fiery son Harold beaten by police in Depression riots, and then as CCF leader had the premiership snatched from him by lieutenant-governmental diktat, turned alcoholic in despair and then, recovering, became serene.

I don't think Senator Mike Mansfield of Montana, one of the wisest men in Washington and later ambassador in Japan, was personally ambitious.

Nor was Senator William Fulbright of Arkansas, Bill Clinton's personal hero, founder of the celebrated Fulbright scholarships that sent American college kids all over the world, enlightening them. While he doggedly fought against the White House with its Vietnam insanity.

I don't think Tommy Douglas, somewhat vain of course as a lightweight boxing champion in his native Scotland and a Baptist minister, who became Saskatchewan premier so he could introduce the first medicare system in North America, was doing it because he was "personally ambitious."

There is one thing that is greatly misunderstood, apparent only to those of us who must face up to politicians day upon day.

That is the belief that everyone who goes into politics is insanely ambitious, devoted to trample over their grandmother, if necessary to get to the top.

This is not true. There are those determined types, of course—a

Nixon, a Mulroney for example, a Parizeau perhaps, a Bouchard who belonged to four different parties, even a Churchill who knew he was divined for the top—who will hang in there in the belief that the goal will arrive.

There is also a second type, as any occupant of any press gallery anywhere can tell you. There is a very strange second layer of politicians. They are those who are in politics because they are personality-defective.

Left alone in society, lonely and bereft in an atmosphere where they have no real talent, they exude bombast from a podium, delighting in acolytes who love the excitement of a political rally and are content to lick stamps and plant lawn signs.

Modesty prevents listing their names, but they populate the front benches of the present Liberal government, blow-dried pomposities who could not exist without a Lear jet.

But there are actually real live human beings who exist within politics without a desire to take over the world. Jan Brown of the Reform seems to be one. Sheila Copps seems to be not one.

John Schreiner, you're a good reporter. But I think you're wrong.

## Americans
• See "U.S. of A."

**ARGOS** Do you ever get the impression that the owner of the Toronto Argonauts is running the country? There is, in the genial incompetence of the gang that couldn't govern straight, a distinct similarity to the country's funniest football team.

Bill Hodgson, in 1978, was a caricature of the capricious sports mogul who has a new toy but doesn't quite know how to wind it up. He possessed enough smarts to have made himself a million dollars while also owning the emotional maturity of a seven-year-old. He would do well in Ottawa.

A student of serious humour never knows whether to turn first to the sports pages or the heavy political stuff. Hodgson, who fired coaches faster than he changed his shirts, after firing the humble Leo Cahill confessed that perhaps he made a mistake in firing Russ Jackson, the coach he fired before he fired Cahill. With hindsight like this, you sometimes wonder what type of moxie is required to become a millionaire.

The prime minister has the same problem. The cabinet blunders on, resembling on most days the Argo backfield on a messed-up Statue-of-Liberty play. Exchange the entire Liberal cabinet for the Argo backfield. The more I think of it, the more convinced I am that it is a good idea.

**ARMSTRONG, LOUIS** The single seminal figure in America's own art form was Louis Armstrong, the waif who was sent to a New Orleans orphanage at age eleven for firing a pistol in the air.

A few eons ago, when the world was young, I went out to Vancouver airport one day to interview the arriving Louis Armstrong and ask him about his proposed trip to Russia. "That Khrushchev cat is welcome in Old Satchmo's dressing room any time," was the reply.

I remember phoning the story in on deadline and the young English girl on the rewrite desk who took it exclaimed, "Boy, what a lead!" In those days, Louis could give quotes in his sleep. He was going to "fracture them Russians," he said—and "a little happiness music should bruise those cats."

The phrases rolled off him and into the grateful typewriters of a world press.

But pure musicians warned that, like Ernest Hemingway, Louis was in danger of becoming a caricature of himself. Some members of his race accused him of becoming an Uncle Tom, with his Aunt Jemima smile and clowning roles in white man's movies. Spurred by the criticism, when news came from Arkansas of Governor Orville Faubus and dogs and cops blocking blacks from public school Satchmo angrily cancelled his U.S. State Department–sponsored tour of Russia. In a most un-Satchmo-like way, he told his government to "Go to hell."

These were the days, it must be explained, when black entertainers still were not welcome everywhere in the home of the rave and the land of the spree, and many of them found a welcome oasis in Vancouver nightclubs—the Cave and Isy's—where Lena Horne and Sammy Davis Jr. were frequent visitors.

One day I went to Satchmo's hotel room to wake him up. It was early afternoon—early morning for him—and his breakfast as usual was that special unfathomable mix of brew that undoubtedly led to his final kidney and liver problems. "Just to loosen the pipes," he explained.

He'd gone into a coma and had nearly died of pneumonia in Italy three months earlier but now he brushed it aside, as he always brushed aside any cautions on his insane schedule of one-nighters. "It was nothing but a chest cold," he growled through his burlap voice and through those steak-thick lips. "They played up the coma and all that jazz. Man, only rich people go into a coma. I was in a trance."

It was one of the great occasions of radio on July 6, 1971, when the father of all jazz died. Vancouver night disc jockey Jack Cullen devoted three solid hours to the guy. He played all his old bootleg tapes of Satch in action locally, in defiance of the prissy pedants of union officialdom.

There was a tremendous recording of Louis going out to

Kitsilano High School one noon hour in 1952 and sitting in—with the nervous school band—playing and singing a favourite, "Give Me a Kiss to Build a Dream On."

It was Louis who offered the ultimate definition of jazz to a matron who asked him to explain it: "Lady, if you have to ask, you'll never know."

**ATWOOD, MARGARET** Margaret Atwood has written that the beaver is the only animal that, to fend off pursuing enemies, will bite off its own testicles and leave them as a delaying method. That is Canada. Thank you, Ms. Atwood.

**AUF DER MAUR, NICK** What every city needs is a salon, a gathering spot for those who like to exchange information, rumours, lies and innuendoes. In other words, gossip—the lifeline of a civilized community. In London and all the grand cities, there has always been down through the decades a salon where the gifted and the malicious gathered to delight in fine talk and wicked assassination of the reputation of one's enemies. Oscar Wilde or Noël Coward, over a thin sherry, would dazzle and dominate while the bitchiest women in town exchanged the worst about their friends.

Every city should have one. For many years Montreal's equivalent was whatever bistro Nick Auf der Maur, the famed boulevardier and perennial mayoralty candidate, also known as the Red Adair of the Olympics movement, chose as his designated drinking spot. As he got into a fight with management and moved his floating crap game elsewhere, the salon automatically moved with him, sometimes including cartoonist Terry (Aislin) Mosher and Mordecai Richler, depending on their current attitude toward the gargle. Since Auf der Maur's death a few years ago the city has not been the same.

**BALONEY, MYRON**
- See "Mulroney, Brian."

**BARRETT, DAVE** Dave Barrett was the Buddy Hackett of Canadian politics, shucking his jacket, loosening his tie, on occasions in past reincarnations taking off his shoes, zinging punch lines that would do well in Las Vegas, sending his loyal pseudo-socialists into raptures, an entertainer who didn't cost the customer a cent in the local church basement.

Short, fat, profane, he has John Diefenbaker's timing crossed with Lenny Bruce's vocabulary. He quaffs Chinese food by the bushel, plays rugby (where he is in constant danger of losing his pants) and tells lady reporters to bleep off.

He is a passionate man, tutored by Jesuit scholars in U.S. universities. A unique Canadian politician in that his formative years were spent there, where he became a hopeless fan of Franklin Delano Roosevelt and his New Deal. Dave Barrett, in 1983, still preached the ethic of the New Deal. He ran up against, and stubbed his tongue on, the voters of 1983.

In 1972, Dave Barrett became the first NDP premier of British Columbia. One of his initial acts was to summon the heads of all major B.C. mines to his office. He took off his suit jacket, threw it in a corner, rolled up his sleeves and then threw at them every obscene word he had ever learned, boasting that he was going to fix their robber baron ways. That finished his relations with the business community.

Dave Barrett, the Lost Wages one-liner, had a great time ridiculing the Socred taunt that underneath his carefully tailored pinstripe suit he still wore red shorts. He waved his underwear in public. It was great show biz, but unfortunately he also waved his tongue in public.

• See also "political suicide."

**B.C. POLITICS** It was Angus MacInnis, a founder of the CCF, who once said that in the Maritimes politics was a disease, in Quebec a religion, in Ontario a business, on the Prairies a protest and in British Columbia entertainment.

To understand, you must remember it was no surprise that within a year of Premier Dave Barrett taking power in 1972 a cabinet minister had to be sacked for being caught *in flagrante delicto* in a car within a fifty-yard view of the Premier's office window. Or that the social hostess of the stately Empress Hotel complained about the two NDP ministers, installed in a suite close by the one reserved for Prince Philip, who were cooking their meals by hotplate and leaving the beer bottles rolling about the Persian carpets.

Premier MiniWac Bennett, Son of Wacky, had his troubles, despite spending a gazillion dollars on Expo 86 in an attempt to get re-elected. All around him, otherwise sane ministers stumbled into bedrooms or their stockbroker's office—neither a place where a minister loyal to Her Majesty should spend much time. If you could set it to music (as someone inevitably will), it would make a good Broadway farce.

All of this, of course, is in keeping with the great traditions of

B.C. politics. Voters in the nethermost province have been weaned on kooks, from the day a hundred years ago when an itinerant from the California gold fields, William Smith, felt his name was too commonplace. He changed it to Amor de Cosmos (lover of the world), became B.C.'s second premier and once delivered a speech lasting twenty hours. Down through the years, the longing for slightly deranged statesmen has persisted. There were the crowd-pleasing antics of Phlying Phil Gaglardi, the evangelical speed freak who while upholding the law as highways minister was convicted of speeding and careless-driving offences, had his license suspended, was fined $1,000 for contempt of court and once sped away after running over a dog, only to be overtaken by an irate motorist (and voter). The Reverend Gaglardi, in a passionate plea for understanding in the legislature, one day cried, "If I tell a lie it's only because I think I'm telling the truth!"

There was Wacky Bennett himself, an abstemious teetotaller who dressed in a black homburg and a funeral director's suit but who in some perverse way collected around him a Technicolor retinue of flakes, touts, rounders and sycophants. One went to jail for forging his signature, another used his name to call phony press conferences for mining promoters and a third wrote a fawning book that was so dreadful it almost won, unentered, the Leacock medal for humour.

And there was the celebrated Agnes Kripps, a gushing Socred who one day aroused snoozing MLAs with a speech explaining there were too many sniggers about the word "sex" and that she proposed replacing it with an entirely new word—bolt—for Biology Of Living Today. There was a thunderous clatter as MLAs of all parties sat up with a start. "I'm bolt upright just listening to you," cried an NDP backbencher. As poor flustered Mrs. Kripps tried to flounder on, a Socred shouted, "It's okay for the bolts, but what about the nuts?" Mrs. Kripps, refusing to quit when she was behind, finally attempted to silence the hilarity all about her by pleading to the chair: "Mr. Speaker, Mr. Speaker, won't you please bang that thing of yours on the table."

Please, do not judge British Columbia by its current spate of prurience and forgetful bank accounts. Judge it by its past. It has a proud tradition it must maintain.

• See also "Barrett, Dave," "Bennett, Bill," "Bennett, W. A. C.," "Harcourt, Mike" and "Vander Zalm, Bill."

• See also "Victoria."

**BEATTY, PERRIN** It's a big bad world out there on the international scene, filled with intrigue, regional hatreds and mindless conflicts. Wherever one looks, from Bosnia to Somalia, there are nothing but complications. To survive, one needs the cunning of Henry Kissinger, the skills of a Metternich, the talents of a Talleyrand.

It is no place for innocents, as a younger Joe Clark discovered when he decided he was going to immediately move the Canadian embassy from Tel Aviv to Jerusalem.

Into this international minefield Canada sent a naïf. In one of the more puzzling decisions to come out of Ottawa in Prime Minister Kim Campbell's months, a hurried cabinet shuffle made Perrin Beatty our external affairs minister.

This was sending a lamb to slaughter. A seamless, fresh-cheeked product from downtown Fergus, Ontario, Beatty is a Boy Scout, a tourist wandering in the casbah of Casablanca, ripe to have his pocket picked and his American Express card filched.

Two years previous, Beatty was made communications minister by Brian Mulroney—this after his brilliant stint in Defence where he was going to buy all those billion-dollar submarines.

Let us set the scene. The new genius allowed into his office a reporter from a serious national newspaper. Let us quote:

"Beatty—who is a self-acknowledged 'techno-junkie'—is fascinated by the mix of creativity and technology that the department must juggle. And last Saturday, before he learned of his new appointment, he happened to buy a compact disc that he thinks provides a neat paradigm of the two sides of the communications department.

"'Do we have fifty-nine seconds to spare?' he asks, before making his way to a CD player behind his desk. He presses the play button. One hears a breakneck version of Chopin's Minute Waltz, with thunking noises in the background and scratchy sound quality. As a recording it is terrible; as a document, Beatty points out, it is unique: the pianist is Frederic Chopin himself.

"'This is the oldest recording in existence, 143 years old,' says Beatty, and explains its origin. It was found in the summer of 1990 by construction workers digging in a suburb of Nohant, a town in central France. They found a steel box, containing a glass cylinder and a barely legible letter from an eccentric inventor named Hippolyte Sot, who perfected a primitive method for recording sound, and tried it on his neighbour Chopin in 1847—twenty years before Edouard Leon Scott, who is assumed to have invented recording, conducted his experiments.

"'I think there are three wonderful ways in which this relates to this department,' says Beatty, who has photocopied an article recounting this story in time for the interview. 'First, you have the act of recording something, the artist performing his work as he wished it. Second of all, the technology affected that artistic choice, since the cylinder could take only about a minute of sound, and the type of piano Chopin was playing on allowed him to play more quickly than we can on modern pianos.

"'And finally, we now have a technology that allows us to optically scan and digitalize it, and bring this to life again. The inventor himself had no way of playing the cylinder to see if it worked, and had to bury it in his garden. He was forced to wait for technology to catch up with him.'"

As more than one reader of the terribly serious paper quickly pointed out, Sot in French means fool. The record label was the previously unknown Xoha, an anagram for Hoax.

The article in the excellent British magazine *Classic CD*, revealing the world scoop on the buried Chopin, explained that the catalogue number of the historic CD was 010491 (April 1, 1991).

And this is the baby we sent out on the world scene? *O tempora! O mores!*

**BENNETT, BILL** Bill Bennett has four sons. They have inherited from him, as he inherited from his father, a fiercely independent spirit, and some of them decided they could make it away from home, heading for those then-heady days in the Alberta oil patch. Things were not always that rosy, and one day one son called home to Dad in Kelowna saying, "We're down to the beans." Premier William Richards Bennett replied, "When you're out of beans, let me know."

The guy who shocked his province by quitting his job is a tough guy, as his decision to retire—at the height of publicity, at the height of Expo's great success—indicated.

He used to fight fiercely with his father over the dinner table about politics, and when he finally did enter the legislature on his father's retirement, he explained that he had needed to wait until that moment—that the two of them could never be in the same arena together.

Bill Bennett, though a millionaire, is in a funny way a product of the Depression, born in the year 1932 just three months before the New York Dow Jones average hit its lowest point after the crash of 1929. He was so impatient, in ways that would interest Dr. Freud, to prove himself to his autocratic father that he didn't even bother to finish high school, casting aside his grade twelve diploma so as to make a buck and prove himself—in a family where he didn't have to prove himself.

He was mocked by Barrett, a social worker from the East End ghetto of Vancouver, as a silver-spoon clone. In fact, by the time MiniWac entered politics at the advanced age of forty-one, he was a richer man through real estate and finance company dealings than was his hardware merchant, twenty-year-premier father. He wanted to prove something to his family first and then, in his relentless, dull, unforgiving way, to prove it to his voters. The message: there ain't no free lunch.

Bill Bennett, through all his eleven years as premier, toughed it out in the atmosphere of being one Canadian premier—as opposed to all those lawyers and lawyers and lawyers—who had never gone to university.

He was a tough little athlete, but never allowed to prove it. He couldn't play on his school's sport teams because it was insisted that he report for work at the family hardware store immediately after school. He once confessed that he had only come to the middle-class sports—tennis and skiing—in his thirties because there was never enough time before.

After being hand-picked for his father's vacant seat in South Okanagan and being hand-arranged as his father's successor as leader of the amorphous Social Credit Party, he absolutely hated his three years as opposition leader in the B.C. legislature. "Bankers," Bennett said one day in disgust, "would go great in opposition. They can always tell you why something can't be done."

In public, he is wooden, a characteristic he shares with other politicians named Stanfield and Clark and Liberal Don Johnston. In the words of a visiting female journalist subjected to two hours of his good looks, he has "a relentless dullness" and is "eminently forgettable." Another female reporter, in the midst of a TV profile on Bennett designed to reveal the real man behind the political mask, demanded in frustration, "Don't you ever *indulge* yourself in anything?"

"Well, yes," replied MiniWac solemnly, "peanut butter sand-wiches." He held his fingers apart before the camera to indicate the sinful thickness of the crime.

In private he has a deadly, cynical wit. He once got himself involved in a celebrated B.C. lawsuit when he tossed off a remark about those who have Scotch with their cornflakes—a reference that everyone in the press gallery readily understood.

He has no friends in politics, at least not in Victoria politics. Bill Bennett, in his entire term as premier, lived alone in a penthouse atop a hotel a few blocks from his office, while his wife remained in the blissful family home on Okanagan Lake with the tennis court and the fruit orchards, his weekend retreat.

As Brian Mulroney offered, one of the most important things about politics is knowing when to leave, something that Mila thought about a lot. Another wife, Audrey Bennett, ran the switchboard when Bill bought his first motel early in their marriage. She was promised long ago by her husband that he would stay only two terms in office. He stayed part of a third. He kept his word, if only a little late, and that is also very tough.

• See also "Bennett, W. A. C."

**BENNETT, W. A. C.** All the great ones have a certainty of purpose. It would never *occur* to them that they might be wrong. They press on, secure in the knowledge that the rest of the ignorant world will eventually catch up with their mental processes. William Andrew Cecil Bennett had that certainty. Like John Diefenbaker, he was defeated a half dozen times in attempts at public office before he could get elected the first time. Tries for federal Conservative nominations, for provincial seats, for local Tory positions. All fell flat. As with Dief, all it did was strengthen the resolve.

When W. A. C. Bennett was a neophyte politician in Victoria, representing Kelowna, whenever any of his children contracted measles or mumps he would move out of the family home and check into a Kelowna hotel. He had more important priorities than to get sick. Destiny awaited.

When Bennett finally did achieve power, it mattered little to him that the vehicle was a kooky populist collection of funny-money artistes under the grab-bag title of Social Credit. The vehicle was unimportant; the man and his mission were paramount.

The man known to the rest of Canada as "Wacky," pictured by cartoonists as a bumpkin in a homburg, governed British Columbia for twenty years and never wavered from his sweeping concepts. His tactics were often mean and petty, but the design was vast. Critics were too trifling even to be answered. Over the years that this reporter had the chance to sit in his office for a chat—the same reporter who gleefully caricatured his party as a bumbling gang of woolhats and numbskulls and who referred in print to the man on the other side of the desk as Premier Whack C. Bombast—Bennett never once even acknowledged that he knew what my occupation was, or that he had ever read a single word I had written. Newspaper carpers, in the sweep of things, were insignificant. He never whined, never complained—he used instead the most effective weapon any politician can use: he pretended you didn't exist.

From afar he appeared a clown. Up close, he was the most shrewd politician ever produced in B.C., a bookend of the country along with that other sly showman, Joey Smallwood.

He had the simplicity of someone who drew his strength from small-town virtues. "City states always collapsed," he said. "They did in Greece, and they will anywhere else because they're built on themselves." One day in his office he swept a contemptuous arm at a mention of all those businessmen in high glass towers in Vancouver: "Know what they're doing? All they're doing is cross-filing sawdust through a knot hole." A classic description of modern office life that will always cling.

He purposely sought the enmity of the Establishment, knowing that was the key to the kingdom. Nobody liked him but the people. He was eccentric, stubborn, proud—just like the province he loved.

• See also "Bennett, Bill."

**BERGER, TOM** Tom Berger, ex-politician, ex-judge, ex-media hero, is the man who made Canadians rethink their North. A man with vast promise, he has gone through several careers and is still fighting for the two forces that have shaped his life: native peoples and the environment that sustains them.

Berger was always destined to be a name. Son of a Mountie who had been wronged in a pension dispute, Berger was a socialist-in-a-hurry (though a Liberal while at university). He arrived in the House of Commons at the same time as another ambitious MP: John Turner. He lost his seat within a year during those quick

Dief-Pearson election years, but turned to the provincial NDP and by stealth and guile overthrew the incumbent leader in much the same way that Brian Mulroney stalked and then slew Joe Clark. The man he killed off, a shrewd and civilized former Scottish carpenter called Bob Strachan, had a surprising comment about the rival who deposed him. Tom Berger, said Strachan, some day will be the youngest man ever to become chief justice of the Supreme Court of Canada.

That seemed a good bet. After Wacky Bennett destroyed him, he returned to his law practice and, at thirty-eight, was a surprise appointment to the B.C. Supreme Court. The man who appointed him? One John Turner, minister of justice. It was another Liberal, Northern Affairs Minister Jean Chrétien, who picked him as the royal commissioner who was supposed to, as all royal commissioners, spend several years obfuscating and delaying so the government and the oil companies could get on with their business of screwing the North. Berger instead turned around the snoozing Canadian attitude toward the fragile northern ecology, dragging adoring media figures behind him as he slept in Indian cabins and held all-night meetings while the CBC broadcasted his hearings in local dialects.

The return to the mundane duties of the B.C. Supreme Court after all the national attention obviously paled. The man who was the great admirer of Chief Justice Bora Laskin for his civil rights reputation could not abide the kitchen-sink scrambling of the Trudeau government over patriating the Constitution and spoke out over the cynical exclusion from the Charter of Rights and Freedoms of women and native peoples. Laskin denounced him and Trudeau, that other civil libertarian, turned establishmentarian, dumped on him in public. (While they criticized his effrontery, the Ottawa hypocrites quietly brought into the Charter the very things Berger advocated.) The battler had had enough and, his dreams of being chief justice of all of Canada denied, he quit the B.C. bench after twelve years to return to private life. As the coal miner said in that immortal *Beyond the Fringe* sketch, "He didn't have the Latin for the judgin'."

**BERTON, PIERRE** There are half a hundred people—mostly women—who have sat beside Pierre Berton at a banquet and have concluded, due to his silence throughout, that he is essentially a shy man. There could be another opinion. Could you say a father named Pierre who named his children Penny, Pamela, Patsy, Peter, Paul, Peggy Anne—and an adopted daughter Perri—just possibly might have an ego?

Someone said all journalists are really shy egomaniacs. That is true, and so Berton fits comfortably into both categories.

All we know is that he is one of the more interesting Canadians this country has produced. He is passionate, he is bumbling, he has extraordinary energy—and he doesn't fear anything. What he hates is Canadian complacency.

Pierre Berton has enraged every self-respecting newspaperman in this country by walking away from the newsroom and the stale coffee and burnt-out editors and rising so disgustingly to the top of the professional personality heap. Slip into any press club in the land and you can hear how Berton is overrated, the king of the recyclers, derivative, grasping and guilty of a dozen other sins.

I know. I was there. (A 1968 review of *The Smug Minority*: "shallow, superficial, insulting to the intelligence...") I recognize the standard progression on Berton: from awe to envy to resentment back across the spectrum to awe and then respect.

There was the shameless Berton of trenchcoat fame in the

1940s when sleaze was a page one staple, almost a caricature out of *The Front Page*.

The series on which he made his national reputation, the mysterious Headless Valley in the Yukon where bodies supposedly disappeared, was largely written before his ski-plane landed in the remote valley scarcely long enough for a photographer to take the necessary on-the-spot photos.

Jack Webster, the best reporter in the country wasted on radio and TV, says, "Berton taught me one thing. Never write a story before five minutes to noon. That way the only space left was page one and they had to play it there." The contrite Berton of later years, seeking redemption, confided, "Everything that was wrong with the newspaper business was wrong with me."

He's now, of course, a national icon.

The big gangling redhead, now progressed to blow-dried white, is almost *reeking* of respectability, garlanded with the musk of Keeper of the National Identity.

Berton's father passed up a faculty spot at Queen's to chase the 1898 gold rush to the Yukon, where Pierre was born. The big galumph who was raised in the mythical Yukon gold-mine town, has indeed lived with history. He has covered everything. In Korea as a war correspondent, he was reviled for having his own jeep, driver, interpreter and bodyguard. He did Hiroshima, the Berlin Wall, China, Hollywood, Antarctica. In the shadow of the Sphinx, he and CBC producer Daryl Duke—waiting for an interview with Colonel Nasser—end up in a belly-dancing joint that featured two half-naked seven-foot Watusi. Berton asks Duke how he likes the local drink, arrack.

"It's more like pop," says Duke. "It's had no effect on me."

Berton: "Then why are we dancing on the table?"

He is hated, of course, by academics because he has hijacked their monopoly: he has made history readable. Early on he was asked on television what subjects he would suggest to young writers. Berton said there were dozens of fascinating stories out there—the Dionne quintuplets, the CPR, Niagara.

Twenty years later, he gleefully recalls, they were still sitting there, untouched. Result: three more best-sellers. On October 1, 1972, he had four books on the best-seller top ten: "That record has never been exceeded and, I suspect, never will be."

The big guy—so shy and diffident among strangers, so overpoweringly egotistical among roistering buddies—is a gem, if only our natural envy could concede it.

## BIG RED

- See "Creighton, Doug."

**BLACK, CONRAD (ALSO *KONRAD BLAST*)** Conrad Black, the Darth Vader of Canadian journalism, ruled fifty-eight of the daily newspapers in Canada. That's a pretty fair hunk of the population—more than Hearst ever had in the United States, more than any one tycoon ever had in Britain.

In short, he's a major threat to our sanity.

Conrad (he is now known simply as Conrad, as in Madonna or Elvis) is in deep danger of becoming a caricature of himself. Lord Almost, as Dalton Camp has dubbed him, would follow, of course, in the storied tradition of Canadian interlopers who lusted after British titles. Max Aitken, of downtown New Brunswick, who left Canada under a cloud over a suspicious cement cartel, was knighted at age thirty-two and by thirty-seven was Lord Beaverbrook. The gormless Roy Thomson ("owning a TV station is a licence to print money") bought his title to the House of Lords and willingly gave up his Canadian citizenship.

So why does the brilliant Lord Almost covet a spot in the pasture land of chinless wonders and spavined fox hunters. The answer, so sad, is that Lord Almost is a bully—as are most types born to wealth and power—and he wants it both ways.

Konrad Blast likes to run Canada from London. On swallowing up the Southam chain, he said he wanted to publish its newspapers at the highest standards possible. "And that means separating news from comment, assuring a reasonable variety of comment, and not just the overwhelming avalanche of soft, left, bland, envious, mediocre pap which has poured like sludge through the centre pages of most of the Southam papers for some time."

I like that. Soft, left, bland, envious, mediocre pap... sludge. I used to work for Southam and I guess that's what I produced.

Some of us, told that the turnips are off the menu, can switch to carrots instead. A tire is flat? Take the bus to work instead. These are the mighty choices most of us have in life. Not Conrad Black, boy tycoon. His choices are more global. When he can't become a press baron in one country, he simply goes off and buys another country. Not exactly a country, I suppose, but purchasing the London *Daily Telegraph*, the largest-circulation quality newspaper in Blighty, is roughly equivalent to grasping that tight little island by the short and curlies.

Actually, I like and admire Conrad. I admire anyone who has an IQ of 203 and is the only man in the world who has a larger vocabulary than William F. Buckley Jr.

A decade ago, when I was with Southam in Washington, the Smithsonian Institution for some strange reason asked me to mount a lecture series for their night programs. Conrad at that time was practically unknown in the United States and I invited him to appear, eager to witness how the insular White House press would be dazzled by his command of the language and his general arrogance toward anyone who was not lucky enough to be Conrad Black.

He kindly agreed to come, mainly because he wanted to savage a "soft, left, envious" Washington correspondent for a London paper, but unfortunately the whole project was cancelled when the Smithsonian became suspicious of my "mediocre, sludge-like" intentions.

In London, he has graciously donated his driver and Jaguar to deliver me to my hotel from his Canary Wharf office. In Toronto, I always invite him to my parties, which his secretary always politely declines, explaining he will be out of the country, which he now controls.

As mentioned, once denied a bauble in one country, Conrad simply switches oceans. A terribly literate man with a taste for power that goes back to when he was eight, he worships Napoleon. Making money has always been a trivial bother; he vowed to become a multimillionaire by the age of thirty and hit it easily. Now, his main interest is becoming a press lord. He is one of those strange rich men who is sort of a press club groupie. His friends include Toronto *Globe and Mail* London correspondent John Fraser and the CBC's Brian Stewart, with whom he shared school backgrounds. He was great friends with the Montreal *Gazette* boulevardier Nick Auf der Maur, whom Black liked, one suspects, because of a similar raffish approach to life—one plush, the other bereft.

Conrad has only one problem, two actually. The first is accuracy. When he gobbled Southam and was shucking most of its independent directors, I had lunch with one, a fine gentleman. He mentioned that he had read Conrad's autobiography, as any wise Southam director would. He said there were five incidents in which he was personally involved, and all five were inaccurate.

I know of what he spoke. In the same book, my buddy Conrad has a tale about this innocent that is completely untrue. When the book publisher pointed out that it seemed like an improbable tale, Conrad replied, "Let him sue." Me sue Conrad, who spills more money on the Concorde each week than my Fothlets need for college? Get serious.

The second problem. My lunch companion explained it. "Conrad," he said, "is a bully." He didn't say it bitterly, resentfully. Matter-of-factly. Bullies, as in the schoolyard, can dish it out but don't like to take it. When the CBC's sophisticated Joe Schlesinger did his calm, non-hysterical two-part look at Black, Conrad ordered all of his fifty-eight papers to print his overheated reply— which was essentially a hilarious claim that he never interfered with any paper he owned. They fell down in the press clubs all over the land with that one.

• See also "Auf der Maur, Nick" and "Thomson, Ken."

### BLOC QUÉBÉCOIS (ALSO *BLOCKHEADS*)
• See "Bouchard, Lucien" and "Duceppe, Gilles."

**BOUCHARD, LUCIEN** Lucien Bouchard is a singular man, probably the best-read MP during his time in Ottawa. More intelligent—in a cerebral if not practical sense—than Mulroney, his literary and classical references putting him near the Lévesque and Trudeau level.

Lawrence Martin's tome—*The Antagonist: Lucien Bouchard and the Politics of Delusion*—is a brilliant primer for anyone seriously interested in the mind of the man who wanted to ruin the country. One suspects Martin wishes some anonymous sneak had not leaked the front-page sensation about Saint Lucien and the Shrink.

Here he is, having written a very serious book about the man who would destroy Canada and it is reduced to pop psychobabble over whether the then-premier of Quebec is nuts or not.

That overheated front page junk—a psychiatrist's off-the-wall assessment of a man he has never met—is nothing compared with the calmly assembled dissection of the man by a good reporter who spent two years interviewing some two hundred friends and family of this brilliant and dangerous man.

Martin's best witnesses are Bouchard's own brothers. They note his traits early in life: a reasonable, mannered personality ninety-five per cent of the time who can suddenly burst in the remaining five per cent into an earthquake-prone figure who goes bananas. That's not nuts. That's just Lucien.

He has the attention span of a hummingbird. In his memoirs (he began to write his life story, *On the Record*, on July 1, 1991, the day after the founding of the Bloc Québécois—who writes his memoirs at this early stage?) he confesses that he first supported the Liberal Trudeau, then secretly kept his Parti Québécois membership card while ambassador to France, joined the Mulroney cabinet and then birthed the Bloc Québécois.

That's four different parties while an adult. He's an adjustable sort.

Intelligence, of course, never excludes nonsense. In a foreword added for the 1994 edition, he writes: "Quebec sovereigntists do not want to destroy a country but to build a better one"—the non sequitur of all time.

Bouchard's tale is a remarkable one, a man whose life has seemed to have been in search of a cause. Rushing to be in the front ranks on Charles de Gaulle's memorable visit to Quebec City, he was crushed by the crowd, fell face first into a steel wire barricade and in pain looked up at the general: "He held out his hand, I grasped it eagerly." He tells of watching his father, who never

went past the fourth grade, attempting at the kitchen table to
write to the first of his sons who went to study in France and
finally dissolving in tears and crumpling the sheet of paper in
despair after a half-hour, surrendering to his inability to write and
communicate "with the son who had left to follow his own
dreams."

What impressed schoolmates of Bouchard was his obvious intelligence and his aloof bearing—reminding one friend "more of a
Latin cardinal or a Renaissance philosopher." He danced from
Trudeau-admirer and party worker to Parti Québécois card-holder
into the arms of Mulroney.

At law school at Laval University in Quebec City, they were
drawn together—two small-town boys from working-class backgrounds. Mulroney wanted the aura of Bouchard's intellectual
gifts. Bouchard wanted the immeasurable Mulroney charm that
led to so many political contacts. Like two scorpions, doomed to
poison one another, they used each other for their own aims.

Since being "stupefied" by the No vote in the 1980 referendum,
this has been a bitter man. He does not seem to see the
hypocrisy—while keeping his PQ membership alive for fifteen
years—of accepting Mulroney's gift of an ambassadorship to Paris,
a safe Tory seat and passage into the federal cabinet.

He had a most telling comment when reporters asked him if he
would apologize for his eyebrow-raising complaint that the "white
people" of Quebec weren't having enough babies. "Apologize? I
never apologize," he announced imperiously before disappearing
into an elevator. There goes a man with a bulletproof ego.

An intelligent francophone commentator has pointed out
that—while anglophones puzzled over his multi-party-switching—
Quebeckers simply see that as a pragmatic man adjusting to
changing conditions.

The first Bouchard, with his stonecutter's tools, arrived in Quebec city in 1650. Lucien Bouchard's father died without ever seeing the old country and left Quebec only twice, to see the horse races at Saratoga and Maurice Richard play in a Stanley Cup final in Boston.

But three of his sons earned doctorates in France. Unfortunate that Lucien Bouchard cannot see that Canada proved not too bad for his truck-driver father.

**BOURASSA, ROBERT** Well, one thing we know. Robert Bourassa read my column.

The suggestion in this space that he could very well be a major factor in the October 1993 federal election was followed, of course, by the announcement of his coming resignation. The wily premier always recognized sound journalistic advice when he saw it.

He did not resign immediately, instead, he stayed around until early in 1994, still able to be a most influential bystander in a crucial Canadian election. He was not a bystander, of course, at all. He was a player, and even more so by the long warning of his coming disappearance from the public scene.

There is no question that Bourassa was the wiliest politician on the Canadian election scene, provincial or federal. Former Ontario premier David Peterson was entirely correct in stating that, "He made the rest of the politicians in the country look like cowboys."

Peterson should know. He sat beside Bourassa at the 1993 federal-provincial conferences and was, it seems, one of the cowboys. We won't even have to try the comparison on a Don Getty.

Bourassa had the resilience of a Mackenzie King. His apprenticeship in the job happened to coincide with the October Crisis, and he never really seemed to recover from that experience—Pierre Trudeau treating him disdainfully from then on. He was Quebec's youngest-ever premier at thirty-six, reviled for doing an about-face on the Victoria Charter in 1971, laughed at by the press for using his bodyguard as his hairdresser (or vice versa), leaving the country in disgrace after a humiliating defeat by René Lévesque's Parti Québécois in 1976.

He lasted six years, and when René Lévesque and the Péquistes toppled him, Bourassa went into what he calls his "political purgatory"—in self-imposed exile first in Europe, then at Harvard, gathering himself for his remarkable recovery.

He in fact came within hours of joining the separatist faction that left the Liberal party. The night before the crucial party convention, Lévesque and followers planned their dramatic challenge to the party in a meeting in the basement of Bourassa's home. By morning he had changed his mind and they went their separate ways, to meet only at the ballot box.

After a year of self-imposed exile in Europe, where he studied models of federalism and the monetary union, Bourassa returned to Quebec in 1978 as a part-time university lecturer and business consultant.

The ex-premier was immediately flattered to find that Quebec reporters, who had loved to hate him for so many years, were chasing after him for interviews.

Over the next two years, Bourassa was in increasing demand as a public speaker. Despite a cool relationship with Liberal leader Claude Ryan, he began to take on some important assignments for the party. During the referendum campaign, he played a leading role as critic of the PQ's proposal for a common market and monetary union between a sovereign Quebec and Canada.

It was an extraordinary turnaround for the forty-seven-year-old, independently wealthy economist. In four years time he went from "the Richard Nixon of Quebec politics," widely despised by

Quebec voters for running a corrupt and inefficient government, to one of the most popular politicians in the province.

His second term proved he knew his timing well. So did the timing of this farewell.

## BOY TYCOON

• See "Black, Conrad."

## BRADLEY, BILL

One day, on a drive from Vancouver to Washington, D.C., I took Old Blue, my trusty steed, down to a little town called Crystal City on the banks of the Missouri River before it turns into the Mississippi.

Simply because I wanted to see it (it was very ordinary), because that is where Bill Bradley, my candidate for president, grew up.

Bill Bradley—knowing that I was pulling for him—was finally making some remarkable gains on Vice President Al Gore—Al Bore—who was the (if you'll excuse me) slam-dunk cinch for the Democratic nomination for 2000.

In the meantime, the equally dull Bradley just kept shuffling along, refusing to go on the TV chat shows, staying away from CNN, just talking to the folks.

He's certainly a thinker. At six-foot-five, he was a basketball All-American at Ivy League's Princeton. Always a team player, in his final college game at the NCAA tournament his coach urged him to go for it. He scored fifty-six points, then a tournament record.

Despite the lucrative entreaties and pleadings of the New York Knickerbockers—dying for a white star in a black man's game—he won a Rhodes Scholarship instead and went off to Oxford.

When he returned, on his own timing, he was an integral part of the famous starting five for the Knicks on their championship teams during his ten years with them. While also being known as the worst dresser (and cheapest tipper) in the NBA.

He was elected to the Senate from New Jersey (home of Princeton) in 1978, 1984 and 1990, before taking some time out to think.

An only child back in Crystal City, his school-dropout father went to work at the local bank "shining pennies" and rose to become president. He had calcified arthritis of the lower spine. Young Bradley and his schoolteacher mother had to dress him every day, tie his shoes, attach his suspenders and pick up his newspapers from the floor.

Everyone wondered why Bradley, having retired from the Senate, was not going for the presidency. The year 1992 was not a good one. His wife developed breast cancer, had a mastectomy and six months of chemotherapy. His father went blind and received radiation for skin cancer. His mother had advancing emphysema. His secretary of fourteen years took leave to fight ovarian cancer. Two friends died in plane crashes, and another friend committed suicide. No wonder he took a couple of years out to think.

He's a serious guy. One year, after a particularly grisly loss that knocked the Knicks out of the playoffs, an eager young sportswriter approached Bradley, who sat slumped at his locker.

"So," the kid burbled, "how do you feel?"

Bradley didn't answer at first. He just sat there, head down, sweat-soaked towel around his neck, and then gradually looked up, red-faced and stared the scribe hard in the eye.

"You have a stupid job," he said.

• See also "sportswriters."

## BRAMPTON BILLY
• See "Davis, Bill."

**BRITAIN** My digs, the Stafford, is the best small hotel in the world. It is like a boarding house—where they take plastic. The lone elevator breaks down every day. One morning, there is no hot breakfast—"the gas" has disappeared. The unbuttered toast, as always, is stone cold even when there is gas.

Outside the door, there is a narrow paved shortcut that opens onto Green Park, one of the three lovely linked hunks of grass—in between St. James's Park and Hyde Park—that are "the lungs of London."

Turn left down Queen's Walk and about one hundred metres along, intercepted only by a punker with green spiked hair flogging a magazine, is the wonderfully named lane, Milkmaids Passage. At the end is an ugly pile of yellow brick: St. James's Palace, built in 1532 by Henry VIII, home last week to the shattered corpse of the young lady who even in death changed the monarchy forever.

Out front was the perfect image of a country that can't decide when it will enter the modern world. A lone redcoat, wearing a busby before a sentry box, carrying erect a submachine-gun that was topped by—what's this?—a bayonet. A bayonet! To counter nuclear missiles, no doubt. There is the great confusion of Britain, a faded empire now desperate not to give up the tourist trade.

- See also "Diana, Princess."

## BRITISH COLUMBIA (ALSO *BRITISH CALIFORNIA*)

British Columbians, one must understand, view all other residents of Canada with an air of amused pity. Anyone so stupid as to not live in Narcissus-on-the-Pacific absolutely deserves the lousy weather elsewhere. The vaster forms of contempt are reserved, of course, for Ontario, the fading linchpin of Confederation, where all the bucks are siphoned and inside every office clerk is a Conrad

Black struggling to get out. When a proper Torontonian is nose-deep in paperwork at 5:30 quitting time, eager to earn the company bonus, which will give him a swimming pool shaped like his ulcer, his British California equivalent is long gone into the hot tub, doing underwater research with his secretary.

The concept of British Columbia as a world unto itself, a unique retreat facing towards the Pacific and away from the rest of the nation, has always puzzled most Canadians.

B.C. has always been spiced from afar. It was formed and shaped by forces from abroad rather than the usual drift westward of Canadians. The first industries of B.C. were linked to these points of origin—capital found in London and San Francisco rather than in Toronto and Montreal.

But British Columbia, as history students will recall, was a British colony long before it joined Canada. It, of course, reeks with its British heritage. Victoria, the capital, honours a Queen who didn't have offspring mixing with doxies or parading their bouts of horizontal delight with strangers before the television cameras. The very nature of the province, the warp and the woof, is a result of the English Fabian socialists who sailed around Cape Horn and settled there.

It's why, to this day, B.C. has the most resilient and aggressive NDP remnant—along with the agrarian radicals of Saskatchewan—in the land. Only in those two provinces is the present-day NDP, bastard son of the CCF, an option for power each election.

The famous river, fierce and dangerous, tumbles out of the rocky gorges of the Fraser Canyon at the town of Hope and settles down for a leisurely, meandering flow to Vancouver 160 kilometres away. This is the Fraser Valley, lush and green with dairy farms, fruit, hops, and at its delta mouth on the Pacific, spreading soil as rich as that of Holland.

It is also the home of the Bible Belt, spreading perhaps sixty-five kilometres from Chilliwack to Langley in its middle section, redolent with fundamentalist true believers who worship at the Social Credit shrine and are loyal Tories at federal election time. The fleshpots of evil Vancouver, with its temptations and NDP supporters, could be light-years away.

There was that eruption of emotion from the province a few years ago when the loopy thinkers in the Chrétien office—regarding a constitutional veto—tried to toss B.C. into a mélange called Western Canada. A movement was set afoot—committees, petitions, letters-to-the-editor—demanding that the archaic "British" be dropped, leaving "Columbia" pristine and naked all by itself.

Well. This is a matter of great import. What would Ontarians think, point out the proponents, if it were called British Ontario? Wouldn't go down too well in Toronto's classier restaurants, ninety-seven per cent of which live on pasta.

British Saskatchewan? Doesn't quite ring true. British Prince Edward Island perhaps, where the pasta has not yet replaced the potato.

British Columbia, of course, is a bit of misnomer when the new name for Vancouver is Hongcouver. (At the moment, one-quarter of the town's population is from across the Pacific.) No one can figure out why Vancouver, named after a British sea captain who discovered the place, is not on Vancouver Island, where Victoria is. Americans still confuse the province with British Guiana, which happens to be somewhat farther south.

Your agent was once ensconced on an island off the coast of British Columbia where bare feet and insults are the order of the day. When the days are not idyllic, they are merely poetic. The bottle-green mountains rise steeply across the sound. One of the familiar local sites is a formation of peaks that look exactly like

Charles de Gaulle deep in sleep. The deer, none bigger than Bambi, come down and nibble in the garden. It is a pleasant sight at breakfast.

The fat white ferries, cruising through the waters with the serenity of Queen Victoria, are more numerous than the Canadian navy's vessels—which ain't hard—and drop brisk bicyclists, pastel pensioners and the ubiquitous camper trucks like detritus as they glide into dock after dock.

High on a cliff, a proud and defiant original cottager—someone says he is such a gentleman that he would rather be caught without his pants than his tie—flies the White Ensign. Once you had to have a certain high rank in the navy to fly it.

There is the ritual grass-hockey game, played with hockey sticks and tennis balls, but the standard of violence is generally of the same level as that of Australian Rules football. There is the standard roughrider ride up the side of a mountain in a jeep, through streams and over logs, teetering on bluffs and frightening the sheep, a journey that would terrify Rambo.

Best of all is the juxtaposition of water against mountain, sunlight against tree, the forest primeval with green fern and dark moss, a soothing balm for a man who has listened to too much bafflegab over a year and yearns to see deer that are, each November, plucked off occasionally by a chap with a large beard and biceps like thighs who—as required by law—can use only a bow and arrow. His wife has made him a Viking helmet with horns, and tourists who have come across the sight are still fleeing to Iowa.

British Columbia is its own ineffable self because it pulls the protective blanket of the Rocky Mountains over its head and has no need to look out. Alberta is as foreign as is New Brunswick. It has never produced a native of the province who has been elected prime minister. It has no need to. It is unique.

It was Bruce Hutchison, who achieved international recognition as a brilliant journalist while refusing all his life to leave his province, who invented the label "Lotus Land," derived from the Greek mythology of the lotus-eaters. The ancient Greeks ate the fruit from the lotus tree, containing the property of making people forget their country and friends and remaining idle in the lotus land. Doesn't that sound like B.C.? Of course.

• See also "B.C. politics," "Vancouver" and "Victoria."

**BROADBENT, ED** Edward Broadbent, the intelligent, earnest and hard-working leader of the Few Democratic Party was once the most puzzled man in Canada. At a time when the Liberals were reviled and the headless Tories were running around bumping into each other—the NDP could never gain any ground.

The answer to Broadbent's puzzlement lies in Marshall McLuhan. The good doctor, no longer with us, taught us long ago that television is a "hot" medium that requires contrast and variation from its performers. It's why Pierre Elliott Ego was such a superb TV artist—one never knew from appearance to appearance what one was going to get: little-boy sulk, arrogance, flippancy, perhaps a finger if we were lucky, statesmanship. It's like reaching into a fortune cookie—mystery awaits.

Broadbent, trying desperately for his thirty seconds on the nightly news smorgasbord, felt he must be angry and strident in the short time allotted to him in Question Period in the Commons each day. The same pitch, the same hardball, there were no curves, no change-ups, no spitballs. The viewer, who gets his *image* and his *perception* of public figures from the boob tube while getting his *news* from print, sees Broadbent as shrill. Well-meaning and honest, but shrill. If you must know: *bor-ing*.

The solution lies within the Criminal Code. Broadbent (who

was the most academically qualified of leaders: a Ph.D. won on scholarships) should delve into it. He would find, to his astonishment, that there is no statute making it illegal for a politician to be funny. Broadbent, when he arrived in Ottawa, was a sardonic, cigar-chewing professor who resembled an academic crossed with a waterfront boss. He spends his private moments with staff in cutting wit but muffles it all in public. Joe Clark is the same, owner of a swift spear in private that owes itself to some distant newsroom, but in public surrenders to that mock-Diefenbaker pomposity.

The strange thing about Broadbent's reluctance to unveil the wit he can show over a drink is that he has such a shining example before him. Tommy Douglas managed to produce the most progressive and humane government on the continent, when the CCF transformed Saskatchewan, while maintaining his reputation as the funniest thing ever to hit a church basement. His wit didn't harm the courage he displayed standing up in the Commons, alone, against the War Measures Act. No one questions Broadbent's courage—or his intelligence or his diligence or his disgust for the smug band of pork-barrel artists in government. One only wonders what his reaction would be if he were locked in a studio with forty hours of his own tapes to review.

Adlai Stevenson once made a stirring speech, and an admirer rushed up declaring that it was the greatest speech he had ever heard and would get him the vote "of every thinking American." "That's no good," Stevenson replied. "I need a majority."

If you travel Canada and listen to the humour—the Prairies with its sly debunking, the Maritimes with throw-away innocence, Quebec with resigned cynicism—you realize that the country as a whole is far funnier than what should be our star performers, our politicians. We are in the hands of men, and women, of overwhelming self-importance—trumped-up puritans with tongues made of burlap.

**BROWN, ROSEMARY** "Take away her race and her sex and what have you got?" one NDP regular said disparagingly soon after Rosemary Brown declared for the leadership of the party in 1975. When the remark got back to her, Rosemary said, "Take away my race and my sex and what you've got is a socialist."

Rosemary has never counted on easy acceptance. As she likes to say, "To be black and female, in a society which is both racist and sexist, is to be in the unique position of having nowhere to go but up."

The family of Rosemary Brown's grandmother were indentured East Indians brought to Jamaica by the British after slavery was ended in 1848. But by the time Rosemary was born in 1930, she was part of one of the first families in Jamaica. The Wilson family bought land, reinvested, and bought more land.

Grandmother was a founder of the People's National Party and helped lead the universal suffrage movement. Rosemary handed out leaflets for the cause, listened to speeches, and by eleven was writing letters to newspapers and government officials.

Rosemary was sent away to school in Montreal at nineteen— "Canada was considered next best to Britain, the U.S. was never considered"—and she was naturally put in a safe residence, Royal Victoria College, for her studies at McGill. After McGill, she headed west to take her Master's in social work at the University of British Columbia.

Elected as an MLA in 1972, it was not what you would call the background of the average Canadian socialist.

She is annoyed by nosy newspapers prying about her supposed "wealth."

"The thing that bothers North Americans is my supposed *vast* wealth and my British private school upbringing. Because I didn't come out of a ghetto or wasn't a hooker, they seem offended. I don't fit the stereotype. That's why they're offended.

"When you've had three hundred years of British oppression, you learn that they are best at sadism. They did it with a grace and eloquence that North Americans can't accomplish."

Her face, which means her personality, can only be perceived after those sly one-liners, when the eyes come alive and she laughs. Rosemary Brown's laugh may yet resurrect the phrase "a peal of laughter."

Many years ago, when you and I were young Maggie, I used to transport Rosemary Brown around in the back of my red MG, along with a gaggle of other giggling social workers I had fallen in with.

In 1975, we are in an Airwest plane, reminiscing and talking about feminism, when she says, "You've come a long way, Allan."

"Well," I say, "I had a long way to come."

"You're right. It has been a long journey."

Naive in many ways, haughty in some, Rosemary Brown is a conscience tugging at a party. She has, like Woodsworth and Coldwell and MacInnis, that cool, evangelical certainty, never hurried, never insulted, and sure of ultimate "victory"—which may in fact be prodding others along to the goal, not power unto themselves. She is, in the end, what Eric Kierans was to the Liberals, asking the questions that the party does not want to hear. Power to the Imagination.

**BUCHANAN, PAT** There are many goofy things that go on in politics (ask Glen Clark) but there's always the assumption that the powerful people control events.

The Grand Old Party, the Republicans, proved that wrong.

Here is the party of the rich, the party of the corporate elite, the party that represents all those at the top of the heap in the wealthiest nation on earth. But in 1996, the Republicans got themselves in an awful fix with wild man Pat Buchanan, who will never get the presidential nomination but chewed up the party while failing.

How bad is Buchanan? Colin Powell, the chap the party wanted, said flatly on CNN that if Buchanan ever got the nomination he could not vote for him.

Buchanan is a fighter. His problem is he will fight with anyone. His fiercely Catholic father hung a punching bag in the household basement and made Pat and his six brothers go at it four times a week—each of them doing a hundred punches with the left and a hundred with the right. At Georgetown University he got in a fight with two cops and broke his wrist.

When he ran in 1992 he ranted on the platform of the threat of Japanese cars. Reporters pointed out that both he and his wife drove a Mercedes. He no longer drives the Mercedes, but the senseless, isolationist rants remain.

Buchanan is as antediluvian as Barry Goldwater, who led the Republicans to their worst disaster. As with Goldwater, the nutty extreme comes easily to him. The Great Wall of China, he says, seems "a good idea" to keep Canadian trade at bay.

To him, it is the 1930s again, America cowering behind tariff walls, holding off the damn furriners who are stealing jobs from those whose votes he seeks. It would be all so ludicrous were it not for the fact he tapped into the anger of the blue-collar Americans who are sick of "downsizing."

He lashes out at anything. He's against gays, against abortion, against immigrants, against foreign trade, against it seems almost everyone in his own party. Illustrative of what happens when you let a newspaper columnist into politics.

**BURPIES** "Big, Unintellectual Rural People," also Eugene Whelan's support base in the 1984 Liberal leadership race.
• See also "Whelan, Eugene."

**BUSH, GEORGE W.** The most puzzling thing about the last American presidential race is the winner, George W. Bush.

The Republicans, who lost the last two attempts at the White House, finally succeeded with a man who has been in politics for just over five years. He's really done nothing much with his life on his own and admits himself that he does not rank very high on the IQ scale. The biographers and profile-writers are trying to dig deep, but they can't find much. His party, with millions in campaign donations, went into battle with a man with nothing much but charm.

"Dubya" was sent to Andover, the elite New England prep school where his father went. His only mark was as head cheerleader. At Yale, where both his father and his grandfather went, he was president of Delta Kappa Epsilon, the hardest-partying fraternity on campus. He confesses he was an unserious student.

He avoided the Vietnam war by getting family help to jump the queue and get into a Texas National Guard unit. As a pilot on weekends he would, as someone put it, "guard Texas from Oklahoma."

Five years after he finished Yale, he applied to the University of Texas law school. He was turned down. This is a president?

There were attempts at the oil business. At the end of a decade, with all his family connections and access to capital, he had only a few hundred thousand dollars to show for it.

Always a hard party boy, he was drinking so much that he (or his wife?) decided that was that. He hasn't had a drink since age forty.

He was saved by an old fraternity brother who had made his fortune in Disney movies and needed some charmer as front man in a bid to buy the Texas Rangers baseball club. Dubya was the right ticket. The taxpayers in Arlington, Texas, were persuaded to put up all the money for a new stadium, and he suddenly had the big name to run for governor in 1994. Not a bad entry-level job.

The answer is that, in Texas, it's not much of a job. The legislature is allowed to sit only 140 days every other year. The governor doesn't even have a cabinet. The lieutenant governor presides over the Senate and chairs the board that writes the budget and is more powerful than the governor. Only 137 people report to the governor—in the second biggest state in the union. The governor of Arkansas has 1,400 bodies working for him. The mayor of Chicago? Some 42,000.

Nicholas Lemann pointed out in *The New Yorker* that Dubya has come to the presidency with a lighter résumé than anybody in at least a hundred years. Even among the "lightweights," Harry Truman had been in public office for two decades before becoming president. Warren Harding was in public life from 1899 until he became president in 1921.

JFK was in the House and then the Senate from 1947 until he went to the White House in 1961. Ronald Reagan rose on his own to become a prominent actor, labour union head, two-time governor of California and a three-time presidential candidate before he won. Dwight Eisenhower liberated Europe. And so on.

"The idea of Bush as president," writes Lemann, "runs counter to the American tradition of giving the job to someone who has spent a lifetime being outstanding."

There is a smart guy in Denver who's become an instant millionaire by printing up a zillion bumper stickers that say, "He's not my President"—meaning an easy audience of fifty per cent of America's 275 million. There were all the expected jibes about the Frauduration Ceremonies on January 20 when "The Shrub" from Texas was sworn in by the Chief Justice of the Supremes, who, in effect, chose the new president.

Dubya is a strange choice. He campaigned with this remarkable platform of "compassionate conservatism." This is the governor who has presided over 120 executions in Texas since taking office and, in the midst of his struggle against Arizona Senator John McCain, refused to interfere in the fatal injection administered to a sixty-three-year-old grandmother.

Gush knows he doesn't have a mandate. When Bore surpassed him in the popular vote. When he very well knows, as the newspapers under his brother's Sunshine Law will eventually reveal, that he lost even Florida. When he knows that American opinion is turning against the death penalty. And, especially, when he knows that less than eight per cent of blacks voted Republican. Which is why his first three appointments were Condoleezza Rice, born in segregated Alabama, as national security adviser; Colin Powell, as first black secretary of state; and Alberto Gonzales, a Hispanic judge, as White House counsel.

It's all about catch-up. It's all about lack of a real mandate. George Bush, no intellect, can at least do arithmetic and knows he is only fifty–fifty in the Senate, with a bare majority in the House of Representatives and—arithmetic again—more Americans voted against him than for him.

**CAMP, DALTON** The view from the large, airy house with the triangular roof and the massive double-glazed windows drifts down over the eighty acres to the winter-grey trees and the restless white ice of the lake itching for spring. The apple trees outside the window are brittle and wizened and one fears the tiny birds on their branches, grateful for the March sunshine, will snap their frail support. In fact, their perch will endure like this muddy earth and these people outside Jemseg in the woods-and-water solitude of the lonely land called New Brunswick.

This is the home of Dalton Camp, the best known politician-in-exile who is captive in Canada. The Tories' own version of creative starvation sits and crinkles his eyes with laughter and regards the world with an expanse of bemusement.

Dalton Camp is not only the most persuasive stylist writing on Canadian politics today, he has been a major figure in Conservative politics for forty years, most famous for being the only Tory who would bell the cat. As president of the party he forced a leadership review that eventually brought down the increasingly eccentric John Diefenbaker, a born-to-be-opposition-leader who never knew how to be prime minister.

In a nervous party still infested with cobwebs of anti-intellectualism, he exists as an abandoned resource, somewhat of an imaginative leper, allowed to meet his peers only under cover of darkness, a scarlet lady of the mind.

The wisest man in Canadian politics is reviled, still, in half of the country as a devious, slippery practitioner of the trade. The previous wisest man in Canadian politics, Bruce Hutchison, who died in 1992 at age ninety-one, once gave this scribbler some advice.

If, he advised, at the end of one's life you take all your acquaintances and multiply by six and divide by twenty-seven and subtract thirteen—if you have two close friends, your life has been a success. By that measure Dalton Camp's life has been a triumph.

Some 240 friends and admirers gathered in a Château Laurier chamber one evening in February 1994. The excuse was his induction into the Order of Canada the following day. The real reason was the celebration for the wisest man in Canadian politics, then seventy-three.

Much of the affection for him has something to do with the fact that the previous May he was within hours of death, his wonky heart giving out. By a happenstance, he was the only heart transplant candidate within reach when the bruised heart of a nineteen-year-old woman that could not be transported elsewhere became available. An admiring Peter Gzowski—just then recovered from a heart problem of his own—sent him a joking note at the time: "Can I have your old one?"

Camp is a son of the manse. His childhood led from New Brunswick to California where, due to a freakish and prolonged encounter with basketball shoes that were too tight, the teenager spent months in a hospital bed. His father would arrive each week with an armful of books, the world's classics from Dickens backwards and forwards.

Frank Mankiewicz, who has been a friend of Camp's since they attended the Columbia Graduate School of Journalism in the late 1940s, testifies that he and Camp spent most of their time in New York at the Yankees' ball games. They made a $20,000 bet as to which of them in their future fame would be on the cover of *Time* magazine. No egos there.

Camp went on, as his Red Deer enemies may not believe, to study at the London School of Economics under the celebrated socialist guru Harold Laski, who turned out such other well-known socialists as John F. Kennedy and many another scion of millionaires.

Dr. Wilbert Keon, one of Myron Baloney's GST senators, and the chap who sliced Camp's chest open, claims to have said "Jesus," on viewing the blue blood spurting forth, "this guy really is a Tory."

On his mantel, above the double-faced fireplace that stretches from the expansive sitting room clear through to the dining room, there is this dreadful moustache cup of one John Diefenbaker. Camp, one understands, is a collector of kitsch. It is a work of atrocity committed by a luckily anonymous Victoria artist who thrusts such abominations on unknowing Yankee tourists. Camp loves it.

He lives in splendid isolation on a hill overlooking a lake in Jemseg. He's an old geezer with a new heart, a man who has more friends than he knows what to do with.

**CAMPAGNOLO, IONA** Iona Campagnolo, who enters a room as if borne on an Egyptian chair, rose through broadcasting and the civic political ranks of the rough northern British Columbia town of Prince Rupert and became an MP in 1974. As minister of fitness and amateur sport, she promoted herself and honed her body around the world. My mother says it's a tacky remark, but I cannot tell a lie; she had the flattest belly of any fifty-year-old I know. She was defeated in 1979. Iona, an early participant in the women's networking system, was the attractive female star of the Liberal cabinet just when feminist issues came to play.

The most intriguing aspect of her 1982 bid for the Liberal leadership was not her kidnapping of the presidency of the party, nor Judy Erola's attempts, with her own leadership aspirations, to block her, nor the dull Canadian male having to encompass the concept of a woman trying for the top job in the land; but his brain (not to mention other threatened parts of his anatomy) having to conceive of two top female contenders.

**CAMPBELL, KIM** My favourite Kim Campbell story is a night in 1983 when she ran for Social Credit against the incumbent NDP in Vancouver Centre in a provincial election. An all-candidates meeting was scheduled in a rough end of the riding, filled with welfare and poverty groups. A man in the audience rose and demanded of the young academic, "What do you know about hardship?"

Kim Campbell stood up and said, "My ambition was to be a concert cellist." And sat down. The stunned room was silent.

You've all seen the official photograph of our first woman prime minister in the book *Portraits, Canadian Women in Focus.* The photographer, Barbara Woodley, confesses that she didn't want our, at the time, justice minister to pose in her robes because she had already taken Supreme Court Justice Beverley McLachlin's portrait that way.

Woodley, instead, suggested that Kimmy (may we call you Kimmy, Kimmy?) hold the robe in front of her on a hanger. "She knew what I was going to ask next before I opened my mouth," allows Woodley. Kimmy whipped off her blouse without hesitation, with the speed of a Madonna.

Kim Campbell, a sharp-tongued mini-Thatcher with an alarming ability to leap wherever ambition leads her, has been at times a great gossip item for those on the inside in Ottawa. After flaming upward like a rocket and then flaming out, and reducing her Tories to two seats, she had no real prospects in life.

The shrinks would probably put the restlessness and constant shifting of dreams down to her unhappy childhood, her mother disappearing overseas for ten years when the bright and energetic Avril Phaedra Campbell was only twelve.

Fellow politicians knew she hadn't even served in the Commons long enough for the exceedingly generous (only six years required) pension plan. She really, despite the advertisements, never had the graduate degrees that would give her a university post. After her flighty and brief career in a law firm in Vancouver, no legal beagles were interested in her.

She tried hotline radio. Her attempt at book writing was roundly trounced. Twice divorced, her relationship with her Russian inventor of spring-bounced shoes seemed to be over. A former prime minister—however brief and disastrous—should not be left with a tin cup and pencils. But it's always nice to have friends in high places, and Jean Chrétien, that great philanthropist, sent Kim Campbell to Los Angeles at about $130,000 with a mansion and a swimming pool.

His earlier attempt to ship her to Moscow as ambassador was killed (thankfully) by the horrified diplomatic professionals in Ottawa. And so? A soft landing in La-La Land, representing us all at Hollywood premieres and hopefully a session at Vic Tanny's.

Someone who boasts, as Kim Campbell does, that she can sing the mezzo-contralto role in all but one Gilbert and Sullivan opus must realize that the whole elaborate political apparatus is a game, a farce if viewed properly. By taking that perspective, she may survive.

**CANADA** One of the abiding myths out there in Vacuumland is that Canada is the dullest place on earth. The British press dwells on it. Everyone in Washington believes it. The French in France can't believe the Quebec accent. They are of course—all of them—out to lunch. As Pierre Berton and Peter Newman have tried to tell us, Canadian history is, in fact, so interesting that not even high-school teachers have managed to dull it.

Our first prime minister and father of the country was so consumed by gin that he used to upchuck while at a campaign podium. Our longest-reigning leader, who never married, used to commune with his dead mother and his dog. John Diefenbaker used to pretend he was a teetotaller while he was not. Joe Clark lost his underwear. And so on.

The myth of blandness continues today. This is an extremely goofy country, as bananas as Ruritania or Transylvania. It is only the overlay of weather that gives the impression of ennui.

The whole concept doesn't make sense: twenty-nine million people strung out in a narrow ribbon over some five thousand miles with a population density less than that of Saudi Arabia. And with a northland, larger than India, speckled by fewer people than attend a baseball game in Yankee Stadium.

If it weren't for emotion, there wouldn't be such an illogical thing as Canada. It's emotion that has kept this unlikely bundle of geography intact. The building of the CPR, when you think of it, was an emotional, daring act of the imagination to bind a nation. Every morning five days a week for many years an equivalent emotional binding—Peter Gzowski's brilliant *Morningside*—brought emotion and patriotism into every kitchen and car radio, a concept unheard-of in the United States, where such a thing as a state broadcasting service is viewed as vaguely socialistic, which of course it is. Barbara Frum's original *As It Happens* was all emotion, insisting that

Canada's reach was the world. Read Bruce Hutchison's book, *A Life in the Country: To Canada with Love and Some Misgivings*, an eighty-seven-year-old man's passionate affair with his woodlot on Vancouver Island. Emotion. All emotion. It's something the bean counters in Ottawa's counting house wouldn't understand.

This country dull? The overpaid boffins sitting in Ottawa offices have so frigged up the counting of fish off Newfoundland that they now whiff grapeshot across the bows of Spanish ships.

The government of all the people killed the Crow, thus stopping the railway subsidy that encouraged Prairie farmers to ship their product to either Thunder Bay and up the St. Lawrence Seaway or to the Pacific ports of British Columbia. This will result in the wheat going down south through the Mississippi to New Orleans. This is regarded as progress.

This is the only country in the world that has two football teams in the same league with the same name. This is the only political jurisdiction known that has a party with the oxymoronic title of "Progressive Conservative."

It contains the only place in the universe—Ontario—as far as is known, where you have to go to one place to buy beer and another place to buy fiery liquid. Dull? Canada?

It cannot be a dull and boring land after having invented the game of hockey, and then allowing it to settle into those manic ice havens of Tampa Bay, San Jose and Anaheim, and now making the Canadian Football League the toys of millionaires in Memphis, Jackson, Peoria and possibly Selma, not to mention Cucamonga.

Any country with a population of a mere twenty-nine million that has some forty cabinet ministers, while the Yanks with 260 million can get along somehow with only twelve, cannot be described as blah.

This is a unique country, the ruling Liberals being actually conservatives, while their only opposition is a Quebec rump that wants to break up the country and a Western rump that tries to pretend Quebec doesn't exist.

Dull? You've got to be kidding.

• See also "Canadian humour" and "Canadians."

## CANADIAN BROADCORPING CASTRATION

• See "CBC."

## CANADIAN DOLLAR

Known on Wall Street as the Hudson Bay peso.

**CANADIAN HUMOUR** There's a strange thing going on in this strange country. Proof that yet another Liberal minister in the Cretinite government admits that the government lies is small beer. We expect that like the sunrise, like the understanding that there will usually be a traffic jam at 5 p.m. No big deal.

What is apparent is that Canadians, as a whole, accept such balderdash and persiflage. We are a self-flagellating nation, knowing that the twits we elect have flannel in their mouths, eager to emit any piffle until the moment they have to admit they, uh, weren't telling the truth.

The way we get around this is by admitting we are Canadians— i.e., fools. A look at our favourite broadcast items shows this to be true. *The Royal Canadian Air Farce*, *Double Exposure* and *This Hour Has 22 Minutes* have ratings that private broadcasting would die for.

What is best, of course, is that all the shafts at government and their stupid politicians are conducted on a government-funded broadcasting system. It's a fine Canadian tradition—handed down from the Brits.

We can see it in the difference between the hours when Canadian satire and American satire are seen on the boob tube. American savaging of their politicians is relegated to the nether regions of the night when most sensible folk have collapsed to sleep or sex. In contrast, the satirical shows that savage our eminently savageable goofs are in prime time in Canada, supposedly the Shy Capital of the World.

This is the strange thing about this strange country. Canadians, as the mouse underneath the elephant, understand the only solution is to laugh.

**CANADIANS** There are certain pure crystalline moments, altogether rare, when all that is fine and decent about being a Canadian is outlined against the sky. Such a one came in 1980 with the caper of the Canadian embassy in Tehran. Six American hostages were smuggled out of Iran "disguised as Canadians."

There are few instances in history when an inhabitant of this insignificant international backwater can make the world stage, but that reference hit a trigger straight to the brain—lives being saved due to the fact that the diplomats could fool the steely-eyed Iranian passport snoops because they were camouflaged as that exotic breed that could flummox any airport cop: your basic indigenous Canadian.

One imagines the first Yank-fake-Canuck brazening it past the airport checkpoint: flopping about the terminal on snowshoes, carrying a hockey stick, the jug of maple syrup over his shoulder, yodelling "Rose Marie." Would fool 'em every time.

I fumble about the world, seeking anonymity, but forever am brought up short by strangers, all foreign, who point at me on London sidewalks and in Spanish bistros alike. They exude a tone of recognition and incredulity—they have spotted a recognizable

Canadian who, despite whatever subterfuge, obviously reveals his heritage.

This, any reasonable person would maintain, is the chief asset of the Iranian caper, despite the Tory claim that it turned Joe Clark in twenty-four hours into an instant statesman, somewhat like Jell-O pudding mix.

Our shy belief has been that the real Canadian, if modelled in Madame Tussaud's, combined the sexiness of Leonard Cohen with the grace of Jean Béliveau, Pierre Trudeau's ability to swear in both official languages blended with the carriage of Karen Kain—all of it topped with the cultural panache of a Harold Ballard. Perhaps we've been wrong?

What else remains, undiscovered, of our psyche? Well, there's the Canadian belief that Wayne and Shuster are funny, that the most patriotic move is to drink Canadian Club and listen to Rich Little imitating George Burns, that Florida is an adequate substitute for Ottawa and that Toronto now possesses style.

United Nations statistics have told us that Canadians (a) talk on the phone more than any other people; (b) use more energy than anyone else per capita; and (c) lead the world in joining organizations. This is basically fair: an image thrust before the world of a chilly gabber who seeks succour in the Elks. Bang on. Mix in the national drink, rye and ginger, and fit it with a satin bowling jacket with the name "Fred" embroidered on the shoulder patch and you've limned the nation of Sir John A., Laurier and Paul Anka.

**CARSTAIRS, SHARON** In 1988, Sharon Carstairs was the new star in Canadian politics and our eardrums were preparing to take a lot of damage. Her voice has all the charm of fingernails being dragged over a blackboard. The first woman ever to be an opposition leader in Canada, she had twenty Liberal seats in Manitoba to the shaky Conservatives' twenty-five and it seemed clear she would be premier within a year whenever she and the NDP chose to topple the minority government.

That voice made her nationally famous. *The Royal Canadian Air Farce* was given a prewrapped gift. Her voice made us forget Joe Clark's ears and Brian Mulroney's chin. She has her trademark and no amount of speech-coaching can erase it. This is not the throaty husk of Judy LaMarsh. Not the Highland fling of Flora MacDonald, nor the languid baritone of Barbara McDougall. This is a piercing twang that goes right through your head bone and comes out the other side. Carstairs's tonsils in full flight could not only shatter glass but topple a minivan.

Do not change, Sharon. No one needs a TV set or a radio. We can hear you from here.

## CBC (ALSO *CANADIAN BROADCORPING CASTRATION*)

It's a terrible thing to have one's prejudices confirmed, to see myths come to life. It's like finding out there really is a Santa Claus or that Eugene Whelan actually exists. A chap flogging a book across the land, like a four-dollar hooker, finds that the cartoonists' view of the CBC is startlingly accurate. Enter a CBC studio and one is immediately struck with the thought that the Salvation Army must be in boom times, since it has obviously shipped all its old furniture to the Holy Mother Corp. There is a standard CBC uniform which could be called stained-sweatshirt chic.

The spectacle is so apparent to the eyeball because of the contrast afforded by their colleagues in private, dollar-a-holler radio. A day spent hopping from CBC studios to private stations back to the CBC is like travelling in a space machine that transfers you between foreign cultures. A private radio or television station is all glitz and plastic, including the hair on the receptionist. It is heartening to see that so much junk on private radio can come from such rich surroundings. It takes money to be so bad.

The grumbling taxpayers who moan about CBC waste should know that the sloth does not include the surroundings.

Society has its own rules of conduct and what it feels constitutes fair play: bear-baiting is no longer legal in this country, cock-fighting is regarded as cruel and unusual punishment and the spectacle of torturing small animals in public for private amusement is regarded as outside the law.

Would it be permissible to say something in defence of the CBC? One never appreciates the clumsy, ponderous Corp. so much as when one is deprived of it. A man trapped for two weeks in California eating tennis balls felt as if he had been deprived of his pacifier, Linus without his blanket, when he realized how much he missed his daily hit of information. As a news junkie, requiring frequent injections of blab into the veins, one realized how much one relied on *World Report*, *The World at Six* and then *As It Happens*. U.S. radio is aimed basically at a fourteen-year-old with the attention span of a gopher, and U.S. television is dominated by news hosts whose weekly hairstyling and dental floss bills would founder the economy of Chad.

It's right, of course, to be annoyed at having to defend the need for Canadian broadcasting while we are being inundated with pabulum for the mind from our rich neighbours, who prosper in the puzzling belief that there is only one use for the airwaves that can transmit electronic images: profit. So we get *Laverne and Shirley*, *Love Boat*, *Three Jiggling Stewardesses*, *Three Jiggling Private Eyes*, *Three Jiggling Sportscasters*. It's the triumph of mammary over mind.

Now, as someone who occasionally allows his winsome visage to be captured by the cameras of the People's Network, I am more than well aware of its lumbering, paperwork-encrusted deficiencies. It is, granted, a hidden cave for large clutches of incompetents who would be thrown on the bread lines if ever exposed to daylight or the free-market system.

All the same, Herschel Hardin argues in *A Nation Unaware* that just as much as the Americans have a genius for private enterprise, the Canadian genius is for public enterprise. His prize examples, of course, are Air Canada, the CNR and the CBC—forces that were needed at the time to bind the country together.

What the CBC needs to fend off the slavering yahoos of the hotlines is not fewer powers but more: the confidence to have a sensitive tyrant at the top who will clean house and clobber the career cobwebbers. One thing that is supposed to distinguish us from the Yanks is our modesty and undue respect for authority. One thing that really distinguishes us from them is a more responsible broadcasting system.

**CHAREST, JEAN** When Jean Charest addressed the venerable Empire Club of Canada in the 1993 Tory leadership campaign, the head table included a mix of corporate elites and a turn-away, standing-room-only crowd of some 650—mostly downtown Toronto businessmen in dark suits—and they warmed to the guy, giving him a standing-O at the end.

Charest has an easy manner, comfortable with himself, a style that makes an audience immediately on his side. He speaks beautifully in either official language—only problem, he doesn't know what to say. He's hard to dislike and, as he says, the questions about his age disappear within five minutes when he starts speaking.

He has a casual, throw-away sense of humour that the women in the room—mostly business types or Tories here to inspect the horseflesh—especially liked.

There is a difference between wit and a sense of humour. Wit is directed at others; a sense of humour can encompass oneself. The Irish have wit, the English have a sense of humour, Pierre Trudeau had wit, Robert Stanfield had a sense of humour.

A modern election campaign, as we know, consists of desperately flying across five and a half time zones trying to target possible key ridings and landing often enough for a fifteen-minute photo op. And then aloft again. So what does sitting in a silver cigar seven miles high for a month do to Jean Charest?

Aboard the Charest campaign plane in 1997, his face has hardened, grown more mature.

How did he lose twenty-five or thirty pounds before going into this campaign? "Actually, it was forty." He started the project in 1994 to downsize. A better diet, the stationary bike and weights did the trick. As a kid, soccer was his sport. He still skis.

He's been reading *How the Irish Saved Western Civilization*, a quirky, serious book that has drawn a lot of critical attention. His mother is Irish.

He has seen his kids only twice since this both boring and exhausting campaign began. There are the girls, fourteen and seven, and the nine-year-old son.

The eldest has shown interest in science and has considered going into medicine. "She once talked about journalism. I tried to dissuade her," he says dryly.

He ponders who is the best speaker he has ever heard. "I used to do criminal law. I learned a lot, appearing before both judge and jury. You must be yourself, if you want to persuade others to your point."

Does he see himself, at only thirty-eight, spending a lifetime in politics? "I hope I will be wise enough to know when to go." (As, the scribbler muses, Dief wasn't.) "As long as I'm still relevant, I'll be around. You just have to ask yourself the honest question—and hope you give the honest answer."

He won the campaign, but lost the election, and left it a gentleman.

**CHARISMA** What Northrop Frye says, shrewdly, is the Greek translation for ham.
- See also "Mulroney, Brian."

**CHINA** Mitchell Sharp and your scribbler were reminiscing recently about 1972, when Old Mitch was sent by P. Trudeau to conduct foreplay for Canada's recognition of "Red China"—before then-president R. Nixon made his own peace offering to what was then Peking.

There was a gang of some 250 Canadian businessmen who mounted a two-week trade fair in the Chinese capital. Practically every night was a state banquet with the finest food I had ever encountered. (The Chinese, who were perfecting sauces when the Europeans were still swinging from trees, regard the French as promising apprentices in the field of cuisine, and feel that, with time, they will come along.)

We met with Chou En-Lai who, to this day, ranks with P. Trudeau and Muhammad Ali as the three brightest people I ever met. (Sorry about that, Mel Lastman.)

Trying to flee the businessmen, your scribbler applied to Peking officialdom to get out into the countryside, meet some real people, perhaps get to fabled Shanghai. Each day, the message would come down the pipe: possible, probably tomorrow. Each day went by, until one got the drift—the Chinese water-torture method, drip by drip.

Finally, in desperation to see something of the world's most unfathomable nation, your desperate agent took a train, from Peking headed for Hong Kong. It was a steam train. Coal-fired. About the same vintage as the ones waiting (with Pierre Berton) for The Last Spike.

From the rolling kitchen, manned, at first, by white-coated waiters, came the finest meals. At each stop, men carrying wooden buckets filled with water would board. Inside the buckets were live fish. As the miles piled up, the windows opened in the August heat, the soot from all that coal coming in, and we all began to look like Al Jolson smiling in a minstrel show. The waiters' white coats appeared as if they had just emerged from a Welsh coal mine.

The journey from Peking to Hong Kong was roughly the same as from Vancouver to Kenora. Over four days, four nights, outside the window there were always people—in the fields, on the sidewalks—always people. I had read that you could never hope to understand the Chinese until you realized almost everyone in that country, from birth to death, is never not within sight of another person. It is true.

**CHRÉTIEN, ALINE** Aline Chrétien, the most important political figure in the land, is working quietly on the task that she sees in fact more clearly than all of us, however frustrated we are. The fading powers are too apparent. He has got to go.

**CHRÉTIEN, JEAN** Joseph-Jacques Jean Chrétien is where he is today because of two women. One wonders whether they know it.

On the evening of June 16, 1984, Iona Campagnolo came to the podium at the Liberal leadership race in Ottawa and announced the vote that made John Turner the new leader of the party. She then, in offering commiserations to the runner-up, praised Jean Chrétien as second on the ballot "but first in our hearts." The convention roared in tribute.

It was an astonishingly silly—if sentimental—thing for a president of the party to say: perhaps the final revenge of a strong feminist for the bum-patting controversy she had gone through with Turner. It indicated that while one guy won, we really liked the other guy better. And Chrétien became convinced that he had been somehow cheated of the crown. To this day, the two men have never made up.

The second woman is publisher Anna Porter. She came to a certain reporter one day and asked if he thought there was a book in Jean Chrétien. This brilliant scribe assured her there wasn't, that he was dead meat. She didn't agree, having just met Chrétien for the first time. She saw something there the political expert didn't.

She hired Ron Graham, a felicitous writer, to tape-record Chrétien and then turn out a book in his name. The result, *Straight from the Heart*, became the best-selling political confession ever "written" in this country. On his nationwide book tour, Chrétien was treated like a hero and by the end of it he had forgotten Graham's name, having convinced himself he had actually written it. Good for him.

So he waited out Turner, he waited out Brian Mulroney, he waited out Kim Campbell and today he's boss of the land. Good for him.

Chrétien, son of a machinist, was the eighteenth of nineteen children, only thirteen of whom survived childbirth. He was kicked out of four schools until, at eighteen, he met his tranquilizer. Her name was Aline. She was sixteen, guarded by the chain-link fence around her convent school. He would walk on the outside, she on the inside, their fingers tracing a trail of love through the fence. He plighted his troth through wire mesh.

When Chrétien first went to Ottawa as an MP in 1963, he was

practically unilingual French. Mitchell Sharp spotted his spunk and later made him his parliamentary secretary. After Chrétien became a junior minister, the finance minister escorted the young MP to his first cabinet meeting. When they emerged three hours later, Sharp remembered that he hadn't warned his neophyte of the rules on strict cabinet secrecy. "Doan worry, Mr. Sharp," said the rookie, "I didin' understand a God-damned ting."

Once a junior cabinet minister, Chrétien found himself one day flying with his social opposite, the worldly and intellectual Pierre Trudeau, a man he held in awe. Chrétien sat by the window, Trudeau on the aisle. Trudeau immediately buried himself in his briefing papers. A half-hour went by in silence.

Raindrops began to speckle the window and the nervous Chrétien, trying to get something going, said, "It's raining outside." Trudeau, never lifting his eyes from his papers, said, "If it's raining, it has to be outside." The flight finished after another half-hour in silence.

In the summer of 1975, Chrétien bumped into Joe Clark in a House of Commons washroom. They were both young MPs and Clark allowed as how he, for all his inexperience, was toying with the idea of running for the Conservative leadership. He wanted Chrétien's advice. "I'll tell you one thing for certain," Jean replied, "if you don't run, you can't win." Shocked into common sense by Chrétien's rough logic, Clark ran and of course won. I wonder if he's ever thanked him.

The Huck Finn of Canadian politics, Jean Chrétien is impossible to dislike, unless you are in favour of depth. The funny thing about his populist reputation is that he is not really a populist at all. He was raised in the region famous for populist politicians with a colourful style, the St-Maurice valley, which produced Maurice Duplessis, Maurice Bellemare and Réal Caouette and Camil Samson of the Créditistes: "Since I had to fight populists, I learned from them and even tried to outdo them" with the slang, emotion and jokes that made him "pay a political price among the intellectuals of Quebec." But the little guy from Shawinigan in truth is not really a populist. He supported his mentor, the right-wing Liberal Mitchell Sharp, in the 1968 leadership battle against Trudeau. He never challenged the Establishment in his troubled stint as the first French-Canadian finance minister. His campaign manager in his leadership struggle was a vice president of Power Corp. His daughter has married into the family of multi-millionaire Paul Desmarais.

In Ottawa, Chrétien is famously impatient over detail, every department he has ever worked in reporting that his attention span won't go beyond three pages of written text. Is he in fact a Ronnie Reagan, who delegated everything, didn't want to know the boring facts, but was loved by the voters because he had about three simple ideas and stuck with them? Or has he reached the heights, politics being his life and his only interest, purely by hanging around so long that all others have dropped from the vine from fatigue?

Any man who can make Ron Graham disappear in his own mind may be capable of astonishing things. After all, Doug Henning, the magician, made the Conservative party disappear.

Considering where Joseph-Jacques Jean Chrétien came from, he done good.

**CHURCHILL, WINSTON** There is always fascination when history sets a deadline for men. When the time and the individual come together for a fateful match, rather like a long-awaited prize-fight. The spectators rub their hands together in the glee of anticipation. Churchill grumbles away in various second-stage roles at Westminster, switching parties, underestimated by all, until Britain finally made its date with destiny with him in 1940—when he was sixty-five.

Winston Churchill was born in 1874. He was an MP by 1901 at the age of twenty-six. He was in the British cabinet by 1908. He was in Cuba with the Spanish forces; he served in India, in the Sudan. In the Boer War in South Africa he was captured and escaped with a £25 price on his head. As he later wrote, "Nothing in life is so exhilarating as to be shot at without result."

He was first lord of the admiralty in 1911. He was a colonel in the British army in France in 1916 in the First World War. He was minister of munitions by 1917. He was chancellor of the exchequer by 1924.

In a policy difference with his Conservatives, he crossed the Commons floor to sit with the Liberals. He returned to the Tory benches eventually with a typical Churchillian remark, "Anyone can rat, but it takes something to re-rat."

After he became prime minister in 1940, he met twice with Roosevelt in Quebec City in 1943 and 1944 to plot the war strategy. Defeated in 1945, he returned as PM in 1951 and lasted four more years in the post.

Every one of his wartime speeches, as a general said, was worth a regiment. After the greatest of all—"we shall fight on the beaches...we shall fight in the fields and in the streets, we shall fight in the hills; we shall never surrender"—he said in an aside to the New York *Herald Tribune*'s Dean Hewlett Johnson, "And we will hit them over the heads with beer bottles, which is all we have really got."

He fancied himself a poker player. After the war, in Washington, he asked President Harry Truman to arrange a foursome. After several hands, it was clear he was a lousy poker hand. When Churchill excused himself to go to the loo, Truman issued a command. "Lose," he ordered the table that included David Brinkley. "This guy saved the world."

Churchill never had any real money. Out of power almost all his life, he had to support himself in journalism and on speaking tours of North America. He once arrived in Vancouver, to be met at the railway station by young J. V. Clyne, eager young lawyer, later chief justice of the B.C. Supreme Court and then chairman of MacMillan Bloedel.

Winston announced he was headed for the top of Grouse Mountain to paint (his great hobby) the famous Vancouver harbour and would need a bottle of Scotch. As Clyne later told the story, he nervously explained to Churchill about Prohibition.

No tickee, no washee. No speech.

The sweating Clyne, having found a bootlegger, walked all the way to the peak and Churchill, hearing the bushes swaying behind him, never raised his eyes from his palette, and said, "Got the whisky?"

Accused of drinking too much, Churchill once said, "I have taken more out of whisky than whisky has ever taken out of me."

I used to live around the corner from Churchill, in Knightsbridge just off Hyde Park, and on his birthday, we would go around, while the Fleet Street photogs gathered, to pay our respects. Bleary-eyed, he would wave through the window, his wife Clemmie at his side.

When the war-weary Labour voters tossed him out within months of saving the world, he had only this to say, "Trust the people."

**CLARK, GLEN** Glen Clark is not someone of personal acquaintance, but of sound reputation from afar. Quite obviously of what could be called the Jack Russell terrier breed of politician. A brain, one suspects, not in the realm of Bertrand Russell or John Kenneth Galbraith, but fuelled by street smarts. One can see him coming out of Brooklyn. Or East Vancouver.

Son of a union organizer, he somehow was allowed to convert himself into a defender of the middle class. The middle class in Vancouver is someone who has a sailboat and a cottage at Whistler when finding time to get off the tennis court.

**CLARK, JOE (ALSO JURASSIC CLARK)** Be nice to people on the way up, as the man says, because you'll meet them on the way down. That's what the chaps at the *Edmonton Journal* were thinking in March 1976 because Joe Clark, then the youngest leader of a federal party since Confederation, and later the youngest prime minister of Canada, started out as a copy boy on the paper. *Joe Clark* from *High River*? Representing the riding of *Rocky Mountain*? Sounds like an invention of W. O. Mitchell's.

The first time I met Joe Clark it was 1975, over breakfast in a small delicatessen, and his fingers trembled so much in nervousness I immediately wrote him off as a serious contender for his party's top job. So much for delicatessen wisdom.

Watching him carefully at close range over an extended period of days, one gets the impression of Cecil Trueheart, the second lead in a Noël Coward play set in the landed-gentry belt of Kent.

Clark himself, who in private is devastatingly analytical about himself, even knows the reason why. High River, Alberta, despite its Gary Cooperish name, was one of those prairie towns populated in early days by remittance men—the semi-failed heirs of the English genteel. In High River, of all places, they played *cricket* when Clark grew up.

Clark is a man who gives the impression that he is never quite sure what to do with his body.

Everything seems out of sync when he walks, his arms swinging to the beat of a different drummer, the wrists and hands only vaguely connected to the arms. You want to shove a chair at him to put him out of his agony.

All this physical awkwardness has nothing to do with the ability to govern, of course.

If ambition is the criterion the kid from the big sky has had a long apprenticeship. There were those university days in Edmonton forty years ago when Joe was shouting in squeaky-voiced fashion across the floor of the University of Alberta mock parliament as leader of the campus Conservatives. Who was shouting back? Little Jimmy Coutts, leader of the campus Liberals, and eventually principal secretary to Prime Minister Pierre Elliott Himself.

In the pomposity that always fills university politics like acne, Joe Clark met Brian Mulroney. They were both teenagers and they were both eager and they were both Tiny Tories with much in common. Each, since that day of meeting so long ago, had his eye on a goal that would exclude the other: leader of the Progressive Conservative party and prime minister of Canada.

J. C. Superboy is not bashful. He was editor of *The Gateway*, the student newspaper, and led the first student march in history on the Alberta legislature. Joe calmly took his troops from the campus, out over the high-level bridge and onto the impregnable fortress of three decades of lordly Social Credit rule. The student demonstration—over some minor dispute about student fees—demanded an appearance by aloof Premier Ernest Manning, who finally did talk to the long march of chairman Joe.

Joe Clark has the sonorous tones and premature solemnity of Richard Nixon—as if by being one of the early courageous ones who called for the downfall of John Diefenbaker he somehow inherited by bad luck the waggling of the jowls. In taking the squeak out of his voice he now sounds like Jimmy Stewart, masticating the end of each oratorical sentence to wring the last meaty juices out of it.

No one can ever recall a Joe Clark quote, though he has been in politics all his adult life (his best lines actually are in wry wit in private). Otto Lang once said that Joe Clark has never explained why he should be prime minister except that he wants the job. There was a reason for Pierre Trudeau in 1968. There was a reason for John Diefenbaker in 1957. The public has no real sense of what Clark stands for, what he represents, save for the fact that he seems a decent fellow from a small western Canadian town who had the perseverance to teach himself French.

Public opinion tossed Pierre Trudeau from office and installed Clark as prime minister of Canada in 1979. It was a minority government, it is true, but Canadian voters expected him to get on with the job. Instead, he announced he would govern "as if he had a majority," which is like saying he would assume that two and two equalled five. Because he couldn't count, he was booted from office in the single most inept decision made in the Commons this century.

When afterwards he was confirmed as Conservative leader by a vote of more than two-thirds of party delegates in Winnipeg, he for some reason called a leadership convention and lost it to Brian Mulroney.

He was one of the chief cheerleaders for the Charlottetown Accord that was so roundly buried by the Canadian population.

Despite this remarkable record of bad judgment and bad decisions, Joe Clark has the resiliency of a Brillo pad. He is sincere, he is honest, he is a dedicated patriot. But he has a track record unblemished by success.

**CLARKSON, ADRIENNE** Those of us in the media mob have
been rather rough on Her Excellency Adrienne Clarkson in her
early days as our newest governor general in this silly role of representing a queen of a foreign country from a castle across an ocean.
In rugby, it's called "piling on"—and rates a severe penalty.
Margaret Atwood claims the attacks have been "racist and sexist,"
something a male candidate would never have to endure.

The *Globe and Mail*'s rapier-like Jan Wong, born in Canada of
Chinese parents, bashed her because she kept her ex-husband's
name and can hardly speak Chinese—"just as phoney as her newfound appreciation of matrimony." When it became known that
she wished to be known as "Madame Clarkson," the Reform party
designated hitter Deborah Grey smirked that she knew what the
traditional title of "madame" meant. Meaning actually that she
couldn't differentiate between "madame" and "madam."

The CBC cameras panned over all the celebrities and high
mucky-mucks packed into the chamber of the Canadian Senate for
Clarkson's investiture. Don Newman and Peter Mansbridge picked
out all the famous faces and honoured guests for those watching
the tube. They missed perhaps the most significant one. Her
name is Carmen Viera. She is from Portugal. She is Adrienne's
cleaning lady.

Well, I think a governor general who puts her cleaning lady in a
star seat among all the other ladies is okay. Carmen, beautifully
coiffed and dressed, was introduced to the prime minister by John
Ralston Saul that night at the Rideau Hall banquet. It was the first
time she had ever been to Ottawa.

Adrienne Clarkson has not always been quite as knee-jerk regal
as she now appears. One night in Toronto, over some wine at the
home of fashion editor Beverley Rockett, the two of them along
with Heather Peterson—wife of junior cabinet minister Jim

Peterson—dressed up in old full-length beaded gowns from the Rockett wardrobe, hired a limo and wound up in the whee! hours sitting around a piano bar in Yorkville.

Rockett once heard me boast that I knew more about fashion than most women (true) and challenged me to assess all the women from Mila Mulroney to Barbara Amiel to Clarkson. Most of them didn't speak to me for two years, and a 1983 issue of the now-defunct *City Woman* had my assessment: "The woman I admire most. I can't imagine ever seeing Adrienne when she did not look dressed for the occasion, whether it's weeding the carrots or whatever. She has the gift of looking as though she doesn't spend a lot of time on how she dresses, even though she does."

I suspect within eighteen months she's going to absolutely hate the mind-numbing ritual and constant travel to Wawa and Otter Haunch that forced Roméo LeBlanc to quit early.

Carmen Viera used to be my cleaning lady, too, at one time. She told me: "At Rideau Hall she didn't treat me like her cleaning lady. She treated me as a friend." Carmen's out of a job now, of course, Herself having rented out her ultra-chic Yorkville digs for five years. "But," says Carmen, "she told me in five years I'd be back with her."

**CLINTON, BILL** The story of Bill Clinton, like the stories of all of us, can be found in his roots.

He was born William Jefferson Blythe III, one month ahead of schedule by Caesarean section, in Hope, Arkansas. His mother, daughter of the town iceman, smoked two packs of Pall Malls a day, bathed in a sunken tub, was an irrepressible flirt who spent most of her days at the racetrack. Her father would give her swigs of whisky when she was twelve.

When she married Clinton's father, travelling salesman Bill

Blythe, six weeks after meeting him, she didn't know that he had been married to a seventeen-year-old (sent her clothes home in a suitcase), then to a twenty-year-old, then to the first bride's sister, then had a daughter born to a Missouri waitress to whom he also might have been married.

He almost immediately went off to war and then, trying to drive from Chicago to Hope overnight, died in a ditch when his Buick overturned. Billy, whose mother was with his father less than six months, was born three months later.

When he was one, his mother left for New Orleans for two years to train as a nurse-anaesthetist. He was raised by his grand-mother, who worshipped him. While he was in his high chair, she taught him with homemade flash cards containing letters and numbers. He could read at three.

Mother then married car dealer Roger Clinton, who came from the fleshpot gambling town of Hot Springs, Arkansas, where Al Capone had a corner suite and kept a machine-gun in the closet. He was a drunk and beat her, until the fourteen-year-old future president, towering over him, warned his stepfather never to do it again.

He drove a four-door finned Buick to Hot Springs High School. At sixteen he was already six-foot-three and over two hundred pounds. Clumsy and awkward, he could never make a sports team and so took up saxophone in the school band.

He was so bright no one in high school can ever remember him studying. Sent to Washington with an elite group of boy leaders, he shoved his way with his bulk to the front of the line in the Rose Garden to get the now-famous photo of him shaking hands with his idol, JFK.

Moving on to the prestigious Georgetown University in Washington, the hillbilly kid from the hick state easily became president of the freshman class over all those Ivy League preppies, and sophomore president. A favoured professor told him that great men in history slept no more than five hours. Clinton returned to his dorm and set the alarm clock to begin sleeping five hours a night.

While he was on campus, his drunken stepfather died. *Washington Post* reporter David Maraniss noted, it was "two fathers dead—and in a sense he knew neither of them." He had been raised, in reality, by two mothers who competed for his love and attention.

Even his closest friends at Georgetown laughed when he applied for a Rhodes Scholarship—founded by Empire fanatic Cecil Rhodes for bright boys who demonstrated "fondness and success in sports." Clinton simply stick-handled his way into chairman of the Student Athletic Commission and dazzled the Rhodes interviewers with his charm.

At Oxford he was one of an elite of thirty-two Americans. Half of them thought Clinton "a classic southern glad-handing politician." Brits were astounded that, within forty-five minutes of meeting, he convinced them he was going back to Arkansas to be governor or senator or a national leader.

As the astute Maraniss figured out, even these contradictions co-existed in Clinton: "considerate and calculating, easygoing and ambitious, mediator and predator."

As I told my buddy Pam Wallin on one of her TV gigs, his acquittal was the greatest miscarriage of justice since Jesus Christ was nailed to the cross. Monica Lewinsky has confessed: "I have lied my entire life." They made a perfect pair.

**CN Tower** The interesting cities have certain identifying birthmarks. In Montreal, it is the Maritime Bar in the basement of the

Ritz-Carlton Hotel. In London, the muted windows that encase silk ties and prim tweed hats in the narrow confines of Jermyn Street and Duke of York Street, back of Simpson's just below Piccadilly. Paris? The polished gold trim around the windows of the expensive shops on the Rue de la Paix that slants up off the Tuileries Gardens to the Paris Opéra.

Toronto? The pride of place is an entry in the *Guinness Book of Records*—a collection of concrete that is piled higher into the sky than any other pile of concrete. It is called the CN Tower, the "tallest freestanding structure in the world." *Hot* dog.

Observing Toronto's almost frenetic slavering over this outdoor Meccano set has been one of the more surprising (and melancholy) experiences of a long-time Toronto-watcher.

The most degrading aspect of all is that the "world's tallest freestanding structure" of course is not any height record at all—even at 1,815 feet, 5 inches. Toronto, coughing nervously into a public relations handkerchief, adds the "freestanding" codicil in an attempt to overcome the TV tower in Plock, Poland, that reaches 2,119 feet, but is secured by guy wires. Is this really the way one struggles for pre-eminence? By getting into a shoving contest with Plock, Poland? Does New York push around Chilliwack, B.C.? Does Moscow take on Bognor Regis?

The city, by going bonkers over vulgar statistics, is a prime example of a community indulging in municipal masturbation. Toronto has dropped its sensibilities and exposed itself in public.

• See also "Hogtown" and "Toronto."

**COHN, ROY** God must love the common man, so goes the saying, because She made so many of them. With their numbers, you would think, in a democracy, they could fashion rules and laws so that the very uncommon people could not stick it to them. We have before us an example of a very uncommon chap who not only sticks it to the common folk but revels in it, boasts about it, is completely contemptuous about the whole matter. He is a charmer, this guy, one of the most despicable men you would ever want to meet.

You remember Roy Cohn? He was one of the two nasty little lawyers who were the henchmen for Senator Joe McCarthy some three decades ago when that unprincipled unprintable was terrorizing innocent people with his Commie-chasing witch hunts. When the televised McCarthy hearings revealed to the public what a bully this headline-grabber really was, lurking in the background in every shot was the fanatical face of Roy Cohn.

Now the fierce young lawyer with the Red-hating views is a social lion in New York. He lives in a thirty-three-room townhouse on the Upper East Side. He has a house in Cape Cod, next door to Norman Mailer. He has a villa in Acapulco, a condo in Miami Beach, his own plane, a twenty-foot motorboat and a forty-two-foot motor yacht. There is just one unusual thing about Roy. He does not pay taxes. Or his debts.

He is the senior partner in Saxe, Bacon & Bolan, which has such clients as New York Yankee owner George Steinbrenner and "Fat Tony" Salerno, but Cohn insists he is merely a "contract employee." The law firm picks up most of his tabs. Everything is in someone else's name. In the 1960s, he was three times indicted, and three times acquitted, on such minor little charges as bribery, obstructing justice, extortion and blackmail.

This is the kind of man who absolutely thrived under the Reagan philosophy, which has been described as free enterprise for the poor and socialism for the rich. He's a cheat. He doesn't really believe in democracy at all.

**COPPS, SHEILA** Sheila Copps, the principal export of a town based on persiflage, hyperbole and obfuscation, livens up any campaign, as she does any brawl. She has managed to clean up her act, but still can't shake the image of a teenage harridan.

When John Crosbie referred to Ms. Copps and quoted from a song, "Pass the tequila, Sheila, and lie down and love me again," the remark was downright dumb, considering the fact that Mr. Crosbie had earlier provoked Ms. Copps's considerable wrath, and helped her become a best-selling author, by calling her "baby" in the Commons.

Her made-for-*The National* anger in Question Period is better than most things you could see on Broadway—and you don't have to pay seventy-five bucks for a seat. The Opposition is delighted to see her, regarding her as their ticking time-bomb weapon.

**COUTTS, JIM (ALSO MR. CUTES)** It is always nice to rediscover a cute face out of the past. We all enjoy bumping into long-forgotten acquaintances from high school or the French Foreign Legion or whatever—trying to gauge how much they have aged, whether they've still got that old snap and crackle, whether they've been a success or failure in the great game of life.

How welcome then, one day, to pick up the paper and find one of my favourites, Jimmy Coutts, doing tremendously well. The well-known "political fixer"—as the Toronto *Globe and Mail* calls him—is no more conning reporters as Pierre Trudeau's long-time principal secretary, no more active actor in periodic cabals to overthrow poor old John Turner. The ever-baby-faced Jimmy, who resembles Mickey Rooney in every way save the fact that he has never married, has a wealthy patron who backed him in an investment and holding company that has something to do with picking up asset-rich companies that are being dumped by corporations.

He is adding to his formidable art collection in his cute little house in the cute little Annex area of Toronto. His circle of fashionable and powerful friends grows ever wider. Coutts is a cherubic little figure who wears red suspenders and clothes that look as if they've been around since the Thirties. He is from Nanton, Alberta, is a great mimic of public personalities at parties, but the little boy image is disingenuous: he has an MBA from Harvard and was a partner in a Toronto business consulting firm before being enticed back to do the biggest consulting job of all—the problem of packaging, marketing and merchandizing Pierre Elliott Trudeau.

Jimmy, who is actually very funny except when his character is questioned, dined out for some time among his Toronto trendies with an amusing story. In my final column in February 1980, before the election that returned Mr. Trudeau to power, I discussed Jimmy's reputation among the press types on the campaign plane. As a result, he "sued."

This scribbler happens to know a lot about libel suits. The lesson was learned well during the salad days of the W. A. C. Bennett Social Credit regime in British California when, strangely enough, libel writs would fall like flowers upon my publisher's door just before the legislature opened for its spring session. When Honourable Opposition members rose to pillory Her Majesty's Government about the charges raised on this typewriter, they were always informed the matter was "sub judice." The opposition was muzzled, the papers couldn't mention the subject further—and no one ever proceeded. My lawyer grew rich.

It is the same with Mr. Cutes.

All he wanted, his story goes, was enough from the libel award to buy a baby grand for his cute little house. To it he was going to attach a brass plaque: The Foth. And then he was going to ask his

white-wine-and-Perrier friends around on a Saturday "for a tinkle on the Foth."

A good line. In retaliation, I let it be known that if the case ever came to court, they would have to shift the venue to Maple Leaf Gardens, that being the only arena able to encompass all those who might want to comment on Jimmy's character.

**C P R** The dear old CPR, the stingiest gang of robber barons we've ever had, now calls itself just Canadian Pacific, in trying to clean up its image. There is one thing you can say about the grasping tycoons of the United States: once they have made their boodle, the old guilt complex moves them to hand some of it back. The Carnegies and the Rockefellers and the Fords set up foundations and libraries and galleries and endowed universities and spread the moolah around. The CPR, given the richest land in the country, turned into a pinch-faced band of Pecksniffs.

No grand foundation or soaring art gallery bears its name. It's still roundly hated on the Prairies and quietly resented in British Columbia. It was so parsimonious in providing airplanes and slow to wake up to reality that its air arm—Canadian Pacific—was suddenly swallowed by little PWA of Calgary. The CPR has hidden all its massive land holdings under something called Marathon Realty, and it now attempts to eke every buck it can out of all that real estate property it received courtesy of the Canadian taxpayer.

The story goes back to Confederation, when the CPR was given huge land grants in return for building a rail line to tidewater on the Pacific. After stopping at Port Moody at the first sign of the waters of Burrard Inlet, CPR officials later decided that a more propitious port could be built at the settlement of Gastown, at the opening of the inlet. Political numbskulls then decided to bribe the CPR to do something it planned to do on its own anyway, offering up all the waterfront land in what is now Vancouver harbour, plus all the rich residential land that is now Shaughnessy Heights.

The ugly rail lines have defaced the waterfront for a century, and downtown Vancouver had to build behind them so as to get a view of Stanley Park, the sea and the mountains in the most magnificently sited city in the world. Once, Marathon proposed a $1-billion development that would wipe out the rail lines and would "open the harbour to the public." What it meant, of course, is that it would shut off the harbour to the public view, with clusters of glass towers of hotels and Gucci-Rolex condo cliff dwellings. Anyone in Toronto will recognize the promise. A grand Ottawa pledge for a lakeside park at Harbourfront has turned into a picket fence of towers at the water's edge.

As a man of modest predicting abilities, I can predict one thing with great certainty. Nothing resembling the proffered multi-coloured sketches and papier-mâché models will be on the Vancouver shore. As usual, Marathon held a grand press conference before being granted any zoning or building permits from city authorities. It's the old trick: announce a faked finality and hope public opinion will fight off those picky people called city planning departments and guardians of the environment. Having been given the waterfront in the first place, they still think they own not only it but all the views of it.

Nothing much has changed since Confederation. The CPR was a bully then, and its land-rich offshoot is a bully now.

**CREIGHTON, DOUG (ALSO BIG RED)** Some aeons ago, in 1978, this scribbler found himself in an Edmonton TV studio, facing Peter Worthington and Ron Collister. Collister, the veteran CBC correspondent, had just been named editor of a new newspaper, the tabloid *Edmonton Sun*. Worthington, as one of the founders of the *Toronto Sun*, was celebrating yet another expansion of "the Little Paper That Grew."

This was on Peter Gzowski's long-dead *90 Minutes Live* late-night show, where I was recruited as an occasional hit man. To the astonishment and surprise of Worthington and Collister, the hired assassin ridiculed their brand of journalism as nothing but "tits-'n'-bum" trash that no sensible reader would buy and no self-respecting parrot would have at the bottom of his birdcage.

Gzowski's minions took us all for a scheduled drink afterwards and Worthington just sat there, looking at the floor. I don't think he spoke to me for three years. I could have been knocked over with a feather if anyone had suggested, that night, that several decades later I would be working for the *Sun* people and the best boss I've ever had, Doug Creighton.

You're talking here to someone who is an authority on bosses, having had a lot of them, due to a congenital difficulty in dealing with authority from above, so I know a good one when I find one. Creighton was the last Canadian newspaperman to rise to the very top of the trade.

Big Red once complained to the crowd at a book-launch party—which he was paying for—that I had described him in the tome as dressing like an unmade bed and combing his red hair with a Cuisinart. I said this was clearly incorrect; what I wrote was that he combed his hair with an egg beater. His wife did not speak to me for several days.

The best boss in Canada invented, for his employees, the Blah Day. February, as we know, is a dead month, no holidays, slush and cold and depressing. Every Creighton employee was told to just take an official Blah Day some time in February, stay home, sleep, get drunk or go to a movie.

The best boss in Canada at Christmas gave every employee, from janitors to the highest editors, a week's salary—in cash. Give a Christmas bonus cheque to a stenographer and it has to go into her husband's joint banking account. Give her an envelope thick with bills and it's a wonderful afternoon out zooming the economy.

To celebrate the twentieth anniversary of the founding of the *Toronto Sun*, Creighton rented Toronto's SkyDome, flew in employees from all over the country and threw the party to end all parties, complete with fireworks.

Since our latest great war, the whole trend on this continent has been for newspapers to disappear. Since Creighton, Worthington and Don Hunt invented the *Toronto Sun* they reversed the pattern and actually opened newspapers.

Creighton made millions for his shareholders, created thousands of jobs and treated people as human beings, not ciphers punching a clock.

He coddled his columnists of course, who often disagreed with him, and his cartoonist mocked his lunch habits. Loyalty begets loyalty and that's what it's all about. He had the happiest troops in the four Toronto papers, an industry where sour gloom is the standard mode.

### CRETINITES
  • See "Liberals."

**CROMBIE, DAVID** David Crombie was six years the wildly successful mayor of Toronto. Known as the Metro munchkin, he was acknowledged as one of the great communicators in politics. A room relaxes when he enters. Once picked by *Time* magazine as one of the world's 150 leaders of tomorrow, he dropped out of law school, became a salesman for General Foods, then a social science instructor.

He is married to schoolgirl sweetheart Shirley, the only woman in Canada shorter than he is. He suffered a heart attack in 1979, and is now recovered. He is perhaps five feet, five inches. Despite having the biggest budget of any portfolio (health) and having run Canada's largest city, he was kept out of Joe Clark's inner cabinet by aides who feared his popularity. Problem: Canada is too large a land to go Lilliputian.

**CROSBIE, JOHN** John Carnell Crosbie turned himself into a most skilful actor. The image across the country is of an amiable buffoon with a tongue like a flapping seal flipper, all done up with the Irish lilt of a down-home pub. Actually, Crosbie was to the manor born. His family owns approximately one-quarter of Newfoundland. (Three other families own the rest.) He went to the very best of schools: St. Andrew's, Queen's, Dalhousie, London School of Economics. He has a brilliant mind—the gold medallist at Dalhousie law school.

In 1949, the day the stubborn rock of Newfoundland joined Canada, there was an interesting little tableau at St. Andrew's, the exclusive private school outside Toronto where the Newfoundland rich send their sons in a vain attempt to rid them of their irreverence. The tired seed of the titled watched in wonderment as a clutch of Newfies stood in the dining hall—draped in the laces of their rugby boots dyed black—tears streaming down their faces and bellowing defiantly the words to "Ode to Newfoundland." One of the Newfies was Frank Moores, who some years later became premier of that distinctive island. Another was Crosbie, who would eventually become the only finance minister to graduate from *Laugh-In* and is the real heart of the Tories.

The NDP's Bob Rae called him "Newfoundland's gift to seventeenth-century economics." He was a Liberal, at first, until his route to the Newfoundland premiership was blocked by Joey Smallwood, so he switched to the Tories. When he came to Ottawa, he dressed like an unmade bed, in gee-shucks rich-boy style, but spruced up with national ambitions in mind.

He projects—as all humourists do—a continual morose air, as if despondent at what he sees of life. He sighed the sigh of the damned at the thought of the finance portfolio. "I have no future political ambitions. I'm ready for the scrap heap.

"In 1921 my grandfather was prime minister of finance in Newfoundland with a budget of $8 million. I was a minister of finance in Newfoundland with a deficit of $200 million. Now I'm minister of finance of Canada with a deficit of $12 billion.

"It makes a man proud."

For a chap who was the most intelligent man in the Mulroney cabinet, John Crosbie said some awfully silly things. His problem: the over-serious lad learned to love the roar of the greasepaint, the smell of the crowd.

**DAVEY, KEITH** Keith Davey is the most loyal and passionate
Liberal in the land. He is so devoted to his cause that to this day,
having resigned from his comfortable perch in the Senate in 1996,
he still refers to Lester Pearson as "Mr. Pearson."

Davey's favourite dining-out story involves Trudeau, whom he
also worshipped. He says that he was at home one Sunday night
when the phone rang. It was the PM, who wanted to discuss a
very complicated problem.

"Sir," Davey claims to have said, "could we perhaps talk this
over later?" Trudeau, whose IQ as we know surpassed Mount
Everest, was apparently the only person in Canada who did not
know that the seventh and deciding game of the Stanley Cup final
was on TV at that moment. The senator, nervously, explains this
to the prime minister.

Trudeau: "Yeah? What inning is it?"

**DAVIS, BILL** Expediency is the grease of all politics. Politicians
love to call it practical or pragmatic or "doable"—the current buzz-
word—but what they mean is acting in a way that will get them
votes, no matter how lofty the principle they invoke.

Expediency is one thing. Sleaziness—that unseemly word—is
another. But that seems the only charitable definition of the

decision in 1981 by Premier Bill Davis of Ontario to call an election during the coldest winter of the last century. Was there a burning issue? Was there a governmental crisis? Yes, one could say. The burning issue was that the minority Conservative government—the longest-reigning government in Christendom—had been told by its pollsters that it could snatch a majority on the winds of racism, on the anti-frog vote. And Bill Davis, that pink-cheeked, pipe-smoking exemplar of Brampton churchgoing was the most expedient politician in Canada. Brampton Billy is as enigmatic as the Cheshire cat, also as shrewd.

The Tories of Bill Davis and predecessors had been in power for eleven straight terms, ranging back thirty-eight years, a mandate challenged not even by Bulgaria. They did this by appealing to the most conservative people in Canada, the comfortable, prosperous burghers of southern Ontario.

To keep these burghers happy, Bill Davis ensured that sophisticated Toronto was the only city in major league baseball where you were not allowed to buy a cup of beer. To keep these burghers happy, Bill Davis allowed his film censors to ban *The Tin Drum*, a film based on Günter Grass's novel that won the Cannes Film Festival and an Academy Award. To keep these burghers happy, Bill Davis played on the anti-French vote so as to win a majority in the March 1981 election which played out in the winter slush, snow and sleaziness.

• See also "Ontario."

**DAY, STOCKWELL (ALSO *STOCKBOY DAY*)** The reason why Stockwell Day, the great Right hope, went down to defeat in the 2000 election is quite simple: The voters don't know who he is. And the explanation is: neither does he.

At a time when the nation would seriously like to toss out an arrogant and tired, old-style Prime Minister, the new kid on the block in his wetsuit raises more questions than answers in the puzzlement about whether he has the heft to reside in 24 Sussex Drive.

It is all very colourful, and intriguing, to view his life pattern in preparing for the country's top job. There was his time toiling as a deck hand on a fishing boat. Driving a bulldozer in the Northwest Territories. Collecting bodies for a hearse company. Being an auctioneer. Working for an interior decorator. Actually raising chickens in his car.

Well. Your scribbler used to graft roses in a nursery. And spread peas on a tray in a frozen-food factory (very useful for dealing with politicians later). And worked in a post office. And put himself through university by being a steelworker during summer holidays, not being able to afford the lousy wages newspapers were offering. And unloaded sides of beef from boxcars.

The only difference being that, while this may have been a good grounding for journalism, I don't think it would be the proper preparation for becoming PM.

The Stock, along with his variegated curriculum vitae, briefly dabbled at the University of Victoria, then quit. Dabbled at a Bible college in Alberta, but never finished there, either. Until his bride introduced him to religion, he seemed a smart, glib young man in search of himself.

Mr. Wetsuit destroyed himself. The news that he believed dinosaurs walked with humans, that Adam and Eve actually existed—indicating that he thought *The Flintstones* was a documentary—finished him off even in the rural Ontario ridings where people actually still go to church.

The dinosaurs did it. We all know now that Mackenzie King talked to his dead mother and his pet dog. But that was only dug out much later by historians. And there wasn't television in those days. The dinosaur/Flintstones story? On the air in minutes. Yabba-dabba-doo!

Much is made, in the badly organized Alliance troop, of the fact that their candidate for Sussex Drive was a successful treasury minister in Mr. Klein's flock for years and once, to demonstrate his verbal skills, delivered an entire budget speech without referring to a note.

Yeah, and that's the problem.

**DIANA, PRINCESS** The mob around Buckingham Palace's locked gates and the endless mound of flowers, including a child's crayoned tribute to her "Queen of Harts," were the main objects of attraction. Banks of TV anchor ladies in coiffed blonde hair emote to cameras—the very media mob of bottomfeeders that is accused of driving Princess Diana into her grave.

London never saw a week like it. Winston Churchill, who saved the world for democracy, attracted 300,000 to his funeral cortege when he died in 1965. This untutored girl drew millions, and so shook the royals that they were forced by public outrage to abandon their beloved protocol and bow to their subjects' wishes that they get a life and get involved.

The spontaneous outpouring of feeling from what is supposed to be the stiff-upper-lip isle left the royals, hunkered in Balmoral up in Scotland, absolutely bewildered and in slight panic—gulping and recalling that they had stripped a bitter "Di the Difficult" of the "Her Royal Highness" label.

Columnist Polly Toynbee, descendant of a rather well-known historian, said "the Windsors are behaving as if a revolution is taking place outside the gates of Buckingham Palace. And they may be right." Every morning, as I went out Queen's Walk to buy my ten newspapers, little men in proper blue business suits were headed, a posy of red roses in hand, down to Buck House to lay another wreath—on the dead hand of the monarchy.

The princess who once confessed she was "thick as a plank" has revealed, even more in death than in life, the desiccated, bloodless family she left behind.

**DIEFENBAKER, JOHN** The trial that made John Diefenbaker a legend was the defence of Alfred John Atherton, a twenty-two-year-old CNR telegrapher charged with manslaughter after a train wreck at Canoe River, British Columbia, which killed seventeen Korea-bound soldiers. Diefenbaker discovered early in the trial that the soldiers had been in wooden coaches while officers on the train were in secure steel cars. To his further delight, the prosecutor, the B.C. deputy attorney general, turned out to have the name of Colonel Eric Peppler K.C. At every possible occasion, Dief laid on the references to the "colonel," all the while hammering away at the contrast between the officers encased in their safe steel cars and the men dying in wooden coaches. He won an acquittal for the young telegrapher and marched back to Ottawa to the plaudits of the nation.

The incident is key to understanding John George Diefenbaker and explaining why this strange man is still the only mythic figure in our politics. He had a touch for human emotions which never deserted him—even when he verged on becoming a caricature of himself. He is forever the Outsider in the corridors of power, luxuriating in his exaggerated martyrdom, revelling in the fact that only he knows the truth.

Like all men of surpassing ego, the Chief had few close friends. Only acolytes. (Though he was loyal: both the lawyer who assisted him in that railway wreck trial and the two benchers who eased through his B.C. licence were appointed judges.) He moved about the country like a stately battleship, enjoying each wave he made, his deadly tongue feared, especially within his own party.

He was the raconteur supreme, slowly rearranging the mental furniture, each anecdote sculpted in elaborate sentences, moving sedately to the dénouement, holding off interruptions with a cautionary eyebrow, a threatening finger. With a phrase he could capture a corner of page one. He had a connection cord to the public, a nerve end for simplistic issues: a mailbox, a Mountie, a railway telegrapher.

Of course he was a terrible prime minister, mystified by decision-making, obsessed by his suffocating inferiority complex, never feeling secure, happy only when appealing directly to the public for succour. But he had a gift—a gift shared by few others among us—of spotting totems, symbols, rituals that strike a nerve. He may have been a lousy leader; he was excellent litmus paper.

**DOBBS, FRED C.** It is the clowns who indicate how bitter things have become. Pagliacci grins to hide the sadness within. Fred C. Dobbs, who came out of sort-of retirement in 1993, in his tattered grey pinstripes and shaggy white wig looks rather like Mark Twain after a bad night sleeping under a bridge. He dispenses his sour nostrums at lunch on Wednesdays at Bistro 990, a Toronto watering hole close to Queen's Park, where they keep the inmates.

Brian Mulroney, he tells us, is the only Canadian prime minister who has had a city named after him—Moose Jaw. He orders the diners to stand and hoist a toast to "the greatest Canadian of all time—Northern Dancer." Fred is in the grand tradition of Don Harron's Charlie Farquharson, and in real life is Michael Magee, handsome as a Hollywood star, a refugee from a privileged upbringing who turned into a modern-day Damon Runyon racetrack character.

Michael Magee was born sardonic and has been going downhill ever since. He was shipped around to the best of Ontario private schools, but ended up as a bellhop at the Austin Hotel in Vancouver, a joint of some character, which, as Fred C. explains, "had, um, recreational facilities upstairs." The downtown hotel was full of "lobby generals," who reminded the young bellhop of his uncle, with his wheezy voice and hoary stories, and so Fred C. Dobbs came into creation.

The bellhop listening to the lobby generals graduated to Vancouver's Inquisition Coffee House during the riotous and disputatious sixties, doing stand-up rants.

But with Mulroney in power, Fred C. Dobbs is angry, disobeying the advice of the lady in his life that he has to be more funny than bitter. His contempt for Mulroney is unalloyed, his morose predictions for the land pure dross.

Like Mort Sahl before him, Fred C. Dobbs stands at the Bistro 990 mike with a mittful of newspapers and quotes the obvious nonsense that fills them every day, cabinet ministers emitting obvious lies and world statesmen pouring out piffle.

He finds, in truth, more honesty at the race track, where he knows the nags are often stuffed with more than oats and often blow up on the backstretch when the steroids run out.

Fred C. Dobbs, who is supposed to be a funny man, is bitter. When the clowns are angry, what about the great unwashed? Those in power might pay attention.

**DOUGLAS, TOMMY** Three frisking pinto ponies surge and bump up the grassy slope until they are frozen on the crest against the fathomless blue sky, like a tableau out of a Zane Grey–era canvas. In the picnic ground below, a half dozen miles northeast of Regina, there are those endless straw fedoras, in pastel, adorning the cautious men who wear both belt and suspenders. The plastic folding chairs seek the shade beneath the trees as the old-time fiddle contest begins to tap toes in the rising dust. The horseshoes clank. It is 1978, and for one final time "an old-fashioned CCF picnic," one designed to honour the last of the happy warriors, Tommy Douglas, who will not pass this way again.

Tommy Douglas in the year before he retired, like all men of passionate belief, seemed perhaps twenty years younger than his seventy-three years. There was a tendency to regard with wry amusement his outdated marionette mannerisms and dismiss his pulpit style. One suspects, however, that the painful progress of social justice in this tremulous country spotlights just how much this pugnacious bantam accomplished.

In 1978 he is the same five-foot-six as when he was lightweight boxing champ of Manitoba. That carefully tended pompadour bounces above the chipmunk grin. His style was a little too evangelical, too corny ever to make him truly comfortable in skeptical British Columbia where he retreated in 1962 after his galling defeat in Regina, but this is his turf here, this picnic, these roots.

"If I'd slept on all the kitchen floors of all the farmhouses as claimed here today," he sighs as he chews on his barbecued chicken dinner, "I'd have been around more than Casanova."

Over the distance of time, Douglas's seventeen years as premier of Saskatchewan were indeed a test pattern for what has happened everywhere else: first bill of rights in Canada; first supplementary old age pension; first loan plan for small business; first student aid program; first assistance to the arts—a decade before the Canada Council.

What Douglas (and the CCF) are most celebrated for, of course, is the introduction of medicare. While nervous Ottawa waffled, the audacity of Douglas was rather breathtaking. After hiring Dr.

Henry Sigerist of Baltimore's Johns Hopkins University, the world's top authority on social medicine, to do a report, Douglas asked him who the best man would be to run it. "The best possible man" happened to be Dr. Fred Mott, who was untouchable, as assistant surgeon-general of the U.S. Army. Douglas phoned the U.S. surgeon-general and somehow got a release for Mott, who established a scheme that was followed years later by everyone else in Canada.

There are some 4,000 victims of nostalgia on the mellow Sunday afternoon. Tommy Douglas stands on a picnic table, the pompadour brushing the red-and-white stripes of the tent. The sky is now black and jagged lines of lightning pierce the horizon. His earthy barnyard jokes, dropped with the precision of a pianist, are the more appreciated for being so familiar.

**DRAPEAU, JEAN** Once the greatest mayor Montreal ever had, Jean "the Olympics can no more have a deficit than a man can have a baby" Drapeau is the author of the most disastrous prediction ever made.

The brilliant visionary, who brought us the 1967 Expo that gave Canadians a pride they had never before realized, hired the brilliant French architect Roger Taillibert, who had never experienced or contemplated a Quebec winter. He devised that divine soaring stadium with the, ahem, retractable roof that never worked and does not to this day.

The whole Olympic exercise was a farce. Cement trucks rolling into the stadium site and rolling out the other end, unloaded, to drive around the block and drive in for yet another paid trip. Corruption supreme, payoffs unlimited, a public debt in all of $1.5 billion.

Frail at eighty, when he returned to Montreal after a Mulroney appointment in Paris, Drapeau in his dotage would defend all his imagination. For more than a decade, he made his once-wonderful city the most attractive visit in Canada. So much more vibrant and sophisticated than tight-assed Toronto. So much more worldly and classy than barefooted Vancouver.

Over the years, Montrealers have found fulfilment of their fantasies in the mayor's grandiose projects. And there was no doubt about the mayor's ability to pluck the heart-strings of civic pride in his constituents. As he said in 1980, "There are those who are quick to criticize people with big dreams. I personally prefer the innovative, the daring."

He may have been right.

## DUBYA

• See "Bush, George W."

**DUCEPPE, GILLES** Born nervous, son of one of Quebec's greatest actors. He spent five years as a Marxist-Leninist working as a hospital orderly to organize a union. Brittle, media types know how to press his temper button. Hair net definitely not a fashion breakthrough. He can never win the image battle because he's always needed Saint Lucien to shore up the Blockhead base, but looks like a gopher as soon as Bouchard appears.

**E a t o n' s** The earth collapsed in 1997, just in time for the news that Eaton's, that staple of Prairie life, was broke. Busted. Out of cash. A small Prairie boy can take only so much.

The year revolved around Eaton's catalogue. The selection of Christmas gifts. The arrival of Christmas gifts by mail. For small Prairie boys, there was the added advantage of an early introduction to sex education, gratis the ladies in the underwear ads. Oh, secret joy.

The Eaton's catalogue, never wasted, never thrown out, then moved on to yet another most necessary role—perhaps the first example of the recycling mode now so popular. In the two-holer out back, it lasted almost exactly a year until the new Eaton's catalogue arrived. The family bosses in far-off Toronto must have gauged the thickness of the big bible exactly for twelve-month use.

And so the Eaton's mythology is gone. One supposes the rot started when Timothy Eaton, 127 years ago, pronounced that the filthy weed, tobacco, could not be sold on the premises, and cigarettes for generations—while the world moved on—were banned as a commodity in the largest and best-loved department store chain in Canada.

On Sundays, the blinds were drawn on its street-front display windows, less the sinners passing by might spy the nude mannequins that were having their duds changed. One can't be too careful.

It would be rude to mention, of course, that the venerable family firm that stocked the two-holers of Saskatchewan through all its years of making millions for its heirs managed to keep the unions out of its stores.

Modern commerce is not kind to dabblers. I always thought Fred Eaton of the four boys was the brightest of the bunch until he for some strange reason accepted the appointment from Brian Mulroney as Canada's high commissioner to London. Shortly after arriving, in a speech to an important English audience, he announced that he had no idea why he had been chosen for the post.

A certain scribbler who cannot be identified wrote at the time that if Fred Eaton, a member of a family that rewards the political party of its choice with generous campaign donations, really did not know why he was chosen, he should never be allowed outside the house without his mittens tied on a string.

It's an old standard in the inheritance business that the first generation makes a fortune, the second generation solidifies it and following generations piddle it away.

And so while Wal-Mart strides the land and J. C. Penney lurks as a predator and Home Depot drags in consumers, in 1997 Eaton's went the way of the catalogue that it killed in 1976 (meaning the last two-holer had expired).

**EDMONTON** The most spectacular river town in Canada is Edmonton, the entire personality of the city and its warp and woof dictated by the waterway. The deep river valley of the North Saskatchewan, carved by centuries of flow through the dark northern soil, makes a flat prairie town memorable because of the views across this huge canyon. The country's most imaginatively sited convention centre is built into the north slope, buried in the bank of the river, with conventioneers like so many muskrats in a burrow. (The new Canada Place sail-topped pier in Vancouver? We just take it for granted that everything in Vancouver is stunning.)

To get anywhere in Edmonton you have to wind your way down into the river valley and wind your way up the other side, a pleasant vista that makes the Alberta capital the only prairie city with a faint sense of what it would be like to live among mountains.

In winter, a visitor gazing from his Edmonton hotel window on high sees naught, with vast white plumes of vapor rising vertically from each and every office building, the excess heat from the industrious bodies beneath converted immediately into erect steam. There is a distorted vision of Dante's *Inferno* against the wide blue sky, an allegory of the richest province of all absolutely bubbling in delicious energy and vigour that translates itself into the ozone.

Another vignette: It is Sunday midnight and a bitter wind originating somewhere around the Mackenzie River delta whips across the tarmac of the Edmonton airport. It is –38°C and the snow swirls in furious gusts. And what is that, huddled out there in the frigid gloom awaiting a turn at the swamped unloading gates? A giant jetliner from Braniff airlines of Texas, inventor of the first Technicolor airplanes, and another from the Howard Hughes airline, both no doubt burgeoning with pot-bellied cattle barons and tanned oillionaires, wondering what aberration of geography and climate has dumped them into this inhuman landscape. In my prosaic craft from the People's airline, a clutch of wide-eyed and milk-fed entertainers from a Disneyland troupe in California gaze out the windows in terror, convinced they have landed on the edge of the earth.

**EDWARDS, BOB** The wild and crazy *Frank* magazine of today, which terrifies cabinet ministers and adulterers in Ottawa and Toronto, would love to be half as outrageous as Bob Edwards's Calgary *Eye Opener* at the turn of the century.

Robert Chambers Edwards, the finest journalist Canada has ever had the pleasure of reading, was born in Edinburgh in 1864, educated at a private school and Glasgow University and continued his studies in Berlin, Paris and Rome. Before he was thirty, he had seen most of Europe, had edited a small journal on the Riviera and ended up in Calgary and the long bar of the Alberta Hotel.

For twenty years after 1902, the *Eye Opener* frightened the bejeezus out of Calgary, while reaching a peak circulation of just 35,000. It could—and did—make or break politicians. R. B. Bennett blamed his 1904 federal defeat on Edwards. The mayor of Calgary declined to run for re-election when the *Eye Opener* opposed him.

At one stage, the *Eye Opener* was denied the mails. The CPR banned it from its trains. The only fight he could never win was against the bottle. "Every man has his favourite bird," he wrote. "Mine is the bat." When the *Eye Opener* failed to publish for several weeks, the whole town knew Edwards was drunk.

**EGO, P. E.**
• See "Trudeau, Pierre Elliott."

**ELECTIONS** In Viking mythology, the Valkyries were the warlike virgins who rode the skies at the behest of the god Odin and were known as Choosers of the Slain. The flickering light they emitted lit up the northern skies and produced what we know as the aurora borealis. As the John Turner 1988 campaign jet, known as LiberAir, took off in search of a victory, on every flight one of the wild animals of the television techies would unleash his boom box and the dramatic sounds of "The Ride of the Valkyries" would resound through the silver capsule while he bounced flickering lights off the walls of the cabin. It was an eerie, ghostly opening to every flight, as the press and politicians grew silent, very symbolic and accurate for the suddenly warlike virgin of Bay Street who had turned populist.

There were many weird images in that campaign. There was the rather unusual introduction of foreign leaders, helpfully coming to the aid of a panicking government party. Ronald Reagan checked in with his hint as to how Canadians should vote, followed by Maggie Thatcher with one of her classic imitations of the Sunday school teacher lecturing the heathen in the colonies. All we needed was the Pope to contribute his thoughts on free trade, to go along with his musings on condoms.

The previous, in 1984, was a bore of an election, not so much a questioning of the public mind as a litany of apologies. If it wasn't John Mulroney doing the mea culpa on his fuzzification of muddifying the facts, it was Brian Turner backtracking on jokes. The only thing missing was Ed Broadjump apologizing for his distressing habit of shouting a lot. It is a pity no one will get down in the trenches and tell us the real facts of life, the matters that the puzzled electorate actually wants to know.

In 1993, the terrified Tories had a genie in a bottle and were afraid to let her out. They were trying to win that most discouraging and unappetizing election with a candidate who said, on silencing journalists: "I mean, it's a perfectly legitimate technique to seal them off from communications to try to force them out, perfectly reasonable." Kim Campbell was a politician who told it like it is—and her handlers were petrified. "I will sell my soul to get re-elected," she advertised.

Now this is good stuff. Who needs the Jean Chrétien bafflegab, the man who announces on CBC Radio that he wants an election "the better the sooner"? This is the best material since Sir John A., addled by too much firewater and the hot sun, barfed his cookies over the edge of an outdoor stage and then wiped off his chin and continued his speech: "So much for my opponent's platform..."

It was almost sad, viewing Stockwell Day up close on the campaign trail in 2000, to see day-upon-day the at first irritating, then exasperating, then defeatist response to the daily assault by the assassins of the national press, i.e., the Ottawa Press Gallery regulars who have been conditioned by the farce of Question Period. The Stock's a nice guy, with an even nicer wife, but you don't win credibility by having frat-house pillow fights with the press at the back of your campaign jet. Mackenzie King, Pierre Trudeau, Lester Pearson having pillow fights on the press plane?

After a dismal election that degenerated into purposeful divisiveness and bigotry, the best place in the world to be in the early summer, I discovered, is the lush green hills of Bali. The volcanoes are always a threat, there is the corrupt government of Indonesia in the archipelago that provides the fourth-largest population in the world and, somewhere off on another island, is Bre-X. Such a retreat is most useful in providing a distance that encourages contemplation. The best place to observe Canada, as it celebrates another year of survival, is halfway around the world from it.

In the coming year, Canada, the jurisdiction the United Nations feels is the most blessed on earth, will ignore the fact of its abundant resources that every foreign rival envies.

Quebec is not going to separate, the inhabitants being sick to the teeth of any mention of the topic. Since 1992, the Québécois have had to go the polls five times—two federal elections, a provincial election, the Charlottetown referendum, a separation referendum—a punishment laid upon no other Canadians.

Gilles Duceppe will say something stupid. Sheila Copps will say something stupid. Bill Clinton will escape jail, while the world puzzles over the naïveté of its only superpower. Washington lawyers will grow rich. Meaning richer. And Canadians will complain.

British Columbia will complain that Ontario, because it has a larger population, puts more MPs in Parliament. The Atlantic provinces will complain because their inhabitants can no longer work for ten weeks and then relax on the pogey for unconscionable drifts of time.

There will be tragedy and starvation in Africa. There will be further turmoil and consternation in the Balkans. And Canadians will complain to each other.

### Ennui-on-the-Rideau
• See "Ottawa."

### Establishment, the
There are several characteristics of the Canadian Establishment. It is feudal in nature. It is very protective of its own. And it is WASP. Most of all it is White Anglo-Saxon Protestant—and determined to stay so. It is the Orange Lodge in pinstripes.

Robert Campeau, the millionaire Ottawa developer who set out in 1980 to take over Royal Trustco, Canada's largest trust company, knew it before, and then had his nose rubbed into the fact. The Canadian Establishment always plays by the rules, but it plays dirty.

Robert Campeau should have talked to Paul Desmarais, another non-WASP. By 1969 the Sudbury outsider had acquired ten per cent of the stock of Argus, the home of Bud McDougald, E. P. Taylor and, later, Conrad Black—the home of WASPdom. He expected to be invited to join the Argus board.

The two French Canadians could have asked Sam Bronfman before he died. Bronfman, of course, was an outsider who had made too much money out of whisky and was trying to buy his way into the Canadian Establishment. He wanted to become a governor of McGill, the tony WASP university where, incredibly, Jewish males had to have averages of at least seventy-five per cent, rather than the usual marks, to be admitted. He was blocked by the veto of sugar magnate John McConnell. Bronfman tried to purchase a seat in the Senate. The Liberal party, the government branch of the Canadian Establishment, did not have the courage to appoint the country's first Jewish senator, but it was not averse to taking Sam's money.

Over a decade he contributed some $2 million to the Liberal slush fund. They cleverly waited until Bronfman was seventy-five (legislation the previous year made that the upper limit for appointments) and then appointed a more acceptable Jew, Lazarus Phillips—who had just thirty-one months left before his own seventy-fifth birthday.

In *The Vertical Mosaic*, the brilliant book that proved Canada still operates under the class system, sociologist John Porter pointed out twenty-five years ago that "the world of the economic elite appears as a complex network of small groupings interlocked by a high degree of cross membership. Throughout this network runs a thin, but nonetheless perceptible, thread of kinship."

Ask Robert Campeau. Ask Paul Desmarais. Ask Sam Bronfman, still muttering in his grave.

## EXCITED STATES OF AMERICA
- See "U.S. of A."

## EXPEDIENCY
- See "Davis, Bill."

## EYE OPENER
- See "Edwards, Bob."

**FEW DEMOCRATS**
- See "New Democratic Party."

**FISHER, MATTHEW** If I had a son who wanted to follow me into the "black art"—as Kipling called it—of journalism, I would suggest he try to find some time to spend with Matthew Fisher. Matthew Fisher is the second most interesting guy in Canada involved in what we in the trade call "typing and spelling." The reason he is so interesting is that he almost never is in Canada.

He spends his life making airlines rich. He's been to 143 countries. He's covered fourteen wars and revolutions. He has a deadly wit, fears no one and doesn't drink. He says "it's not necessary."

**FORD, GERALD** The only man to occupy both offices without ever being elected vice-president or president, Gerald Ford was so aware of his tenuous hold on the White House he inherited from the disgraced Nixon that he ordered the Marine band in the Rose Garden never to play "Hail to the Chief" when he walked in.

**FOURTH ESTATE**
- See "Journalists."

**FRASER, JOHN** John Fraser, former editor of *Saturday Night* magazine, is a darting little magpie with lively dark eyes and a tongue, hinged in the middle, that waggles at both ends. I believe it was Peter C. Newman who once described him in print as the most promising young journalist in the country. He is the biggest gossip in Canada—a great gossiper is one of the things that makes a good journalist. (Pick out the gossip in your high-school class and you'll be anointing a future journalist.)

Wee John, having gone to the best private schools, has had a most unusual and bemusing rise upwards. He went to Memorial University in Newfoundland. He became ballet critic of the Toronto *Globe and Mail*. As that, he was intimately involved in the defection of Soviet star Mikhail Baryshnikov—and wrote a book on the dancer. From ballet, he moved to China as his paper's correspondent—a leap attesting to his versatility—and wrote a book on that.

Balletomane, sinologist, coffee-house teller of tall tales, when he was the correspondent of a little-known Toronto morning newspaper, he darted about the streets of London like a water bug with a mission. He is the owner of a new dark hat, brim turned down all around, that makes him in his greatcoat resemble the second lead in *The Phantom of the Opera*. His dark eyebrows rising in horror and shock behind his librarian glasses, he is chockablock with delicious gossip about the high-and-mighty. The low do not interest him. He is a proud member of the Reform Club on Pall Mall ("Pell Mell" in the local argot), a chilblained pile of stone where the stuffed remnants of British Liberalism—some of them still breathing in the slow-motion manner reminiscent of the Victoria Conservative Club—gather at lunch for warm gin and slow waiters.

As usual, a drifting mob of refugees from the Great White Waste of Time (as Fleet Street refers to our land ruled by Ennui-on-the-Rideau) speckles the place and pecks away at its impervious underbelly.

**FREE TRADE** In the great scale of things, it is hard to decide which is the most bothersome type of people—liars or meddlesome characters. Liars are at least consistent, if they have a virtue. You just take as a given that everything they tell you is untrue, and you pay no attention and you get on with things. If, periodically, they come out with a truth, and you refuse to believe it or trust it and they suffer as a result—well, that's tough titty. Meddlesome types are worse trouble because they won't go away. (We are leaving aside here even more loathsome specimens such as bores or whiners.) Needless to say, the worst fate that can befall anyone is to come upon a meddlesome who is also a liar.

This is pertinent, because the liars who negotiated the free trade agreement turned out to be meddlesome also. Ottawa lied to us by claiming that cultural factors were not on the free trade bargaining table. The emasculation of Flora MacDonald's film distribution policy—Flora's bones picked clean by the Mulroney cabinet that bowed to White House pressure—proved that. Another triumph for public trust.

The problem the proponents of free trade have is that they are all numbers and figures, statistics and dollars, quotas and tariffs. They don't really understand their own country at all. If Canadians were really interested in trying to equal the American standard of living—dollar for dollar, crime rate for crime rate—they would have opted long ago for complete integration, surrender as the 51st state. They didn't because they realize there is something more important than mere numbers and figures.

Calvin Coolidge once said, "The chief business of the American people is business." But the business of Canada is not business. It is figuring out how to survive as an independent entity next to the richest and most powerful nation in the history of what passes for civilization.

There is the silly analogy with the European Common Market and how it hasn't destroyed national identities. Aside from the fact that those identities have been nurtured for countless centuries and not 134 years, there is another small matter. There are fifty-seven million people in Britain. Fifty-six million in France. Eighty-two million in Germany. Fifty-seven million in Italy— before you even start to count the junior partners. That has nothing to do with a cockamamie scheme that puts a country that has the same population as California into bed with a giant of 250 million.

The business mindset of the free trade boys charges that those who oppose the deal are arguing on emotional grounds. Right!

**F R U M ,   B A R B A R A** Barbara Frum made *As It Happens* famous, ranging the world for insightful and tough interviews by phone, abiding no fool, accepting no bafflegab from some faraway tinpot tycoon. She became a national treasure on *The Journal*, insisting in all her journalism, that Canada's reach was the world.

• See also "Jennings, Peter."

**F R U M ,   D A V I D** David Frum, son of the late Barbara Frum and real estate tycoon Dr. Murray Frum, is one of the earnest young men who think they have reinvented the wheel and wish to destroy what the Tories, the party that founded this nation, stands for.

These are the neo-cons, descendants of Newt the Nut, firm believers that only they have seen the truth and must press it on the masses.

The main push behind the putsch to Unite the Right is my *Financial Post* colleague. An extremely bright and extremely energetic Harvard grad, he has had the advantage in the past of my sage advice—given free—that he might contemplate deciding whether he wants to be a journalist or an empire-builder. David, a friend who greets my free advice with humour, might be right in his fervour. Who knows? I may be wrong. (The last time was 1938.)

**FULFORD, ROBERT** The reigning intellectual in Canadian journalism.

## GAGLARDI, PHIL (ALSO *PHLYING PHIL*)
- See "B.C. politics."

**GALBRAITH, KENNETH** Someone once described John Kenneth Galbraith and Marshall McLuhan as "the most famous Canadians the United States has ever produced," which is true. Galbraith, with his forty-four honorary degrees and solid credentials as a Harvard/Kennedy family guru, glories in his birth at Iona Station, Ontario, and the fact he somehow graduated from Ontario Agricultural College in Guelph.

He is now in his dotage and still delivers his usual droll asides— "the American war against the poor, having been won…" On the Republican trickle-down theory, slashing taxes to goose investment while also cutting welfare rates: "it all boils down to the slightly improbable case that the rich are not working because they have too little income, while the poor are not working because they have too much."

This, he explains, is "the horse-and-sparrow theory of economics in which if you feed the horse enough oats, some will pass through to the road for the sparrow."

He stretches six-foot-eight into the ozone, and speaking a few years back at the University of Toronto, required the introductory speakers to stand on a pink suitcase so as to reach the microphone that was ratcheted to his oxygen level. He was introduced as "the only economist alive who can make people laugh"—which is also true.

**GERUSSI, BRUNO** The first time I encountered Bruno Gerussi was in 1949 when he, a total stranger, sprayed beer all over me. That would be in a small theatre in New Westminster, B.C., where he was Stanley Kowalski opposite Blanche DuBois in Tennessee Williams's *A Streetcar Named Desire*.

Gerussi had the same vigorous arrogance as Marlon Brando. Watching as I was from a front-row seat in theatre-in-the-round ambiance, I got the remnants of his angry beer bottle all over me.

Bruno—short, funny, egotistical, creative—was a product of what Canada can be. His father was an Italian stonemason immigrant who settled in Medicine Hat, Alberta. His combative son won a scholarship to the Banff School of Fine Arts and honed his gifts with the Seattle Repertory Theater and went on to Shakespeare and national radio.

Some of us thought he never should have left the Stratford Festival, which, on reflection, doesn't pay all that well. Robert Clothier, himself a classical actor and then the Relic counterfoil to Gerussi in the TV series, in his eulogy on the CBC, claimed that Laurence Olivier had stated that Bruno—we'll forgive the exaggeration—was the best Romeo he had ever seen on stage.

Gerussi, an "ethnic" (hello there, Mr. Parizeau), did it all. A widower with two small children, he wisely decided he couldn't continue the roaming life of the itinerant actor and had to raise them. He became the host—after the sparkling Helen Hutchinson—of the three-hour national celebration afterwards hosted by icon Peter Gzowski. The kid from Medicine Hat with an accent became renowned as the star of *The Beachcombers*—an Italian playing a Greek?—but he was more than that.

The guy had a bigger ego than Sylvester Stallone. His swagger was his eventual downfall at the CBC, where he was nibbled to death by ducks. The cheese-paring twits at the CBC, who can't stand stars, of course killed the show because it was too successful. Gerussi was mobbed when he travelled to Australia. Germans loved it, naturally—confirming their belief that every Canadian wore a lumberjack shirt. One of his kids married one of Pierre Berton's kids, the two old bears always arguing over who was the real grandfather.

A stonemason's son from Medicine Hat who became a Shakespearean actor and then an accomplished radio performer and then, after a playful gig as Celebrity Cook, a star for nineteen years on one of the most successful CBC series ever, which played in thirty countries. Bruno Gerussi represented everything that Canada can be: expansive, reaching out, unlimited expectations.

**GETTY, DON** Proof indeed of premature senility was the amazing announcement by Quarterback Don Getty of his retirement from the political gridiron. Brilliant! After threatening to lie down on the carpet and kick his heels in the Constitution-hatching cottage industry, threatening to veto Quebec unless he got his useless Senate, he then decided to turn himself into a lame duck in 1992 as the real struggle on a national referendum approached. A class act.

The follicularly disadvantaged Getty, who has never met a golf course he didn't love, provided a prime example of psychic distancing. After threatening to veto any idea of Quebec as a distinct society and getting, as a result, his goofy elected Senate on the agenda, he rides off into the sunset on his motorized golf cart, leaving the remains of the confusion to the purse-lipped Presto! Manning, who in the accurate words of the PM is such a leader that he had to poll his membership before deciding whether he would support the Anne of Green Gables accord.

For some time, those of us who are still sane have had the deep suspicion that too much Constitution-watching can be damaging to the brain.

**GIBSON, GORDON** Gordon Gibson, the wealthy Vancouver figure and Fraser Institute guru, used to be as Liberal as anyone could get. Gordon Gibson Sr. was a rough-and-ready timber baron, the "bull of the woods." As a Liberal member of the B.C. Legislature, he unearthed the bribery scandal that sent to jail Social Credit's Robert Sommers, the first cabinet minister in Commonwealth history to be put in prison for using his job for criminal gain.

Young Gordon went to Harvard. As a parliamentary assistant in Ottawa, he was the first backroom boy to start the excitement that led Pierre Trudeau to the Liberal leadership in 1968. At the surprise wedding to Margaret Sinclair, he was to be the best man; but the PM judged him not properly dressed at the church and had the Trudeau brother stand in instead.

Gordon Gibson became leader of the B.C. Liberal Party. He ran as a Liberal, unsuccessfully, for the Commons. Today, he cannot stand the Ottawa Liberals. He has complete contempt for them, and has since turned himself into a columnist (the highest calling).

In his writings—in the *Globe and Mail* and now with the *National Post*—one can trace his gradual embrace of the Alliance cause, the frustration with the Natural Governing Party and its arrogant reliance on the Montreal-Ottawa-Toronto cabal.

He eventually went over the wall and called on his beloved

province to separate. Forget Quebec, B.C. has no place within Confederation. It was the utter despair of a serious man who has gone from being an Ottawa insider to someone who thinks there is no hope for those outside the cozy system that has Ontario supplying all the MPs necessary to keep the Grits in power forever.

**GLIBERALS**
- See "Liberals."

**GLOBE AND MAIL, THE** A society, if it is to survive, must have certain verities, some icons, some concrete in the basement. There must be rocks we can all cling to, some glue that holds us together as a nation. It has long been established that a mature country needs, among other things, a national press to transmit common thoughts throughout the land. It is what has made Britain such a literate nation: a tiny country with a large population that reads, from Land's End to John O'Groats every day, all the national dailies. Canada, because of its sprawling geography spread over five and a half time zones (the world will end at midnight; in Newfoundland, at 12:30) has always been denied this unifying force. That is, until the magic of the satellite and Lord Thomson's North Sea oil zillions brought us our first national newspaper, the *Globe and Mail* of Toronto.

Bouncing its electronic wisdom off a satellite into printing plants in Vancouver, Calgary, Ottawa, Moncton and waypoints, the *Globe* now proudly flaunts its title as the national newspaper, earnest of mind, ponderous of tone, dripping in the dignity of Lord Thomson's oil. What then, does one make of this:

*Attractive, shapely redhead, 30, seeks a generous businessman for discreet afternoon encounters. Enclose phone number. Box 2294, The Globe.*

The eye boggles. What is the redhead doing in the classified section just beneath Educational, Schools, Colleges, Tuition and ahead of Gas Saver—"get 80 to 200 miles per gallon carburetor"? Is she offering discreet Berlitz lessons or a primer in Latin verbs? Tips in lubrication or a motor overhaul? How much of your gas could she really save? Astonished, a reader fights his way through the daily accounts of Question Period and the "Report on Business." Back behind all those one-column pictures of clean-jawed executives getting promotions at Amalgamated Widget, one finds:

*Exceptionally gorgeous blonde of French extraction wishes to meet very selective, affluent executive for discreet daytime encounters. Please reply with phone number to Box 2796, The Globe.*

What is going on in Canada's national newspaper? The glue that was going to bind us all together? It's becoming very pliable glue. What do they do in discreet afternoon encounters in Toronto, one imagines? Bowling dates? Movie doubleheaders? A look at the Blue Jays should indeed be discreet, for fear friends would question your taste. The thought that satellites and Lord Thomson's oil are being used for this method of bringing the nation together should concern our journalism schools. Would Roy Thomson, whose only discreet afternoon encounter was with his wallet, approve of the way his fortune has been used to enrich shapely redheads and exceptionally gorgeous blondes? One doubts it, strongly.

• See also "Paper Wars."

**GOTLIEB, ALLAN** Allan Gotlieb, later Canada's ambassador to Washington, was once Larry Zolf's summer camp counsellor, and—Zolf claims—sat up in a tree reading Schopenhauer while children drowned all around him.

**GOTLIEB, SONDRA** In the U.S.A. a Canuck is assumed to be a dull Canuck until he can be injected with some Yankee verve. It is a conceit the Americans own and one that we usually accept. Official Washington, therefore, never quite figured out what to make of Sondra Gotlieb of Winnipeg, she of the sharp tongue and sharper pen. Wives of Canadian ambassadors are not supposed to act like a cross between Lucille Ball and Dorothy Parker. They are not supposed to be able to draw the cream of Washington society to intimate little dinner parties for fifty. The Great White North is supposed to be dull, dull, dull.

But it is formal Washington that is dull. The rules of behaviour are written down like a papal bull. Everyone arrives at parties at the same time and everyone leaves at the same time (i.e., early, since they must get up early and Lead the Free World). Allan and Sondra Gotlieb, when they were in Ottawa, used to throw some of the best parties in town in their big Rockcliffe house because they used a Mixmaster when choosing their guests: a smorgasbord of politicians who were witty (a scarce commodity); journalists who owned a tie and did not drink out of the finger bowls; and a snippet of the swivel servants with the most interesting wives. By transferring the same simple recipe to Washington, the Gotliebs hit town with a bang. Sondra, shortly after her arrival, turned to a man at one of her parties and asked, "And who are you?"

Replied Caspar Weinberger: "I'm your guest of honour."

Such openers would spell finis for some Washington hostesses. Instead, they have created a sort of instant fame for the perpetually wide-eyed Ms. Gotlieb, who affects an air of constant confusion but actually is watching the world with the careful eye of a social surgeon.

Ms. Gotlieb said she had discerned the basic rule for advancement in Washington: "Kick below, suck above." Allan Gotlieb, a former Rhodes Scholar who went to Oxford with John Turner and has the detached air of a professor, smiles quietly to himself and goes about the business of perusing the guest list.

**GRAY, HERB** Herb Gray was once famed as the most ardent nationalist not presiding in the Trudeau cabinet. Bounced by the Trudeau brain trust for unnamed intellectual sins, Gray spent his years in the wilderness busily peppering the cabinet and every journalist in the land with his tomes on economic nationalism and the party's dreadful drift to the right. Then when the brain trust, fearful of NDP gains in Western Canada, lurched back to the left, Gray was restored to above the salt again and made minister in charge of Canada's coughing industrial machine in 1981—just in time to look ridiculous as the man who must shovel buckets of taxpayers' money into the insatiable maw created by that epitome of American dinosaurism: Chrysler. As an MP from Windsor, which will disappear into the Detroit River if Chrysler folds (as it deserves to), Gray the nationalist found himself desperately thrashing about to save an obsolete American branch plant disguised as his own seat.

Herb Gray is the owner of the only surviving crewcut in the Western democracies. He last told a joke in 1957. Laughs twice a year, whether he needs to or not.

**GREED**
• See (under "X") "Bre-X."

**GRETZKY, WAYNE** Class. You can't buy it, you can't teach it, you can't even inherit it. The gangly—"too thin, too slow"—kid from Brantford, whose working-class dad built a makeshift rink in the backyard as soon as frost hit, somehow acquired it.

The remarkable thing about Gretzky is that he was hired as a seventeen-year-old in the World Hockey Association by Nelson Skalbania (just released from prison after a theft conviction) who then sold him to Peter Pocklington (now near bankruptcy and in disgrace in Alberta) who then sold him to Hollywood's Bruce McNall (now in prison for fraud)—and was never touched or tainted by any of them. His inner core remained intact.

My favourite story about Gretzky, who at the age of ten scored 378 goals in 68 games, was when his coach decided to rest his never-off-the-ice star after his team fell a hopeless three goals behind in the third period.

The furious young Wayne fumed on the bench until the coach finally gave in to his entreaties. "Do you want me to win or tie?" the angry kid demanded. "A tie would be nice," the amused coach replied.

In five minutes, Gretzky scored three goals to tie it, just as the bell sounded. A kid on the bench turned and said, "Coach, you made a mistake. You should have told him to win it."

Wayne Gretzky never once swore at a referee, never whined about a call, never kvetched to the press about anything ever written, never swung a stick at some jerk's head, just played the game with the joy he found as a three-year-old on that jerry-built rink in his dad's backyard.

The best description, ever, of Gretzky was from Russia's national hockey coach who exclaimed in wonderment at first encountering this magician on skates: "He appears from nowhere, he passes to nowhere, and there is a goal!"

• See also "hockey" and "Orr, Bobby."

## GROPE AND FLAIL
• See "Globe and Mail, The."

**GZOWSKI, PETER** There was a feeling, when Peter Gzowski ended his fifteen years at *Morningside*, that he could have been elected prime minister—such was the thin gruel offered to us at the polls in 1997. He was taking more farewell tours than Harry Lauder (or Karen Kain?). The best thing on the crippled Canadian Broadcorping Castration is radio, and the best thing on radio was *Morningside* and the rumpled guy who can't read a sentence without stumbling.

There was all the usual de-Stalinization, mainly in the Toronto press, over the amazing discovery that Gzowski, off air, isn't a terribly nice man. Who said he had to be? Some of us are saints at the typewriter, but somewhat less than that away from it.

Don Harron had several seasons as host of the show—as did Helen Hutchinson and Bruno Gerussi—and a senior staffer at *Morningside* once explained the difference between Don and Peter. Harron, a Shakespearean actor at Stratford before evolving into Charlie Farquharson, was a bit of a smart-ass on air with his quick wit. Off air, he is the most shy and quiet man you will ever find at a party.

Gzowski, she explained, has the on-air personality of an awkward innocent when in real life he is quite arrogant and abrupt with his staff. Who cares? All Barrymore had to do was be good onstage.

Just as the CPR bound the nation together with a ribbon of steel, Gzowski and *Morningside* tied it together with "a ribbon of reason." At a "Save-the-CBC" benefit, I once recited a letter to the editor from an Alberta woman who had set out in her car for a new life in Nova Scotia where she knew no one. The yapping kids in the back demanded usual junk rock until, fiddling with the dial in New Brunswick, she came upon the deep-chocolate voice of

Gzowski and—I choked up a bit with the sentiment—she knew she "was in Canada again."

This scribbler has known Gzowski, sort of, for decades, since he was causing trouble at the University of Toronto student paper and your humble agent was doing the same at the University of British Columbia.

We've never once had a serious conversation over those decades. As a matter of fact, I don't think we actually like each other. A female friend calls it "pecker-stretching"—her contemptuous phrase for male rivalry. My friend didn't listen to Gzowski, didn't understand Gzowski. That's because she's from Toronto and Toronto isn't a Canadian city. The Big Pickle enviously wants to be American.

That was the whole key to *Morningside*. It was an *anti-Toronto* program. It was perfectly appropriate that Gzowski's farewell show came from Moose Jaw, Saskatchewan.

He's a great treasure.

**H A R C O U R T ,  M I K E** Well. It first of all must be admitted that I
invented Mike Harcourt. (Of course I also invented Brian
Mulroney and Paul Martin, but that's another book.)

One night at a party in Vancouver (in the home of a prominent
Tory backroom type), I told his beautiful Norwegian wife Beckie
that her husband—then a young alderman in city council—would
become mayor, then leader of the provincial NDP and then premier. She told me I was nuts (not an original theory).

The night he achieved the latter role, I faxed her a note containing only three words: Told you so.

Harcourt, the son of an insurance agent, is a thoroughly middle-class product who paid his way through university as a
summer waiter in a CN dining-room car and was turned on to
socialism by a passenger named Tommy Douglas who fascinated
him on a three-day train trip.

He was the first lawyer in Vancouver to open a storefront office
and always thought he was out there on the cutting edge of social-
democratic thought.

He has grown a beard now, as most bald men eventually do at
the advice of their wives and their hairdressers. I tell him he looks
like he sleeps under a bridge with a bottle of cheap wine in a
brown paper bag, but that's okay.

One would think a retired provincial premier, well out of politics, would calm down and let bygones be bygones. Instead, he wants to get even with a Victoria media mob that he clearly feels drove him from office—unfairly. He calls them "the scrum of the earth." A good line, admitted.

At various times in his five years in office, he points out, he was referred to as "awkward," "disinterested," and a "vacillator." He was given the titles of "Mikey Milquetoast," "Premier Bonehead," and "Premier Blockhead." The premier of British Columbia was called names by Vancouver columnists that newspapers would not use in reports about convicted felons.

Plaintively, Harcourt cites one columnist's description of himself: "He is an honest man. He is a nice man. He is a reasonable man. Worse insults could not be paid a political leader."

No one ever described Trudeau, or Napoleon, as a nice man.

**HARRIS, MIKE** It was not too long ago that a chap known as a political back-room fixer phoned your humble agent. He asked if I would do him a favour. Ever charitable, as always, I said, "Sure."

His request, as it turned out, was that I would have lunch with him and his candidate to become the new leader of the leaderless Ontario Conservative party.

I went to Bistro 990 in Toronto, then my hangout, and the hired hand walked in with a large man and introduced him. About ten minutes later, I remember saying to myself, "Oh boy, this is going to be a long lunch." I thought the guy was a dolt. Several months later, to my astonishment, I picked up the paper one morning to find Mike Harris is the new premier of the biggest and richest province of all.

First impressions, as we all know, are the best impressions. My ten-minute assessment of him was correct. He is a clumsy dolt. He only takes his foot out of his mouth to change feet. An apology a week is now a staple of the papers, as familiar as the comic strips and the truss ads.

Harris the golf pro has a tin ear. He can hear the thwack of driver off the first tee, but he has the sensitivity of a Clydesdale.

There was a time when you had to serve an apprenticeship for politics. John Diefenbaker was defeated six times for public office before finally making it to Ottawa, serving thirty-nine years as an MP while winning thirteen straight elections.

William Lyon Mackenzie King went into exile in the United States, working for the Rockefellers, while plotting his return to the path that put him in the prime minister's chair. Sir John A. was a professional politician. Laurier, too.

John Turner was groomed by his mother from birth to become prime minister. Both Joe Clark and Brian Mulroney, at age seventeen, aimed for the 24 Sussex Drive slot they eventually reached.

These days, these times, they is different. Voters toss into office neophytes who are so wet behind the ears they drink out of the finger bowls at the inauguration banquet.

He got elected by delighted suburban and rural voters by beating up on inner-Toronto welfare mums. Proof that he always misses a beautiful chance to keep his mouth shut was his now celebrated remark that he was cutting a cheesy $37 grant to pregnant welfare mums to prevent it going "to beer."

His cloddish treatment of the sad and tearful Dionne sisters led him, in panic—while his PR advisers headed for the exit—to fly to Montreal to deliver to them a coffee cake. Thereby just ensuring there would be more headlines about his goofus behavior.

Premier Harris has said, "While some knowledge can be a good thing, sometimes too much is a dangerous thing almost, in some areas, in my view." This is splendid thinking, it was a warming harbinger of things to come in the Harris regime. Harris, as the declared enemy of knowledge, is a delight to cover from the press gallery.

Tory boys, put Mikey in a cave. Roll up the rock. He's the original Piltdown Man. In London, Ontario, the incumbent mayor in 1998, having been fined by a human rights body for refusing to declare Gay Rights Day, announced she was going into hiding for the entire mayoral election campaign. She won in a landslide.

**HATFIELD, RICHARD** There are too many politicians, as we know, in this country, the most over-governed country on earth. It's probably because of the vast, underpopulated space—the politicians feel they should be portioned out on a per-square-mile basis, the people being secondary to the acreage. There are not enough politicians who are unique, who are special. Richard Hatfield was one of them.

Hatfield, as his friends have pointed out since his death, was the rare (the only?) Canadian politician who did not separate his public persona from his private life. He never tried to be what he was not. He enjoyed life too much and, as proof of his philosophy, was closer to more journalists and good friends with more journalists than any other high political leader in the land.

He was the only Canadian guaranteed an invitation to Truman Capote's parties. His fellow premiers of course didn't like him, because they didn't understand him, their wives least of all, knowing that while their husbands were on the golf course in Palm Springs, Richard was in Morocco and probably having more fun. Only Trudeau sort of appreciated him, because of Richard's stout support for the bilingualism principle. When the Liberal Opposition dug into the travel records and found that he had been in his province only 168 days the previous year, he told his friend Dalton Camp that "I was elected to run New Brunswick. No one said I had to live there."

Hatfield said his decision to enter politics came at the behest of his brother; he then took to his bed for three days to agonize over the decision, then had to ask his mother's approval.

One-time Opposition leader Charlie Van Horne ended his political career by once sneering at Hatfield as "a mother's boy." It was his largest mistake. Van Horne ended up selling real estate in Arizona and the mummy's boy laughed his way through four terms, the dean of Canadian premiers. New Brunswick knows where its values lie. You can be a tosspot and a layabout in this province but all will forgive you if you are known as being "good to your mother."

He lived alone in a beautiful home filled with contemporary art, soft, collapsible furniture and huge, limp rag dolls, the only premier in Canada never to marry. I once tried to persuade him to marry a lady he liked very much. He simply grinned and refused to respond. He was married to politics, right to the end.

The best obit of all came on the afternoon of the day he died. The ineffable Vicki Gabereau, finishing off her CBC Radio show, said simply, "It's going to be dull, dull, dull without you, honey."

**HEARNE, SK** Your blushing agent was borne in Hearne, Saskatchewan, named after Sir Samuel Hearne. Born in London 1745, he was sent out by the Hudson's Bay Co. and in 1771 became the first European to make it to the Arctic Ocean overland. He became chief of Prince of Wales Fort, where he was captured by the French and taken to France. His release from jail was negotiated on the unique condition that he publish an account of his travels.

People from Hearne are called Hernias. In fact, the town is

so small we couldn't afford a village idiot—everyone had to take turns.

## HIMSELF, PIERRE ELLIOTT
• See "Trudeau, Pierre Elliott."

**HISTORY** A history professor from a distinguished Canadian university once wrote me, asking for help. This department, as all readers know, is only too glad to offer aid and assistance to lofty academics—since politicians somehow manage to ignore my advice. His problem, as he explains, is that his students inevitably ask, "Why study history?"

Well, this is simple. I could never figure out how algebra and chemistry were going to help with getting a job—columnists only have to have one string to their bow—but history is a little more useful. As George Santayana said, those who don't learn from history are doomed to repeat it. Caesar was done in with a dagger from his friends, and so was Maggie Thatcher. Nothing ever changes. They just switch the names around.

Students of history will find that most of the famous historical quotes in fact never were spoken. Marie Antoinette never said: "Let them eat cake." The Duke of Wellington never said that the Battle of Waterloo was won on the playing fields of Eton. He said it was won "in the classrooms" of Eton, which is an entirely different matter. One thing a student of history will learn is never to attempt to destroy a myth: once it's up and galloping it can never be caught.

That is why history is so fascinating (unlike algebra and chemistry, which never change). The fat Sunday editions of the London papers are filled, week upon week, with aging generals and admirals always fighting the last war. Young men die so old men can give their version of it. Britain's death as a great power came not in the Second World War but in the First World War, when the flower of its youth perished in the muddy, rat-filled trenches of France.

The arrival in 1997 of the replica of John Cabot's frail craft in Newfoundland reminds us that remnants of a Roman galley have been found off the South American coast. Proof indeed that others, undoubtedly Leif Eriksson and the Vikings, touched these shores long before Christopher Columbus (see, never touch a myth).

Someday the historians will be writing about how the Conservative party of Canada went from two successive majority governments to two seats and how the province of Quebec, which has supplied Canadian prime ministers for twenty-eight of twenty-nine years, is threatening to separate and how the Supreme Court of the United States ruled that its president appear in court before a reservations clerk who claimed she can testify as to certain unusual features of his genitalia. No one will believe any of it.

**HOCKEY** It was seven minutes into the second period in the Regina Agridome on March 1 when eighteen-year-old Brad Hornung of the Regina Pats cut for the net. As he raced toward the Moose Jaw Warriors' goal, he spotted Craig Endean open on the left and dished the puck across to him. A lot of hockey players would then wheel away from their check.

Instead, Brad Hornung tried to cut behind the net and come around to get back into the play in case of a rebound. That was his style and Troy Edwards of the Moose Jaw team, who had played Hornung many times before, knew that was his style. So, from behind, he gave Hornung a swift chop in the back with his hockey stick, propelling it outward with both hands as you would a barbell.

Brad Hornung went headfirst into the boards. His helmeted

head snapped back. He was unconscious when he hit the ice. When the team trainer reached him, he discovered the boy had swallowed his tongue and was choking to death. His jaw was locked shut and the trainer couldn't reach into his mouth to yank his tongue back. With the player flat on his back on the ice, with 6,000 fans in the stands suddenly deathly silent, doctors slashed his throat open so he could breathe and they could recover his tongue. Brad Hornung now is in a hospital bed, where he will remain for the rest of his life, his spinal cord crushed, permanently paralyzed from the neck down, needing a respirator to help him breathe. There was no penalty on the play.

Who's responsible? Simple. The callous morons who own and run the National Hockey League. They are the greedy jerks who have taken the game which the Soviets and the Czechs still know how to play in its pure form and have turned it into roller derby—since they have determined that fans like violence. Troy Edwards is not to blame. He has been taught since so-high to cross-check from behind, since referees never call it any more—and now we've got yet another paralyzed eighteen-year-old.

He is not the first, and he won't be the last as long as the millionaires set the pattern for the game at the top for the boys who want to graduate there.

In Saskatoon in winter, with the steam trails from the chimneys tracing the night air over the South Saskatchewan, a stranger to town, chewing over his pork ribs with pleasant companions and gazing through the restaurant's vast glass doors, suddenly spies across the road a scene out of a boy's dreams. A clutch of youths, perhaps eight or ten, ranging from six years old to teenage hulks, all in their favourite hockey jerseys, are skating in the dark in those never-ending pick-up games on a formless little rink, their breath hanging in the air.

To the stranger, it brings it all back. Skate all after school, skate all night. Mothers pleading through the back doors to come in for homework or warmth or fear of frostbite and chilblains, all of the warnings meaning nothing since a role as left wing on the Toronto Maple Leafs was surely in the future.

The stranger finds it hard explaining all this to his pleasant companions, feeling like a dinosaur from the swamp, attempting to evoke an era when every boy on the Prairies, his Beehive Corn Syrup coupons going in to someplace in Ontario to return a stand-up photo of Bob Davidson—stick flat on ice, no helmet, no visor, hair slicked down like Rudolph Valentino—a guy who probably made up to $6,000 a year for being the checking forward to Apps and Drillon.

One wonders, as the wine flows, whether these tads outside the window dream in their reverie of wearing—some day!—the famous sweaters of the Anaheim Flying Ducks. As they fly over the snow-bank boards of their imaginary rink, do they lust in their hearts to be in some future heaven wearing the livery of the Tampa Bay Lightning?

Is there a single one of them, as their mothers call one last time from the back stoop, who want in their secret dreams to be a San Jose Shark? One wonders and ponders.

• See also "Gretzky, Wayne" and "Orr, Bobby."

**HOGTOWN** Toronto got all excited, a decade ago, by advertising itself as a "world-class city." Cities that are world-class—minor burgs such as Rome or Paris—don't boast about being world-class. They know it and never think about it.

Come the last recession that brought juvenile Toronto to its knees we assumed such piffle was forgotten. Alas, not so. The self-imposed disease, something like measles, is broke out again.

Dr. Anne Golden, an enthusiastic thinker, in 1996 produced a 269-page report about a powerful, single economy—the GTA—whose wealth-generating potential would allegedly rival that of some countries.

Dr. Golden, obviously an intelligent, educated woman, announces that this vast urban area is "the world's most multicultural area." Hello? Smell the coffee. Where has this expert ever been?

Toronto papers, with a straight face, printed this piffle with blind belief, never once questioning it. It has become a growing myth in Toronto for some years now, based mainly on the evidence that when Italy wins soccer's World Cup the streets in Little Italy are filled with crazed fans hanging out the windows of cars that block traffic.

Has Dr. Golden ever travelled so far as New York, an hour's plane ride away? Has she ever been to London? Anyone who actually believes that Toronto is the most multicultural area on earth should not be allowed to write a report on a city's future.

That's okay. Urban myths endure. Only in towns insecure about their worth—wanting to be New York wannabes—are they allowed to flourish and survive.

In 1992, the tourism board launched a $1.4 million TV campaign aimed at Americans, featuring the official slogan: "Toronto—there's no place like it on earth."

For once, we agree. A columnist asked readers for alternatives and has received such suggestions as: Toronto—the city of angles. Or: Toronto—where we know how to spell potato. Or: T.O.—the city that never wakes. Or: Toronto—unlike any American city yet. But we're trying. Or, my favourite: Toronto—come meet your relatives!

There is definitely something wrong with Toronto. The city that every loyal Canadian loves to hate has gone soft. More than soft, it has lost its nerve and its spine. Its Hogtown reputation was built (honestly) on rapacious lust for the buck, arrogance and a blissful conceit that it was No. 1.

A blow to civic pride came from Paris, when a Toronto delegation—after spending $1.5 million—lost out to Lisbon in a bid to play host to Expo 98. This followed Toronto's failed attempt to get the 1996 Summer Olympics, where it was out-hustled by Atlanta, a non-city that is built around an airport and has the worst crime rate in the United States.

All this demonstrates a strange lack of zip in Toronto's quest to be something.

Montreal, as we know, has staged a fabulously successful Expo and a fabulously expensive Olympic Games. Vancouver put on the most celebrated Commonwealth Games of all with Roger Bannister and John Landy in the Miracle Mile—and has recently tossed up an Expo.

Calgary put on the Winter Olympics. Winnipeg has done the Pan-American Games. Edmonton has done the Commonwealth Games. Even Hamilton, for heaven's sake, did the same back when they used to be called the British Empire Games. Toronto? Zilch. Zippo. The Big Zero.

Why this is so is not a hundred per cent clear. But the country can afford only one city as a failure. Ottawa fills that bill very nicely. To fill the vacuum, Toronto must return to its previous role. Bring back Hogtown.

• See also "Toronto."

## HOLY MOTHER CORP.
• See "CBC."

**H**OME **OF THE RAVE AND LAND OF THE SPREE**
- See "U.S. of A."

**H**ONGCOUVER
- See "Vancouver."

**H**UDSON **B**AY **PESO, THE**
- See "Canadian dollar."

**H**UMOUR
- See "Canadian humour," also "Broadbent."

**H**UTCHISON, **B**RUCE The old man raised his head from his pillow on a sunny afternoon. "Since Mr. Fotheringham is here, Mrs. Veitch," he instructed his housekeeper, "you'd better bring us something with an alcohol content." This was Bruce Hutchison, the most remarkable Canadian journalist of his century, several weeks before he died in 1992.

This was the essential Hutch, pretending to be sardonic, a mask that disguised his warmth, faking a dreary view of a world that had gone wrong but still getting some humour out of it. At his cozy little house smothered in foliage on the fringe of Victoria, he was glad to see the scribbler he used to label "the frumious Bandersnatch of West Coast newspapering."

Hutchison was an idol to those of us who knew him, not only for the languorous ease of his writing but for the astounding—miraculous—way he conducted his entire career. The miracle was never going to the office. A genius! No semi-literate editors to deal with. No fools at the next desk. No niggling accountants badgering over some expense account.

He became internationally famous while staying in his beloved cottage at Shawinigan Lake on Vancouver Island and chopping wood. He edited the *Winnipeg Free Press* at one time and the *Vancouver Sun* at another by understanding there was a thing called the telephone. He was the first journalist to recognize— as everyone with computers now does—that you don't have to leave home.

Hutchison, like Pierre Berton after him, wanted to be a cartoon- ist. As a young man he supported himself by selling fiction, illustrated by himself, to the popular magazines in New York. For decades he had a column in the respected *Christian Science Monitor* of Boston—his dispatches pecked out two-finger style on that bat- tered Underwood by the woodpile.

After a half-hour, Mrs. Veitch, who is "pushing eighty-three," brings a large bottle of Hiram Walker Special Old rye whisky and sets it on the bedside table. Hutch pours himself a healthy dollop and orders his visitor to mix his own poison. Mrs. Veitch settles for a Drambuie.

On the walls of the Victoria Press Gallery are the yearly official photographs of the inmates, going back to the 1920s. There are the overstuffed and weather-beaten old pros and there is the young Hutchison, all tweeds and serious pipe. The studious and industrious young reporter, on his way to becoming a confidant of prime ministers.

There is the famous story of the tiny Victoria Press Gallery, in Prohibition days, being invited to attend a well-oiled legislative banquet where they fell into the grape with some abandon.

All five of his typewriting rivals, records Hutchison in his mem- oirs, "lay down on the floor and went to sleep, which led me to believe they were drunk." The youthful and abstemious babe of the gallery thereupon sat down and wrote five separate stories for their Vancouver clients, each one in the varying style and political slant of the sleeping ones, marched down to put them on the midnight ferry to Vancouver—and saved five jobs.

Hutch was the only person ever encountered, with the possible exception of Stephen Lewis, who speaks in a manner so that you can not only see the paragraphs, you can sense the beginning and end of sentences—the *semi-colons*.

His mind is still as sharp as ever, demanding the latest nuance on the Constitution, worrying over a colleague whose wife is very sick, wondering dolefully as ever what is going to happen to his country. He dominates the conversation, as usual.

The sunlight streams through the trees into the main floor bedroom. His father died in this room and his mother died in this room and he feels content at the end of a prodigious life. "I don't need to live any longer, Fotheringham," he rasped. "Ninety-one years is long enough, for Christ's sake."

No it wasn't. Not for him it wasn't.

## HYPOCRISY

• See "politics."

**I, FOTHERINGHAM** There is a time when one must be honest with one's readers. Invisible out there in the void, faithful and uncomplaining, they deserve some insights. The columnist, hiding behind his computer, has an unfair advantage, protected by his kindly editors, guarded by his sensitive lawyers. At some stage, it is best to 'fess up and reveal the secrets.

I was born in a tiny Saskatchewan town, twice the size of your living room, called Hearne. However, my parents eventually moved to British Columbia and this improved the IQ of both provinces.

Past experiences include grasshoppers, hail, drought, blowdirt, gophers, the Depression and relief packages. This has proven extremely useful in later life in dealing with politicians, stockbrokers, lawyers, aluminum-siding salesmen, pollsters and waiters named Bruce.

I lead a simple life, stealing secrets from politicians and conning dumb public relations officers. I write a simple column. I receive several dozen letters a week attesting to just how simple it is. They rest here before me on my desk.

On October 20, 1975, in the second column this here scribbler ever scribbled for *Maclean's* back page, I set out to set aright the confused Tories as to their selection of a leader in their upcoming convention. There seemed to me, in the stakes to succeed the well-known sex symbol Bob Stanfield, a certifiable lack of excitement. Such as Paul Hellyer and Sinclair Stevens were pushed. Along with someone called Joe Clark. "Too young," I told my few readers. The man they should go for, I suggested, was someone I had never met. One Brian Mulroney of Montreal, thirty-seven, bilingual, crime-buster, the one chance the party had to break into Quebec. (The "too-young" Joe Clark reminded me, on next meeting, that he was exactly three months younger than the mature Mr. Mulroney.)

When I first spoke with Mr. Mulroney, I asked, "When did you decide to run?"

"The second time I read it in your column," he replied.

It is the least I can do to help save the country. If a chap doesn't like the leader of the ruling party, one might as well invent an imaginative leader for the other party.

It is a struggle keeping the country intact single-handedly, but God knows somebody has to do it. It took the Regressive Convertibles a full seven years to take my advice, but they finally fumbled their way to it.

The ponderous editorials do not raise a blink from those of us (former editorial writers) who now scrabble in the field and are prisoners of the genius of mankind, i.e., computers. Let me tell you a story.

There was a day when, young and foolish and carefree, I could roam anywhere in the world, burdened only with a small Hermes portable typewriter enclosed in a metal case. I loved it. I had a relationship with it surpassed only, possibly, by my relationship with my expense account. It was durable—you could drop it, kick it around a bit, and it always performed.

Kick-started into action wherever the meandering scribe alighted, it produced. All that was needed was a piece of paper, easily obtained in most of the Earth's civilized jurisdictions. Next, all that was needed was a telephone. At the other end was a marvel of humankind, a young lady at the *Vancouver Sun* who could type faster than I could talk. I called her Magic Fingers, and she never missed a comma. We had a link that was made in heaven, mainly because the system worked, and the column appeared, unblemished (i.e., untarnished by the genius of science) in the paper every day.

The years roll on. The day of the computer in newspapering arrives. The truth of it all hit me one day, on a sweating stop on some sweating campaign plane chasing some forgotten prime minister, when I was wrestling into a phone booth a "portable" computer approximately the size of a one-holer. I expressed the usual mild, even-tempered observation to my mate Charlie Lynch—lugging the same embarrassing contraption—that this really didn't seem an improvement on my trusty Hermes and Magic Fingers.

(And as for Magic Fingers, somewhere out there in Vancouver now dangling babies, I have just one message. Still love yuh.)

To tell the truth, my major ambition in life is to have a radio show. However, I apparently lack the required prerequisites. That would be leather lungs, preferably a Scottish accent, an ability to mouth commercials for pantyhose and mufflers and an ability to carry on lengthy conversations with morons. I regret my deficiencies, since I could be rich doing it.

I am no engineer, seer, McLuhanite, prophet or phrenologist. All I know is what I get. No country that provides, free, John Diefenbaker, Wacky Bennett, Phlying Phil Gaglardi, Joe Clark, Harold Ballard, Eugene Whelan, Myron Baloney, Charlotte Whitton, Lord Thomson and, an import, John Ziegler, needs any help from me.

How can one possibly poke fun at politicians who invent a "revenue-neutral" GST, introduce free trade and concoct something called Meech Lake? It's an impossibility.

As a mild-mannered lad, whose even temper is well-celebrated across the land, I seldom complain, as you know. The personal satisfaction that I receive from my writings is that I am the luckiest person in Canada—I am the first to read my jokes.

## JAW THAT WALKS LIKE A MAN, THE
- See "Mulroney, Brian."

## JAMES, STEWART
Stewart James was considered the Einstein of the magic world. An eccentric recluse, he lived a strange life in Courtright, a tiny town of 600 outside Sarnia, Ont. His parents did not allow him to play with other children. They did not exchange presents even at Christmas. His mother kissed him twice in his life. His father forced him out of school at fifteen to work in his tinsmith shop.

In the James household the only art on the walls was old photos of dead relatives in their coffins. When he went off to war in 1942, his mother gave him a peck on the cheek (the second one).

His father dead, his siblings fleeing, James was left to care for his mad, hypochondriac mother. He became the local 5 a.m. postman, home at 9 a.m. to minister to her. She hated magicians—was known as "the bitch" to everyone—and screamed at him from upstairs whenever he had one around.

In 1947 he received a letter from a young Allan Slaight, the man who would later own Standard Broadcasting and a media empire of radio stations from Vancouver to Montreal. James, who was thirty-nine, wrote a long, encouraging reply. Thus a forty-nine-year devoted friendship began.

In 1989, Allan Slaight and collaborator Howard Lyons published *Stewart James in Print*, the largest magic book ever printed. In August 2000, four years after James's death, seven world-class magicians flew into Toronto from all over the United States to worship at the shrine of Stewart James and demonstrate his genius by performing some of his magic tricks.

Stewart James had to play postman until he was seventy and take care of "the bitch," who stubbornly did not die until she was ninety-seven, in the house he had lived in since he was nine. He died in 1996 at eighty-eight.

 • See also "Slaight, Allan."

## J. C. SUPERBOY

 • See "Clark, Joe."

## JEMSEG, THE SAGE OF

 • See "Camp, Dalton."

**JENNINGS, PETER** Now the first thing you've got to look at is the tie. Peter Jennings is the only anchorman brave enough to abandon the outmoded, square Windsor knot that is supposed to be so appealing to Mr. and Mrs. Front Porch out there in Peoria. Dan Rather and Tom Brokaw, who should be ashamed of themselves, wear this stale relic that was named after the Duke of Windsor. These things are important. By their tie knots shall ye know them. And so it's terribly vital to realize that Peter Jennings—whose other "handicaps" are that he is a Canadian from Ottawa and a high-school dropout—has become the most popular anchorman in the U.S. of A.

By far the most accomplished reporter of the Jennings-Rather-Brokaw rivalry, Jennings is doing rather well. His cool mid-Atlantic accent, his sophisticated wardrobe and his calm delivery make the CBS millionaire and the NBC milk-fed boy appear rather too all-American.

Jennings has authentic roots as a ham. His father was Canada's first national radio newscaster. Charles Jennings was one of the first four announcers hired by the Canadian Radio Broadcasting Commission, predecessor of the CBC, in 1935. He went on to become a vice-president of the Holy Mother Corp.

So young Jennings had no excuse when he started his professional broadcast career as a "horribly pretentious" nine-year-old for a national network Saturday morning hit parade show, *Peter's Program*. I happen to have it on good authority from a former girlfriend of his that at age fifteen Jennings announced that his ambition was to be a major network announcer.

He bounced around the CBC for a while, then became CTV's Parliament Hill anchorman and covered the fall of the Diefenbaker government in 1963. Unbeknownst to him, ABC took the feed in New York and offered him a job. They sent him to Mississippi to report the integration turmoil, and two carloads of Ku Klux Klan members chased him in a wild 105-mile-per-hour chase that still leaves him with miserable thoughts about that state.

He was briefly ABC's anchorman in New York, hated it because it took him away from the field and the action he loves and soon returned to the safari-suit-and-bullets role and headed up ABC's first Middle East bureau, working in Rome and then Beirut.

He actually was quite prepared to come home when he heard about the CBC's plans to establish *The Journal*. He expressed interest—and waited around for a year without hearing back. Pity.

**J E W I S O N ,  N O R M A N** A miniature lemon tree, perhaps two feet high, sits on the patio at Malibu, thirty minutes above Hollywood.

There are seven lemons on the stem, four of them ripe and ready for picking. Sitting on the patio gazing beyond the pounding surf out at Santa Catalina Island off in the mist is Norman Jewison.

Don Rickles lives next door. Burgess Meredith was four doors down. Johnny Carson lives around the corner. Things ain't bad— just like those ripe lemons—for a runty little guy from the Beaches in east-end Toronto.

Norman Jewison doesn't actually sit and gaze. He's got too much energy for that. He's seventy-three, looks sixty-three, and has the fire of fifty-three. He's about, at this moment, to take off for a three-set tennis bout with Malibu carousers.

In all the fuss about Canadian nationalism and the brain drain, Norman Jewison remains an icon. If you can make it there, he can make it anywhere. The little guy from the Beaches grew up being called "Jewie" and "Jewboy" because of his name—he laughs in glee; his family is Anglican.

He did it all: son of a shopkeeper, after University of Toronto, he struggled as a young bohemian actor, wrote scripts and acted for the BBC in London, did a puppet show on the CBC, produced TV specials in New York for Judy Garland and Harry Belafonte. He was scheduled to meet with his friend Bobby Kennedy the night RFK was assassinated in that Los Angeles hotel.

Jewison, who never stops laughing, is one of the most serious men you will ever meet. Bobby's useless death was one of the reasons he fled America in 1970. "Nixon was president!" he rages. "Reagan was governor of California! I'd lost my sense of humour!" He talks in exclamation marks.

He not only moved to London—spending the next eight years making movies in Yugoslavia, Israel and Germany—he tore up his green card, the cherished Excalibur for American employment. Worse! He tore up his wife's and those of the three children. He laughs now. Probably a dumb move. He now gets into the U.S. on a special visa.

It's probably one of the reasons why he didn't get an Oscar for his latest Hollywood blockbuster, *The Hurricane,* starring Denzel Washington—after *The Russians Are Coming! The Russians Are Coming!*, after *Fiddler on the Roof* and *Jesus Christ, Superstar* and *Moonstruck*, with Cher winning the Oscar as best actress.

The "grunts" in Hollywood—meaning the cameramen, technicians, et al.—are understandably disgruntled that their jobs are going north.

Norman, with his usual sardonic laugh, a man who finds laughter in all human activity, points out there are now 45,000 people employed in various ways in making U.S. films in Ontario. Because of the cheap Canadian dollar (the Hudson Bay peso) British Columbia's film and TV industry ranks only beneath Los Angeles and New York.

This is the same Hollywood industry that makes up that strange Academy "Arts and Sciences" polling body. Norman, heading off to London and then Berlin and South America on demand for his *Hurricane*, wasn't expecting to make the cut.

But not bad from the Beaches to Malibu Beach.

**JOHNSON, BEN** The country's shock and horror over the Ben Johnson scandal was mixed, beneath the surface, with chagrin—the slow realization that the Ottawa-funded attempt to push the nation's sports profile on the world stage has been done at the expense of imported talent. Canada has a professional track team, almost all of it from the Caribbean, running for the glory of the Maple Leaf. Ben—poor, dumb Ben—was merely the most exploited.

In all the sports funded by Sport Canada (i.e., taxpayer) dollars, foreigners have been hired to shore up the sports (unlike the indigenous specialty, hockey) where Canada has lagged behind in international arenas.

That's okay. If a country barely a century old feels ashamed that it can't compete in gymnastics or Greco-Roman wrestling with such countries as tiny Bulgaria and minuscule Romania, let the ebullient bureaucrats of Ottawa unleash the funds to put athletes on full-time salary—as has happened.

What is not okay is the blatant hypocrisy of the bureau-jocks on the Rideau who nervously didn't want to challenge those around poor, dumb Ben because of Ben's growing success. Can any sensible nit explain how Johnson, the rumours already rampant, was allowed to get through the Canadian Olympic trials in the summer of 1988 without being tested? Government (bureau-jock) greed for international acclaim? Government hypocrisy?

For the latter, we have the swift prime ministerial phone call to the CBC booth in Seoul containing the confused young man, doom almost written in his eyes even then.

Swiftly thereafter, the same government banned him "for life" from the Canadian team (the International Amateur Athletics Federation banished him for just two years) and harrumphed the announcement of a government inquiry at which he will be invited to appear. Johnson is not a criminal. He was stupid, but he's not a criminal.

More stupid are those who have used him, doctored him like a race horse with strange substances, hoping to cash in on a $4-million bonanza.

Diane Clement, one of the officials of the Canadian Olympic team in Seoul, said that the Johnson scandal had "set Canadian track and field back twelve years." Well, maybe not. Perhaps it has set ahead, by twelve years, the thinking of the applause-hungry politicians and the bureau-jocks in Ottawa—with the realization that when you hire others to do your work for you, you reap the results.

**JOHNSTON, DON** Don Johnston was the only candidate in the 1990 Liberal leadership race, along with Jean Chrétien, who was in the same race the previous time. He represented law firm buddy Trudeau against the Meech Lake lead sinker. Most entertaining man in any private gathering, he suffers the Robert Stanfield disease: he cannot translate his personality to the public. Twice as smart as Chrétien, with half his charisma.

**JOURNALISTS** Every new prime minister needs advice and helpful suggestions, as any sensible voter would agree. Especially when it is constructive advice, as all contributions from this desk always are. The advice: ignore the press. Forget it exists. Act as if it had never been invented. There is no law that says a prime minister has to reply to every attack, justify every mistake, respond to every supposed slight.

The abiding myth that the powerful press (and powerful press personalities) somehow hold sway over a simple-minded electorate is one of the astonishing fairy tales of our time. The belief that a Hearstian decision, arrived at over the press club bar, can affect in the teensiest way the polling booth is a thumb-sucking refuge, the Linus blanket, of the immature.

There are examples cluttering the landscapes of history. Franklin Delano Roosevelt, the raging pinko of his time according to rock-ribbed traditionalists, was vehemently denounced for four elections by ninety-five per cent of the American press—owned by good Republican owners. For four terms he laughed his way to the ballot box. W. A. C. Bennett, the shrewd old con man, for twenty years in power courted the enmity of the four daily papers of Vancouver and Victoria. You can't fly a kite in dead air. You have to have the wind going against you. For a politician to succeed, he explained with a delicious chortle, you had to have the foaming press against you.

John Turner once confided that he was given some very valuable advice by W. A. C. early in his career: never answer back to the press. And, if you'll recall, whatever his other weaknesses, he never did.

"Journalists and reporters," according to Ekos Research, check in at thirty-two per cent trustworthiness, far ahead of the twenty-four per cent given to lawyers in a 1996 poll. Not to mention the politicians who follow up the rear at fifteen per cent, lobbyists at eleven, and car salesmen at seven.

This indeed is a sea change in public thinking. (A "journalist," as any reporter will tell you, is a reporter who is out of work.) But the thought that those of us who are mere scribblers have at last risen above those who defend us in libel trials is an event that must be observed with some seriousness.

Those of us who are minor typists have always assumed that, in the public mind, we were regarded as lower than aluminum-siding salesmen, let alone liars on used-car lots. I always tell my lawyer friends (some of my best friends are lawyers) that the last time I checked, there were more lawyers in jail than journalists. You could look it up, as Casey Stengel used to say. The fact—pollsters never fib—that we have risen above the legal profession in esteem almost moves us to rush to the nearest pub for a tiny little tipple, which real journalists—as opposed to reporters—almost never do.

Get any three reporters together in a bar and within twenty minutes there will be a fist fight over the nature of journalism. Is it a profession? A trade? A calling? Or what? Kipling had it best when he described it as "the black art." It is history-in-a-hurry, neither high literature nor low comedy.

The pollster's view of the rating of scribblers in the great scheme of things must be viewed in perspective. In Britain, given the slavering tabs, reporters in dirty raincoats are regarded as those you would let in only by the servants' entrance—along with the butcher, the mailman and the pizza delivery boy.

In Washington "journalists" are regarded in the highest of rank. Any Georgetown matron who cannot attract a Peter Jennings or a David Brinkley to the gin at 5 p.m. will soon be struck off the social list.

We are not as despised as the chaps in London in dirty rain-coats who lurked about Lady Di's back alley in hopes of detecting which rugby player was climbing out her window. Neither are we sought out for every White House dinner table beside the wife of the ambassador from Spain whose cleavage would rival the Rockies.

The Canuck scribe, manfully bearing the burden of being more trustworthy than the lawyer who may or may not be a loan shark, is perturbed at his responsibility. There he is, nudging up behind the banker in the trust ladder, not wanting to fall so low as to the rank of a politician, not really knowing what it's like to be invited into the living-room. It's an awesome burden to bear.

The only solution is to take the accolade with grace. If there is one thing scribblers have in surplus, it is humility. Any poll that puts us above Sheila Copps, Lucien Bouchard and Jesse Helms we will accept with gratitude.

• See also "Amber, Arnold," "Creighton, Doug," "Hutchison, Bruce," "Lynch, Charlie," "Nichols, Marjorie," and "Webster, Jack."

• See also "press, the" and "sportswriters."

**KIERANS, ERIC** Eric Kierans, the wise old sage, was once the most intellectually stimulating minister, along with his then-buddy René Lévesque, in Jean Lesage's Quiet Revolution cabinet. He headed the Montreal Stock Exchange, served in the Trudeau cabinet, and now, in supposed retirement in Halifax, dispenses semi-jaded nostrums on a country that has lost its nerve.

**KING, WILLIAM LYON MACKENZIE** The news that William Lyon Mackenzie King was the best prime minister we ever had will confirm what the rest of the world thinks of Canadians. We're dull, monosyllabic, don't smoke, don't drink, with little interest in sex—and talk not only to our dead mothers, but our dead dogs.

Some twenty-five of our most esteemed academics and historians were asked to rank all twenty of our previous leaders and decided, in their wisdom, that the little short fat guy ranked at the top. This will astonish all Canadian schoolchildren who are taught that Sir John A. Macdonald, the Father of Confederation, automatically got the top spot by any reckoning. At least he drank, rather enthusiastically we'll agree, but he had to put up with a tragic family life and persevered and acted like a real person, warts and all.

To think, as academics do, that a lifelong bachelor who tried to commune in the heavens with a dog and his mum was the exemplar for all Canadians is a bit rich. If he were alive today, he'd be interviewed on Oprah, not to mention Geraldo.

One can just imagine what *This Hour Has 22 Minutes* and the *Royal Canadian Air Farce* could do with King. William Lyon Mackenzie King goes down in the record books, of course, for his most famous quote: "Conscription if necessary, but not necessarily conscription."

This defines the ethos of this country. Why did the Canadian cross the road? To get to the middle. That is the Canadian way. That is the Mackenzie King way. That is why he is our best, our idol, our leader for all time, someone that schoolchildren must be taught to look up to.

The twenty-five scholars cite his great political skills and devotion to unity. The devotion to unity, which one would think would be the duty of any prime minister, consisted of not stirring the pot. Perhaps that was the only way during the war, but he never gave Canadians great inspiration, burning passion—as Trudeau did—or a sense of personal warmth.

Arthur Meighen called him "the most contemptible charlatan ever to darken the annals of Canadian politics," but we know the language was more colourful then (damn it).

The great Bruce Hutchison in his book on our prime ministers wrote that "in King's long, pious and oily speeches the listener could detect little substance, precisely as the speaker intended. He blandly disregarded the platform laid down by his party, he disregarded his own book of left-wing social theory as meat too strong for the electorate, he disregarded the wartime Liberal schism..." And so on.

Long, pious and oily. Yep, that figures for a Canadian hero.

**KISSINGER, HENRY** There was something typically Canadian—
i.e., obsequious—about the audience gathered in a hushed theatre
at the National Arts Centre in Ottawa in October 1980. Charles
Lynch, the newspaper columnist and celebrated harmonicist, had
just asked Henry Kissinger the very justifiable question of why
Kissinger had been involved in transporting the Shah of Iran into
the United States, ostensibly for medical reasons, when it was clear
the act would only inflame the mad priests running Iran. Henry
the K., with that weary European charm he has perfected,
protested about all these anti-American "clichés" being dredged
up—and a little burst of applause sprang from the plush seats.
So typical. A clutch of high-priced Canadian civil servants and
academics were siding with an American hired gun against a
Canadian journalist. Diplomatic blood runs thicker than
nationalism.

Kissinger, a mercenary-with-mouth that will travel, is Mr.
Shiftiness, the one who carefully escaped without any of the
Watergate glue on him.

As the Canadian diplomats fawned on him, Kissinger's fabulous
skill as an escape artist was apparent. Oozing charm from every
pore, he oiled his way across the floor at a private lunch ($305
extra on top of a $195 seminar fee). It was abruptly announced
that the occasion would be off-the-record. The mouth for all seasons was nonetheless safely sandwiched between Mitchell Sharp
and Flora MacDonald and contented himself with whispered gossip. The man who is shrink to presidents and favourite dinner
companion for the Beautiful People has good reason to be shy at
Ottawa dining tables. On a previous visit, at an External Affairs
banquet, a microphone at his table was accidentally left open and
transmitted to the astonished tape recorders in the press room all
his salacious gossip about Elizabeth Taylor and slurs on Nixon.

When the *New York Times* reported in 1969 that the U.S. was
secretly bombing Cambodia, a neutral country, Kissinger phoned
the FBI director, J. Edgar Hoover. That afternoon a wiretap was
placed on the home of Morton Halperin, Kissinger's assistant for
planning. The tap, and others that immediately followed,
infringed the limits of the law and marked the first of the domes-
tic abuses of power now known as Watergate.

What is so remarkable is how the man escapes so quietly while
all around him remain stuck in the glue. At the Ottawa love-in
he didn't want to talk much about wiretaps or Cambodia, since it
was 3 p.m. and the private jet was to zip him off to Cleveland and
presumably another $15,000 for his standard latter-day-Metternich
speech which serves wherever the Chase Manhattan jet will
speed him.

He's a nasty man and it's not nice to watch the elite of the
Ottawa Establishment elbow one another to clutch the hem of his
pinstripes.

**KLEIN, RALPH** So, the high-school dropout, once-divorced guy
who says he drinks only one bottle of wine per day, son of a pro
wrassler, is now the most powerful premier in the country.

Ralph Klein is master of all he surveys, the No. 1 spokesman for
Western Canada in its wars with Ottawa and the coming show-
down (yet again) with Quebec. With his massive sixty-two per cent
approval from his adoring voters, he has a more commanding
mandate than Mike Harris in larger Ontario.

He's killed off his opposition, ended its leader's career, he has
no sales tax, no unemployment and so much moolah from booming natural gas revenues that his province will soon have no debt.
He might be able to afford a better brand of wine.

Klein's poppa, Phil, is now eighty-three. In the ring, in his day, he went under the label of the Phantom, the Mask and Killer Klein. Of his pudgy son, who can wrestle a vote out of thin air, he says, "He won't back down from any kind of fight." Poor Nancy MacBeth and her Liberals never stood a chance, losing not only half her caucus but her own seat. She was dead from the moment the Ralphies started calling her "the Honourable Member from Holt Renfrew."

Nobody said politics was pretty. A university study shows that for every $100 his Conservatives get in campaign donations—mainly from his Calgary energy executives—the Liberals get $33 and the NDP limps in on $10.

Klein, only five when his parents divorced, was raised mainly by grandparents. He quit school at grade ten, tried the RCAF before ending up at a Calgary business school where he became a teacher, and then principal. Then he morphed from being a radio reporter to Calgary mayor, where he hosted visiting firemen in the basement beer parlour of the St. Louis Hotel.

One good thing to be said about the premier of Alberta. As a grade-ten dropout, Ralph Klein will not add to the glut of lawyers who led us to such entangled disasters as Meech Lake and the Charlottetown accord. He may even learn five words of French, thus surpassing the previous Prairies record held by John George Diefenbaker.

• See also "Tories."

**LALONDE, MARC** The key to the character of Marc Lalonde is what he found when he first began taking the train from Montreal to Ottawa to do legal work for the government.

He found the conductors on the publicly owned CN train couldn't speak French and the security guards in Parliament couldn't converse with him in his own language.

Marc Lalonde set out, with Pierre Trudeau, to set that situation right. Due in part to Trudeau alienating most of western Canada when the Official Languages Act became law, between 1969 and 1979 the percentage of francophones in decent jobs in the federal civil service went from ten to twenty-five per cent.

Lalonde served Trudeau as justice, finance and energy minister and his moral imperatives were as deeply rooted as was Trudeau's icy Jesuitical mind.

The only member of his family ever to go to university, after Oxford he embraced the youth arm of the reformist Action Catholique and spent volunteer time amidst poverty in India. Enormously charming and witty on private social occasions, he is a humourless Jekyll-Hyde when on government business (which is, when you think about it, dealing with other human beings). Lalonde's family has farmed the same land on an island in the St. Lawrence for eight generations and he has inherited that granitic

stubbornness. More important, he is—like Pierre Trudeau—someone who came to the governmental process as an unelected official
and back-room brain and retained (like Trudeau) a thinly disguised
impatience with the bothersome business of accountability.

A man, in Christina McCall-Newman's lovely words, who has
"a face as long as Lent," he is not even really "political" in the old
sense of the word. His passion is in getting on with the job, and
therein lay his unfortunate flaw. It is because he asserts he is personally honest—and he is—that nothing he could have done
could possibly be wrong.

There is in that assertion the basis of the fervent reformist
Catholic conviction that pushed Lalonde into active politics in the
first place. Unfortunately, there is the overlay of the Liberal arrogance that, since they stride the bicultural nature of the country
like no other party, they have the absolution of divine rule.

Marc Lalonde is most of all a moralist, someone who in the
words of McCall-Newman has the "self-confident piety of the
worker priest he might have become."

**LaMarsh, Judy** One April evening in 1968 in the Ottawa Civic
Centre—it was two days after Martin Luther King was shot and the
night they decided to burn down Detroit—I witnessed one of the
more astonishing sights of my youthful malehood. The sight was
Judy LaMarsh, in thigh-high plastic boots, appearing in the Paul
Hellyer cheering section in the fight for the Liberal leadership. I'm
not sure whether I've ever recovered. The next day, during the
furious power stroking after the second ballot that saw Hellyer
trailing both Pierre Trudeau and Robert Winters, my frail little
body was crushed in the stampede of thrusting microphones
around the insanely stubborn Hellyer as Judy pleaded passionately
with him to throw in his lot with Winters to stop "that bastard"

Trudeau. It was one of the more well recorded—and honest—assessments of our time. Judy LaMarsh did not like Pierre Trudeau.

In 1979, the obstreperous lady published her first "novel." To call it a novel is to call a stiletto a paring knife. *A Very Political Lady* is a careful evisceration of the most proud, the most vain—and the most masculine—members of the Liberal party which dear, deadly Judy once served as a cabinet minister.

As an author, she is somewhat like Anne of Green Gables crossed with Harlequin romance. But as the proprietor of a literary slaughterhouse she had everyone in Ottawa buying.

There is Prime Minister Jean-Jacques Charles, whose ways "were not to be questioned. Enigmatic and haughty, his eyes glittered, and his facial muscles worked, drawing the pebbly skin over the high cheekbones." Anyone you remember?

That is kind, considering some of the other carcasses carved up. Jim Coutts, the PM's principal secretary, is "'Boots' Jamieson, short blond, with a cheery face." Keith Davey is "the shaggy-haired, stoop-shouldered Senator David Kirke." This is not even to mention the beautiful, naive woman (guitarist Liona Boyd crossed with someone else) whom the PM marries. Some of the bedroom scenes featuring Hume Frazier—whoever *he* is—and his frigid wife, I would not have wished on Gerald Ford.

Judy LaMarsh couldn't write her way out of a chequebook, but she could lead a knee-capping squad in a banana republic.

**LÉVESQUE, RENÉ** There can be nothing more descriptive of the strange country called Canada than the fact that a state funeral was awarded to the man who tried to break it asunder. René Lévesque loved his province and its people so much that he was prepared to jettison the whole country. *Le Monde* of Paris said some years ago that only in Canada would a man that intelligent not be prime minister. His rumpled manner and his obstreperous outbursts—some rude, others outrageous—camouflaged for English Canada his real intelligence.

The country misunderstood René's background. Everyone assumed that the nervous, jerky little man in the rumpled suit, the world's greatest walking advertisement for lung cancer, was the product of the streets, an urban animal. In fact, the man with a face like a used gravel pit was of rural roots, raised in a little town called New Carlisle on the underbelly of the Gaspé peninsula. His formative years were spent closer to Halifax than Montreal.

The lady who was his family's neighbour in little New Carlisle says he had to be tied to a tree on a leash because he fought so much with the other kids. The amateur shrinks, of course, attribute the bellicosity to the well-known Napoleonic syndrome. Lévesque was perhaps five feet, six inches on a good day.

He obviously could have been a brilliant lawyer, as his lawyer father wanted him to be. But the legal profession (to its relief) lost him when a law professor at Laval—Louis-Philippe Pigeon, later a Supreme Court justice in Ottawa—ordered him out of his third-year class until he returned sans his constant cigarette. No one—especially future Supreme Court judges—orders René Lévesque what to do, and so he went off and joined the U.S. Army.

As a correspondent for the U.S. Office of War Information, he went through the London Blitz with Walter Cronkite, Edward R. Murrow and the other storied broadcast people. He crossed the Rhine with General Patton. He was one of the first people into the Dachau death camp. He was present when Mussolini and his mistress were strung upside down, their heads battered into watermelons, in a Milan square. He went to Moscow with Lester Pearson and interviewed Khrushchev.

As the CBC's man, he roamed the world explaining international issues to a Quebec audience on his popular public affairs show, which made him a celebrity and gave him a vaulting box into politics. The guy had been around.

Claude Ryan once told this scribbler that he believed René Lévesque knew and understood Canada better than Pierre Trudeau did. When I put it to him once, Lévesque enthusiastically agreed. "You know why? He never worked a day in his life. He knew more about the Constitution—that *bum!*—than I did, but I knew the country because I had to earn a living." Lévesque had his conversion in a national experience—his discovery of Anglo Ottawa's indifference and arrogance over a Radio Canada strike turned him from an objective journalist into a passionate politician.

The subtle anti-French prejudice that still obtains in so much of Canada both east and west of Quebec's borders painted him as a bit of a demagogue who operated by his own rules. I was talking just days before Lévesque's death with a premier who said that in the closed federal-provincial conferences Lévesque would openly laugh at Trudeau—as the others gaped. He was far more a democrat than Pierre Trudeau, which is probably why they clashed so early, a personal feud that poisoned Canada for too many years. But as Brian Mulroney himself has pointed out—a rare confession of admiration from one politician to another—Lévesque built a movement that in Mulroney's words is the "most democratic" party in the country. The little guy was so passionate about doing things the democratic, proper way that the more impatient nationalists shattered his party when he felt the mood of his public was to go slow on the essential, fading dream of an independent Quebec.

Like most journalists, he hated doctors and hospitals, and we have now learned that he regarded his end carelessly. He was treated, in his going, by politicians eager for applause almost ludi-crously as somehow a Father of Confederation. But his beliefs turned out, in a way, to be a Krazy Glue that bound us together.

He wrote his own best epitaph in his memoirs: "But at least they deigned leave me—to the very end, in my case—the essential title of democrat." Wherever he has gone, mark it as a given that there is a bilingual smoking section.

**LIBERAL LIONS** There is nothing like the last Liberal lions, growl-ing while rubbing one another's fur, as they gather over cocktails. While knowing they could do better than the present lot—they luxuriate in their memories, content that they knew better.

This would be the collection of the Liberal Party Establishment, on a terribly snowy night in 1997, collected to honour the Rainmaker himself, just-retired senator Keith Davey who epito-mizes everything that the Natural Governing Party has known for almost all this century—it was born to rule.

When Franco died in 1965, there were the usual moral cluck-cluckings from the editorial pages over the fact one regime ruled Spain for thirty-six years. What is strange is that no one drew the parallel with another regime that had dominated one country so thoroughly—the Liberal Party of Canada. The Liberals at that time had already ruled Canada 38 of the previous 49 years, 43 of the previous 54. The Liberals, of course, use a different method of sus-taining themselves in power than Franco did, but it is just as successful and in its own way destroys the parliamentary system.

The Liberal method is to co-opt talent from the civil service, put it into political life, then return it safely to its own secure reward back in the civil service. It is Tinker to Evers to Chance, the taxpayer paying for it every step of the way. It accounts for the bloodless technocrat cast to the Liberal front bench, since so many of its predominant figures were drawn from the civil service. When Trudeaumania died after 1968, there were thirty-eight government MPs defeated or retired in the 1972 election. The Liberals managed to fix up twenty-six of them with jobs.

To see and be seen. This is what such gatherings of the Liberal establishment are for. Whose jowls have slipped another notch? Who is in last year's fashions? The last Liberals must check the faces to see who is still faithful, who is still kicking.

There is half a Trudeau cabinet. Alastair Gillespie, once the most handsome man in Canadian politics, now merely the most charming. The towering Donald Macdonald, his head above the crowd. All the old fund-raisers, what they would call in Chicago ward-heelers. Pressing bodies as usual surround Pierre Trudeau, looking taut and old. Lurking at the back is John Nunziata, the skunk at the garden party, turfed out of the stern Chrétien party by daring to state over the GST that the emperor wears no clothes.

Someone remarks that in this room, over the scotch, you could probably construct a cabinet that would be better than those party junior clowns now so besmirching the Liberal name in Ottawa. As the snow keeps falling, all safe and warm inside there is this contentment, this serene belief that these guys would never have fallen into the current government's magnificent bollix with apologies that aren't apologies flying about and everyone dodging blame.

The usual Liberal-watchers lurk, looking for insights. The *Toronto Star*'s Richard Gwyn. Massey College's John Fraser. *Toronto Life* gossip meister Patricia Best. The *Globe*'s John Gray and Andrew Cohen. All the academic greats look down, in their scarlet gowns, from their expansive portraits, on Hermes-draped disciples of Galbraith and Davey and Trudeau. Tom Axworthy, Trudeau's amanuensis in a thick academic sweater, is here, down from Montreal.

There is an air in the room that—look around us—this was indeed the best and the brightest, the gang that kept Quebec in Canada, the last of the Liberal party before that province deserted for the only time one of their own who, after all, is prime minister of the realm. Unspoken, of course—save for the raised eyebrows and the mutters in the men's loo—were the embarrassing, clinging thoughts of all. How the predicament of those dummkopfs on the Rideau wouldn't have happened under our watch. And the snow continued to come down.

## LIBERALS (ALSO THE *NATURAL GOVERNING PARTY*)

"The philosophy of the Liberal party is very simple—say anything, think anything, or better still, do not think at all, but put us in power because it is we who can govern you best."—Pierre Trudeau, *Cité Libre*, 1963.

You look puzzled. Let me explain this, slowly. The NGP (also known as the Natural Governing Party, alias the Liberal dynasty) always goes outside for its leaders—always aware of the inexorable facts of the Insatiable Maw—that voracious beast with iron teeth, electrodes for eyes and typewriter keys for innards has to be fed. They went outside to get that kinky little cutie, Mackenzie King, who was languishing in the United States during World War I as John D. Rockefeller Jr.'s closest adviser before being brought back to run as a Liberal. When he was used up, they reached into the musty world of Quebec corporation law for Uncle Louis St. Laurent. That finished, did the NGP resort to the old party pols, Paul Martin (Sr.) and all those too-familiar faces? Of course not. Ever aware of the Insatiable Maw, they plucked a dewy-cheeked ex-second base-man from External Affairs. When Mike Pearson had had his fill, he wisely gazed past all the panting graduates of the Rideau Club and instead knighted a strange little bachelor from Montreal.

The compliant Canadian voters, Pavlovian to the end, faithfully followed.

Davey, O'Hagan and Coutts. Sounds like a double-play combination in the Three-Eye League? A plumbing outfit perhaps? A small law firm in Eastern Ontario?

Davey to O'Hagan to Coutts of course was the sleight-of-hand gang assigned to keep slipping past your unwary ballot that master of masks, Pierre Easily Trendeau. Knuckleball artists, all. They'd never steal a hot stove or a boxcar. All three were leftovers from the Pearson years, all passionate in the belief that the world will rot and wither away, the soil will turn putrid, small children will grow faint and rickets will infect the adults unless the Liberals are returned to power. Forever and ever. Amen.

When they write the history books on the inventory of the Just Society, they will unfortunately conclude that the perks and the patronage and the pork barrel were just for Grits. Trudeau was the clearheaded, fine-minded academic idealist and innovator who was going to sweep the sleaze from politics. In fact, his record of patronage and blatant jobs-for-the-boys is the worst of any modern-day prime minister. You could call him Pierre Porkbarrel and make an easy case to prove it.

Hovering at the end, like a white-haired vulture, was Senator Keith Davey, the rainmaker, watching, assessing, trying to decide when to call Mr. Blue Eyes, John Turner himself, in from the bullpen.

An assessment of their years in power shows a party so cynical and arrogant that it has achieved a wondrous status in the Canadian mind: its devious behavior has been accepted as the norm. The Liberals, it should be granted, are the political equivalent of *Jaws*. They have had the skills, over the years, to devour all philosophic thoughts to the left and right of them. Socialists, as decreed by Mackenzie King, that piranha masquerading as a dolphin, were merely "Liberals in a hurry."

Fear does not produce humility. Failure does not result in diluted arrogance. Threatened humiliation somehow doesn't manufacture a softer, more likable stance. If it's Liberal, it must be good, and there can't be anything wrong because Liberals have your best interests at heart.

A scribbler sits in the press gallery looking down at the House of Commons and is embarrassed as a citizen at the spectacle of the current prime minister making sport of his party's cynical actions over the GST. He smirks, he reads facetiously from the joke that is the Red Book, he sits down with a self-satisfied look on his face, knowing that he is invulnerable, his party is invulnerable, because opposite him sit the remnants of four parties that will never be government.

The arrogance of the Liberals has not been equalled since the C. D. Howe/Pipeline days. It is understandable. The interlopers of the Bloc Québécois, who would destroy Canada, lost all relevance with the disappearance of the messiah, St. Lucien. The Reform/Alliance, hived into just British California and Alberta, have no chance of becoming a national party. The NDP and the Conservatives are more to be pitied than described.

It is with such hubris that the Cretinites, with careless ease, can make a martyr and a hero out of John Nunziata, one of the more dislikable MPs who ever trod the hallowed halls of Ottawa. What is so remarkable about this remarkable cabinet, full of dolts, dunderheads, no-hopers and never-will-be's is that the arrogance flows on, as water runs downhill. They suffer from mental drip: the superiority that flowed through the cranium of C. D. Howe down through the ego of Robert Winters and the intellect of P. E. Trudeau now rests in shallow catching pools.

There's a reason for this. The Liberal party seeps through the underbelly of this country like a nuclear submarine in the deep. In 1955, when the Liberals modestly acceded to the twentieth anniversary of uninterrupted rule in Ottawa, the shrewd political scientist Paul Fox noted that: "The Liberal government aims at operating noiselessly, like a respectable mammoth business operation which fears nothing more than making people aware that it is there. The shadows flit silently along the wall, as in Plato's cave, and the citizen is never sufficiently disturbed to turn his head."

Some fellow made the remark the other day that there was small difference between the Liberal and Conservative parties. There is all the difference in the world. One is in and the other is out.

• See also "Liberal Lions."

**LONDON (ENGLAND)** The man who is tired of London, said the good Dr. Johnson so accurately, is tired of life. The best town in the world does not assault you but just sits there like a large lump, absorbing the wandering pilgrims. The problem is that exhaustion is brought on by the energy of the colonials who have adopted the place and move at a pace slightly above that of the locals. As usual, a drifting mob of refugees from the Great White Waste of Time speckles the place and pecks away at its impervious underbelly.

Canada, in fact, was invented in this place, Lord Durham writing his celebrated report in the comfort of the Reform Club on Pall Mall. He is recorded on the walls with a large portrait, right next to that of Lord Grey, who donated a cup of some football fame in the colony across the pond.

The soggy English, who lost their seed in two wars, are susceptible to raiders from across the sea. Rupert Murdoch, the Dirty Digger, has conquered Fleet Street, as Fredericton's Beaverbrook did once before. Conrad Black, the cold-eyed Toronto wordsmith, purchased a London house, as befits an owner of the *Daily Telegraph* on his way to the House of Lords (Lord Dominion?).

London, for all its charms, did nothing to improve Roy McMurtry's baggy suits, haircut or half-mast eyes. The Canadian high commissioner, in his retreat on Grosvenor Square marked by two tiny trees, was in his usual benign humour in 1987—needed when one greets a Bourassa one day, a Vander Zalm the next, a Joe Clark sandwiched in between. It is a movable cafeteria.

A visit to Buck House reveals that Vic Chapman, formerly of Vancouver, graduate of Britannia High School, B.C. Lions punter and baggage-smasher for P. Trudeau, and here the front man for Bat-Ears and Lady Di, is out of the residence on duty and therefore unable to provide champers.

There is a most unusual tone to the town. It is blue sky and sun, heretofore invisible at this time of year, a daytime so clear and bright as to almost match the Technicolor hues of the punk-coiffed louts of all three sexes who slouch through the streets, displaying their angst and advertising with their sharp elbows their contempt for Maggie Thatcher, the Iron Lady of 10 Downing.

The class warfare that divides Britain as no other nation continues unabated. The colonial invaders, not understanding class, gallop through, unimpeded.

• See also "Britain."


**LOTUS LAND**
   • See "British Columbia."


**LOUGHEED, PETER** The woman in the coffee shop with the Loni Anderson hair and the black leather pants says to the waitress, "I hope Pete goes for it."

To proud Albertans, two years before he retired in 1985, Premier Peter Lougheed is just plain "Pete."

It symbolizes the fact that they feel they own him, that he is their boy and will protect them, and the surprising thing is how many of them in 1983 seemed willing to give him up if he chose to go to Ottawa. Most everyone you talk to in the Oil Patch seemed to agree with the lady in the spun-candy hair. The Alberta newspapers were urging a draft. All that was needed was for others to create the conditions that would have the bedraggled and confused Conservative party come to him in their leadership search.

Sometimes as insular as Calvin Coolidge, he has devoted his whole political career to restoring Alberta pride from those Depression days and making central Canada respect his province.

This is the celebrated Fortress Alberta feeling that has subsided somewhat now but is still palpable. There was something eerie in his grandfather's maiden speech in the Senate when he intimated that Calgary could in time replace Ottawa as the capital. Senator Lougheed went on to state that the province's resources "when developed, I am satisfied, will eventually make [Alberta] the dominant portion of the Dominion." That was, dear friends, in 1889, in the last appointment to the Senate Sir John A. would make.

In his childhood, Peter Lougheed's insistence on setting up constant competition gave him the teenage nickname of "the Demander." Harold Millican, a schoolmate and later oil heavy, says "All of [his] games, whether cowboys and Indians, table tennis or football, were set up as win-or-lose situations."

Political scientist Larry Pratt, in *The Tar Sands*, wrote: "What Peter Lougheed articulates so well are the politics of resentment, the frustrated aspirations of a second-tier elite for so long dismissed as boorish cowboys, as yahoos with dung on their boots, by the smug, ruling Anglo-French establishment of Ontario and Quebec."

In 1938, a ten-year-old boy broke into a twenty-six-room house in Calgary. The mansion, known as Beaulieu, was up for public auction the next day, having been seized for tax arrears. The boy was Peter Lougheed, and the reason he broke into the house was that it had been owned by his grandfather, and it was a symbol of the family fortune and reputation that had been destroyed.

The house—filled with teak and brass and eight Italian marble fireplaces—had once entertained British royalty and now was being stripped. Peter Lougheed, from his secret hiding place, saw the entire library—volumes bound in leather—go for $22. Peter Lougheed has a long memory. Anyone of us, one suspects, would be the same.

A prominent Calgary woman who knows Lougheed well and has worked with him says, "Peter never makes a move until every block is in place. That's the story of his whole life in politics."

**LYNCH, CHARLIE** A bunch of the boys were whooping it up in the press club saloon one night in 1994, and nobody shot the piano player. There were there to roast and toast Charlie Lynch, a freak of journalism because he always believed you can have fun while going about a serious business. On D-Day in 1944, Lynch somehow found a piano on the tub carrying him to the Normandy invasion. On the way to the biggest military adventure in history, he merrily plinked away and led the lads in raucous verse.

Lynch was the undisputed dean of the Ottawa press corps. He did it all. He was a correspondent for Canadian Press in South America. He drank with Hemingway in France, two war correspondents who didn't like one another. In Paris he once found himself running the cash register at a whorehouse, the sex-famished army boys beating down the door.

He covered the Nuremberg war crimes trials. He covered the United Nations. The carrier pigeons he loosed in Normandy to carry his dispatches to London all took off and flew in the opposite direction. Right along with his cathouse trick, he was the first Canadian scribbler who made the leap into TV.

He talked as he wrote—offhand, never ponderous, not pretending to be a deep thinker. There are witnesses who claim to have seen him write a column without taking off his hat. He wouldn't know a thesaurus if it fell on his foot.

At the large thrash in his honour at the National Press Club, Charles presided, at seventy-four still battling with cancer, just as he had every day at lunch at a regular table with similar reprobates.

Jean Chrétien dropped in for a while, hoisting a large flagon of beer. Robert Stanfield sent his regards and affection, as did Paul Martin and a host of others. Herb Gray's letter said: "Ottawa without Charles Lynch will be like summer without black flies, rock 'n' roll without the Monkees, hockey without Don Cherry."

**MACDONALD, DONALD** Donald Macdonald, one time Liberal finance minister and aspirant for the Liberal leadership, was appointed in 1982 to head a three-year commission of inquiry into the economy. The Macdonald commission wasn't going to change anything, except for the diminution of the otherwise straightforward reputation of Don Macdonald.

Don Macdonald, in all his career through Ashbury College, University of Toronto, Osgoode Hall, Harvard, Cambridge, the Liberal cabinet and Bay Street, proved an unstinting worker, a great family man, loyal to the party in unrequested tasks (where Turner was not).

He laboured dutifully and long for the Liberal government, early and abrasively as House leader when the Grits felt they needed a Thumper to speed up Commons business, later as a finance minister, he had no more success with the economy than did John Turner—or Jean Chrétien, or Allan MacEachen for that matter. He is a lawyer whose talents were used by his Toronto law firm as a high-profile boardroom figure representing prestigious clients. Walter Gordon was at least at the centre of the Canadian business establishment when he set out on *his* odyssey into the unknown. Macdonald had no such solid economic background.

Why should anyone have taken serious Don Macdonald seriously in this appointed role? The essential point is that the Trudeaucrats were never really serious about this Royal Commission. The shallow interest of the Trudeau Liberals in this allegedly critical study was apparent. The misjudgment of Macdonald in his own reputation was supreme.

**MacMillan, H. R.** All great corporations—like all great newspapers—flow from the personality of the person on top. H. R. MacMillan, of MacMillan Bloedel, was a giant of a man who dominated every room he entered and was as well-read as any professor. He made modern British Columbia.

He was born a Quaker in obscure poverty on a small farm north of Toronto. At Ontario Agricultural College in Guelph he finished sixth in his first year behind the head of the class, John Bracken, later premier of Manitoba. MacMillan seemed more interested in poetry, but then went on to Yale, the only Canadian there to study forestry.

Shortly after he graduated, he was diagnosed with tuberculosis. In 1908, there was no medical cure for the disease. He was twenty-three. He spent three years in a sanatorium in the Laurentians. A year later, he was the first chief forester in B.C.

The old joke was the H. R. walked the length of B.C., noted every single tree, then quit government service and bought all of them. He established the first locally owned lumber export company. Fifty cents of every B.C. dollar came from timber and H. R. dominated the industry.

He was a huge man, well over two hundred pounds, and his fearsome countenance, all eyebrows and glowering, actually looked like a Douglas fir. When Arthur Erickson, Canada's premier architect, built MacBlo's downtown headquarters on Georgia

Street, he shaped it thick at the bottom, tapering upwards, with sunken windows giving the impression of bark, so the whole structure looked like a tree. In essence, really, like H. R.'s face.

H. R. was special. When his favourite daughter, Jeannie, graduated from Stanford, for a graduation present he gave her a trip around the world for two and asked her who she wanted to take. The answer was simple: "You." They sailed to Japan on the *Empress of Canada* in 1939 and took four months to tour the world. She phoned him every single day of her life until he died in 1976.

## MAGEE, MICHAEL

• See "Dobbs, Fred C."

## MANITOBA
Manitoba, a province that can't really decide whether it is connected to dolorous Ontario or is a card-carrying member of Western Canada.

• See "Winnipeg."

## MANNING, ERNEST
Ernest Manning, a cross between Oral Roberts and Mackenzie King, ruled Alberta for twenty-five years, 1943–68, the second-longest term of a Canadian premier.

Manning's death in 1996 took up three-quarters of the front page of the *Calgary Herald*. Follow-up stories were the only ones on page four. The editorial was top to bottom, floor length. Tributes consumed the entire op-ed page. The only portion that was missed was the sports pages.

The Alberta esteem for the senior Manning could only be compared with Quebec's outpouring of grief on the death of Maurice Duplessis. They were equal giants on their own turf. The reverence in which the man, eighty-seven at the time of his death, was held is best illustrated by a tale told by his son. The 1968 day on which he retired, Preston arrived at the Alberta legislature in Edmonton to pick him up.

Ernest Manning emerged carrying two boxes of personal files and papers. As Preston points out, "He'd been going to that building for thirty-three years. I've known some political types who'd require three moving vans to haul away their memorabilia. All he had were the two boxes."

The reason he needed to hitch a ride with his son was because he had already handed in his government-owned car.

When Manning turned down the entreaties to become national leader that role fell to Robert Thompson, remembered only for his celebrated quotes: "You've buttered your bread and now you'll have to lie in it." And, even better, "The Americans are our best friends whether we like it or not."

The man who balanced a budget a record seventeen years in a row never would have been in Alberta but for a mail-order radio he bought in 1924. As a teenager he was bouncing around his father's farm in Rosetown, Saskatchewan, in a Model-T Ford that had no muffler, no windshield, no headlights. It cost fifty dollars. On the radio he heard the Calgary evangelist Bible Bill Aberhart. He became the first graduate of Aberhart's Prophetic Bible Institute. In the landslide election victory when Aberhart embraced the goofy Socred theories, Manning became the youngest cabinet minister in the Commonwealth at twenty-six.

A non-smoking, teetotaller Christian, he was most private. After first elected, he told reporters he didn't have time to think about the opposite sex. Shortly after, he married Muriel Aileen Preston, organist at the Bible Institute.

In 1968 he worried about the "strong socialistic sympathies" of Pierre Trudeau. In 1970 Trudeau appointed him to the Senate.

Beneath the puritan soul, there was dry Prairie wit. He, after serving there, said, "a lot of people think senators are entirely pre-occupied with protocol, alcohol and Geritol."

In his retirement speech to the Socreds he said, "Over the years I have been portrayed by newsmen and commentators as an enigma—reserved, dour, cold and void of emotions. I am happy to report to you that none of these afflictions have ever caused me any pain."

Peter Lougheed says, "He gave to the citizens of Alberta a feeling of calmness, a sense that things were under control."

Oh, that we could find that in Ottawa today.

## MANNING, PRESTON (ALSO PARSON MANNING)

Journalists are really amateur anthropologists, digging into the midden that is a politician's soul. One rumbles about, kicking over a spare bone or two, finding a piece of skull and examining it, hoping beyond hope to stumble upon a personality or even a clue to character.

The microscope (disguised as a shovel) is upon Preston Manning, the organist who would be a rock star. He even went so far as to offer up his body as a sacrifice to Michael Jackson: turn me into something I was not.

The spin doctors of politics and the surgeons of the operating room combined to wipe that Prairie Ichabod Crane visage from reality. A chameleon emerged for the real goal in life—the urban Ontario voter without whom the most bendable Reformer could never reach the Holy Grail, 24 Sussex Drive.

He really is Presto! Manning. Leaping Hugo boss and Armani with a single bound. Speeding from hairdresser to dentist to voice coach faster than a silver bullet. One feared turning off the TV set hourly, so swiftly did he transmogrify into another being.

The man who would have led us into the Promised Land

confessed that he had laser surgery so he could throw away those geek glasses. A lovely hairdresser whose name is probably Bruce reconstructed his soup bowl haircut and tinted his locks.

He allows that he had his teeth fixed, just as any aspiring bimbette does when she first hits Hollywood looking for a casting couch. He had a tonsil doctor work on his voice box, to eliminate that squeak that always gave the impression his underwear was too tight. And the boys in the back, the Edgar Bergens to this Charlie McCarthy, shucked the bib overalls and gave him threads that any self-respecting stockbroker would wear.

Now, all this image-making of course is not sinister, not even illegal. Like stealing hubcaps or selling smokes to underage teenagers, everybody does it, has always done it. Pierre Trudeau arrived at a Grey Cup game in Toronto's Exhibition stadium, to do the traditional ceremonial kickoff granted to a prime minister, garbed in a cape and a grand hat that made him look like an artist from Montparnasse off on a lunch break. Churchill had his famous cigar, which he brandished more than he smoked. Dwight Eisenhower, on his days at the West Point military academy, confessed later in life that he had "studied acting" for three years under the celebrated General Douglas MacArthur, who tried to convert the corncob pipe into the presidency.

The difference is that all these towering personalities created their own images, however artificial. No hovering press agent was required, no focus groups necessary to remake their visage, no eager aides paving the way to a dentist here, a hairdresser there, a tailor down the block.

Murray Dobbin's volume entitled *Preston Manning and the Reform Party* is a studied look at this suddenly popular, unknown (popular because it is unknown) "grassroots" development that so worried both Grits and Tories on the Prairies at the beginning of the 1990s.

His insight is not that Ernest Manning, father of Presto!, was Social Credit premier of Alberta for twenty-five years. It is that when Presto! enrolled at the University of Alberta in Edmonton in 1960—not-rocking and not-rolling with such campus contemporaries as Joe Clark, Jimmy Coutts and future provincial NDP leader Grant Notley—he went into the physics faculty. Sign of a strict, disciplined mind, one might assume.

The young Manning at twenty-six went to California to spend half a year at a high-tech military firm to study "systems analysis." From there, he went to Vietnam to study the then-popular American theory about the "domino" effect of Communism.

There is, Dobbin discovered, an interesting link with the career development of Brian Mulroney: aside from one failed foray into federal politics in 1965, Presto! had never run for any office before becoming leader—not provincial, not municipal, not for school board. Not for anything.

Here is Dobbin: "It is very unusual for a person with such strongly held convictions to stay completely out of the democratic process in his broader community. Yet at no time did Preston Manning attempt to engage in the normal day-to-day political life of his community. He believed that the country was moving dangerously in the direction of socialism, yet he did nothing in any democratic forum to stop it."

The contention is that Manning's narrow focus and political isolation have denied him the opportunity to work with a wide variety of people: he can't make judgments about their character.

Presto! Manning and his Reform magicians came into hard times before long, the phenoms who must be brought back to earth.

'Twas ever thus with those who rise so far so swiftly, the thin oxygen in the ozone going quickly to their heads, seemingly unaware of the vipers of truth lurking down below, their sabres waiting to thrust into the soft underbelly of the faith.

## MARATHON REALTY
• See "CPR."

**MARGARET** As the well-known vice-president of the Defend Margaret League—an old friend from teenage days—your humble scribe felt that her published tome, *Beyond Reason*, was unfairly maligned for telling us more about P. Trudeau than it did about M. Trudeau.

Well, we finally had to resign from our role, rolling our eyes into the moral ozone and sucking our teeth at her continued blabberings at the ongoing excuse of making a buck.

Margaret's sin, in the public eye, had nothing to do with the fact that Jack Nicholson taught her one evening just how much room there was in the back seat of a Daimler. Or that she spent a week in bed with Ryan O'Neal ("he had a nice maid who brought us breakfast in bed and told me that I was the only person she had met, aside from Ryan, who never, ever, wanted to get up").

The coy hints about Senator Edward Kennedy ("a secret I intend to keep") by now are tiresome. Christopher Reeve, alias Superman? The Peruvian playboy? The Texas cowboy with the burns? The Pillsbury Doughboy? Who cares any more?

The reason so many Canadians could not stand Margaret Trudeau in 1982 was that they realized, subconsciously, that she still had an effect on the political future of this country. It would have been all very well if she had disappeared into the demimonde of the Gabors, or even a sort of teenage Elizabeth Taylor, fit only for the *National Enquirer* and the hairdressers. Alas, the world's youngest and most beautiful slurp-and-teller was still a factor in the tortuous lifestyle of our most tempestuous prime minister.

Margaret Trudeau—unlike the myth—is a very intelligent woman. Her insights (on Kosygin, who cried on leaving her, on Brezhnev, on Ivan Head—"that pompous and somewhat self-important man," on Ottawa, on Chou En-lai, on Nixon) are shrewd. She will have to answer to herself and her children for her silliness and destructive vanity. But it all gets down to Pierre Trudeau's motto: "Reason before passion." Unwittingly, this scandalous lady epitomized many an election issue. She left the marriage convinced that "Pierre's solution to subjugate everything to reason and will was wrong." Another small clue to the unfathomable puzzle of the man we once faced on our election ballots.

**MARJ-PARGE**
- See "Nichols, Marjorie."

**MARTIN, PAUL, JR.** Some years ago, a political insider whose name is long forgotten wrote your humble servant with a quiet "tip." Keep your ears open and your eyes sharp, was the tip, because Paul Martin Jr. wants to be the leader of the Liberal party. Paul Martin Sr., of course, was a giant in the party, but as for Jr., I didn't have a clue.

He was, it turned out, doing very well in Montreal after making a million bucks with his shipping empire, but no one had ever heard a word about any political ambitions. I dutifully burst this astonishing news on the world in my column and it dropped like a stone, no one paying any attention.

We eventually became social friends on visits to Montreal, where he always mused about the decision whether to go to Africa and do good works—or try politics.

He was rather nerdish then, with thick, horn-rimmed glasses. He has solved that with contact lenses, has got rid of the "Jr." and, after being a terrible speaker on entering the Commons, has now become one of the smoothest put-down artists in the joint.

He worshipped his father, and may be acting out his father's failed dream. Paul Martin Sr. twice tried for the top ring and slipped, not entirely his own fault.

As the architect of his party's social security philosophy, he felt he deserved the Liberal leadership when Louis St. Laurent left. The party instead turned to a political neophyte it had plucked from External Affairs, Lester Pearson.

When Pearson left, Paul Martin Sr. was too old—his instant dyed hair for the leadership campaign an indication—and the party again turned to another flashy newcomer, Pierre Trudeau. Martin Sr. was a legend in his Windsor seat, unbeatable there. There's the hoary old political story of a reporter riding in a car with Paul Martin Sr., past a Windsor cemetery.

Paul Martin Sr. automatically took off his hat and placed it over his heart. "An old friend?" inquired the reporter.

"No," said Paul Martin Sr. "They all vote for me every election."

Paul Martin Jr. was the most silent man in the last election. With good reason. He is now regarded everywhere as the strong-man of a very weak cabinet. As finance minister patiently waiting, he knows the most powerful politician in Canada (Aline Chrétien) will eventually quietly but firmly take her man out of the action. Martin knows TROC wants a non-francophone to lead the battle if there is another referendum. With his Montreal base, he would be an anglophone inside Quebec fighting for TROC. He is the best bet for the Liberals. And for the country. His long wait will be rewarded. And please his father in Heaven.

**MASSE, MARCEL** In order to display its wit, the Mulroney government took the elegant Marcel Masse, who goes around in a cape, from his cultural portfolio and pitchforked him into the defence ministry. As Marjorie Nichols wrote, his only possible affinity with the armed forces would be those cute uniforms of the military band, with all the brass buttons on the tunics and the ostrich feathers protruding from their helmets.

**MCDONOUGH, ALEXA** In the 1997 federal election, Alexa McDonough looked like a Before and After in a *Chatelaine* makeover contest. Horrified NDP handlers got her out of the 1950s in a swift move to a design consultant. She is the only political leader in the land who has never learned to speak, even in Question Period, without looking down at her notes. As a long-ago church companion said about a United Church preacher who thundered from a prepared text, "If he can't remember it, how can he expect us to?"

The daughter of a millionaire socialist, she lives too far, on the fringes in Halifax, from the NDP core vote in British Columbia. She is handicapped by being the second successive female NDP leader. Voters can't tell the difference.

**MCDOUGALL, BARBARA** Barbara McDougall, former journalist, former Bay Street, former Mulroney cabinet inmate. Ms. McDougall is deadly on her feet.

**MCHAGGIS, BLATHER**
• See "Webster, Jack."

**MCKENNA, FRANK** Frank McKenna, the shrimp from New Brunswick with the squeaky voice, boss of the only officially bilingual province, runs it as the hijack capital of Canada, stealing high-tech giants such as telephone companies and UPS from Bay Street and Toronto, where one might think they would be more naturally sited. He is aggressive, ambitious and—not too inclined to fall asleep reading Shakespeare—has been positioning himself over the past decade for a run at the big job in Ottawa.

**McLAUGHLIN, AUDREY** When Audrey McLaughlin first entered the House of Commons from the romantic North, she sat watching the men bellow at each other in the farce known as Question Period. After several months of observing the posturing and insults, she was reminded of her favourite episode of the *Murphy Brown* TV sitcom.

"The men in the newsroom are having a huge fight that's all about their egos," McLaughlin recalled. "Murphy watches them in disgust for a while, and finally she bursts out, 'Oh, why don't you all just drop your pants and I'll get a ruler?' "

She grabbed attention before the Tories and the Grits had the guts to select a woman leader.

**MEECH LAKE** Blind pettifoggers, the tiny politicians titillated the world—and the dollar on international exchanges—with their stagy obfuscations on the dreaded M-word, the Meech Lake Accord, which even now has such a bad name that even Honda is thinking of changing the name of its car.

Television is largely to blame—not just the constitutional lawyers who made their living trying to pick fly shit out of rice while wearing boxing gloves. Never in our short history, since this country was stillborn 134 years ago, have such minor players been given such national attention. Strutting their small stuff on the stage, they revelled in the slavering attention of the TV cameras outside the old Ottawa railway station each evening while their mothers proudly watched.

When was the last time (or the first time?) anyone in Canada knew what Gary Filmon looked like? Did you know before Meech Lake how short Joe Ghiz was? And how squeaky Frank McKenna's voice is?

Was it part of your knowledge, while longing for the boring Stanley Cup finals as Peter Mansbridge and Don Newman got ever more excited, that Don Getty was part of that unfortunate section of maledom that drives the paste-over style of hairdo? Was it really worth Meech Lake to have this revealed not just to his family and his hairdresser but a wondering nation?

It is not that the country is going to fall apart. It's not, despite what the experts on the *Washington Post* editorial page assert. The sadness is how our provincial satraps, given their hour strutting upon the stage and bowing before the graven image of Peter Mansbridge, knowing in their smarts they had a labour negotiator rather than a prime minister at the head of the table, played so shamelessly upon regional prejudices.

These guys were turf-guardians, not really big people. It did not help (in fact guided the picture) that the prime minister was just seeking for a middle way, a middle way that could never come without leadership and toughness at the top.

As everyone in Moose Jaw knows, this turkey trot will go on and on, there being no need to call out the militia just yet. There are further Meech Lakes to come, as painful as this is to predict and record. Yet-unknown and ignored lakes to be made famous in history for the fact they were the sites where eleven men in suits spent yet another all-night session—fuelled by coffee, cancer sticks and Confederationspeak—and wrestled with the equation, punched the pillow, tried to nail jelly to the wall.

In the never-ending mission to save the nation, perpetually on the edge of self-immolation, one should ignore the obvious signs of disintegration. Disdain the paperwork. The predictable blatherings of the bureaucrats. Cast not an eye on the Meech Lake documents, the Allaire report, the Spicer papers, the incomprehensible Doobe-Beaudoin tablets handed down from on high.

Watch the players instead. Real human beings. Documents mean nothing. The quarterbacks make the decisions. Trust moi.

**M o n t r e a l** The best possible place to be for a Canadian who is an optimist is Place Jacques Cartier on St. Jean Baptiste Day. This is the cobblestoned square sloping down past a grain elevator to the St. Lawrence from the turreted balcony of Montreal's City Hall, where Charles de Gaulle shouted his famed "Vive le Québec libre." Circles of whey-faced teeny-bleepers, zonked on substances not liquid, hunker down cross-legged on the cold stones, waving aloft the blue-and-white Quebec flag.

With small exultation, thin boys drag in cardboard beer cases labelled "O'Keefe" and "Molson's" and there are cheers as they are flung on the makeshift bonfires in the centre of the 15,000 beer-swigging celebrants. Ah, the Anglos to the torch.

There is a wealthy Montrealer, now in his sixties, who shakes his head ruefully over his drink and remembers that he was past seventeen before he knew that there were French Canadians populating the city he grew up in. Beneath Mount Royal, beneath the private school and the case-hardened racial barriers, he was never given any hint or clue that people who were, well, *different*, dwelled down there on the flat sweeping out to the St. Lawrence. That was, recall, only a decade after we had finished a war. There is a semi-wealthy Montreal lady of fine legs and WASP combativeness who, in an argument with a Parti Québécois stalwart, is told,

"Only people who are rich or happy can have a sense of humour."
The PQ, being unhappy, is ruled out.

Montreal, still the most interesting town in the country, has
geographic layers unlike any other. Over on Crescent, in downtown Montreal, Glenn Miller, that famous Québécois figure,
pours his trombone sugar from the amplified speakers, enabling a
fortyish lady, swinging a large white purse that hasn't been seen
since Rita Hayworth, to waltz with her husband on unfamiliar
pavement.

Halfway down Place Jacques Cartier are the comfortable
awnings of the Nelson Hotel, a familiar backdrop for the TV cameras as the home base for Robert Lemieux, the lawyer who
represented the FLQ in those now-dreamy forgotten days. It is the
statue, most ironically, of Lord Nelson that dominates this square.
The inscription commemorating the Battle of Trafalgar, in unconscious stiff-upper-lip parody, tells of Nelson wasting the combined
fleets of France and Spain.

One can remember a St. Jean Baptiste Day in the 1970s. The
same square, the same demographic slice of youthful Québécois,
filled with beer and holiday abandon. Police were massed in hidden alleyways on the perimeter of Old Montreal. Riot clubs and
plastic face masks were the holiday garb. A threatening police helicopter swooped back and forth over the heads of the crowd, its
blinking red-and-green lights in the twilight mixing with the
coloured balloons sent aloft by defiant denizens of the drinking
cafés that line the square.

Now, that anger has been vitiated. Finally, oh, finally—the message has got through to the descendants of the Westmount
Rhodesians: this holiday is not *theirs* but *ours*. It is not mere cultural homage to the patron saint of the French-Canadian voice; it
is now Quebec's *fête nationale*.

There is, in Montreal, the sense that the boil has been punctured.

• See also "Auf der Maur, Nick" and "Drapeau, Jean."

**MOOSE JAW** There is, we know, the standard whipping boy when you want to make fun of the Prairies: Moose Jaw. Ranking up there with Otter Haunch, Alberta, and Gopher Breath, Manitoba.

Moose Jaw (believed to be from the Cree word "Moosegaw," meaning "warm breezes") has taken the abuse valiantly over the years, providing amusement for passing travel writers and stand-up comedians. It has scarcely complained. Now it's getting even.

It's got a secret past and, like the scarlet lady, is letting everyone in on the facts. For some seventy-five years, city fathers denied the rumours about a mysterious network of tunnels running underneath this quiet little city.

Only when a heavy truck collapsed the pavement on Main Street and disappeared into a large hole did the juicy truth come out.

When the CPR was stretching steel to the Pacific, dollar-a-day Chinese labourers were welcome. Through the treacherous Fraser Canyon, a commission later estimated, up to four Chinese per mile perished through rock slides and drowning in the 1880s.

When the "yellow peril" hysteria hit Western Canada, panicky Ottawa imposed its infamous head tax, which rose to $500 per Chinese immigrant by 1903. By 1911, 162 Chinese had made it to Moose Jaw. By 1921, there were 188, only 11 of them female.

Unable to pay the head tax, the Chinese went underground, using the tunnels under buildings in downtown Moose Jaw and doing work for above-the-ground cafés and laundries. They raised children in rat-infested darkness. The tunnels snake underneath what is still the main drag in town, good old Main Street.

It was all changed by booze, also known as Prohibition. By that time, primitive little Saskatchewan contained 406 bars, 38 wholesale liquor dealers, 12 clubs and 23 "dispensaries." As luck would have it, Saskatchewan ended Prohibition in 1924, nine years before the Americans did. That left Moose Jaw, smack on the Soo Line that ran south to the United States, a convenient bootleg retreat for the Chicago Mob.

Quiet little Moose Jaw? The town that had become known as the Buckle on the Wheat Belt turned into the Sodom and Gomorrah of Saskatchewan. The tunnels were now full of gamblers, prostitution and bootleg warehouses. Brothels lined River Street.

Things were helped along by chief of police Walter P. Johnson, the most infamous lawmaker in the West, who took his cut from the bootleggers. Nancy Gray, a Moose Jaw local, has written that her late father, Bill Beamish, a barber, used to be called to the tunnels to cut Al Capone's hair.

Okay? Got it? No one makes fun of Moose Jaw any more. That's an order.

• See also "Saskatchewan."


**MOP AND PAIL**
• See "Globe and Mail, the," also "Paper Wars."


**MULRONEY, BRIAN** If you want to pick a fight with an Irishman in a bar, first make sure he is the only Irishman present. If the Irish have one common trait, it is that they are loyal. Veteran Mulroney-watchers have found that the consistent thread in the record of Martin Brian Mulroney, the Jaw That Walks Like a Man.

As someone who invented Brian Mulroney back in 1975 as the MP from Whimsy, as a means of getting rid of the hated Liberals (it worked, didn't it)?), I understand how his cranium works. It sits before me as clearly as the written Korean instructions on how to assemble a garden chair. It is a mind that leaps about like a water bug, relying as much on Irish intuition as it does on political expediency (as in all politicians).

In *Mulroney: The Politics of Ambition*, John Sawatsky points out that the exact reason why the 1984 Mulroney government came unstuck so soon is that the secretive lad from Baie-Comeau took into his Ottawa inner circle only those locker-room mates he had known since university days, a gang of amateurs who sort of remind you of those barstool familiars on *Cheers*.

His No. 1 adviser was diminutive Montreal lawyer Michel Cogger; they've been pals since Laval University law school. His chief Quebec organizer was Jean Bazin, a sly adviser since buddy days at Laval. His tap to Toronto money, Michael Meighen, grandson of a prime minister, another friend from Laval days. His closest friend is Sam Wakim, a Toronto lawyer, briefly a Tory MP in the Clark government, Mulroney's roommate back at St. Francis Xavier. His long-time adviser and confidant, Peter White, was another Laval pal who is a close associate of tycoon Conrad Black.

When Brian Mulroney was in search of delegates on his way to the Conservative leadership, he had a particularly hard time in Pembroke, Ontario, winning over the serious young lady who was leader of the riding's youth delegates. Tiny Tories are very heavy on policy, and Mulroney, as is his wont, was cleverly stick-handling his way around any firm stands on the great issues of our day. She kept pressing him, and he kept evading. He was therefore amazed—and delighted—on arriving at the Ottawa shinny rink for the June convention in 1983 to find the same young lady plastered with Mulroney buttons, a loyal supporter. Intrigued, Mulroney dispatched one of his flunkeys to ascertain, discreetly, which of his policies had won her over. The aide returned with the truth. The young woman explained that it happened over the delegate breakfast that Mulroney threw in Pembroke. The scrambled eggs and bacon arrived. Mulroney immediately reached for the ketchup bottle and tilted it over his eggs. Nothing happened. He then took his knife and stuck it in the bottle. "Anybody who would stick a knife in a ketchup bottle," explained the new supporter, "can't be all bad."

The point is that Brian Mulroney was the only national political leader who could tell that sort of story on himself. ("It wasn't NATO," he says, "it wasn't the Constitution, it was *Heinz*!")

Mulroney is truly in the American mould: our first working-class prime minister. No silver-spoon Trudeau this one, no Rhodes scholarship, no Rockefeller-lackey Mackenzie King, no elegant Laurier or plutocrat Bennett. Mulroney is a real truck-driving, sweating, dirty-finger guy, son of an electrician; he is proud of that.

Thumb-suckers as disparate as Dalton Camp and Bob Rae made the same point about the puzzling person who is Martin Brian Mulroney. In private, he is the best of companions—funny, charming, generous, loyal, a joy to be with. In public, he came across as pompous, stiff, insincere, never really relaxed.

Martin Brian Mulroney developed his fatal flaw because he grew up in the back rooms of Quebec politics that cherished bombast. Because he entered real politics so late—never earning his warts as an alderman, a city councillor, a provincial legislator, a junior cabinet minister, a senior cabinet minister—he emulated those he worshipped as a youth.

His personal hero to this day remains Daniel Johnson, the Union Nationale premier. They used to drink together at the Château Frontenac in Quebec City when Mulroney was a law student at Laval. The boy student, fatally, learned old Quebec church-basement bombast.

The reason why Brian Mulroney was driven out of office by public opinion was exposed—though he didn't realize it—in his resignation news conference. Not content with graciously bowing out, he told a national television audience that, in fact, he and his wife had planned to leave in 1990 but that grievous responsibilities—Meech Lake, the Gulf War, Oka, etc.—had forced him to remain at the wheel.

In the following days, this curious reporter asked some fifty or so people—inside my trade, outside, strangers, one respected ex-premier—if they believed that statement. Of course not, was the near-unanimous judgment. Even in resigning, he could not resist braggadocio that wouldn't pass muster at mother's knee.

History is going to be kinder to him than the present public mood is. He kept that ever-fractious Conservative caucus together—because he could do it all behind closed doors once a week. That charm and humour and boyish sense of life that was denied the public was available only to those in the party "family."

Because he was a child and a product of the back rooms, he could never manage to get into the living rooms of the nation.

But the real assessment came from his Montreal friend Nick Auf der Maur after his first election in 1984. "He's a typical Irish fraud. It's a positive thing, not a negative thing. He's not trying to make you believe in his fraudulence. You know exactly why he's doing it and how, but you can't help but be charmed by it."

**MULRONEY, MILA** The important thing to realize about the person we once elected to run the country, Mila Mulroney, is that she was our first immigrant prime minister. Yes, indeed, John Turner was born in England and so was some forgotten PM at the turn of the century, but Mila put the final stamp of approval on the post-war wave of immigration from Europe.

Mila was born in Yugoslavia, in Sarajevo, the product of a solid European professional class. Her grandfather was a lawyer, and her father became a lawyer to keep the family happy, but when he came to Canada he decided to become what he really wanted to become, a psychiatrist, went back to university and started all over again. Mila was an engineering student at university in Montreal when the chap who assisted her in running the country swept her away. She was nineteen at the time.

Thirty-one when her husband became PM, fourteen years younger than her husband, she is five-foot-nine-something and, if she is ever out of work, could earn her groceries as a model. She enters a room as if she owns it, and her smile could power the James Bay turbines. During her husband's Regressive Convertible leadership campaign, she was advised to tone down the jewellery on their countrywide junkets in search of delegates, but, when they hit Alberta, flash all the diamonds in her possession.

Mila Mulroney can "work a room" better than Lyndon Johnson or Milton Berle. To work a room is an esoteric political term mean-ing the art of pressing the flesh of a ballroom full of total strangers, leaving each of them with the impression that he or she was the only guest present. It means not lingering but moving, not sprinting but tarrying, appearing as natural as if you were just strolling through the supermarket and leaving everyone all gaga.

She has only two rules for her three children. They are not allowed to say "I can't" and they are not permitted to yawn at the table. She calls her husband "Muldoon."

This ex–prime minister of Canada is years older than her chronological age and down deep she is tougher than Air Canada steak.

## NARCISSUS-ON-THE-PACIFIC
- See "British Columbia."

## NATIONAL POST, THE (ALSO *THE NATIONAL PEST*)
- See "Paper Wars."

## NATURAL GOVERNING PARTY (NGP)
- See "Liberals, the."

**NEW BRUNSWICK** It really is good to know that there are some governments with the proper priorities. There are so many silly and unnecessary projects financed with public money that only occasionally do we encounter an initiative that we can all applaud. I refer, of course, to the decision to build a $9.4-million underground bunker in New Brunswick where government leaders would live in a nuclear war.

Elsewhere, all around us, nearsighted politicians with no vision are concerning themselves with welfare reforms and unemployment benefits and the debate over abortion. Out in Fredericton, they've got their eye on the real issue—how to provide a ping-pong room for the premier and his pals while nuclear destruction levels the rest of the earth. Good thinking.

Dug into a hill about five kilometres from the New Brunswick legislature, the Regional Emergency Operations Centre will have fully equipped living quarters for up to three hundred people. There will be thirty-five bedrooms, including two executive suites, fourteen bathrooms, a lounge, an exercise room, a games room and a fully equipped kitchen with a walk-in freezer. There will be a ping-pong table, stationary bicycle, treadmill, weights, a large-screen television, a washer and dryer and an ice-cube dispenser. There is no mention of the gin.

It seems a number of "high-powered-rifle-resistant doors" are being installed, apparently to prevent unauthorized persons from entering it once it has been sealed. Does Richard Hatfield own an Uzi? How many irate wives of cabinet ministers, shut out, might take drastic action? Does Mrs. McKenna make the list of three hundred? I wouldn't want to be one of the Elite. Rosedale cocktail party pecking orders are bad enough. Things could get vicious around Fredericton.

Even more droll is the fact that N.B. conned Ottawa into paying for it all. Only Ottawa could plan for three hundred people lining up for fourteen bathrooms. It's federal constipation, as usual.

There's also the matter of the number of bedrooms. How do you fit three hundred into thirty-five? "The structure is unique in Canada," says Dave Peters, operations director for Emergency Preparedness Canada in Ottawa. It certainly is, if someone can decide who gets the summer camp bunk beds and who has to stretch out on the ping-pong table.

The news that there are three hundred people in New Brunswick worth saving will come as a surprise to the rest of the country. Think about it. Say you live in Ontario, which has some nine million people ever ready for nuclear war. Can you think of three hundred Ontarians worth saving? Ben Johnson's trainer haps, the premier, Patti Starr's lawyer, Farley Mowat and Ed Mirvish. After that, the imagination tends to run out. The thought that little New Brunswick actually has three hundred precious bodies due to survive the nuclear holocaust is impressive indeed and causes one to think. Perhaps we've been underestimating old N.B. all these nuclear-free years.

• See also "Hatfield, Richard."

**NEW DEMOCRATIC PARTY (ALSO THE *FEW DEMOCRATS*)** There is something terribly useful about the Few Democrats holding a convention to decide who will lead the rump party that used to be the conscience of the nation. One walks into the aircraft hangar that goes under the name of the Winnipeg Convention Centre and—suddenly!—the 1960s are born again. Every macrame-knitter from Saltspring Island is there. Oxfam polemicists abound. Antiwar posters proliferate. Every ill-kept beard in Canada is in residence. The corridors of this bloodless concrete cave resemble a flea market in Cairo. The most progressive party of all loves to wallow in nostalgia.

Conventions of the Regressive Convertibles may be all about bagmen, and gatherings of the Gliberals are meetings of yuppie lawyers, but this event is the only convention overshadowed by a shoplifting charge. As usual, Central America plays a large part, although as far as can be determined there are no voting delegates from that region. The folkies sing about them, and brave men from El Salvador are given the microphone. Among the leadership banners on the walls is an Oriental screed, puzzling an onlooker as to whether Chairman Mao or David Suzuki is a late entrant in the lists. Not too many delegates from Nanaimo can decipher it.

Stephen Lewis and Bob Rae and Gerry Caplan are joined at the hip, power brokers who pretend they're not, plotting the drift of the convention. Dave Barrett, the man of the people, in his theme portraits wears a red cashmere sweater. Audrey McLaughlin— adapting quickly to the genre—takes on the frozen mask of an Inca model as the TV cameras try to catch a glimpse of emotion as she sits in repose listening to the Barrett pyrotechnics.

The concrete cave is kept alive by the chair, a lady from Newfoundland, who calls wearily for another vote on an obscure argument over Robert's Rules of Order, complaining that "skinny people look like hands to me." Elijah Harper, an Indian from Manitoba, reluctantly given time to make a plea from Microphone One and reminded that he has just three minutes, says: "You give me three minutes. We've been waiting a century."

Crazed cameramen, chasing Barrett and McLaughlin down the aisles, trample the macrame salesladies in their mandatory sneakers. The best lapel button of all: "Vander Zalm's mother had No Choice."

This is the most educated gang ever to contest a party leadership. Howard McCurdy has four degrees. Steven Langdon and lawyer Ian Waddell both have three. Audrey McLaughlin has two degrees. Barrett has two degrees from universities in Seattle and St. Louis. Simon de Jong, who started out in a Japanese internment camp in Indonesia, has a degree. Even the beachcomber candidate, Roger Lagasse, has a degree. This mob has more degrees than the entire Social Credit cabinet of British California.

Perhaps this is the reason why they think there is a new law against humor on the political platform. There is not a guffaw in a carload.

Life is grim, but does socialism always have to be *this* grim?

**Newfoundland** When I become prime minister (as I may), there will be enacted a new law applicable to all Canadians. It will be that all citizens of the land not already living there be compelled to visit Newfoundland at least once before they croak. You cannot really be a Canadian until you have seen the Rock, where it all started, have talked to the Newfs and had your sinuses cleaned out with a little shot of Screech. Newfoundland reminds us that there is something older than a shopping plaza in Edmonton, that there are more serious things in the land than Harold Ballard.

St. John's harbour is timeless, appearing today as it must have when John Cabot or whoever sailed in around 1497. Cabot's real name was Giovanni Caboto, and he was born in Genoa, but I digress. Water Street is the oldest street in North America, as some of the fish-and-chip shops seem to testify. High on the hill sits Joey Smallwood's legislature building, looking like a miniature version of an early New York skyscraper, the only legislative building in Canada built on the vertical scale, as if Newfoundlanders yearn to struggle toward the sky, out of the bleak reality of the Rock.

We are, for purposes of research, at Murray's Pond Fishing Club, a spot of roast beef haven outside St. John's where the gentry retreat when the cares of the week fall on their foreheads and gentle relief (i.e., raucous behavior) is the only solution to the torments of the soul.

Downstairs, it being full of lawyers and therefore incipient politicians, there is much talk of Dick Hatfield and Bob Coates. The jokes have a Newfoundland twist, and therefore are unrepeatable. Upstairs, the beer flows. A poet in a flattened black cowboy hat and beatific smile tears the music out of a fiddle. An actor with a munificent belly holds forth on a tiny flute. There are several accordions and much mirth. All the old Newfie songs are dragged out, and most everyone knows the words. It is dark and close and intimate. You can feel the culture of the island, sniff it like the salt air.

This is Newfoundland, 1985. The country club set waiting for the riches of the Hibernia oil fields to arrive. The other set upstairs desperately trying to hang on to the past. The fish, slumbering outside beneath the ice of Murray's Pond, seem blissfully unaware of the contrast within, but the two floors of the late-evening revelry illustrate perfectly the layers of Newfoundland society, one affluent, the other pensively trying to consolidate something.

**NEWMAN, PETER** When a small group of Toronto's media heavies were gathered on a Saturday night at the cottage home of Peter Gzowski, the host proudly showed a guest around the beautiful landscape of the old mill town and, on returning to the house to pour drinks, heard a familiar strain of conversation. "Oh my God," he cried in mock despair. "Are we into Newman stories *already*?"

Gather three journalists together and within a few quaffs there will be new Newman gossip—some imagined, some real. I've seen little book-representative girls reduced to tears at lunches when they can't get the author they are nervously escorting to quit swapping Newman stories with the reporter who is supposed to be inquiring about the *book*—while the expense-account gin flows.

Peter C. Newman is without doubt the most eccentric journalist around. The stories are legend about how he falls asleep at 9:05 at 9:00 movies. His painful inability at small talk, chitchat and what is now called interpersonal relationships fuel a thousand anecdotes. He seldom drinks, claims to have invented Perrier water and has the appetite of a hummingbird. He used to play drums in the Ottawa Press Gallery band and writes his books with ears encased in headphones blasting the esoteric rhythms of Stan Kenton. His journalistic infighting is often described as Byzantine. His personal affairs are sometimes tempestuous. And he makes—oh, sin—too much money.

One day in the autumn of 1975, when he was about to morph

stately old *Maclean's* into a newsmagazine, Newman sent a letter across the mountains to me in Vancouver. In it he offered me "a job of your choice." I flew down to Toronto to have a chat. I told him I couldn't move, for family reasons, to dreaded Central Canada but would do a national column for him from Vancouver. He immediately called in his senior editors to sound them out on the idea.

Managing editor Walter Stewart, an old friend, said "No frigging way. You can't cover Canada from Lotus Land." Newman went around the table, never saying a word himself. Three, four of them—all of whom I knew well—said the same, regretful thing: it would be impossible to write, from the Wet Coast, a column on national affairs.

Newman, puffing on his pipe as usual, listened in silence and then spoke. "You're all wrong," he said. "It may not be a national column, but it will be a Fotheringham column. Allan, please file your first column next week."

I sent off my first epic for the October 6, 1975, debut, and rushed out to the newsstand on Tuesday morning, when the mag arrived in Vancouver. A man of small ego, I instinctively turned to the opening pages, expecting my brilliant opus to be on page two, if not three. It wasn't there. I leafed through the mag with sinking fear; it wasn't in the first twenty pages. Nor the next twenty.

Crushed in the realization that my first effort had been rejected, I finally—completely deflated—turned to the last page, there to find my orphaned piece. It turned out to be the most inspired positioning ever in Canadian journalism. There isn't a self-respecting journalist in Canada today who wouldn't give his left one for that spot.

History will better judge the most controversial editor of his day. What is overlooked in the most gossipy trade of all is that Newman refashioned journalism in this country. As a privileged child in Czechoslovakia who saw it all go down in the Nazi sickness, he sees Canada's potential more than those of our complacent bent who were born here. He is not so much a journalist as a propagandist. He has used his magazine to push his causes—as perhaps you and I would, though in more subtle ways. He pushes because he cares, passionately, as converts always do.

The man changed the face of political reporting in this country and is in large part responsible for reviving Canadian magazines. He cares about what he believes in.

**NICHOLS, MARJORIE** Marjorie Nichols, the immensely talented, immensely troubled Ottawa journalist who died too early at the age of forty-eight, was one of my two best friends in life.

Marjorie was dying of cancer—perhaps knew it, valiantly fought it off for three years—the inevitable result for someone who, like her friend Jack Webster, once used to smoke five packs a day.

When her lung cancer was discovered in early 1988, she said "It's not fair. I got the alcoholism. Why couldn't have Webster got the cancer?"

She was the only person I have ever met who was, congenitally, incapable of uttering a single sentence without there being within it some wit, some nuance, some pun, some innuendo—arms thrashing, rage on her face, all body language, all energy.

Here's Marj-Parge at her best, on "why we have such cruddy contemporary reporting. Reporters today think that scandal-mongering is journalism. They're wrong. The art of journalism is the art of synopsis, and that art form has been lost. It's sort of like stone carving. Cave wall painting. It's gone. What's happening now is that you don't have to have information pass through your brain to be a reporter. All you have to do is have a tape recorder and a long arm." Pure rage. Pure Marj.

She fought, it turns out, all her life with her father, an American wealthy, on his land outside Red Deer, Alberta. She was so wild as a child she went to live with her nearby grandmother, a lady she adored.

She did everything in excess. Holder of Canadian speed-skating records as a teenager, touring Europe in meets against the Russians.

In a profession that produced characters in a casual stream, she became one at a tender age, and a top journalist as well. It is not only that she established an Ottawa reputation despite the fact she was published farther from the capital than any other columnist, and the Vancouver *Sun* naturally is not seen in Ottawa on a that-day basis. It is not just that she was the only woman columnist and the best woman journalist on Parliament Hill; at thirty-three she was the youngest national columnist among Ottawa heavyweights that included Geoff Stevens of the *Globe and Mail*, Charles Lynch of Southam, Doug Fisher of the *Toronto Star* syndicate and Richard Gwyn of the *Toronto Star*.

One day, on the ferry to Vancouver Island, B.C. Premier Bill Bennett felt a plop on his thinning hair and reached up to discover the worst: a seagull's revenge. He gazed aloft and said to a companion, "I didn't know Marjorie Nichols was flying to Victoria today."

She was never a frail flower, we can assure you.

**NIXON, RICHARD** A man who has seen the twenty-fifth anniversary of Watergate marvels, in retrospect, at Richard Nixon's supreme contempt for his country. The power and dignity of the capital meant nothing to him; he placed above it a "second-rate burglary" and lied and corrupted the highest office in the land for two years while slipping and sliding in grime. He cared nothing for America when you think about it. He cared only for Richard Milhous Nixon.

Well, he ain't done bad. The man who had less than $500 in his chequing account on the day of his resignation is now a millionaire. He lives in a fifteen-room, $1-million mansion among other millionaires in a plush retreat in New Jersey, across the Hudson from Manhattan. He still gets $119,000 in pensions and $300,000 in government expenses. He still has his Secret Service guards, who drive him to his Wall Street office every day.

He was Tricky Dicky when he started out in politics in California, smearing an opponent with allegations about being a Red, and he never changed. That unctuous smile reeked of insincerity, and his insensitivity, on leaving the White House by helicopter that August day in 1974, had him holding his fingers aloft in the "victory" salute. In effect, it was his own version of the uplifted index finger.

**NOVA SCOTIA** Johnny Carson, the noted one-liner, is an expert on tennis and alimony. He plays hard at both. He attends Wimbledon every year and, during a break in play, a television commentator asked him, if he could do it all over again, whether he would like to return in life as a tennis pro. "Actually," replied Carson, "I'd like to come back as a divorce lawyer." Well, when I am reincarnated, I want to come back as a paint salesman in Nova Scotia.

It would seem to me the easiest route to becoming a millionaire. Everybody in Nova Scotia, it strikes me, paints their house at least once a year. One reads incessantly about how poor and destitute are the Atlantic provinces. Perhaps, but if so, the last dollar seems to go to paint. White clapboard, blue clapboard, green clapboard, occasionally purple clapboard. But always clean and, it seems, painted just yesterday. Oh, for that salesman's job.

Your faithful researcher is always being assaulted by good down-east types who complain that this space devotes little attention to their region. This is true, mainly because I know nothing (as with most Canadians) about the area. My total knowledge of the Atlantic provinces covers a dinner table surrounded by Richard Hatfield, Dalton Camp and Finlay MacDonald, with time out for a half-hour sprint around Mike Duffy, along with brief acquaintance with a terrible gang of ruffians at a fishing club in St. John's, Newfoundland. This is not an extensive body of knowledge.

One of the great assets of Nova Scotia is the high price of electricity. One can drive for miles and miles in the peaceful country and never see a neon sign uglifying small towns. The newspapers are dreadful, and K. C. Irving owns everything, a circumstance that may be more than coincidence.

The proper summer drink to request, this being Nova Scotia, is dark rum and soda. Visitors, this being work-ethic Nova Scotia, are forced to sing for their supper. This consists of digging in the garden. No one makes any money in Nova Scotia, but everyone is made to work. This is most puzzling, since no one in Toronto works much, but everyone makes money.

I suppose this is why Confederation works.

**O**LIVER, **C**RAIG There are, as we know, highly endangered species on the planet Earth. There is the duck-billed platypus. And the three-toed wombat. There is the honest public relations man. Not to mention the politician who knows how to make a twenty-minute speech. Most rare, however, is the Fiftyish Professional Bachelor, a cherished specimen that should be preserved in aspic and—as anthropologists of sexology will attest—must be mourned when it passes from existence.

There was one such passing in December 1988 with the demise of one of the flowers of the breed. Craig Oliver, the burbling presence of *Canada AM* and CTV Ottawa bureau chief, bit the dust. Went to his fate. Walked down the aisle, thereby cancelling bets in every press club in Canada, astonishing not only himself but his bride and her parents, who had almost given up hope.

Those of us who attended the fateful ceremonies (mainly worried about our bets) applauded the nervous groom's final ability to chew the bullet. It was Dr. Johnson who said the definition of a second marriage was the triumph of hope over experience, but Craig, white of face in terror, marched into the teeth of hell with good humour, knowing that the honest dollars of our transcontinental bets rested with him.

My favourite Craig Oliver story (of which there are a thousand) is when he was a young radio announcer in Prince Rupert, from whence he whelped. His mother, who was then driving a taxi, was cruising the docks one day when up pulls this humongous white yacht and, staggering down the gangplank, come who else but Bing Crosby and Phil Harris. They went up the B.C. coast every summer, salmon fishing.

Craig's mother waltzed them around on their chores, the liquor store and other vital matters, and allowed to them that her tender little boy worked at the local station and if they dropped by, pretending to know him, it would speed his progress to stardom. Of course, said the besotted Hollywood twosome. They walked into the station and the station's staff goes mouth agape. Guess what? It is Craig's day off. "It took me five more years to get out of that God-damned town," he remembers.

His father once gave him some very good advice. It was that whenever he sat down to a poker game, look around, because there was always one sucker at the table. If he couldn't pick him out, get up and walk away—he was obviously the sucker.

**ONTARIO** One evening back in 1981, Dr. Stuart Smith, the highly intelligent leader of the Ontario Liberal party, delivered an impromptu, searing message from the soul to a clutch of fellow Liberals in the basement of a motor hotel in suburban Winnipeg. I upped to him afterwards and said, in admiration, that if he talked like that at home he would be premier of Ontario. He snorted at my ignorance. "If I talked like that at home," he said, "I'd lose my own seat." As someone raised in Quebec, he had always thought that to be "passionate" was a compliment—a person who felt strongly, who was eager and had energy. In Ontario, he found to his eventual sorrow, a "passionate" individual was regarded as slightly unbalanced, demented, if not deranged. "I've only just learned this," he explained. "And I'm a psychiatrist."

Ontario takes itself very seriously, as we know, viewing itself as the brood mare from which all Canada flows. The province still sucks its collective thumb, feeling the universe revolve around it, seeing those without its borders as lesser breeds who have never glimpsed the glories of a forty-seven-car pileup on the 401. Residents of Ontario feel superior for the obvious reason that all the banks are now located there (all but one in bloodless towers that have all the imagination of a vice president's eyes). Since banks are the soul of Canadian life, and the skyline of Toronto proves it, Ontario takes heavily its responsibility of being the Canadian leader in dullness.

The interesting point in this age of illusion is that Ontario is living a myth. It is the myth that Ontario, the province with the money and power (Alberta has more money, but no power), can proceed with the shifting principles of Brampton Billy or Mike Harris.

It's Alberta East now, sitting on Lake Ontario, taking its lead from the Klein revolution on the bald Prairie. Toronto, no longer the leader, is now the follower, aping its rural cousins. Winston's, mark my words, will have to install spittoons.

The triumph of the "Common Sense Revolution" of course was remarkable for its lack of common sense. People, known as voters, will believe anything, even if it is baloney—because baloney is a substitute for the real thing, as any student of salami knows.

It is entirely appropriate that the premier of the biggest and most confused province of all is a former golf pro and proprietor of a ski hill. This is what angry white guys like to do—play golf with other angry white guys all day Saturday and sit in the bar on the slopes to watch the ski bunnies. Ain't gonna find any of them welfare mothers in a painted-on ski outfit.

The reason Toronto is confused is because it no longer controls its own fate. Those who sit in the Albany Club—where they still show visitors the framed luncheon bills rung up by Sir John A.— those who dine at the Toronto Club and the York Club have fathomed that their fate now rests in Markham, where a tree has yet to sprout, and tackily named compounds on the suburban fringe where the votes are. The voters who put Mike Harris in power now number some 2.5 million in the suburban fringes that in a half-moon umbrella pin Toronto to its lake.

A few years back your blushing agent was asked to get on his hind legs and give a speech in London, Ontario, that hide-bound bastion of insurance companies and Holiday Inns. Unwisely, an acceptance was transmitted, mainly because I had never seen this strange medieval redoubt and was curious about the elements that make up the mind-set of the southwestern Ontario denizen.

The voters of Ontario, you must understand, are not voters like any others. They move like fudge. Caution is their password. Careful is their motto. Someone once asked Bill Davis why he was so bland. "Because it works," he replied. Ontario is writ bland, a large lump of conservatism that views with some wonder the experimental things going on in more venturesome provinces. It was the Prairies that invented the reform parties, the United Farmers sending MPs to alien Ottawa aeons ago. The Regina Manifesto created the first federal socialist party and Regina later provided the first socialist provincial government.

The three-humped camel called Social Credit was spawned in Alberta and spilled into British Columbia, where it still breathes, if faintly. Quebec can flirt with separatism and social democracy and even Farley Mowat, if you can believe the twits of U.S. immigration, has a Newfoundland Revolutionary Party—armed with one rifle. None of it touches Ontario, which could never be mistaken as the land of the rave and the home of the spree.

- See also "Davis, Bill" and "Harris, Mike."
- See also "Ottawa" and "Toronto."

**ORR, BOBBY** The most interesting thing about Bobby Orr is that, like all great artists who have inherited powers not their own, talents that they can summon but not fathom, he can always show something new.

He was at the Pacific Coliseum in Vancouver one night, the second time in the 1971 season, playing with the casual insolence of someone who, at twenty-two, knew he was the finest player on the finest hockey club alive. By closing one's eyes slightly to induce a blur, there was the impression of a group of men playing floor hockey on foot, with one casual figure floating about on roller skates. On the ice he seemed to play a private little game of his own, with his own puck—while all around him, friend and foe, struggled in another arena.

The attraction of hockey is that men, with artificial aids added to their feet, are transformed into different beings. They are indeed *super*men in the fantasies of the audience, given a speed that is allowed to no other performers in sport. The artificial surface lends a grace to their movements that is denied foot-bound traffic in all other sports—even dance.

There is the violence that sedentary American audiences seem to need in their pro football, plus the primitive grace of the rough people who populate the rough small towns of rough, untamed Canada. The patrons who packed the Vancouver Coliseum even to watch a last-place club play equally inept expansion opponents, *relate*, because for the most part they are from those same small towns across the country.

In the final period, frustrated at the clutching tactics lesser players employ to drag the great ones down to their level, Orr lashed out at a Vancouver player who had pinned him against the boards, and was penalized. A strange thing happened. As he skated slowly to the penalty box, there was a tentative wave of boos, then more confident ones, until all joined in with a relieved, cathartic enthusiasm. His brilliance had been too much to abide. It was grateful acceptance of the fact that at least rules could tame him, where mere men couldn't.

For the rest of the evening the audience, bolstered by confidence when dealing with genius, lustily booed him to the rafters whenever he touched the puck. Someone had belled the cat and now it was safe to decry his uncommon talents. Unfortunately, the same bravery did not apply on ice. Near the end, with Vancouver easily deserving a win, he made a rink-length rush and danced about unopposed, his aura going before him and protecting him.

As if a magic circle enclosed him, both opponents and colleagues backed away to let him, in his own serene privacy, blast in a slapshot that unfairly tied the game. No one dared intrude on the territory of a god.

• See also "Gretzky, Wayne" and "hockey."

**OTTAWA (ALSO *ENNUI-ON-THE-RIDEAU*)** It happens as soon as you get off the plane and enter the Ottawa airport terminal. It hits me in the face each time as surely as if it were a tepid face cloth. It is the miasma of Ottawa. My blood congeals, my heart sinks, my pulse rate slows, a melancholy lassitude overcomes me. I know, sadly, that once again I have been immersed in the all-pervading blahs of the capital of the country. Ottawa, the town that fun forgot.

You may think I exaggerate, but most all other refugees from the outside world report the same symptoms. There is something about the town—the atmosphere, the people, the palpable feel to the air—that is discouraging, that is disheartening. If you wish to understand why the government that governs you doesn't govern very well, you have to understand the dismal backwater that is Ottawa. The main problem, of course, is its isolation from reality. That very quality is endemic to the mind of the civil servant, as we know, but silly Queen Victoria reinforced it by perversely plunking the capital down in a spot on the globe where no one really wants to go and no sensible soul would stay.

The Europeans, not being beset by overly democratic urges, know better. Rome. Paris. The MP in London, who emerging from Westminster has to fight for a subway seat or a taxi along with the ordinary unwashed, gets a sense of the ordinary daytime struggles of the ordinary taxpayer.

The Ottawa MP or swivel servant—recipient of the most richly endowed-thanks-to-taxpayers city in Canada—has no daily reminder of how most Canadians live. Our own little Ennui-on-the-Rideau is a capital out of touch with the land it is designed to serve.

The problem with Ottawa is that it is inhabited by only three types of people: civil servants, who have no interests; politicians, who have no principles; and journalists, who have no manners. They all talk about the same things, the same gossip, the same stale speculation, the same jokes. They drink their own bath water so much their innards, not to mention their thought processes, grow rusty. After about three straight days in Ottawa I tend to develop the yin-yangs, a condition brought about by running into

my own rumours that I started several days previously.
In Ottawa you continually bump into yourself coming around
the corner.

The place is impervious to outside influence. None of the
verve of Montreal, only 120 miles away, seeps through. None of
the grasping voraciousness of Toronto. Ottawa has a cachet all its
own. Every place in town seems just too far to walk but not far
enough for a cab. The Sparks Street mall, a brave idea, is lined
with second-rate restaurants. There are no decent shops, as every
guilt-ridden conventioneer trying to buy a salving gift for wifey
has discovered.

Ottawa, allegedly a city, is in fact a theme park to amuse and
coddle those who live there. No other jurisdiction in the land has
such a surplus of pleasant park space, bicycle paths, jogging paths,
cross-country skiing tracks, the world's longest (and free) skating
rink, swimming pools, tennis courts, squash, canoeing, the
National Arts Centre, two superb new museums. In short, everything needed for upper-middle-class white-collar people who are
subsidized by the rest of Canada.

The sad fact is that none of its material cushiness has
improved the personality of the town. It has resulted only in a
more expensive type of dullard, even more smugly reluctant to
stray once one's nose is securely in the public trough. There's no
flux, no movement. If you leave the press, you move into government flackery. If you are defeated at the polls you are fixed up
with a job.

At the base of Ottawa's dullness is the beastly weather. The
village that aspires to be a city is at the mercy of nature in mid-
winter; the swirling snow making visibility difficult. One moves
about the town by Braille, guided only by the knobs on the foreheads of the most prominent deputy ministers. The snow along

the streets is a deep grey, resembling the hue of the government's policies. Only in Rockcliffe is the snow a pristine white, since the high mandarins who live there all drive non-leaded Volvos and actually prefer to arrive at what is laughingly called work by cross-country skis to separate themselves from the common herd.

In summer, thanks to Queen Victoria's genius in picking a swampy area at the junction of the Gatineau, Rideau and Ottawa rivers, where mosquitoes can breed unmolested, an oppressive blanket of moist air hangs over the city. Mandarins keep fresh shirts in the desk drawer so they can remain kissin' sweet until cocktail hour.

Frigid in the winter (second-coldest capital in the world next to Ulan Bator—you can look it up) and sweltering in the summer, it is no place for a grown man to make a decision.

• See also "Parliament."

**O XYMORON** Progressive Conservative.

• See also "Tories."

**PAPER WARS** Richard Gwyn, the veteran *Toronto Star* columnist, recently made a trip to his native England after a long absence. He came to an astonishing conclusion, after reading for several weeks London's ten national dailies, that Toronto and Canadian newspaper readers are getting better quality than Fleet Street.

The increased quality and readability of Toronto's press is, of course, due to the Paper Wars. The city has now four ferociously battling papers—two of them fighting for the national market. It's nonsense, naturally; New York, with three times the population of Toronto, is now down to three papers.

Toronto cannot last with four, but it's fun for the reader—while it continues. (This scribbler, as can be imagined, operates with a clear conflict of interest in this commentary, being a writer for one of the four.)

The Paper Wars have been fuelled by Lord Almost, Conrad Black, the Don Quixote of millionaires. His birthing of a national paper—a very good paper—set off a duel that will end, as always, with one death.

There is, you see (my patron), the paper-of-record, the *Globe and Mail*, fondly known as the Mop and Pail, or the Grope and Flail. There is Conrad's invention, the *National Post*, fondly known as the National Pest. The one thing that is known is that any Toronto businessman who tries to read both papers will not get to work until 11 a.m.

The reason readers are served better, as Gwyn knows, is that the threat of the Pest has made the *Globe* a better paper, shaken out of its superior attitude. And the Pest is invigorated, knowing that it has become a threat.

There is the *Toronto Star*, the largest circulation in the land only because Hogtown women buy it for its ads, looking for bargains. It no longer has Pierre Berton or Ron Haggart as a "must-read" columnist, save for those readers who love the language and have Dalton Camp, the best stylist still. It is going sideways.

In some trouble is the tabloid Toronto *Sun*, with its double-breasted daily Page 3 Girl. It has lost its best feature, Christie Blatchford, to the *Post*, who writes longer than a Florida court judgment and fascinates women by laying out in every column every single personal emotion she can confess. Another prominent columnist (ahem) has fled lately.

Most pertinent to those of us keeping our heads down in the trenches is the advent of corporate owners. BCE, which took over CTV, will control the *Globe*. Izzy Asper's CanWest empire now owns fifty per cent of the Pest—Conrad, while wanting to dictate Canada's future, now no longer wants to own all of it.

Neither BCE, nor Izzy, one suggests, will abide forever their mutual debts while chasing the same advertising dollar. Just as Canada is too small to support two national airlines, it (i.e., the Toronto advertising market) is too small to support two national papers.

All I know is that in two to three years there will once again be just one national newspaper, one of the duellists having surrendered. Most likely the *Post* will revert to a fine national Sunday newspaper like the Sunday *Times of London*—badly needed—or go back to its roots as a daily financial paper, as is the *Wall Street Journal*.

The *Globe* will survive, supreme again. I am, as is obvious, completely objective.

**PARIZEAU, JACQUES** The rain in Spain stays mainly on the plain. The delusion in Canada for many years resided mainly in the brain of Jolly Jacques Parizeau, the man with the belly of a banker and the chortle of a pub keeper. He has become a victim of his own propaganda, a man walking around in a vacuum of his own creation.

Jacques Parizeau is a delightful man to view. Highly educated, with an Oxford accent and a vocabulary that would put most Canadians to shame, he has the certainty of an economist—an economist once being defined as someone who is good at numbers but doesn't have the personality to be an accountant.

Some think of him as looking like the villain in a French movie: the drooping moustache, the heavy-lidded eyes, the ponderous speech. A shrewd letter-to-the-editor gets it more right—with his ample girth and ponderous manner he is Jackie Gleason, caricaturing himself in *The Honeymooners*. He is a joy to watch, almost as entertaining as the man he will never match, René Lévesque—now almost a saint in his province.

He is not as cuddly as Lévesque was, but being a trained economist was thought of as having a steel-trap financial mind that could leap complicated constitutional questions in a single bound, and was considered likely to be a more formidable foe.

Where was the grand vision? The mighty declaration of an independent state? Turns out he wanted training wheels instead. He wanted to keep the Canadian currency. He wanted to keep the Canadian passport.

In essence, what the Rotund René wanted was to turn Quebec

into a Puerto Rico, a piece of flotsam in the American currency stream, with no powers of its own to control its own money supply.

Parizeau's fear of asking a simple Yes or No question on separation was natural. He was stunned into incomprehension on election night in December 1994 when the number of voters came within a nanosecond of his own followers. He was so stunned, his wife wrote most of his "victory" speech.

After that, he was treading water, a dangerous activity for such a large man.

Jacques Parizeau, as it turns out, was simply a fatter René Lévesque. In his great scheme to put Quebec in the UN General Assembly along with Chad, he revealed himself—boring, boring— as another true believer in divorce with bed privileges.

One wonders what the doorman at the UN building on the East River in Manhattan would do when the new President of the Republic of Quebec turns up and shows as his credentials a blue Canadian passport that bears on its cover the Canadian coat of arms and "a mari usque ad mare" (from Rimouski to Hull?) and states: "The bearer of this passport is a Canadian citizen." How is the guy going to find a seat?

Oh dear. Jolly Jacques was a confused man. Because he thinks the numbers work—that Quebec has the resources, the smarts to be a new Sweden—it can automatically become so. Because he was a civil servant before stumbling into politics, he thinks only financial logic matters. He doesn't know passion, he doesn't know patriotism, he doesn't know love—all of that coming from the TROC he doesn't understand.

**PARLIAMENT** It was Dalton Camp, the sage of Jemseg, New Brunswick, who pointed out that if mastery of the procedural mumbo-jumbo of the Commons was the criterion of success in this country, Stanley Knowles would have been our prime minister long ago. Learning the arcane rules of parliamentary procedure and grasping the petty little debating tricks is rather like learning to ride a bicycle, Camp pointed out. It seems unnerving and devilishly tricky to the youthful novice but, once learned, is something you never unlearn. Lester Pearson never could get very interested in the nuances of this once-important chamber, which on too many days resembles the cafeteria of a boys' private school when they start throwing the cake and the overdone roast beef. He was sheltered by the trickery of such as Jack Pickersgill and Paul Martin Sr., who found their Peter Principle at that level.

Show me a man who is truly obsessed with the parliamentary pea-shell game and I will show you a man who fails to become leader. John Diefenbaker thought the world started and ended in that chamber but he could not organize his own office, let alone his lunch. Joe Clark came tumbling down because he was pitifully uncomfortable in any area of the realm except in that confined space. Pierre Trudeau was clearly bored by it. Mulroney knew instinctively how far the Commons (and Ottawa in general) has fallen in public respect over the years and the pettifoggers and nitpickers have turned it into the irrelevant institution he was accused of not mastering.

The thing about Ottawa, as you know, is that it suffers from a surfeit of talk. Talk and paper are the only products produced by the town that fun forgot. Verbal flatulence envelops the city like a thick layer of smog. Chaps who couldn't attract a crowd to a church basement in Wawa are allowed to stand on their hind legs in the House of Commons and emote on chicken subsidies to an extent that forces even their best friends to retire to their offices to watch Oprah on the square eye. The whole capital suffers from slack lips.

You see, I know this political person in Ottawa. She has seen it all. She knows who the bagmen are. She has been acquainted with prime ministers.

She is well aware, in both the House of Commons and the Senate, who are the drinkers and who are the womanizers. Her father was a politician himself and she grew up in the trade, cabinet ministers in the kitchen for breakfast, cheerful wives of high politicians blurting out their fears and frustrations.

She thinks she knows which of the inmates of the press gallery one can trust and those one cannot—there being ample supplies of both. She knows more than she tells. In other words, she knows where all the bodies are buried.

She has a theory, you see. It is a shrewd one, and probably true. The problem with Ottawa is that everyone there is tired. Walking zombies in the corridors of Parliament Hill. Strong men falling asleep in committee meetings. Guys in the back benches catching flies with their mouths open as they snore.

The reason for all this, she explains, is that the country is too big. Because it is too big, every otherwise intelligent legislator headed for Ottawa is zonked out by the time of arrival.

This is why, my political operative points out, there are a lot of really stupid comments coming out of MPs whose brains have been warped by too many free flights from too far away.

No MP from Ontario or Quebec knows what it does to the body—let alone to the cranium—when an otherwise sane individual has to travel half the length of Africa and then get off a plane and say something intelligible to a media scrum.

That is why (their brains scrambled) we have had one Reform MP from Alberta talking about studying caning in Singapore. And another from far-off Vancouver Island advising on how irritating minority types could be shipped to "the back of the shop" for fear of driving away customers. And another Reformer from Alberta agreeing with him, bringing down the wrath of poor Parson Manning, whose travels at 35,000 feet perhaps affected his voice box.

There was time for considered views in Ottawa when those from the bald Prairie and beyond went there by the iron horse. Splendid dining cars with silver service and lace, the calming clickety-clack of the rails inducing sleep, knitting up the ravelled sleeve of care. The MP arrived beside the Rideau a rested soul, his mind fully in gear.

No one seems to have noticed that Jean Chrétien, with a piece of plastic he never had in Shawinigan, travelled the world more in his first years as PM than the Jaw That Flew Like a Man, Brian Mulroney.

His grey matter is in permanent jet lag. We can't account for Sheila Copps's lengthy journeys to and from Hamilton, but that's another matter, involving aliens from outer space.

What goes on in the Commons the Canadian public regards as slightly above the phenomenon of mud-wrestling. The battle is being fought, and won, out there in the great ozone known as the mind of the Canadian public.

• See also "Ottawa."

**PAWLEY, HOWARD** A man so quiet you can hear the integrity tick.

**PEOPLE'S AIRLINE, THE**
• See "Air Canada."

**POLITICAL SUICIDE** It is, one would think, one of the more difficult recipes in the world to concoct. How does a government throw away a near landslide mandate—thirty-eight of fifty-five seats—in just three years? It takes real imagination to devise such efficient self-destruction. It is a remarkable feat, if one can manage it, because the voter—while not overly sophisticated, not stupendously intellectual—is essentially fair, being more tolerant than the carping press.

To demonstrate how tough it is to commit public suicide as quickly as the Dave Barrett government of British Columbia, there hasn't been a provincial regime since the war that disappeared so swiftly. The Dave Barrett brave new world of 1972–75 saw the art of kamikaze raised to perfection. The government fell on its own sword voluntarily: it willingly, willfully called an election with two full years to go on its mandate and cheerfully was swamped by the collection of feckless car dealers, undertakers, turncoat Liberals and claim-jumping Tories collected around the inexperienced Bill Bennett, a man who had been in politics only two years. In retrospect, it now seems so simple.

First of all, what you do if you are intent on jettisoning the position of ruling the most affluent portion of the world yet to vote in socialism is thumb your nose immediately at the bewildered voter. That means instantly doubling the salary of all members of the legislature. Next, as premier you surround yourself with a callow, shallow personal staff. As a man educated in the United States, you never had the chance to develop a network of university contacts, so you stick with old cronies, despite all the signs of impending doom, with the same crew that inspires only derision in the reporters who view their performance.

The public is allowed to get the impression that a genial air of carelessness abounds. There is swaggering locker-room mentality around some of the NDP cabinet that allows one female columnist to write that a certain minister "has more toothbrushes scattered around town than Squibbs."

When a $100 million overrun in welfare costs is discovered, you dismiss it at first as "a clerical error." The public, head spinning at the runoff of dollars, boggles and watches. To make sure the public gains the impression that a group of children are loose in the candy store, you quickly travel to Europe twice, to Japan, to China. The trade minister goes to Sweden, the resources minister to Belgium, the welfare minister to Israel, the consumer minister to Australia. (Of the caucus of thirty-eight, twenty-two crossed the oceans.)

Throughout it all, a steady stream of innovative legislation is produced—farmland frozen, consumer laws beefed up, pharmacare and mincome for the aged, a better return on forest royalties, protection of the family farm, better transit systems and the legal system streamlined. But no one bothers to explain it, the NDP being secure in its evangelistic fervour that the rightness of its actions will automatically shine through. To make sure the message does not get through, you foolishly tie yourself down in Victoria with a double portfolio—attempting to handle not only the premier's job but the finance post as well. It means that your party's best weapon—your communicative gifts and showmanship—is anchored to a desk.

Then to make the picture complete, you refuse to punish the casual incompetents who speckle the cabinet—the fumbling mines minister who moves his lips when he reads, the tense education minister whose hands shake when she attempts to face the press, the communications minister who won't answer questions in the House and grins instead. The social worker as premier: too loving to be able to cull the deadwood.

To make the suicide efficient and clean-cut, the election was called without waiting for redistribution which would have sliced up the bulky suburban ridings saturated with upwardly mobile NDP-haters. Even worse, Barrett did not wait for his election expenses act which would have shored up the other minority parties and put stiff curbs on the lavish Social Credit slush fund.

It was a most impressive kamikaze mission.

• See also "Barrett, Dave."

**POLITICS** The taunt comes often, to a columnist who makes a living by instructing, lecturing, hectoring and advising politicians how to do their job: "If you're so smart, why don't you run for politics?" The answer is always the same: "A journalist who wants to be a politician is like a jockey who wants to become a horse."

The essential ingredient of politics, of course, is hypocrisy. Grown men stand unblushing, facing cameras and microphones, mouthing words that would elicit soap from their mothers. They would never beat their children, kick dogs, or refuse an entreaty from the Salvation Army. But they regard it as perfectly respectable to damage the language, utter obvious untruths and still go home to a good meal with their consciences apparently unimpaired. It's a strange mental adjustment that would bother ordinary folk.

It reminds one of the old politician who announced to an election rally: "Those are my principles—and if you don't like them I've got other ones."

Men staggering from principle to principle, like drunks in a motel hallway, have been a noble feature of our politics from the start. Politicians fleeing across the floor in pursuit of greener grass, their justifications trailing behind them, have been around forever.

The reason Dalton Camp is so devastating in his critiques of Liberals is that he was once one himself, a vociferous one as a young man before he saw the light and converted. Was not Saul of Tarsus, now that you think of it, the first political convert on that road to Damascus? Dalton would love the analogy.

There was also Pliable, in Bunyan's *Pilgrim's Progress*, an untrustworthy neighbour of Christian's. He accompanies him as far as the

Slough of Despond, then backslides and deserts him. It has led, as you know, to the saying about a friend as reliable as Pliable.

Norm Atkins, the smartest backroom operator in Canadian politics says there are three things needed for an organization to win an election: "The first is friends. The second is friends. The third is policy."

The reason, it would seem to me, why columnists would make lousy politicians is that the whole philosophy of column-writing is the unassailable belief that the scribbler is right on everything. Never take a backward step. You gotta believe in what you believe.

All politics, or course, is the opposite: the art of compromise, the art of the possible. Compromise, prevarication, slow every-thing down, change tacks, reverse principles, make friends with your enemies if necessary, make enemies of your friends if required. It's not a bed for a journalist.

• See also "B.C. politics."

**POWER** "Power is the greatest aphrodisiac of all," said Henry Kissinger. Proof? There it was, seated like obedient schoolboys around the horseshoe table at the 1978 federal-provincial Conference on the Economic Plummet that was impinging on your afternoon soap-opera injection. Who would have suspected the lust that lurked beneath all those bland, barbered faces and safe, sincere suits? The ten premiers who would have represented us in all things, portrayers of the common man, were most uncommon in one field. They are enemies of Zero Population Growth, clear viola-tors of the 2.5 children norm. They crash through, those discreet guardians of our fiscal affairs, all the national averages on what constitutes the Canadian Bedroom Quota.

Look at them! Moores of Newfoundland: eight kids. Lyon of Manitoba: five. Regan of Nova Scotia: five more. Davis of Ontario:

five. Lougheed, Bennett, and Blakeney: four apiece. Even the laggards, Lévesque and Campbell, have three. (Mr. Trudeau, oldest of all the first ministers, and obviously shamed into catching up with his prolific juniors, had three in four years.) Even throwing in the bachelorhood of Hatfield of New Brunswick, this energetic ten averages a brood of 4.1, quite clearly men who establish as a group the validity of the Kissinger theorem. Power means progenitors.

Next time you sneer at politicians' inability to solve inflation, unemployment and foot itch, heed Dr. Kissinger's shrewd dictum.

**PRAIRIE, THE** The trees on the road west from Winnipeg are gold, stolen from the brush of Cézanne. The prairie at this time of year, suspended in Indian summer, is not dull and bland at all, but delicate and beautiful. A traveller on the road west, swallowing the miles between the glimpses of civilization, contemplates only one fey wish. It is that the stern intellects in the cabinet could travel this road just once to comprehend what distance means to the West.

In these fathomless miles, skies stretching to the horizon in all directions as if a Plexiglas bowl had been plunked down on this portion of mankind, is the basic Western Canadian belief in land and property and resources. Distance from one's neighbours creates a feel for the earth. Geography becomes a friend, not an enemy.

It is a concept not easily grasped by sophisticated men from tightly packed urban centres in Montreal or Toronto. The miles pound by, the dead porcupine by the road, the squished skunk, the small animals melded into the asphalt. In Central Canada, one gets on an airplane to travel short distances. Out here, one must travel the land. The argument over resources is between men who sit in offices and men who have a feeling for the earth.

The road dips and waves past Portage la Prairie. Towns called Sidney and Melbourne—how did they get here?—disappear behind. Carberry, Justice, Two Creeks. We miss Pope, Snowflake and Rapid City.

Outside Wapella, past Red Jacket, an object lesson thunders by. A fright train headed back east, its lengths and lengths of automobile carriers empty as it heads to Windsor and Oakville for its next load. One can almost imagine Peter Lougheed smiling. His point, exactly. Hewers of wood and drawers of water.

At Oakshela, the sky darkens, the wind that warns of approaching winter whips the loose soil from the fields, creating a Sahara dust cloud. The wind dies, the windshield reappears. The big trucks dominate the road creating their own slipstream and a shuddering blast of air as they thunder by, their jockeys perched on high, steering their rigs like captains at sea, a sea of stubble and hay that stretches as far as the eye can see. The tourists are gone, the swaying trailers fled safely south.

Another train heads by eastward, tank cars from Alberta Gas Chemicals, destined for distillation in the East rather than the West. One imagines Peter Lougheed's smile expanding to a smirk.

Summerberry goes by. Sintaluta. Peebles, Odessa and Kipling are left. Stockholm. Gerald and Esterhazy to the right. The farmers sit on their space-age machines, Technicolor in hue, five-figure in value, air-conditioned, tape deck in the earphones. There is no longer awe for men in vests in Ottawa offices that have double doors for security's sake.

The road reaches west. Outside Indian Head, a small airfield holds private planes for these newfound entrepreneurs and landholders who zoom away to the potash fields and, one suspects, Arizona. There is no inferiority complex left from the dust-bowl days. Only a sort of weary contempt—and sadness—those from less-changing surroundings who have no idea how once-colonial regions have changed.

## PROGRESSIVE CONSERVATIVE PARTY

## (ALSO *REGRESSIVE CONVERTIBLES*)

- See "Tories."

## PREMIERS

- See "power."

PRESS, THE The thing I worry about is the press. The arrogant, lovable, cheeky, oblivious, harum-scarum press. They are breeding too fast. They are dividing and multiplying like paramoecia. They dominate the events they are meant unobtrusively to cover. When the bit players outnumber the participants, you know something has gone scroogy.

The apogee of the art came at the Montreal Olympics when it was discovered there were 7,886 members of the trade present to cover 6,934 athletes. At the same time, in Madison Square Garden in New York, the 5,000 delegates and alternates to the Jimmy Carter love-in were outnumbered by 5,500 media types milling about in search of a new angle on Amy's lemonade stand. That may indeed be true journalistic democracy—a reporter going one-on-one against every delegate with a few left over to sleep off their hangovers—but one wonders if a bit more of the manpower and expense accounts might not be spent more fruitfully elsewhere.

The fact of the matter is that any large gathering these days, be it smoke-filled or sweat-stained, is a media event. Conventions are as much a gathering of the clan among journalists, who haven't seen each other for a year and have a need to exchange gossip, as they are among legitimate conventioneers. It becomes the celebration of one's self, the press itself more a participant than an observer, sucked into the process and often dominating it.

The paraphernalia of TV—both human and mechanical—is

such that it takes half an acre to accommodate the foot soldiers, stragglers, handmaidens and spaghetti entrails sufficient to put one cliché-encrusted commentator into your living room. The total creative output per body would not threaten a dachshund, but the carcasses clutter the view.

The point that those of us who practise the "black art" tend to ignore is that the public is getting exasperated with the mob scene that merely obscures their view and adds little to their perception.

The first chipping at the feet of clay was done in a sympathetic way, but it was nonetheless devastating. In The Boys on the Bus by Timothy Crouse, a day-by-day chronicle of how the working press covered the 1972 U.S. presidential campaign, the public got a readable, understandable explanation of how news decisions are made, of how pack journalism works, of how the boys waited to see how the Associated Press man played his lead, which ones drank, which ones were lazy, how the photographers always got the stewardae and other esoteric details they never taught you in journalism school.

Dr. John Porter, in his classic The Vertical Mosaic, laid down an indictment that unfortunately still applies, "There is, of course, nothing professional about the role of newspaper reporting."

The excessive numbers of scribes wouldn't be bad in itself if it bred diversity of opinion. It doesn't. It merely encourages mono-lithic thinking, group conclusions, herd clichés. It is journalism by press conference.

• See also "journalists."

**PRESS GALLERY, THE** One of the vast amusements of the Western world is sitting around conventions listening to some of the flaky resolutions that emanate from the foreheads of the semi-sozzled conventioneers, just in off the Greyhound. So there was a

great ripple of amusement rising from the press pews at the
Constellation Hotel in Toronto during a Liberal policy conference
at an idea that was designed to vault the Grits forward into the
post-Orwellian era.

The resolution, received heartily by the faithful on the hard
chairs, would see to it that the expense account elite of the Ottawa
press gallery be indentured, like some early bit actors out of *Roots*,
to serve several years in the boondocks of the nation. The scribes
to have their prejudices recycled, as it were.

A jolly good idea, as a matter of fact, with about as much
chance of achieving life as a conversion of the Liberals to a sincere
belief in freedom of information. The suggestion, naturally, caused
large merriment among the entrenched aristocrats of the gallery,
who grow nervous once outside an eighteen-mile circumference of
the parliamentary dining room's subsidized meals. It is impracti-
cal, of course, to separate the national press from the lair where
their sources are dug in. It is the same in any national capital—
London, Washington, Moscow—the journalistic cognoscenti piled
on top of one another in a degree of incest surpassed previously
only by some of the nestings among Kentucky hillbillies. (In such
Dogpatch surroundings, the products of incest often emerge with
six fingers or three toes. In the journalistic variety the product is
interchangeable copy born from self-induced rumours.)

What makes Canada different (and what arouses such resentment in the delegates from the deep bush) is that in other such
lands the national capital at least is a major, civilized centre. But
Ottawa is such an ingrown repository of middle-class minds that
the national press, perforce, is off in one insulated backwater, safe
from the ferment of what is really going on amongst the
unwashed taxpayers. It is as if the U.S. capital were in Terre Haute,
the British one in Bognor Regis, the Russian one in Omsk. No

wonder the goofy resolutions on a compulsory press Ferris wheel spring from the paranoia of the Liberal mind.

• See also "Ottawa."

**PRINCE EDWARD ISLAND** The most valuable advice any mother can give to any daughter is an age-old one: never go to a party on an island. Mothers know best. The floating, away-from-reality aspect of an island reduces inhibitions, tosses away caution, sweeps away sweet care. It's why more mischief is achieved on ocean liners and yachts and cruises than would ever be attempted on dull old terra firma. Islands are sort of like boats. Strange things happen on them.

This certitude is offered for the benefit of the good burghers of Prince Edward Island, the sand dune in the Gulf of St. Lawrence that passes for a province. When they were enmeshed in their punch-up about a fixed link to the rest of the world—otherwise known as New Brunswick, my advice was: Don't do it, guys. You will lose your floating qualities, which are the main reason we love you. Canada's theme park can't remain a theme park if you're linked to us permanently with an asphalt umbilical cord that would allow any common camper van to violate your isolation. As the only virgin province left, we have a concern about your sanctity. Beware.

Off Chester, in Nova Scotia, there are islands that are right out of William Faulkner novels, six thumbs and all. The most individualistic people in Canada live in Newfoundland, a rock that is covered with six inches of topsoil and—fortunately—will never be connected by a fixed link to anything.

One need not even mention Blighty, the Tight Little Isle best illustrated by the famous Fleet Street headline in one of Lord Beaverbrook's papers: "Blizzard Over Channel/Continent Isolated."

The Brits have preserved their kinky eccentricity because of their failure to be inoculated by the bloodstream of other cultures. Prince Edward Island has had the same advantage ever since the chaps in funny hairstyles and coats whelped this pup of a nation into being barely a century ago on Island soil. It has done quite well on its own ever since, producing hardly a hubcap stealer, a major drug dealer or a french-fry franchise, its only blight on the land being the manufacturer of Mike Duffy.

One can see no real good coming out of any link to what is laughingly called reality.

**QUEBEC** On a May weekend in 1980, in the garden restaurant of the Ritz-Carlton, just opened for the late-blooming spring that always astounds a Vancouverite, the white ducks swim endless circles in a pond on the lawn. They are plunked in each spring, idle away the summer, presumably ordered for dinner each fall by the patrons who have watched their mindless paddling. The luckless ducks are somewhat like the beaten-upon Quebec voter.

The chambermaid in the hotel rushes about, apologizing because, as she explains, she must get to the polling booth on time.

The next morning, she is asked if the result pleases her.

"Oh yes," she beams, "I've never told anyone before how I vote. But I was so sorry for Mr. Lévesque. He cried, you know."

This is the province where politics, which means life here, is taken seriously.

A record eighty-three per cent of eligible voters took the trouble to struggle out to the polls on a Tuesday to decide their fate— which only barely beat the previous mark that showed up on November 15, 1976, to elect the first avowedly separatist government.

Still and all, the percentage of Quebec voters who cast ballots is the highest in the country—by most marked contrast with the thirty-five–forty per cent who turn out to elect the most powerful man in the world in the most powerful nation in history to the south of us.

Quebec (unlike the United States), knowing its future rests in the ballot box, takes care to care—and shows up.

As the old town, slumped in exhaustion, tries to recover its equilibrium from the emotional drain of the referendum drama, already the headlines scream about the coming provincial election. The ducks, due to be encased in orange sauce on a silver platter by the fall of leaves, don't know how lucky they are.

• See also "Referendum."

**QUEEN ELIZABETH** I remember it well. Seated on a 1939 curb in Regina (or was it Moose Jaw?) waiting for jiggling hours for a glimpse of King George and his Queen and those glistening, sweating RCMP horses, an address tag around my neck directing the finder to ship me to Mother should I go astray—or run away to become an apprentice footman. Some forty years later and through the magic of the electronic revolution (CTV's Lloyd Robertson doing the commentary for the CBC) I watched the spectacular Silver Jubilee homages to that man's daughter, Queen Elizabeth, who has devoted her life unstintingly to the mind-numbing chores of keeping the monarchy credible and alive.

She is a fine, fine woman, doing a magnificent job of being Queen, but she is not mine. She belongs to Britain, and they currently need her. (I live in Canada, with its own few small problems, and what my country does not need is a foreign queen.)

I have seen the Queen at work, I suspect, somewhat more than most Canadians. I saw her in a Cardiff stadium the day she made the surprise announcement that her son would henceforth assume the title Prince of Wales, and the Welsh, with those voices that send a tingle up an unsentimental Canadian spine, spontaneously broke into the singing of "God Bless the Prince of Wales," some 40,000 voices sending shivers across the Rhondda Valley hills. I watched her at close hand at various chores in Australia, all around London, on periodic jaunts to Canada, and viewed the polite disinterest of the Québécois (the faint, small cheering on her careful forays around Montreal came from little anglophone ladies). It is because I have watched her in so many venues that I admire her so much.

There is a misconception that Good Queen Bess is stubbornly sticking to her crown and selfishly won't give it up to the resolutely underemployed Prince Charles. We are here to disabuse you. In 1981, your agent, for his sins, was ordered to cover the Cinderella wedding of the Virgin Di and the chap with the large ears. I sat some fifty feet from the fairy-tale ceremonies in St. Paul's Cathedral and was struck most of all by one overriding image. It was the glum and sorrowful look on the face of the mother of the bridegroom.

One would have thought—all London aflame with a party passion understandable in a people who lead such dreary lives—that the Queen would be beaming with pride. She wasn't. She looked unhappy. We have shared a glass or two at the off-the-record press receptions on the royal yacht, and, at the time, your blushing republican was struck by (a) her daintiness; (b) the fact she is more attractive in person than in pictures; (c) her understated wit that borders on withering.

Implicit in that was a good humour. The good humour had disappeared by the time of St. Paul's Cathedral. She has never smiled since. The reason she has never smiled since is that, as she gazed at the altar and the fairy-tale wedding, she knew within herself that her son probably would be an old and tired and discouraged man before he ever acceded to the throne she would like to give up.

She would like to, but she's decided she can't. Because of the past, and because of the present conduct of her offspring, she's been advised by her Buckingham Palace advisers that she has to stay, for the survival of the monarchy.

The past of course was her selfish uncle, the Prince of Wales, who abandoned the throne for the conniving and much-married Wallis Simpson—and spent the rest of his life wandering in exile, a pitiful figure. Good Queen Bess can never forgive her uncle Edward for that: the abdication forced her shy father, who didn't want the job, to become king, a task that killed him—and therefore ruined the youth of a twenty-five-year-old bride who had to accept a heavy crown.

If King Edward can junk the job for love, can Elizabeth now do it because she's old? And wants her long-impatient son to have it? Nope. The dangerous precedent cannot be repeated. It's too fragile a myth as it is. The crown is not something you can abandon, willy-nilly, as the coinage would be debased. It's not a job, it's a calling—a lifetime calling.

Little wonder the moody Prince Charles is reduced to talking to flowers and wandering the Scottish woods in his kilt. His mother is past sixty-five and certainly not infirm. The genes are in the family. The Queen Mum is 114 or something and still going strong, with the pearls, the corgis and the gin. He's over fifty and could hit retirement age before his coronation.

She knows the secret to his morose nature and how to lift it: hand him the crown. But she can't, won't, because it would destroy the myth. It's all high-class soap opera, and the British public loves to watch (while Canada is trying to grow up without it).

• See also "Diana, Princess" and "Royals, the."

**QUEEN MUM, THE** Everyone noticed, one trusts, that the Queen Mum visited Saskatchewan in 1985 when it was celebrating its 80th birthday. She was 85. A queen older than a province. Love it.

• See also "Queen Elizabeth."

**RAE, BOB** A young lady who used to date Bob Rae would tell that when he grew bored at parties he would retreat to a corner and stand on his head. That he would go on to do the same thing to accepted politics in this country is entirely appropriate.

In 1990, his Red Hordes have captured Bay Street. The faceless pinkos are in control of the heartland of Canadian capitalism, the richest and most populous province where John David Eaton and Conrad Black did once roam. There is clearly something wrong. When hated Ontario, once the home of the tight-assed WASP, goes for the Few Democrats, one knows that the world has gone wonky.

The press club wits used to sneer that the cerebral socialist was "born in a log embassy"—the inference being that the son of respected diplomat Saul Rae somehow couldn't be sincere, considering his family background in Geneva and elsewhere. The puzzling theorem that to be a socialist one perforce has to be poor carries with it the analogy that to be a conservative one has to be rich. Neither treatise obtains.

Rae's only sin is that he came from an interesting family. Brother John is a high executive in Power Corp. and, as such, the kingmaker behind Jean Chrétien's rise. Sister Jennifer was a celebrated beauty and charmer, a Pierre Trudeau date, in those 1968 days of Camelot-by-the-Rideau.

Premier Bob was a Rhodes scholar, as was that brief prime minister, John Turner. As was NDP icon David Lewis, father of Stephen Lewis. (When David Lewis applied for his Rhodes, the president of the CPR who was on the application committee asked him the first thing he would do if he ever became prime minister. "Nationalize the CPR," replied young David. He went to Oxford. I digress.)

Premier Bob, like the senior Lewis, could not restrain in his early days in Ottawa as an MP his gift for the searing line. He once said Pierre Trudeau "made Judas Iscariot look like a team player." It was more in the mode of the Oxford faculty lounge and made him appear rather too clever for the hurly-burly of the Commons.

He adores, above all things, to be banging away on the ivories at a late-night political party, making up satirical ditties about his opponents. He is also the only politician in the world who has tried to sell to Sony records a song he composed.

There are those of us who thought he was too impatient, and unwise, when he retreated to the Queen's Park leadership rather than wait for the Ed Broadbent retirement—he being the obvious dauphin at the time.

Such is life. Denied an eye-glazing chore as No. 3 in Ottawa, he went on to control the province that controls Canada.

**REAGAN, RONALD** I was on a plane one day in 1984, flying from Tedium to Boring with a stop at Lassitude, when I heard one American businessman talking to another about Ronnie Reagan. One was saying he had read that Reagan didn't work very hard at his job. "That's right," the second chap said, approvingly, "he's sort of like the Queen of England. He just sits up there above the battle and kind of supervises." It is as good a description as any of the old-fashioned man who had just been given such a vote of confidence by an American public unconcerned about his age, his casual work habits or his lack of grasp of detail or mundane facts. The voters simply liked what they saw, an uncomplicated guy with a few simple ideas who just kept repeating them over and over again.

One of the endangered species of our time is the politician. Meaning the traditional type who makes his living at the arcane art, who goes through the apprenticeship and works his way up the system, hoping for the top job finally. What he sees now rather confounds him. The president of the United States, the most powerful man on earth, is not a politician at all but an amateur imported from Hollywood. No hard slogging through the committee rooms, no learning the rules of the game. Bingo, the chap vaults in at the top.

It is, when you look at it, completely loony. The most vigorous and energetic country on earth elected as its boss a guy who would, within weeks of his seventy-eighth birthday, be at the end of his second term equal to the geriatric specimens that coughed through the Kremlin. Reagan overcame all such doubts. He grinned and he aw-shucked, he told stories about himself that, when you check the facts, don't add up, but he made people feel good.

Owner of the greatest landslide in U.S. electoral history, he grew angry and frustrated when he couldn't get his way. He was irritated because Congress wouldn't go along with his plan to ship more military aid to the Contra guerrillas in Nicaragua; so irritated that in a meeting with Republican leaders he banged the table with his fist and proclaimed, "We've got to get to where we can run a foreign policy without a committee of 535 telling us what to do."

The 535, of course, just happen to be the 435 members of the

House of Representatives and the 100 members of the Senate. In other words, the voters, in their fumblings toward wisdom, elected to keep a check on the president. This thing called democracy is a very cumbersome, inefficient thing.

All wild-eyed causes founder on their own excesses. All crazed ideologues eventually crash-land on their goofy extremities. The Reaganauts, with their supply-side economics, were going to remake our way of life. By cutting taxes for business and the upper classes, this was supposed to stimulate the economy so much that unemployment would be eradicated.

The great sin of our times was too much government, too many regulations, too many laws, too many restrictions that hampered the free individual from reaching his true potential and stretching to his financial limit. "Deregulation" was the Reagan litany.

We have seen the result. Some of Reagan's own disciples, irritated by the mere restrictions placed by Congress on monetary and military aid to certain foreign revolutionaries, decided to do their own deregulation. Colonel Ollie North and his cowboys in the White House basement took it upon themselves to privatize American foreign policy and found their own way around the law. Just as the Nixonites did, with a similar contempt for the dull elected people who sit in the House of Representatives and the Senate.

Wall Street took its signal from the same White House philosophy. What capitalism needed was less bothersome triflings from federal overseers. Washington cut down not only on the number of air-traffic controllers but stock-market checks.

The result? As could be predicted, the belief that greed is good for you.

In 1980, the year Reagan came to power, the urge to merge saw 1,889 companies acquired at a cost of $44 billion. By 1988 the takeover and merger mania had risen to 3,356 mergers, at a total value of $177 billion. As a result of the greed, eleven of the best and brightest of Wall Street investment bankers and lawyers were headed for jail. "It was like free sex," said one banker. No one was getting caught, "so the atmosphere grew relaxed."

The one thing Ronald Reagan is famous for in Washington is demanding complete loyalty from his underlings. He supported, without nitpicking, some rather dubious companions, including his attorney general, Edwin Meese III, who gave government jobs to those who helped him out of his financial problems, fudged on expense accounts and seemed puzzled, as the No. 1 law enforcement officer of the nation, about the definition of the word ethics.

When the rot sets in, it goes all through the tree, bottom to top.

**REFERENDUM (ALSO *SEPARENDUM*)** It was clever René Lévesque and his shrewd tacticians who vaulted the turtle, Claude Ryan, into the lead in the 1980 Separendum drama. With just a holiday weekend to go before the vital vote, it was clear the carefully orchestrated Parti Québécois strategy had backfired—with the No forces the beneficiaries (and Canada the grateful recipient).

By forcing all his opponents to unite uneasily under the No umbrella committee, Lévesque unwittingly forged a coalition that overcame the early PQ lead in the battle for the minds of the 4.2 million Quebec voters eligible to cast their opinions on the dog's breakfast called sovereignty-association.

That wasn't the plan, of course. The PQ strategy, laying down by law how the referendum debate was to be conducted, was that with just a single Yes umbrella group and a single No umbrella committee, the warring political forces against the PQ would tear themselves apart.

Could the lords of patronage of the federal Liberals bed with the born-again provincial Liberals, the dregs of Joe Clark's Tories, the refuse of Union Nationale, the funny-money showmen of the Creditistes?

It seemed most unlikely, a perfect formula for divide and conquer.

Instead? The PQ ploy bred, unwittingly, what may have been the most effective propaganda machine ever to march across Quebec. It was a remarkable sight, those phalanxes of the No forces fanning out over the province each day until their larynxes grew ragged with the abuse.

Lévesque, due to his remarkable feat of uniting all his enemies, was responsible for one of the more amazing sights of modern-day political life at a spine-tingling Trudeau-Ryan rally in the Paul Sauvé Arena in east-end Montreal, scene of that euphoric PQ election win on November 15, 1976.

On the stage, united behind the banner of the federalist option, were all the Quebec heavies of the Trudeau cabinet—Chrétien, Lalonde, Sauvé (what was the neutral Speaker doing there?), Fox, Ouellet, and whatever.

And also a dark-haired beauty who stood boldly in the packed stands in a red T-shirt that read: "Not tonight, René. I've got a headache."

A veteran CBC reporter, noting this was the finest Trudeau performance ever in twelve years, confided as the ear-splitting roar rolled down from the sweating throng, "It's the speech that he entered politics to make."

"I'll tell you this," said one passionate No campaigner after the Paul Sauvé audience blistered out an opening and closing "O Canada" that would make any anglophone weep with shame, "never again will 'O Canada' in French be booed in Calgary or Toronto. If it is, I'll throw the first bomb."

• See also "Quebec."

**REGINA** It may surprise most everyone, save those who have passed through Regina, but the legislature building is in the most beautiful setting of any of the ten provinces—surpassing even the wedding cake in Victoria with its harbour nesting. We will entertain arguments, but you are wrong.

Regina, the only important Prairie centre without a river, long ago realized the lack and set out to do something about it. A completely artificial body of water was created and it instantly made the Saskatchewan legislative building into one of the most attractive capitals in Canada. Saskatchewan residents, the most politically sophisticated citizens in the land, learned during the Depression to improvise for themselves (which is why every Saskatchewan family of that generation contains one piano player, a violin player, a banjo player and possibly someone on the accordion), and since Regina wasn't gifted with a river it manufactured the next best thing.

The result is man-made Wascana Lake, surrounded with vast lawns and gardens, a waterfowl park and a woodsy retreat that is a miniature Stanley Park. Geese swoop and ducks paddle. In winter, an automatic ice rink rivalling the celebrated Rideau Canal in Ottawa, where swivel servants skate to what is laughingly called work.

Folded in is the Museum of Natural History, the Saskatchewan Science Centre, the Saskatchewan Centre of the Arts and the university. It's a fine Pile o' Bones.
• See also "Saskatchewan."

## REGRESSIVE CONVERTIBLE PARTY
• See "Tories."

**REISMAN, SIMON** Court jester and pie-thrower, Simon Reisman is a bright man who should never be allowed in a TV studio without a dose of Valium inserted into his veins and a babysitter to calm his tantrums.

**RESPECT** It's hard for cabinet ministers, those pampered workaholics, to face the culture shock of real life.

John Crosbie said on his retirement that he suffered "withdrawal symptoms" and compared himself to Rodney Dangerfield, complaining that former politicians don't get any respect.

It is true that the saddest (and funniest) sight on earth is a Canadian ex-cabinet minister standing in an airport lineup, toting his own luggage, shock written all over his face, his body language exuding embarrassment at having to shuffle along with ordinary mortals.

But no respect? We're not so sure about that. Voters don't have any respect for certain kinds of politics and certain politicians, but they are essentially fair.

I can think of lots of politicians who get lots of respect. Robert Stanfield is one, a man who is treated with deference and affection wherever he goes in this country. Whatever her policies, Audrey McLaughlin gained nothing but respect for the way she handled her doomed election campaign in 1994. When she left the NDP leadership, she took respect with her. Pierre Trudeau's passing shows there is still a lot of respect for him among Canadians, including a large number who didn't particularly like him.

Jean Charest is well respected for the dignified and quiet way he accepted the mess that was the responsibility of others.

There was no one who got more respect from all quarters of the House of Commons—let alone the public—than Tommy Douglas, the only MP who dared to oppose the War Measures Act.

There are lots of politicians who are and have been respected, from Ian Waddell to Herb Gray to Ged Baldwin to Jimmy Sinclair and Davie Fulton.

What Crosbie seemed to encounter was a still-simmering anger at politicians and a political party that came to believe in the divine right of kings, that they and it knew better and would teach us so. As when the free trade deal with Washington was pushed through (only with a massive injection of money from the business sector) with the majority of Canadians opposed to it. As with the Meech and Charlottetown fiascoes drummed into us with rivers of advertising money, telling Canadians that our political masters knew best.

Crosbie himself was always respected, especially when he demonstrated on the podium that he didn't take himself—or politics—all that seriously. It was only when the dunderheads in his cabinet shut him up—made himself "wean on a pickle" as he put it—that he began to be regarded as just another Tory politician and he slumped under the burden.

Respect will come back when honest policies come back. There's lots of respect out there in the public arsenal. The voters are just waiting for someone to earn it.

**RIIS, NELSON** Mr. Blow-dry from Kamloops cowboy country. Perfect TV image. A New Democrat whose tie always matches his suit. He flirted with crossing the floor to join the Tories in the Joe Clark era, whatever his denials. A good Commons performer, the party wonders whether he is ideologically pure. He looks like a socialist you could trust.

**ROBERTS, JOHN** The Billy Bunter of the 1984 Liberal leadership race. How can one run for leadership when one is almost certain of losing one's seat? Winsome John, darling of the cocktail circuit, specializes in imponderables. Cute face, quick tongue, charming guest at dinner tables that launch a thousand quips. Slightly at sea in the real world once away from the canapés. He had no real chance, but what would politics be without ego?

**ROMANOW, ROY** Roy Romanow of downtown Saskatchabush is the real statesman of the current clutch of premiers. Though formally he did not become a premier until 1991, he has been around the block, as we say. His father, an immigrant from Ukraine, was a socialist in his kitchen who, every election, voted Liberal on the order of his CNR foreman who reminded his railway workers of their debt to the party that allowed them into the country. And would they like to keep their jobs, or what?

With Jean Chrétien and Roy McMurtry (Charlie Francis's lawyer), Romanow was a member of the kitchen cabal that brought us a flawed Constitution. After being in power's waiting room longer than John Turner or Paul Martin, he eventually decided he would rather be the next premier of Saskatchewan than leader of a third-place party.

Hollywood-handsome Roy, while waiting patiently to become the premier of his province, an outcome that was inevitable, turned down an offered bribe by the Trudeau government to become a member of the cabinet in Ottawa. The Ukrainian Robert Redford is so vain he is the only premier in Canada who will not reveal his birth date to the *Parliamentary Guide*.

**ROYALS, THE** The thing, being a professional voyeur paid to do royal-watching, is that you have a lot of time for contemplation.

Covering a royal tour, as my cruel employers make me do (when Charlie Lynch would give up both his lunch and his harmonica to do it for free), is rather like being in the army, you hurry up so you can wait.

Aside from catching pneumonia standing in the rain, being infected with a terminal case of Brownies and wondering when they are going to invent a new method of presenting flowers, a royal-watcher spends most of his time watching the royals doing nothing.

They ride through cavalcades brandishing a tired wave and a spontaneous smile. They have to listen to "God Save the Queen" at every fifteen-minute stop. They endure bravely the yokum-hokum of parish pump politicians, they unveil plaques, cut ribbons and ask thrilled ladies in kerchiefs where they're from. Basically, they are there to be looked at. It's a strenuous job, in short stretches, but nothing really happens.

If the Brits had the same regard for the royals as they do for animals, a society for the prevention of cruelty to monarchs would by now have released the Queen from the task.

Some of us loved Dr. Seuss; others, it appears, like their fairy tales live. George Will, the American commentator, noted that "the monarchy is a residue of the infancy of the British people." Alone among European democracies—almost all of them republics—the Brits persist in turning their royals into movie stars (unlike the Yanks, who turn their movie stars into royalty).

There was a time when a royal visit, *vide* 1939, was a national trauma. These were gods. We all palpitated on the curbs of Moose Jaw and treasured the photos for grandchildren forever after. Today? The problem, sorry to mention, is that even the royals breed too much. Such is the product of their loins, such is the shrinking of the Empire, that the poor kids have time to kill, and Canada—simp-faced Canada—is bored to the gills with the prog-eny who have good manners, no zits and nothing to do.

As the public boredom with a foreign family increases each year—as Canada attempts to grow up—the nervous bureaucrats who arrange these things must reach farther and farther afield to find the innocent locals who will go gaga at their arrival.

One can clearly imagine the day when the chief pooh-bahs of the royals will get their official welcome in Inuvik, to be followed by a visit to a daycare station just outside Wawa, with the main banquet hosted by the governor general in Bella Coola.

Only then would the significance of their irrelevance sink in. Only then would we be spared the presence of the clutch of Fleet Street hacks, the camp followers who trek their soggy tweeds along in the slipstream of the chinless wonders, sending back their tired clichés of life among the colonials.

The essential search is to find an equivalent to the waitress at a remote Vancouver Island banquet, some years ago, who instructed Prince Philip, "Hold the fork, Dook, the pie's to come." Such gems decorate London newspaper pubs for decades.

If you must know, I am bored. The surfeit of the royals, desperate for make-work projects so as to justify their teen-age allowance, drives me into eyeball-rolling paroxysms of ennui. What newsprint that could be usefully taken up by accounts of traffic accidents is consumed by slavering details of yet another clean-jawed prince, displaying clone-like replicas of Prince Philip's arch wit, dazzling factory maidens who know no better. Really, do we need this stale titillation?

• See also "Diana, Princess," "Queen Elizabeth" and "Queen Mum, the."

**ROYAL YORK, THE** The Royal York, a Gothic pile of stone across the street from Toronto's Union Station, once thought of itself as the centre of Canada. When it was opened in 1929, at twenty-four storeys it was the tallest building in the British Empire. Vancouver businessman John Nichol, one of the few ever to have the courage to resign from the Senate out of boredom despite having been president of the Liberal party, explained at the time that Grit guru Keith Davey's view of Canada was everything he could see from the roof of the Royal York.

Today, the old hostelry is a rather comic turreted midget surrounded by the sixty-storey Bay-and-King glass-and-steel towers of Mammon of the country's banks, edifices as cold as the hearts of the men who man them. It is still filled with conventions of vacuum-cleaner salesmen and nostalgic travellers from Saskatoon, but modern Toronto has gone elsewhere.

## Saint Lucien

• See "Bouchard, Lucien."

**SASKATCHEWAN** Every province, of course, feels it is unique, the exclusive owner of some magical qualities denied the other nine. It is what makes Canada: smugness divided ten times with enough left over for two territories. Ontario naturally has the morality denied all the others, Alberta the buccaneer spirit of freebooting capitalism. British Columbia has a lock on the loonies and the weather. Prince Edward Island has the most preposterous claims to be a separate jurisdiction. The main export of Nova Scotia and New Brunswick, as we know, is brains—half the universities of the land are populated with presidents who got their smarts near the Atlantic gales. The true base of Canada, however, is the province that happens (not by accident) to be at the heart of the country. All the great ones come from Saskatchewan.

The main export of Saskatchewan is guts—those who survived the rainless Depression years and conquered the spineless competitors in more favoured portions of the realm.

At a black-tie homecoming sponsored by Opera Saskatchewan in 1991, the province's sons and daughters preen themselves before the locals while displaying their credentials earned abroad.

As Dizzy Dean used to say, "It ain't bragging if ya dunnit."

For some reason, the flat prairie produces an inordinate number of chief executive officers of national outfits, the high pooh-bahs who run everything from the Royal Bank to Trizec Corp. Saskatchewan is the only English-speaking province that has produced two governors general: Jeanne Sauvé and Ray Hnatyshyn. As someone said, as you travel east from Saskatchewan you realize that the Wise Men did not come from that direction.

Allan Taylor, chairman of the Royal Bank, tells the crowd how he started as a sixteen-year-old teller in a hamlet and had to hold off irate customers one morning after an exuberant party because the bank manager, who had the only keys to the vault, was having trouble making it to the office.

The teenager who would later rise to his bank's highest chair dared not phone Regina superiors to explain his dilemma for fear of exposing his boss, who eventually staggered in, opened the vault and then passed out in it.

Imperial Oil's CEO, Arden Haynes, is here from downtown Esk. Is there a form of regional nepotism going on? Six of the top executives of the Royal are from Saskatchewan, three of the top Imperial bosses. Does the human rights commission know about this?

Pamela Wallin, the pride of Wadena, the woman every man in Canada shaves with each morning, is present. The province also produced Don Newman, he of the immovable upper lip, the pit bull Eric Malling and Dougie Small, of budget-leak fame. Guts is the operative label. Bill Shatner of *Star Trek* and Leslie Nielsen send their regrets. W. O. Mitchell of Weyburn and Max Braithwaite of Nokomis couldn't make it, and, for some strange reason I couldn't figure out, no one invited poet Sarah Binks, the Sweet Songstress of Saskatchewan. There are an inordinate amount of heavy thinkers from the upper mandarinate class of Ottawa—known in Indian lore as the Place Where the Mind Bends.

It has been known for some time that the upper reaches of the mandarinate in Ottawa are populated almost exclusively by people who spent their early lives snaring gophers. There are entire reaches of Rockcliffe filled with deputy ministers who still know what a pitchfork looks like.

In all, the gang from deputy governors of the Bank of Canada to former Dambuster pilots to president of the Calgary Flames and pipeline tycoons wear their celebritydom warily. They emerged from obscurity and hardscrabble times and, if not exactly still looking over the shoulder, do not forget it.

The graduates of the flat prairie, modest as always, know only one truism. It is that all the great ones come from Saskatchewan.

• See also "Moose Jaw" and "Regina."
• See also "I, Fotheringham" and "Romanow, Roy."

**SAWATSKY, JOHN** About 150 years ago, just after the earth cooled, a young man came into my office at the Vancouver *Sun*. He was a student at Simon Fraser University, Arthur Erickson's celebrated architectural monument on a mountain overlooking the city. He wrote a column for the campus paper and explained that he would like to do research for me nights and on weekends.

I explained that I already had the world's finest English secretary, Miss Framsham, and the world's best researcher, Mizzus Stooz, and couldn't afford any more help. "Oh," he said, "I don't expect any money. I just want to do it for the experience, for what I can learn from you." That was my introduction to John Sawatsky.

Sawatsky is stubborn and dogged. At one stage, to survive in his student years, he put a hot plate and a sleeping bag into a beat-up Volkswagen van, parked it in the Simon Fraser parking lot and lived there. He eventually became the Vancouver *Sun*'s parliamentary correspondent in Ottawa, then left to write books. He is now generally considered the best investigative journalist in Canada.

I once asked him how much it had cost him to give up the Newspaper Guild minimum rate for a senior reporter at the *Sun* for the uncertain income of books that take him years to produce. He didn't care, he explained. That rotting, rusting old Volks van was now settling into the weeds of his father's farm in Abbotsford, British California, and if things got that rough he was quite prepared to retreat there and live in it once again. He's stubborn.

Sawatsky was the first reporter in the country to break the story of the RCMP's break-ins and barn-burnings in the early days of Quebec separatism. It won him the Michener Award. His first book, *Men in the Shadows*, was a best-selling exposé of Canada's role in the grey world of espionage.

It's not too often that the subject of a book illustrates immediately that the book's assessment is bang-on correct. The supersensitive reaction of a supersensitive prime minister to Sawatsky's *Mulroney: The Politics of Ambition* is the greatest compliment Sawatsky could be paid. Brian Mulroney couldn't have done more if he'd stood on the corner of the Sparks Street Mall flogging the best-seller.

The Mulroney PMO sent its hit men and disinformation friends out on the television, radio and press conference trail, trying to discredit a very good reporter who got closer to the truth about the former prime minister than anyone yet. Trying to discredit Sawatsky, a painfully meticulous reporter, is like trying to accuse Mother Teresa of stealing the loose cash.

**SCHLESINGER, JOE** The courtly CBC Washington correspondent known as Joe Schlesinger, the ex-Czecher, has a mind so swift that he can't stand those who can't keep up, with the result that he is one of the few humans extant who went through elementary school, high school (a war contributed some delay) and university without bothering to collect a graduating certificate from any of them.

At the end of his tenure as editor of the University of British Columbia's *Ubyssey*, which has long been the best college paper in the land, Joe Schlesinger stuffed the ballot box to ensure the democratic election of his successor as editor, who cannot be identified other than the fact his initials are A. F.

**SCHREYER, ED** The terrible press, regarding Ed Schreyer's late entry into the 1999 Manitoba election with cries of "Bullshit," began recycling the false story that one year at the parliamentary press gallery dinner the scribes pelted him with buns.

That is not true. We pelted him with sugar cubes.

It was so bad that the French ambassador was in tears, shocked at what he regarded as such an insult to the representative of the Queen.

He was probably right, but Ed Schreyer was no ordinary governor general. As the barrage continued, he looked down from the head table at the chief culprit and warned, "You do that one more time and I'm going to come down there and kick your ass." The barrage ended.

The point is that farm boy Edward Schreyer is one very stubborn guy. He refused to play by press gallery rules.

The annual black-tie banquet in his era, the early 1980s, was the most sought-after ticket in Ottawa, each scribe eligible to invite only one guest—a politician or high swivel servant.

It was off-the-record then, which allowed party leaders to skewer each other and the prime minister with the type of lines usually heard only at a Jackie Gleason/Dean Martin roast.

The CBC's droll jester Larry Zolf used to write the jokes for Pierre Trudeau, the only problem being that the cerebral PM wouldn't get the joke himself and invariably would screw up the punch line.

Schreyer, from rural Manitoba, would have none of this. He persisted in reading a long and moralistic lecture on the responsibilities of the press and TV mob, most of whom by this time (nearing midnight) had demonstrated their responsibility toward the grape. Hence the sugar cubes.

How stubborn is Schreyer? He was so bored with the daily ritual of Rideau Hall that he tried to emulate a Winnipeg judge's feat of reading the *Encyclopedia Britannica* from A to Z.

Those of us who were frequent visitors at his dinner table— Farley Mowat and Don Harron among others—followed his progress with fascination. I think he finally quit at R.

How do you grow to be this stubborn? Schreyer, as a teenager, was sent by his family to be the sole tenant and minder of the animals at another family farm, a far distance from his parents. He was given an account at the store in town, and would ride in once a week, play pool and buy his week's supplies. He knew how to cook only two things and ate those two things every night, alone, until he could shave.

Schreyer's problem is that he is so bright his active life in politics ended when most men would just be coming into their prime. He was elected to the legislature in Winnipeg at just twenty-two. At twenty-nine he was in the House of Commons in Ottawa. At thirty-three he was Manitoba's first NDP premier.

(It was an alert *National Post* reader who caught Adrienne

Clarkson's boast that she was the first governor general from neither of our two founding nations. Never heard, he asked, of Schreyer or Ray Hnatyshyn?)

This simply underlines, does it not, the artificiality of the post, hanging on to Betty Windsor's petticoat. As one constitutional expert has put it, on governors general, "To think they would be political eunuchs for the rest of their lives would seem somewhat unreasonable."

**SEGAL, HUGH** With the regal countenance of a youthful Alfred Hitchcock and the vocabulary of Evelyn Waugh, Hugh Segal is a walking advertisement for the Tory equivalent of Grit arrogance.

**SHARP, MITCHELL** I was walking down an Ottawa street one day and ran into Mitchell Sharp soon before he led yet another puzzling Team Almost Canada to China. As Liberal finance minister under Pearson, Sharp was the one who took Jean Chrétien under his wing and made him parliamentary secretary. He is today, of course, the $1-a-year senior advisor to the prime minister. I hope and believe he took his new wife with him to China; twice a widower, he remarried most recently at age eighty-nine.
 • See also "Chrétien, Jean."

**SHEIK OF CALGARY, THE**
 • See "Lougheed, Peter."

**SHIELDS, CAROL** Several years ago in the town that winter never forgets, I saw an improbable and hilarious play involving four women who had been playing bridge once a week through their courting days, their tired and droll marriage days, on to their grandmother days. Only last week do I discover it was written by

Carol Shields, the American-Canadian who won the Pulitzer Prize
and has spent her entire adult life in Canada and Winnipeg with
her University of Manitoba professor husband.

It is so typical of Canadian chauvinism that newspapers here
never mentioned that she was actually an American and held dual
citizenship. It was so typical of American chauvinism that papers
there never once mentioned that she happened to live in Canada.

**SHRUB, PRESIDENT**
- See "Bush, George W."

**SILVERSPOON, LORD**
- See "Thomson, Ken."

**SLAIGHT, ALLAN** Every man should have a hobby (golf is not a
hobby; it is a serious disease that should be eradicated) and lucky
he who has one that lasts a lifetime.

When Allan Slaight, the man who bought and sold the Toronto
Raptors at a juicy profit, was eight, his parents drove him to
Eaton's Toyland in Toronto at Christmas. He planted his little feet
in front of magician Johnny Giordmaine's act and would not
budge for four hours. An obsession was born.

At sixteen, the obsessed Allan Slaight found himself with his
family in "the magical isolation of Moose Jaw." In desperation, the
lonely boy wrote an outrageously bold, long letter to his new
hero, the living encyclopedia of magic, Stewart James.

The letter finished: "If you do confide a few cherished secrets
with me, you need have no worry of it ever leaking out; for two
reasons—(1) I wouldn't tell it if you didn't want me to; (2) I
wouldn't have anyone to tell it to, anyway. So please write me!"

Slaight, who has built and passed on a media empire, is a lifelong amateur magician. The lone task that has taken up his past ten years is *The James File*, two volumes running up to 1,700 pages (with a third volume containing the index).

"Ten years?" says Slaight. "That's only 170 pages a year. A page every two days. No big deal."

An American reviewer has called it "The greatest work of literature in the history of conjuring." *The James File* collector's edition is $250 (U.S.) and, understandably, only 200 copies were printed.

• See also "James, Stewart."

**SOVEREIGNTY-ASSOCIATION** Divorce with bed privileges.
• See "Parizeau, Jacques."

**SPORTSWRITERS** It is a little-known fact, privy only to those of us who type, but the cream of journalism is populated by types who got their start sitting around lacrosse dressing rooms, listening to the beer caps pop. Before the accountants and computer boffins took over, there was a time when most managing editors and publishers came into their stations with the whiff of old sweat sock still lingering on their new three-piece suits. Cast a glance at the curriculum vitae of most any scribbler of note and you will find that he started it all at space rates, covering the local midget hockey tournament. From Paul Gallico to Mr. Hemingway to Scott Young (Robert Fulford, if you can believe it, started in sports), the lists are sprinkled with graduates of the press box. Scotty Reston, arguably the single most influential political columnist in the world from his platform at The *New York Times*, was once the press agent for the Cincinnati Reds. You can look it up.

Being a broken-down sportswriter myself, I love sportswriter stories, like dumb blonde jokes. Norm Van Brocklin, out of the University of Oregon, became a terrible-tempered NFL great as a quarterback and then a terrible-tempered coach of the Minnesota Vikings. At a press conference one day he allowed that if he ever required a brain transplant he hoped it would come from a sportswriter, that way it would never have been used.

When they tried to keep Mickey Mantle alive, after his dissolute life, with a liver transplant, his surgeon held a press conference at the Houston Medical Center. A reporter asked if the donor of the liver was still alive. The doctor looked down from the podium, paused, and said, "You're a sportswriter, aren't you."

But the reason why sportswriters rise to the top is quite simple. They are born enthusiastic. The reason they go into the scribbling trade in the first place is because they lust to be close to the action, their heroes and the game that fascinates them. It doesn't really matter if they are failed athletes themselves (hello there, mother) or are just slobbering acolytes. Their passion pushes them. They would cover the jocks for nothing, the mere proximity to the demigods reward enough. They care. Compare this with your average young reporter going into straight (i.e., boring) reporting. One cannot really convince me that one is born with an innate desire to learn more about sewer bylaws at city hall or lies awake at night atingle with the next development in the Law of the Sea conferences.

Eventually, sportswriters grow bored with their calling (hello there, boss) and drift upward, levitated by the smarm they have learned consorting with millionaire club owners and low-IQ plutocrats who have been made rich by their ability to discern a curve ball.

Sportswriters have the advantage of meeting, early on, the scam artists of the playground, whose only gift is quick reflexes, and the scam artists of the counting house, who play Scrabble with sports franchises. This equips them admirably for introduction in later life to both types to be found in politics: the silver locks and silver voice concealing a vacuous brain on the one hand, on the other, the artful grifter who survives by working the scams and perfecting the bump-and-run. Stick with the jocks, I say.

**STANFIELD, ROBERT** One day, after a press conference that had died because of Robert Stanfield's dullness, a few of us stayed behind to have a drink with him in his hotel suite. One of the group was Jack Webster, the mouth that roared, who is instant showbiz in any gathering over two persons. Webster went into one of his stories and was just mounting full steam when Stanfield gently skewered him. There was a large hiss as the air went out of Webster. He wound himself up for a second time and launched forth. Just before the punch line came another Stanfield shaft. There was another loud hiss of air. A third time Webster pumped himself up. A third time an incisive, deadly, precise Stanfield line punctured him completely. The ineffectual Bob Stanfield, politics' worst communicator, completely destroyed the toughest talker in journalism. In such close company he is delightful.

At the off-the-record press gallery annual dinner each year, Stanfield's droll speech from the head table completely overshadowed that of Trudeau. In 1975, Stanfield rose and began his ponderous introduction. "Your Excellency," he said turning to Governor General Jules Léger, "Prime Minister, Mr. Broadbent, Mr. Chairman, ladies and gentlemen—and Doug Ball." The place collapsed. It was an in-joke of magnificent self-deprecation since Doug Ball was the photographer who took that famous campaign shot of Stanfield fumbling a football, a devastating cameo that was widely credited with aiding his defeat. There are Tories still bitter over the selective way newspapers played that picture, since Ball supplied Canadian Press with other shots of a surprisingly graceful

Stanfield catching and passing the football. It's a debate still argued in press clubs but only Stanfield had the sense of humour to handle it.

He is a man who sent Christmas cards, signed by himself, to newspapermen who all year brutally chopped him into tiny pieces and then toyed with the remains. It is extremely difficult to dislike such a man.

The final day of the futile 1968 campaign an exhausted Stanfield boarded his lumbering campaign plane in Belleville, Ontario, for the flight home. On the flagstone patio of The Oaks, the Stanfield home in Halifax, the day after the election, Stanfield and the Tories of course have been buried under Trudeaumania, and the pallbearers—Finlay MacDonald, Gene Rheaume, Flora MacDonald and a few others—have gathered for lunch. The gloom is hedge-high. Suddenly Fast Eddie Goodman leaps to his feet. "I've got it!" he cries. The mourners look at him strangely. "We start right now, building for the next time. We start a rumour. We plant it. Get it going right across the country." The Stanfield entourage gazes puzzled at the antics of Fast Eddie, who by now is dancing with excitement. "Here it is," he whispers. "Bob Stanfield comes home for nooners!" Mary Stanfield laughs so hard she falls off her chair into a rose bush.

Late one evening I was waiting for an MP outside the west door of the Commons. Stanfield appeared out of the darkness in his white raincoat, the hunched figure as always appearing shorter than it should be. There was a full moon and we talked while MPs hurried home. We talked and talked and one got the impression this thoroughly decent man would have stayed there for hours. No hurry. No sweat. He had already announced he was leaving and was patiently waiting for the leave-taking, no recriminations, no regrets, no complaints. Just a nice man on a nice night who enjoyed talking.

Clark Gable died shortly after making a movie *The Misfits*, written by Arthur Miller. In a copy of the screenplay given to Gable, Miller wrote: "To the man who did not know how to hate." That will do also as a political epitaph for Robert Stanfield, a gentleman in a ruffians' game.

**STATESMEN** A statesman is a dead politician, and what this country needs is more of them.

**STRONG, MAURICE** Maurice Strong. Maurice Frederick Strong, if you insist, of English, Scottish, German and Irish descent—the vertical mosaic incarnate—is Horatio Alger crossed with Huckleberry Finn.

Born into Depression poverty in Oak Lake, Manitoba, his railway-worker father laid off by the wicked CPR. He left home at thirteen ("I didn't run away from home. I ran to adventure"), tried to join the navy and stowed away aboard a Canada Steamship Line vessel on the Great Lakes. At fifteen, as an apprentice fur trader at a Hudson's Bay post on Chesterfield Inlet, to where he took along a copy of *Maclean's* that analyzed the performance of Canada's hundred largest companies, he formed his own mining exploration company. At eighteen, he went to work for the new United Nations' secretariat in New York (Secretary-General Trygve Lie called him "the kid"). At twenty-three he had made his first fortune with Dome Explorations. Success seems to bore Strong and six weeks after he had lavishly furnished a new home for his wife, the two of them took off on a two year safari around the world. He opened the first service station in Zanzibar and established a graphite mine in Tanganyika. At thirty-five he was the head of Power Corp. of Montreal and then accepted—delicious revenge—

an offer to become head of the Canadian foreign aid program that had earlier refused him a job.

From there it was a minor hop for the Oak Lake boy to become head of the UN environmental secretariat based in Nairobi. The move to Petro-Canada in 1978 seemed small beer to Strong. "Just running an oil company is not what I want to do with my life," he confessed.

The best thing about an anti-hero is his appearance. Maurice Strong has one of those faces of a bit player in a 1930s movie, a moustache left over from Early Postal Clerk. A millionaire several times over, he still looks as if his suits are picked off the rack ("in the dark," a friend once observed). He has the perpetually surprised, pleased look on his face of a small round boy just being given an unexpected piece of candy. On the macho scale, he resembles Caspar Milquetoast out of Mr. Peepers.

Wasting Maurice Strong on such a minor, petty chore as setting up in rather absent-minded fashion your friendly government's excursion into oil and gas development, as some would say, was akin to assigning Michelangelo to design the new McDonald's neon sign. If the Americans had Maurice Strong, he'd be right up there with Betsy Ross, Abe Lincoln and Joe Namath.

## SWIVEL SERVANTS

• See "Ottawa."

**THOMSON, KEN** I used to work for Ken Thomson, 150 years ago on Fleet Street, in a funny little haywire operation called *Canada Review*. It bore unmistakable signs of the Thomson ethos: made up of dupes of Canadian Press copy *mailed* from some Thomson outlet in Canada, the composing room in Edinburgh, editorial offices in London, with the result that the main target of this strange little epistle—Canadian troops in West Germany—got the Stanley Cup results about the time the World Series was starting. Ken Thomson used to come into the office occasionally, a shy, rather insecure man, as most sons of powerful, insensitive millionaires are. He puzzled me then (we weren't exactly intimate pub-crawling friends) and he puzzles me now.

The Thomson "philosophy" keeps cropping up in my life, as I flee across the ice floes with the wolves at my heels, desperate and starving, from employer to employer. Some 200 years ago Roy Thomson, who later bought himself a title in London, came into ownership of a very lively little morning newspaper in Vancouver. The *News-Herald*, under a wise, dry and laconic publisher by the name of Slim Delbridge, employed managing editor Robert Elson, who went on to become general manager of *Life*; future *Vancouver Sun* publisher Stuart Keate; Jack Scott, one of the most literate columnists produced in Canada, a twenty-one-year-old Pierre

Berton as city editor; and a clutch of other survivors who were paid in sacks of coal and two-pant suits.

Roy Thomson owned it briefly—and quickly folded it. The point is that the Thomsons—*fils et père*—didn't like competition then and they don't like it now.

"Each one has to find his own way in the world," Lord (Ken) Thomson said after his closing of the *Ottawa Journal* put 375 people out of work.

Lord Silverspoon, as he is derisively and somewhat affectionately known in the press clubs of the land, had purchased ten papers in the twenty-four months before he acquired the eight major national dailies of FP Publications.

Quickly, my old boss from *Canada Review* melded the Victoria *Daily Colonist* (founded in 1858) with the Victoria Times, sold the *Calgary Albertan* and folded the ninety-four-year-old *Ottawa Journal*. What was his point in buying the chain in the first place? Is there a dog-in-the-manger factor? We buy it simply because we have the money to do it?

The new Lord Thomson says, "You take advantage of your opportunities when they come and where they come." True, of course, but what about your *responsibilities*?

**TORIES (ALSO THE *REGRESSIVE CONVERTIBLE PARTY*)**
In the mail, by roundabout route, there once arrived a fancy envelope from Room 200 at 161 Laurier Ave. W., Ottawa, K1P 5J2. It was a three-page friendly letter asking me to contribute money to the PC Canada Fund—being the slush fund that finances the operations that kept Mr. Mulroney and his friends elected. Included was a nice plastic card: "Here is your personal 1986 PC Canada Fund sustaining membership card." It was engraved with my name—"Fotheringam." My first name and initial are mixed up. It was addressed to a city

where I no longer lived and to an employer where Fotheringam hadn't worked for years. It finally made things clear. If the Tory party actually thought Fotheringam was going to send them a cheque, it just shows how much trouble the party, even then, was in.

The Tories, the dear, blissful, nearsighted Tories, continue to do it to themselves. They proudly boasted about a 1982 survey of their membership which indicated, sad to tell, the exact reasons why they have been out of power seventy of the past one hundred years in the country.

Why anyone would publish an autopsy—proving all we have suspected about the Regressive Convertible Party—is a mystery. The typical Conservative convention delegate, it turns out, is a male between the ages of forty-six and fifty-five, who comes from Ontario and is basically against most of the advances of mankind since the children were released from the mines.

What the survey proves, of course, is what one saw every day sitting in the press gallery, looking down upon the blue-serge-and-grey wasteland of the Tory back benches. The minds were as grey as the wardrobes.

The party that birthed the nation, and now down to a miserable few seats, could have held their 1995 convention in a Volkswagen van, but dragged their bodies across the river from Ottawa to Hull for the mea culpa act.

Did the chaps who approved the celebrated Jean Chrétien ad show up? Would Kim Campbell make it from her redoubt in Montreal—supposedly writing her memoirs? Did anyone want her? In what portion of China or South America was Brian Mulroney making his latest million that week? Did anyone care any more?

The best piece of desperation the Tories encountered since Kimmy told us election campaigns were the last place serious issues should be discussed was the effort to draft Ralph Klein.

Klein might have been their saviour since he is the first politician since Sir John A. Macdonald to like the tinkle of a glass.

This is exactly what the Conservatives need: someone who links them to their proud roots, Sir John A. being the founder of the nation and all Tory prime ministers ever since diminished by his shadow. There isn't a reporter in the realm who hasn't exchanged beers with Mr. Klein in the subterranean depths of the St. Louis Hotel in Calgary, in the days when he was mayor of the city.

Tales of Sir John's bouts with the gargle are by now legend. And bored Ottawa press gallery regulars were praying that Ralphie would come galloping out of the wide prairie and reinvent the party that the earnest Jean Charest failed to revive.

Joe Clark, although an Alberta boy, is no drinker. Robert Stanfield could have been embalmed in rye throughout his political career, but how would we have known? Brian Mulroney, as we all know, saved his career and won the Tory leadership on his second attempt by giving up drinking completely. The suggested merger with Reform would never have worked, since Preston Manning hasn't had a sarsaparilla since 1947.

Ralph Klein, a beer-drinker's sort of guy, could have revived the whole image of Sir John A., a giant who could hold his liquor and still build a country.

"You were selected to receive this card," the direct junk-mail read, "because I believe you share with PC members of Parliament a faith and conviction that Canada can regain its economic health and move toward prosperity and opportunity for our generation and for our children's generation." I have not faith and conviction in a party that actually thinks Fotheringam is going to send them money. Sounds to me like a party on the edge of delirium tremens.

• See also "Campbell, Kim," "Clark, Joe," "Mulroney, Brian" and "Stanfield, Robert."

**TORONTO** There was a wonderful front page one week in the Toronto *Sun*, the tabloid that devotes page 1 only to massive headlines and great colour pictures. "METRO BEST CITY IN WORLD," one side of the page screamed. Alongside was a dramatic shot of a cop wrestling a suspect to the ground while a colleague in blue aimed a large rifle at his head.

Whether this was meant as satire, or the photo editor had gone out to lunch while they wrote the headline, is unclear.

*Fortune* magazine, some years back, decided that Toronto—beating out London, Paris and Hong Kong—is the finest city in the world outside the United States. This would indicate that *Fortune* has the same sense of humour as those sly guys who craft the *Sun*'s front pages. Would this be the same sophisticated Toronto where you have to go to one establishment to buy your hooch and then another building somewhere where they sell beer? Yup. A city that is so classy it holds its massive Santa Claus Parade two months before Christmas, so as to vacuum every bit of commerce it can before a day supposed to be devoted to kids? Where the city council voted to ban all smoking in restaurants and bars—bars being the place I thought you went to so you could smoke? That's the city that used to be called Toronto the Good and has merely evolved into Toronto the Antiseptic.

The first time I ever saw Toronto, as a lad, I arrived on a late plane and checked into the Royal York close to midnight. Never having viewed the fabled resting home of Mammon, I decided to take a stroll around what I assumed would be the adjacent downtown area. After several blocks in the dark, in what I took to be a deserted warehouse district, I returned to the hotel, presuming that it was located on the outskirts of the city. It was not until I ventured forth next morning that I realized the oppressive environs of the Royal York in fact were the lower reaches of Bay Street,

in daytime the very crucible of all that was sacred and dear to
Canada's financial welfare. It was indeed, in those days, a city run
by the tastes of pinched Presbyterians.

Canada, in fact, was first settled by a group of Scots
Presbyterians. Being Scots Presbyterians, they worshipped money
and set up the Canadian banking system, which is the tightest
labour union in Christendom. To make room for all this stored
loot, which the bankers use to buy their six-piece, bulletproof suits
from Harry Rosen, they had to build their numerous tall buildings,
mostly on the same corner, all of which except one have the architectural originality of a Lego set. This is why there are a lot of tall
buildings in Toronto.

Toronto is the only large city in the world that doesn't know
it is built on a lake. Babies are born in Toronto, grow up and die
and go to their graves never having seen Lake Ontario. This has
been cleverly arranged by erecting a picket fence of overhead
freeways and concrete condo caves that successfully render the
water invisible.

All the great cities on the globe are built around water. You cannot travel anywhere in London without having to cross the broad
Thames. A Parisian has to cross a bridge over the Seine every ten
minutes to get around town. The lazy Tiber winds through Rome.
Hong Kong has the most spectacular harbour in the world, rivalled
only by Vancouver. Montreal is an island, surrounded by the
mighty St. Lawrence.

Toronto once had its chance. The SkyDome in fact sits on
land that was supposed to be Toronto's first public park—killed
by political graft and railway greed. In the 1830s, there was a
dream of a green park for the citizens on the lakefront.
Watercolour renderings by Toronto's surveyor of the time show
walking paths and trees and laughing children on slides.

According to official city council minutes, aldermen talked about putting a park south of Front Street as early as 1836. This was two years after the city was incorporated. To achieve the impossible—having a huge lake that no one can see—took some ingenuity, but Toronto has managed it.

I have, however, become somewhat of a fan of Toronto. It is about the only place left in North America that has four lively and competitive and profitable newspapers. The curved towers of Viljo Revell's city hall made it the most interesting new building in the world until the advent of the Sydney Opera House. There are definite possibilities of elegance in the Bloor-Yorkville sector—still the only portion of Toronto in which *walking* is a pleasure. Toronto also has a lot of trees, and therefore squirrels. I think we can say with some sense of certainty that Toronto leads the nation in sea gulls combined with squirrels. It is a good image.

I could even conceive of living in Toronto—if only something could be arranged about the unspeakable weather. However, I understand that is under the jurisdiction of God and I plan to speak with Her about it.

In fact, the art of Toronto-bashing seems to be in a bit of a decline lately, largely, one suspects, because the rest of the country has become bored with it. Once Toronto, in its hubris, decided that it liked being kicked—evidence of its obvious superiority—all the fun went out of the game. The rest of Canada got on with the job of improving the quality of life, deprived as it is of the advantages of gridlock, steamy summers and the Maple Leafs. Toronto, the bully on the block who craves attention, actually misses all the tossed rocks.

• See also "CN Tower," "Hogtown," and "Royal York, the."

## TRUDEAU, MARGARET
• See "Margaret."

**TRUDEAU, PIERRE ELLIOTT** Pierre Trudeau remains as much a mystery after leaving us as when he assumed power thirty-three years ago. He divided emotions as no other Canadian politician before him, mainly because he persisted in keeping his real personality in hiding, a hostage to his public life.

His long-time friend and confidant, Gérard Pelletier, once explained that while Trudeau gave the impression of a daring risk-taker, he was, in fact, a most cautious person. (His long delay in risking the perilous shores of marriage, if nothing else, proved that.) Pelletier pointed out that Trudeau would launch his canoe over a seemingly treacherous stretch of white water—but only after charting and checking beforehand on foot every bit of the route. He took risks, explained Pelletier, but only carefully calculated risks. In fact, little was left to chance. "Reason over passion" was the family motto.

His whole record of serving us confirms a confession he once made at an Ontario Liberal conference in Kingston: "I personally get a fair amount of pleasure from daring people to do certain things. That is why I'm enjoying this period in my political life." He was an emotional roller coaster, dozing between fits of passion. The economy always bored him. He lunged at it only in fits of exasperation. The War Measures Act was his finest hour, bringing out a courageous, tough leader who rallied the nation against an unknown foe with his chilling eloquence and undeniable courage. Trudeau for once was roused and he responded magnificently.

He needed confrontation to concentrate his frozen-in-aspic intellect. The boy in Saskatchewan tossing wheat at him is told he is about to get his ass kicked. The demonstrator in Vancouver is cuffed. The striking mail truck drivers from Montreal are told what edifying diet they can eat as the PM of all the people speeds off in his limousine. The TV reporter on the Parliament steps who presses him on how far he would go in restricting civil liberties in the FLQ drama is told, "Just watch me." Watch me, if you think you can kick sand in *my* face, just watch me.

Pierre Trudeau, in essence, never outgrew the need to be the youth, knotted red bandana around the neck, running before the bulls of Pamplona. He liked to dare to do certain things. The first to wear sandals and an ascot in Parliament. To throw snowballs at Lenin's statue in Moscow. To ride around Montreal on a motorcycle wearing a German helmet. To marry a dazzling beauty thirty years his junior. To be the first prime minister to tell an MP to "fuck off" in the Commons. To do a mocking pirouette behind a queen. Always there is the image of the little boy wanting to stick out his tongue during the formal photography session.

This man of masks, who told biographer George Radwanski that he was so sickly and insecure as a child that he purposely set out to build a physique and a steel will that would repel all outsiders, wobbled between the arrogance seen by the public and the shyness seen by his intimates.

Back in the days when he still spoke to your blushing agent, he once confided to my notebook that the toughest thing to master in his early years as prime minister was learning to be a team player. As a loner who would never touch team sports as a youth and preferred to test his body in single combat with the elements, he suddenly found himself part of a team—thirty or so bodies sitting around a cabinet table—and he had to think as a team player. It wasn't easy, he confessed, to wipe all the solitary mental attitudes developed over his life. As a grown man, he had to re-educate himself.

Tom Axworthy, one of the guests at Trudeau's eightieth birthday party in 1999 at Chrétien's home at 24 Sussex Drive, used to
dine out on the stories of the lofty one's famed disinclination to
remember the names of even his top aides in the PMO.

"I'd been there for two years," he recalled, "and whenever he
wanted to talk to me he would just say, 'get me the fat guy.' "

Paul Manning was a speech writer in the PMO when Trudeau,
his popularity waning, was facing his third election campaign.
Manning, ushered into his presence, suggested he had a bright
idea for Trudeau's address the next day to the steelworkers in
Hamilton. It was that even Hank Aaron, who at the time was chasing Babe Ruth's all-time homer record, having whiffed once and
whiffed twice, still had a chance with a third strike.

Trudeau: "Who's Hank Aaron?"

Manning, clearing his throat, explained Aaron was the baseball
player who was about to break Babe Ruth's record.

Trudeau: "Who's Babe Ruth?

Manning, by now sweating nervously, explained who Babe
Ruth was. Trudeau, finally getting the three-strike analogy,
thought it was a good idea. And so, next day before the doubting
steelworkers, the PM allowed that he perhaps had not been perfect
in his first two terms, but deserved a third try. "Even Hank Aaron
gets a third strike. And you know who he is — the guy who's
going to break the home run record of Baby Ruth!"

Trudeau went through two periods in his life. First, he was a
brilliant loner who walked through life according to his own rules.
Then, he was someone casually thrust into power—almost against
his own will—who then came to enjoy the power very much.

As the emotional reactions to Pierre Trudeau's passing washed
in, it might be remembered that his contemporary as a leader
when he first took power was Charles de Gaulle. Lyndon Baines

Johnson, we tend to forget, was president when Trudeau was prime minister. The Americans went through four presidents during his first tenure. The Brits picked five prime ministers in the same time.

He gave Canada, always the wallflower at the North American dance, something it never had before: a belief and lusty pride that we had a guy we could stack up against anyone in the world.

In 1968, still riding the euphoria of Montreal's Expo 67, we suddenly discovered this reluctant warrior, who confessed to the press that he at first thought it "a joke" that he, of the Three Wise Men brought in from Quebec by Pearson, would be considered a prime-ministerial candidate. But there he was, rich, casual, witty, attracted to attractive women. Further: athletic and effortlessly bilingual!

Lester Pearson, who couldn't really speak French but could fake it well enough for formal occasions, predicted that after he left 24 Sussex Drive there would never be another Canadian prime minister who was not completely bilingual. He was right, of course, and Trudeau's official bilingualism legislation ensured that. The proof (and the victims) of that were John Crosbie and Preston Manning, each in his own time arguably the most intelligent MP in the Commons.

The most poignant moment of Trudeau's successful return in the 1980 campaign came one night in a high school in, of all unlikely Tory places, Prince Albert, Saskatchewan. A tired Pierre Trudeau stood on a stage while a choir of more than a dozen young boys launched into "O Canada."

But: the boys launched into "O Canada" in French and, once Trudeau realized what was happening, it was almost impossible to describe the look that spread over his face. In all my years of watching the moody man, I have never seen such obvious joy on his face.

Here, in the home of "unhyphenated Canadianism" was the proof that it could be done—this inflexible man's dream of portable bilingualism. Beaming (and Pierre Trudeau did not beam easily) as the anthem soared forth in his own tongue, the country's most famous single parent gazed fondly at the younger boys who were about the same age of the three he had left at home.

He was an inspiration, even though he never really understood that seamy grave of politics that lurked beneath the philosophical levels he preferred. George Radwanski, who as a reporter with a law degree and a similar "European" mind-set got closer to Trudeau than any other journalist, concluded that he was "unfulfilled" as a prime minister, a semantic delicacy that may over time be the closest approximation of the truth.

Your humble scribe, one night in Rome after a G-7 meeting in Venice, was smuggled into a party thrown for him by Roloff Beny, the famed Alberta photographer. It was midnight under a moon, on a rooftop garden overlooking the Tiber. Exotic people of all three sexes floated about, serving champagne and smoked salmon.

Trudeau walked in and, in semi-disgust, said, "Oh, Fotheringham, you remind me of Cyrano de Bergerac. You make enemies so easily." And he launched off into a long quotation, in French of course.

"Oh, Mr. Trudeau," I said, "I wouldn't know what you're talking about, naturally, since I'm from Western Canada." He turned on his heel and walked off. We did not talk again for two years.

In essence, the Ottawa press gallery was afraid of him, intimidated by his intellect, very wary of his withering wit. He pretended, of course, never to read the press. But when the lowly scribe, retreating from early Trudeaumania, began to give him some severe shots, on leaving a press conference on the way to his limo out front he would punch me in the gut.

On the day he resigned after the walk in the snow, he dusted off the white Mercedes convertible and rolled up the long drive-way to Rideau Hall, the press mob gathered in hundreds. He eased up at the door, turned gently, and ran over my foot. It was the highest praise.

When his son drowned, I sent him a personal note, father to father. Reporters aren't supposed to write to politicians. I guess that's why he was different.

• See also "Liberals."

**TURNER, JOHN** When John Napier Turner was eighteen years old, he received a telephone call for help. He was in Vancouver. The call came from Lytton, which is at the north end of the Fraser Canyon. His stepfather, Frank Ross, the roly-poly industrial-ist and later British Columbia's lieutenant-governor, and a close friend, Colonel Victor Spencer, ruler of the Spencer department store chain, which was eventually absorbed by Eaton's, had set out from a summer retreat near Lytton and been missing for eight hours in their station wagon. Young John was told to start the search.

He drove all the way up the then-tortuous cliffside road and, sure enough, he came to a break in the guardrail. Peering down the mountainside, he saw the missing station wagon, perched pre-cariously on a ledge above the raging river. Turner scrambled down the mountainside to find the two nonchalant men drinking out of a bottle. "What took you so long?" his stepfather asked.

Turner has always been reliable.

He was born in England, raised as a boy in Ottawa, went to university in British Columbia, married into a proper Winnipeg family, practised law in Montreal, held seats in Ottawa and Vancouver, and has collected directorships like hives in a high

Toronto corporate tower, where the windows are festooned with gold flake.

The Duke of Windsor of Canadian politics, he was our fourth foreign-born prime minister and almost certainly the only one who was the son of a journalist. His father, an English journalist, died when John Turner was a small boy. His mother, whom Turner terms "one of the first feminists," was the first liberated mandarin in Ottawa, a brainy and powerful woman who was one of C. D. Howe's wartime wonders. His mother married Frank Ross, but at his death there was little money to pass on. Turner has always maintained that he has lived on his own income.

He was the Canadian record holder in the 100-yard dash, but a knee injury in a car crash kept him out of the Olympic Games while his track buddies from Oxford, Roger Bannister, Chris Chataway and Chris Brasher, went on to world fame.

He is surprisingly insecure in his personal ways. That accounts for his leftover gung-ho fraternity approach, someone whose zeal at meeting every stranger resembles a teenage George Hees, enthusiasm gushing from every pore. But he's intensely private, a man who is fearful of letting down his guard, which accounts for the George Raft–style machine-gun delivery and the bristling presence that moved Keith Spicer to describe his early leadership demeanour as "Kirk Douglas on speed."

In 1984, at the moment of his greatest triumph, his aging mother, suffering from Alzheimer's disease, was taken from her bed in a nursing home on Salt Spring Island, B.C., and placed before a television set to see John crowned Liberal leader in the Ottawa arena. She did not recognize him.

He is a very old-fashioned person, the youngest man I ever met who still wore garters to hold up his stockings. His old-fashioned (i.e., outdated) mannerisms became embarrassingly obvious in his bum-patting, patronizing attitude to women on his return to politics. He never has been as self-confident as pictured and his nervousness and awkwardness before the TV eventually led to the humiliating sessions with a "media doctor" who had him lying on the floor of his office learning how to breathe properly to cure that loud on-air throat-clearing.

For all the Fleet Street frenzy about the handsome lawyer "who danced with a princess," there was never any chance that Princess Margaret, especially in those days, would have been allowed to get involved with a Catholic. They are still friends, and Turner and his wife, Geills, call on her when in London.

Although he and Mulroney (who once applied for a job at Turner's Montreal law firm) cannot stand one another—one thinking the other a child of privilege, the other thinking the other a jumped-up opportunist—they have similarities. Both want very much to be liked. Turner's early desire to be all things to all people leaving him a politician who never articulated a believable philosophy to the public.

It is not exactly a state secret any more that the reason Turner and Trudeau parted ways swiftly was because the former went into the office of the latter on September 10, 1975, to arrange (a commitment he believed he had been given) a removal from the dead-end finance portfolio. When the prime minister, with the sensitivity for individual relationships for which he is famed, offered Turner the demeaning suggestions of a judgeship (or the Senate!), the proud man who was a decade younger than the PM was so insulted that he resigned and went back to his aides with tears in his eyes.

His pride moved him out of Ottawa at too young an age. His caution kept him on Bay Street too long, and his skills had congealed by the time he came back to a younger press gallery that didn't care about his earlier reputation.

The mean refusal of Trudeau to come to the podium and join hands with him at his leadership triumph in 1984 doomed him to a party thereafter split, and Jean Chrétien with a more populist audience always lurking.

One of the most interesting things John Turner ever said was a supposed joke that in fact was a description of himself. "The definition of a Rhodes Scholar," he told a friend one day, "is someone whose future is behind him."

**U.S. of A.** Why does everyone always look at the dark side of things?

Canadians, in their conceit, always assume that the voracious Yanks want ever more territory and cast covetous eyes this way. In truth, Americans are very insular people. They simply want to be left alone. They are isolationists by nature, being formed by peoples who left other lands because of their troubles and unhappiness there. Having founded the home of the rave and the land of the spree, they know they have discovered Nirvana and are content.

Americans did not seek out world leadership. It was thrust on them, willy-nilly, after the 1945 war because of the collapse of British energy and the rising threat of the Soviet Union. Most Americans resent the burden of foreign aid they have had to supply, just as a previous generation didn't like Woodrow Wilson's championing of the League of Nations. Most Americans, if they had their way, wish the United Nations would get to hell out of New York and go off to Geneva so the Swiss could figure out what to do with foreign diplomats with wall-to-wall limos who refuse to pay parking tickets.

The standard theory up here is that the Americans lust after our water and our resources. Yes, but do they know they would have to take Bill Vander Zalm too? That should frighten them. The thought of having to listen to Jean Chrétien's eloquence—in either language—would give them pause to think.

Americans, you see, spend their lives seated before the evening news, ending with the weather forecast that explains that "a cold front is moving down from Canada." Canada comes across as a rigid lump of ice slightly larger than that which sank the Titanic.

The Meech Lake mess had some silver in its lining. Americans, having watched this incomprehensible mishmash from the outside, were further dissuaded from any aspiration of acquiring our troubles.

Because Americans can't figure out what to do with their black population, their inner cities are being destroyed, drugs and crime are rampant, and a permanent under class is being formed. You think Americans want to inherit Quebec too, not to mention Newfoundland?

The surging Hispanic population is bringing increased pressure on the idea of Spanish as an official second language. Do you think Americans want to wrestle with the problem of assimilating seven million proud Québécois who are accustomed to official language status? Canada can't figure out Quebec after 134 years, do Iowa, Mississippi and New Mexico want to have a try?

One of the hilarious things about the innocent arrogance of John Buchanan was the assumption—given the leaving of Quebec—that the Atlantic provinces could just automatically join the United States. Who says the United States would want the Atlantic provinces?

Franklin Delano Roosevelt was a vigorous, athletic young man who played tennis every summer on his family holidays on Campobello Island, off New Brunswick. After one exhausting day at tennis and boating, he fell into cold water, then helped to fight a forest fire, developed a fever and in the isolation without proper medical care developed polio and spent the rest of his life as a paraplegic, which was withheld from public knowledge when he became president. He was thirty-nine years of age at the time on Campobello.

When John Kennedy visited Ottawa in 1961, John Diefenbaker —against the advice of White House staff—scheduled a tree-planting ritual at Rideau Hall. JFK, wanting to show up his elderly host, vigorously dug in his shovel, aggravated his wartime injury to his back and had to retire to a rocking chair in the White House for regular rest periods the remainder of his life.

An American president did not visit Canada until 1923, when Warren Harding on his way back from Alaska stopped off in Vancouver. He was suffering from a fever and his eager hosts, on a very hot summer day, had scheduled an exhausting itinerary including a golf game. He died on the way to San Francisco, without reaching Washington again.

Attorney General Bobby Kennedy, exasperated over Ottawa's dithering during the Cuban missile crisis, said, "In an emergency, Canada will give you all aid short of help." The Yanks have troubles enough of their own.

Besides all this, there is the simple reality that the Americans don't have to try very hard to own Canada. When you can get the milk for free, why buy the cow?—as a million mothers have warned their daughters.

To a scribe who has spent five years in Washington viewing the American problems (and virtues) rather as a bemused visitor from Mars might do, an American love for Canadian property seems as remote as a complete sentence of English from George W. Bush.

They have got much better things to do with their time, and so do we.

**VANCOUVER (ALSO *HONGCOUVER*)** There is a new landmark in Vancouver, a thin tower just at the entrance to Stanley Park. It is famous for having an elevator for visiting dinner partners. It is a car elevator. Each guest puts his car on the elevator and it is taken aloft. I guess it's for those who want to take their Ferraris to the table. Or want their Lamborghinis with their lasagna.

The humourless men of Royal Trustco Ltd. have financed a survey to determine where the rich of Canada live. To no one's surprise except the residents of Toronto, they live in British Columbia. It is only right and proper. With the best weather should come the best money.

There are so many instant millionaires on Howe Street—where stockbrokers go to die—as a result of the Voisey's Bay miracle strike in Labrador, that you can't buy a Savile Row suit in Vancouver. This is the town where teachers in a suburban high school wryly complain that the luxury cars driven into the school lot by their newly arrived Hong Kong students make the teachers' clunks look like junk. This all fits the glamorous, slightly inexplicable nature of Vancouver where Errol Flynn, arriving with his seventeen-year-old paramour, chose to die after a memorable weekend debauch.

In the 1930s, emulating the F. Scott Fitzgerald days, the town was fascinated by the literary duel between two witty columnists on the opposing major papers. The struggle for circulation was ended one evening when the perhaps more bibulous (or depressed?) of the two filled his suit pockets with rocks, marched from the sands of English Bay into the sea and started walking towards Japan, never to return.

We see this delightful eccentricity today in the plush ads—nationwide—advertising the luxury clutch of condo towers to arise on the edge of Stanley Park, on lands controlled by Westin Hotels' Bayshore Inn.

This would be the hostelry where the loony Howard Hughes hung out in a penthouse in deep security for two months in his dying days, his fingernails and toenails growing to elephantine lengths, while continuing a secret conversation with the publisher of the Vancouver *Sun*.

The condos climb the mountains across the harbour, reaching to the snow line. The only major city on the continent not defiled by a freeway as a result has 3 p.m. gridlock.

No one here gives a fig for the Quebec alleged drama, content in the knowledge that if the province goes, British Columbia will just saw itself off and float off to sea. There's the joke about the Newfie who says he wouldn't care if Quebec separated—all it would mean was that it would take only half the time to drive to Toronto.

Vancouver feels the same in another direction. It is already out in the void, halfway to Hong Kong.

• See also "British Columbia."

**Vander Zalm, Bill (also *Bill Vander Slam*)** Bill Vander Zalm is quite the most unusual premier Canada has produced since René Lévesque. He's run for Parliament as a Liberal, he's run for the Liberal leadership of British Columbia when he didn't even have a seat—and a party card barely warm. He's run for mayor of Vancouver, even though he doesn't even live there. That's called brass, that's called chutzpah. He's impossible to insult, the sly, handsome grin unmasking a set of dentures that calls into suspicion his claim that he had to eat tulip bulbs to keep from starving in wartime Holland.

Vander Zap is a millionaire and, like Lee Iacocca (who was saved by government loans), can't understand why all the rest of us with a little hustle-and-shovel-work can't do the same. He is the Jimmy Swaggart of politics, the Oral Roberts of Confederation.

It has always been my belief that when the Zalm was made B.C. education minister by Premier Bill Bennett, himself a high-school dropout who became a millionaire, it was a sly signal of revenge against all those book-larnin' professors. The confirmation of my theory came quickly when the new minister announced that he was about to reform the B.C. school curriculum because he had come to the conclusion that high-school graduates these days "don't write too good." Everyone ridiculed Willie Wooden Shoes, but one suspects that it was MiniWac Bennett who was giggling.

Vander Zalm is the exemplar of the phenomenon called telepolitics. It is the politician who pronounces in ringing tones that he has principles—and if you don't like them, he has other ones. John Diefenbaker is famous for stubbornly running for office for years, defeated a half-dozen times before finally getting a seat and eventually a prime ministership. But Dief had one cause, one belief—prairie Tory populism—and just one party. Mr. Wooden Shoes, who wears his wooden loafers so as to keep the woodpeckers away from his head, runs for anything, not because he cares for causes but because he's ambitious, because his ego needs another outlet.

The former premier once answered criticism that he is all style and no substance by saying, "Style is substance."

There was a consistent pattern to Vander Zalm's rise. Even while he was a minister in the Social Credit government, he built an addition onto one of his gardening stores without a building permit. Warned by authorities that he was violating a municipal bylaw, he refused to comply. He received the minimum penalty. When his two brothers violated agricultural land-zoning laws, Vander Zalm—then the municipal affairs minister—intervened on their behalf.

When Bill was mayor of the Vancouver suburb of Surrey, his own council once voted to investigate him on conflict-of-interest charges. Two days before the then-NDP government was to bring in a deadline on public-disclosure legislation designed to protect the public from political conflicts of interest, Vander Zalm quit the Liberals and joined Social Credit.

Caught accepting, in the middle of the night in a Bayshore Inn suite, a large brown envelope filled with cash from a Taiwan billionaire, he fled the premiership to write a gardening column—his true Peter Principle posting.

The Zalm, from his retreat in Fantasy Gardens (only in British Columbia, as someone has pointed out, could the premier live in a theme park), once gave a videotaped speech to the U.S.-based Campus Crusade for Christ in which he revealed that Jesus Christ did not have a B.A. from the University of British Columbia.

"Christ didn't have an easy way," the premier who wears his Christianity on his sleeve explained to the video cameras. "He was taunted and ridiculed. He never had a University of British Columbia education. He would have been low in the polls."

Vander Zoom, who explained later that of course he wasn't comparing his own personage to Christ, has never been contaminated by any university education himself. "The application of democracy sometimes gives me trouble," he is quoted as admitting.

His cavalier attitude toward the law is accompanied by another characteristic: stubbornness—which is both a strength and a weakness common to the Dutch. Earlier in his career he lost three times in seven years, running for Parliament in 1968 in hopes of riding on Trudeaumania and running for leadership of the B.C. Liberal party among other things. Later he was to lose yet again when he tried for mayor of Vancouver. He simply came back smiling. He's a hard man to insult. You can't insult a man who doesn't believe in anything.

**VICTORIA** It has to be the water. Victoria, as we know, has the mildest climate in Canada, roses at Christmas and actual palm trees—due to the warming waters of the Japanese Current that sweeps down the Inside Passage.

Victoria has done the most successful job of making a fortune out of pretending it is really British. Yankee tourists, landing behind the Tweed Curtain, delight in an ersatz England, full of tea and crumpets and pet dogs, the Empress Hotel lobby looking as if the Queen Mum and the corgis are just down the hall.

It was the students at Victoria College, back in the early nineties, who tried to do something about this. Vic College was then just a two-year training bra, its graduates having to cross the waters to the University of B.C. in Vancouver to get full degrees.

When the government decided to make it a full four-year university, the students had an idea. Why not, instead of all this British junk, honour the Spanish explorers who probably got there before Captain Vancouver? The salubrious Gulf Islands offshore honour by name some of them—Galiano, Gabriola.

The Strait of Juan de Fuca separates Victoria from Washington State. Why not, said the kids, pay respect to the Spaniards by naming the new institution the University of Juan de Fuca?

Splendid idea, said the faculty. An inspired choice, decided the board of governors as it prepared to make the decision. Alas, the boastful kids let slip too early their real rationale: their planned T-shirts that would advertise "Juan de Fuca U." Result? It is now the University of Victoria.

The languid city of the newly wed and nearly dead hides under its skirts a seething lust for the physical pleasures. Perhaps it has something to do with its fake-English veneer that is designed for the tourists. John Major, as we know, headed for the dumpster after too many three-in-a-bed scandals of randy Tory MPs, including a chap who miscued with a plastic bag over his head while in naughty underwear.

Poor Mike Harcourt, who looks like an aging pharmacist, was done in by loose zippers, just like his philosophical opposite, Major. NDP stalwart Robin Blencoe was turfed from cabinet and caucus after allegations of unspecified sexual harassment while at the Canada Games in Alberta brought by a toothsome legislative assistant, and allegations by two other women.

Senior members of Harcourt's staff have had to be severely spanked after distributing sex-rated e-mail, an Internet chain letter aimed at those "who need to get laid within ninety-six hours."

This brings us back to the water. Previously, we had thought the celebrated randiness of Victoria legislators—stuck off on that island with ferries always being late—had excluded the saintly socialists. The sinful capitalists, it was always assumed, had a lock on lust.

There was Socred minister Jim Nielsen, father of nine, who was caught pressing his attentions on a lady not his wife by the outraged husband, a small civil servant. As the aggrieved chap told the press: "I knocked him down. He got up, so I knocked him down again." Nielsen returned to the legislature with a black eye, his career gone.

There was his cabinet mate, Bob McClelland, a sombre and ambitious minister who used to work for a country-and-western radio station. Depressed at being slighted in a minor cabinet shuffle, he consoled himself with the services (whatever they might be) of one of those ubiquitous "escort services" that exist, yea, even in Victoria, composed of comely young ladies who feel sorry for lonely rug salesmen sitting in hotel rooms looking at the wallpaper, and come up and do Bible readings, or something. This particular minister of the Crown was bright enough to pay for his Bible readings with his Visa card, which just happened to have the Parliament buildings as his address. The cops just happened to be chasing this particular escort service. Whoops!

The Liberals, naturally, drinking that same suspect Victoria tap water, had their own recent soap opera. The farce of then-leader Gordon Wilson and his political paramour Judi Tyabji is too familiar to repeat, leading all the way to the Oprah show and available in book form at your nearest newsstand.

So it is with island life. B.C. lawmakers, their aides, assistants, consultants, forehead-feelers—all have their mind-sets altered whether they know it or not by their transition to the goofy little ghetto by the water, the Empress full of tourists from Omaha drinking what they think is the Queen's tea, the bored MLAs after dark taking their secretaries to Oak Bay—beyond the Tweed Curtain—for sherry by the sea.

Do lawmakers at Queen's Park, in the depths of slogging Toronto, have such temptations? Of course not. Do frigid floggers of reform in Edmonton have such delights before them? Naturally, no. Winnipeg? Where in Winnipeg would one go for a nooner?

Canada, if it were compassionate, would commiserate with the politicians of delightful Victoria, the tiny spot of green that will be forever England and where one can do a knee-trembler in a car in the park in February without any chance of chilblains.

The temptation is simply too much.

**WEBSTER, JACK** In 1983, Simon Fraser U. honoured an unlettered ham actor who was the finest ombudsman (unpaid) in Canada. His name: Blather McHaggis, the Mouth That Roared, also known to his drinking companions as Jack Webster; the only honorary Ph.D. ever to come out of the dockyards of Glasgow.

Dizzy Gillespie, the bebop king of trumpet, once said of Louis Armstrong: "No him, no me." So it is with every hot-line, open-mouth host on the continent. No Jack Webster, no them. Long before Rush Limbaugh, long before New York's Don Imus or Vancouver's Rafe Mair, the burly Oatmeal Savage perfected the medium—an electric chair for guests, disguised as a microphone.

His sixty-fifth birthday coincided with a visit to Ottawa, and Webster being Webster, he invited 150 of his closest friends to drop around to his hotel suite. Vast mobs descended, and Webster, who loved a crowd almost more than he loved lunch, entertained at the top of his sandpaper voice dressed in what looked like a shirt left over from *Gilligan's Island.*

John Crosbie and almost anyone in Ottawa who enjoyed a drink and a laugh showed up, and the host, despairing of taking his friends out for dinner, hit upon the bright idea of ordering up club sandwiches for all. Phalanxes of white-coated waiters, as if on a jungle safari, beat a steady tattoo on the door of his suite, bearing enough sandwiches and chips on the side to feed Stanley's expedition to Dr. Livingstone. Eventually, an anonymous young blonde who had ingested too much gin expired on the bed. As the party raged on she could not be awakened. "Here I am on my sixty-fifth birthday," wailed Webster in self-mockery, "attempting to get a woman *out* of my bed." The room-service bill came to $887.

Webster was always the man for the grand gesture. After he left school at fourteen in Glasgow, he had three jobs, delivering the milk in the morning and then shuttling between copy boy stints at two newspapers. On the streetcar between the two he read Dickens and Shakespeare in the shorthand training manuals supplied to apprentice scribes. At sixty-five, he used his helicopter to drop him on his ninety-four-acre farm on a blissful mountain slope on Saltspring Island in the salubrious gulf between Vancouver and Victoria. The poor boy, become a Scottish laird at last, terrorized visitors by stuffing them in a battered Jeep and plunging through streams and over logs past his subsidized sheep, a rollicking man enjoying his toys.

His flamboyant side tends to overshadow all. He once accidentally burned down his own house when he was a struggling young reporter just arrived in Vancouver. A smouldering couch had been lit by an errant cigarette, and he attempted to throw it out the window, thereby igniting the drapes; racing to a pay phone, he dropped his dime in the snow. His tale of woe on the front page the next day intimidated the insurance company that held his expired policy to pay up. He and a companion once witnessed a waiter on fire in Winnipeg's finest restaurant (being Winnipeg, the restaurant is in St. Boniface) and as the poor man was engulfed by the flambé, Webster explained, "I could have saved him, but I was wearing a new suede jacket."

He was offered political slots by all parties in British Columbia, offers that he loved to court and loved to reject, since it would have meant a diminution of his wallet—and his ego.

Haggis McBagpipe, as I called him, had beneath all the distinctive burr and gruff exterior the heart of a soft coffee cake. Every sidewalk drunk outside his studio in Vancouver's gritty Gastown knew he was the easiest mark for five bucks for another bottle of vanilla extract. The unwashed loved him and recognized him as one of their own, a patriot who shouted, when his wetback qualifications are questioned, "I'm a Canadian by *choice*, not the product of an accident in the back seat of a car on the beach on Friday night!"

One day he and his best buddy Pierre Berton were in a small float plane in bad weather headed up the B.C. coast for their annual fishing trip. "You know, Webster," said Berton, "if this kite hits the drink, every paper in Toronto will have a headline: 'BERTON DIES—Webster also aboard.' And every paper in Vancouver will have a headline: 'WEBSTER DIES IN CRASH—Berton also perishes.' "

It was a good line, but it wasn't true the day after Webster died, surrounded at bedside by his four children. The *National Post* had his picture on page one with a story and a terrific obit inside that took up almost a whole page. The *Globe and Mail* had his picture on page one. The *Toronto Star* had a big obit. He was instantly a lead item on the national news on TV. The next day the *Globe* had an editorial—fittingly opening with a quote from Shakespeare—and finishing with a simple, "Thanks, Jack."

He was *sui generis*—one of a kind. His like shall not pass this way again.

## WET COAST, THE
• See "British Columbia."

## WETSUIT, STOCKWELL
• See "Day, Stockwell."

**WHELAN, EUGENE** In the 1984 Liberal leadership race Eugene Whelan looked about him at other putative chiefs, and laughed. If John Roberts is a contender, why not a green felt cowboy hat? He felt he had a national base through the years of stroking farmers and standing up for them. He speaks a semi-version of one of the two official languages, but one suspects he fakes that corn-pone accent (he actually speaks impeccable Oxford English when at home). He is a cunning politician, a central Canadian who tried to look like a westerner, as befitted his Agriculture post, the Colonel Sanders of Canadian politics. No one tangled with him in the Commons for fear of being drowned in bafflegab.
• See also "Burpies."

**WINNIPEG** Everyone worries about Winnipeg. The hockey club is gone. The winter lasts forever. The town is dying. The Crow has long been killed. The mosquitoes. The place is so conservative it has voted Conservative again and again. Oh dear.

If the truth be known, Winnipeg is the most stable city in Canada. It is stable because nothing ever happens there. Not for The Peg the wild booms and disastrous busts of Calgary, oillionaires flying to Hawaii on their private jets one year and then selling the car the next.

Not for The Peg the airy arrogance of Edmonton, which once thought it was going to be such a surging metropolis that it built its international airport so far out of town that you can't afford a hotel room after you've paid the cab fare.

One of the reasons for the serenity is that the city is not in lockstep with other regions. It is not really a card-carrying member of the Prairies, Saskatchewan and Alberta carrying the ball there. Winnipeg, so much older and more settled, has one foot in Central Canada.

The city where the Red joins the Assiniboine exists on good theatre, the famous ballet company, fur coats and concentric circles of friends who know they're all going to be around for the same parties a decade hence. There is no urgency. Time moves at a stately gait in Winterpeg.

Stately old Winnipeg, where you always feel as if you've stumbled upon some European city frozen in time, is lucky enough to have two rivers (obviously inheriting the one that missed Regina). The Red River curls and twists like a rattlesnake's tail through the town, joining up with the calm Assiniboine. There were few more pleasant spots in the summer in Canada than overlooking the brown waters of the Red in the posh River Heights area where all the grain millionaires stupidly built their mansions facing Wellington Crescent, their backs to the river.

Winnipeg was going to be the Chicago-of-the-North, the railway and grain centre of the nation that the twentieth century was supposed to belong to. It was the headquarters of the Hudson's Bay Co., the oldest incorporated company in the world. The most influential newspaper editor in Canada was John W. Dafoe, advising and admonishing Ottawa from his desk at the *Winnipeg Free Press*.

Anybody raised in Winnipeg is used to the Jewish North End, the Ukrainians, the Mennonites who produced Jake Epp. In francophone St. Boniface, just about where the Red and Assiniboine rivers meet, Louis Riel's tomb sits in the courtyard of the ruins of the magnificent old St. Boniface Cathedral, mostly destroyed by fire some two dozen years ago. Wreaths of bright flowers, red and yellow against the snow, can still regularly be found leaning against the tomb.

An hour north on Lake Winnipeg is Gimli, where every single person is a descendant of the Icelanders who came in 1875 in search of fish and starved to death in great numbers. Despite this, the survivors have grown to enormous heights.

The reason for the quiet town's cultural maturity is this easy mix and—I guess we'll have to include them—the WASPs, from the Richardsons and the Heffelfingers and down to the rest.

Winnipeg is a strange place, run, as quoted by Peter Newman, through "dead men's shoes." Most anyone of importance has left, and the leftover money is managed by heirs of little imagination, personality or national interest. It has a dignity denied Calgary, Edmonton and Regina, but I can't figure out what still keeps it alive.

It is a town that has no outer doubts. Whereas Vancouver poses, fascinated, in its mirror, and Montreal gazes sardonically at grasping Toronto, and Toronto is torn with penis envy of New York, Winnipeg is serene, oblivious, profane. It does not envy any-one. It is civic karma.

Any city that can abide those mosquitoes can cope with anything.

**WINTERPEG**
  • See "Winnipeg."

**WOMEN IN POLITICS** After the remarkable swan dive of Liberal leader Lyn McLeod in the 1995 Ontario election, I feared yet another devastating blow to the case of women in Canadian politics, that the refrain "I told you so" would come from those who think the other sex still isn't up to snuff.

McLeod bombed. Just as Kim Campbell before her bombed. Just as plucky Audrey McLaughlin bombed in her own quiet way.

Yes, there was in this an element of the "angry white guys" backlash against the very idea of a female prime minister or premier. No one suggests the male race should be banned from politics because Frank Miller spectacularly bombed, or Joe Clark bombed in nine months as PM and John Turner bombed as PM in even less time. But women? Can't cut it.

The suggestion shyly offered here is that the only problem has been in selecting the wrong women. For every Frank Miller and Joe Clark and John Turner there have been toweringly successful male politicians.

Charlotte Whitton, the long-time Ottawa mayor, chewed up men and spit them out for breakfast. Male members of her city council were terrified of her because she was tough, fearless—and intellectually superior.

We all know the old joke about Maggie Thatcher taking her Tory cabinet out to dinner. "Roast beef," she tells the waiter. "And vegetables?" he enquires. "Oh, they'll have the same," sez Maggie with a wave of her hand.

Golda Meir in Israel could best any man. Indira Gandhi did the same. Females running Iceland, Norway and Sri Lanka suffered no insecurities.

The first female MP in Canada, Agnes Macphail, sat alone among all the blue serge from 1921 to 1935 before another woman, Martha Black, joined her. For five more years, they could at least see each other, but there wasn't much chance of co-operation, Macphail being a CCFer and Black a Conservative.

In the four decades from 1921 to 1964, only seventeen women

were elected to Parliament. And seven of them got there only because they inherited the ridings of their dead husbands.

All the symbols of parliamentary government are still drawn from the manly arts of war. The chief official in the Commons is the sergeant-at-arms, who carries the mace. His counterpart in the Senate is the Gentleman Usher of the Black Rod.

Iona Campagnolo noted that all the paintings in Parliament's corridors are of men and war and swords and blood. The few female images are British queens, including Victoria, whose statue apparently was first guarded by an imperial lion "in a state of too-obvious virility." In deference to shocked females and curious children, his bronzed penis was sawed off in 1908—"the only emasculation known to have occurred on Parliament Hill."

Of all the calls received by Barbara McDougall's constituency office during the crucial FTA election, there were more about her hair than about the trade pact.

What is a girl to do? The new band of women MPs, cutting across party lines, got a tuck shop carrying things women need—pantyhose and sanitary napkins. Writes Sydney Sharpe, author of *The Gilded Ghetto: Women and Political Power in Canada*: "Within the bustling community of Parliament Hill, with its myriad services aimed at males, women were given less consideration than they would receive in any rural Canadian town with a drugstore."

She devotes an entire chapter to Brian Mulroney, the classic MCP in youth, being educated by his wife and his female Tory mentors, eventually doing more than any PM to advance women in Ottawa. In his first cabinet, when only nine per cent of all MPs were women, twenty-one per cent of his ministers were female.

The problem is that Canadian political parties have been choosing the wrong females. Campbell was not really a politician, as her disastrous brief reign proved, but an opportunist who leaped from lily pad of publicity to lily pad, dooming herself in the party hierarchy by never once learning the two simplest words in the English language: "Thank you."

McLaughlin, earnest and honest, became NDP leader only because the male feminists in her caucus—led by Svend Robinson and Ian Waddell—were convinced the way to the front pages and salvation was to beat the Tories to having the first female leader. The Conservatives at the time clearly leaning toward either Barbara McDougall or Campbell.

It is, the world being not fair, extremely tough to be a woman in politics. It's why the women in our politics who can take the time and energy to survive in it have to be essentially alone. Divorced, as in Iona Campagnolo, Pat Carney, Campbell, McLaughlin. Widowed, as in McDougall, Judy Erola. Or never married, as in Flora MacDonald, Judy LaMarsh, Monique Bégin.

Lyn McLeod, Campbell and McLaughlin are just the first wave of troops out of the trenches and annihilated by the machine-guns on the Somme.

They will be succeeded by tougher, and more experienced followers and eventually the "angry white guys" will discover they have enough balls to elect a prime minister of the opposite sex.

That PM will be my daughter.

## WOODEN SHOES, WILLIE

• See "Vander Zalm, Bill."

**BRE-X** So, a friend in Vancouver reported, three of the guys in his office had their RRSPs cut in half. Two of them put their houses up for sale.

This would be the day when every fax in the land warned their friends: there may be no gold at all in Bre-X.

Just a month earlier, the screaming headline on the *Maclean's* cover had stated: "GREED, GRAFT, GOLD." Where there is gold, there is always greed and graft.

Students of irony will recall the names of those who were fighting fiercely to get control of this obscure hunk of jungle at Busang in Indonesia. Pushed out at the last minute was Toronto billionaire Peter Munk, the Numero Uno gold sharpie in the world, who was backed by his heavyweight directors and shotgun riders, George Bush and Brian Mulroney.

When the ex-president of the United States and the ex-prime minister of Canada—not to mention Mr. Munk—come within an inch of looking like rubes, we have deep comedy.

It is highly reminiscent of the classic 1948 flick, *The Treasure of the Sierra Madre*, starring a younger Humphrey Bogart and the grizzled Walter Huston. In the last frame, as Huston cackles over the mound of gold dust before him, a whirlwind pounces and the whole fortune disappears on the wind.

Huston bursts into anguished tears—and then, as reality sets in, subsides into laughter. Greed, graft and gold. They all go together.

David Baines was not surprised. He said the Bre-X farce is "unique in size," but fits into the genetic scheme.

Baines is the superb *Vancouver Sun* reporter whose tender task has been to cover the Vancouver Stock Exchange and all its wonderful ways.

One of the great VSE scares was the junior stock that had found "diamonds as big as chicken eggs." After a ride, the stock settled at nine cents—which was about the price of an egg.

A few years back, the Toronto Stock Exchange suggested that two characters named Murray Pezim and Earl Glick take their business to Vancouver, the surroundings perhaps more salubrious. I once asked Pezim on television if he knew that he and his partner were known at the VSE as "Sleazy and Slick." The rest of the interview did not go well.

Bre-X? What else is new?

**YUKON** There is something about gold, Robert Service told us, that drives men mad. I don't think it's the gold, actually. I think it's the North. The Yukon, the Klondike. Once under its spell, normal blokes grow a little goofy. Not just in 1897, but even today. The mountains are painted with yellow trees in the extended summer, but the strange things go on in Whitehorse and Dawson City and everyone takes no never-mind.

In Dawson City, the town that spawned the one-man industry known as Pierre Berton, there is Captain Dick Stevenson, who is still attempting to achieve world fame by insisting that no visitor to the town can escape without sampling his "sour toe cocktail." This is a drink contained in a glass wherein a pickled toe rests at the bottom. Stevenson says he and his wife found the original toe, but he is now working on the third successor, an overeager imbiber having accidentally swallowed the first one. He declines to reveal where he gets the toes.

Town fathers, for once growing squeamish, put their fully toed feet down, however, when the captain, never having made it past the Johnny Carson show, attempted to dispense a new drink containing bear testicles.

It is cold and lonely up here in the winter, and someone—the mayor was the suspect—thought of subscribing to Home Box

Office of New York for its service through satellite dish. One membership was bought, under the name of George Dawson, for $19.95 a month, the whole town was hooked up and happy residents enjoyed every channel under the sun until visiting reporters, coming upon soft-porn movies, blew the whistle.

There is Ruby's Place, a celebrated house of ill repute that has been restored—so to speak—under the auspices of Parks Canada, which is turning the whole joint into a picture-postcard town for the tourists. Ruby and those who followed her operated the house of pleasure right into the 1960s. The story is that a group of federal bureaucrats and their wives arrived on a junket, the men arrived back at the hotel rather too late one night and, shortly after, Ruby's Place was closed. The Parks Canada plaque on the front identifies Ruby as a "dancehall girl." So Ottawa.

At the Palace Grand Theatre, built in 1899 with tiers of boxes rising three levels, the prim puritans who took over the place in the 1920s covered over the sinful barroom area. When the theatre was finally restored to its present glory, they panned the dirt covering the lobby to find the location of the bar and found a straight line of gold, indicating where the drinkers had drunk.

The bard of the Klondike gold rush, the man who made it famous around the world, wasn't there to see it happen. Robert Service, raised in Scotland, was a bank clerk in the Yukon in 1905 when he borrowed the name of a depositor to create "The Cremation of Sam McGee." It's not true that he had to slave in the bank while his ballads went unnoticed; the bank manager fired him when he found out that the lyrical clerk was making more money than he was.

The author of "The Shooting of Dan McGrew" ended up a rich man on the Riviera and refused to return to the Yukon "because it was too cold," a sensible poet if not a romantic one.

## Zalm, the

- See "Vander Zalm, Bill."

## Zolf, Larry

Michael Wilson once said that the problem with Canada is that it didn't have enough millionaires. That's not true. The problem with Canada is that it doesn't have enough Larry Zolfs.

Zolf, the ugliest man in the country by his own admission, is the clown prince of Canadian letters. He has a mind as sharp as a tack, proof incarnate that if you want to be a comic you have to be a very serious person.

During his thirty-eight years at the Canadian Broadcorping Castration he has done everything but save it from itself. Everybody in Canadian journalism has a Zolf story. And you don't even have to make them up. They're all true.

He was born, to immigrant parents, as Yehudah Leib Zolf. He was known as Leibel and on the first day of junior high in gritty North Winnipeg the schoolyard roughs chanted: "Leibel, Mabel, poop on the table." When they were called into class, the kid in front of him was named Larry. When the teacher then asked little Zolf what his name was, he answered: "Larry Zolf."

He went to school with Barbara Amiel, he roomed with a young

Joe Clark, he went down to the Excited States of America to work with Bobby Kennedy, he wrote jokes for Pierre Trudeau, he survived cancer and alcohol and now, somewhere in his sixties, plans to stick with the Corp. until he's one hundred—just like the Queen Mum.

When the doxy Gerda Munsinger was unearthed in the Diefenbaker era, Zolf was sent out to bang on the Montreal door of Pierre Sevigny, the one-legged cabinet minister who had been identified as one of her lovers. Sevigny came to the door and, on camera, swung at Zolf with his cane. He now refers to it as his Citizen Cane period.

The parliamentary press gallery dinner used to be the highlight of the Ottawa social season, an off-the-record roast where all the party leaders had a go at one another. Trudeau hated the evening. Zolf wrote his jokes and Trudeau—reading them with the verve of reciting the phone book—walked all over his own punch lines.

The PM five days later ran into the still-steaming Zolf in the Centre Block and asked his ghostwriter how he had done. Zolf: "Well then, here it is. You, sir, couldn't deliver a joke in a Brink's armoured truck." And turned on his heel and stomped off.

One of the more memorable Ottawa disasters was a plush gathering of wealthy donors to the Writers' Development Trust in the Château Laurier ballroom. Peter Gzowski was the MC and the Royal Canadian Air Farce were to be the main event. As a short warm-up act, Gzowski asked Zolf to tell a few jokes.

Unfortunately, there was a comfortable chair on stage. Zolf, a large man, settled in cozily and began to read from his forthcoming book.

Fascinated with his own verbiage, he went on for ten minutes, fifteen minutes. Gzowski looked completely confused. The Air Farce, behind the curtain, stirred noisily. The flamboyant Richard

Hatfield, premier of New Brunswick, stood up, waved his white napkin over his head and shouted: "Stop! Stop!"

Zolf raised his eyes, said, "As the Mormons say, 'Fucketh off,' " and resumed reading. Finally the entire ballroom rose, all waving their white napkins in surrender, at last driving him from the stage. To this day, this has gone down in Ottawa lore as "the Night Larry Zolf Sat Down To Read."

Of his time with Barbara Frum: "I was the first real visible Jew to appear on CBC TV as a reporter, interviewer and host. As such I had this terrible problem. I have a magical false nose and glasses—magical in that the glasses come off, but the nose doesn't."

He's an icon—better than any millionaire.

# INDEX

*Page numbers in bold refer to main entries in the text.*